# LAW AND VENGEANCE

# ALSO BY MIKE PAPANTONIO

*Law and Disorder*
*A Legal Thriller*
(2016)

*Closing Arguments: The Last Battle*
Coauthored with Fred Levin and Martin Levin
(2016)

*Resurrecting Aesop: Fables Lawyers Should Remember*
(2000)

*Clarence Darrow, the Journeyman:*
*Lessons for the Modern Lawyer*
(1997)

# LAW AND VENGEANCE

*A Legal Thriller*

# MIKE PAPANTONIO

SelectBooks, Inc.
*New York*

This edition published by SelectBooks, Inc.
For information address SelectBooks, Inc., New York, New York.

First Edition

ISBN 978-1-59079-436-4

Library of Congress Cataloging-in-Publication Data

Names: Papantonio, Mike, 1953- author.
Title: Law and vengeance : a legal thriller / Mike Papantonio.
Description: First edition. | New York : SelectBooks, Inc., [2017]
Identifiers: LCCN 2017013470 | ISBN 9781590794364 (hardcover : acid-free
  paper)
Subjects: LCSH: Criminal defense lawyers--Fiction. | Women lawyers--Fiction.

  | Revenge--Fiction. | GSAFD: Legal stories.
Classification: LCC PS3616.A587 L395 2017 | DDC 813/.6--dc23 LC record
available at https://lccn.loc.gov/2017013470

Book design by Janice Benight

Manufactured in the United States of America
10 9 8 7 6 5 4 3 2 1

*For Rose, Rhonda, and Richard,*
*who provided me with a limitless amount of material for*
*the creation of wonderful and unusual fictional characters*

# ACKNOWLEDGMENTS

I wish to thank the following people:

Dana Isaacson for the launch

Alan Russell for his remarkable laser focus

Bill Gladstone for his vision

Diana Bailey for her command of details

# PROLOGUE
# WELCOME TO THE NEW O.K. CORRAL

**O**fficer Kim Knudsen turned up the air-conditioning of the squad car. On hot, steamy nights like this, even maximum AC couldn't compete with Chicago's humidity.

"Hot enough for you?" she asked her partner, Vinnie Velez.

"*Muy caliente*," said Velez, showing a smile of too-white teeth. The rookie thought he was a ladies' man. "But some of us like it hot."

The happily married Kim, and mother of two, smiled at her partner's attempt at flirting and said, "I like it quiet."

Of late, Chicago had been anything but quiet. The Windy City no longer felt like the same place she'd grown up in. It had become the murder capital of the US, with up to fifteen homicides every week, and things only seemed to be getting worse. Gangbangers were fighting for turf, and citizens and cops were merely collateral damage. It seemed as if every month Kim had to put on her dress uniform and go to the funeral of yet another CPD officer, where she had to listen to the mayor do his usual lip service.

"Are you up for going to the range Saturday?" Velez asked.

"Sounds good to me. I'll just have to make sure Tom can look after the kids."

When Velez had become her new partner, Kim insisted the two of them spend some time together at the shooting range. She had found it was a good way to bond. Besides, she wanted to make sure her partner had her back. Anything that improved her chances of making it home to her family was a good thing.

"Which range?" asked Velez.

Kim didn't even have to think about it. "The old hall suits me. Libertyville gets too many suits."

Libertyville, Kim thought, almost felt like a club. The police union had pushed for its construction. Kim's thinking was that if something wasn't broken it didn't need fixing. It was the same way with her service weapon. The police union had pushed for every cop to be outfitted with the Sight-Clops—the supposed latest and greatest in gunsight laser technology. She and Vinnie had recently been equipped with the holographic gunsight, and had tried it out the previous week on the range. After the first go-around, Kim with her "show me" attitude had found herself pleasantly surprised by her target practice results.

"Just call me Annie Oakley," she'd said to Vinnie. Then again, even without Sight-Clops, Kim was already an expert shot.

The squawk box suddenly came to life. During patrol, the voice of dispatchers was a constant drone only half-listened to, but they were all ears when it came to hot calls that involved them. Shots were being fired in West Englewood.

Velez liked to complain that Kim drove "like a grandma." That was true enough, until they got dispatches like this one. Kim pressed down on the accelerator of the 470 horsepower Dodge Charger, and hit the sound-and-light show. With sirens blaring and the rooftop showing a "rocket's red glare," the squad car approached warp speed before it came to a screeching stop on South Racine Avenue near 63rd. They could see other squad cars had already gathered at the opposite block's end near 64th and Ogden Park.

The area looked like a war zone. White flight had occurred long ago; that had left the blight of burnt out and ransacked buildings towering over decaying streets. It didn't look like an area worth fighting over, but the two vying gangs didn't seem to have gotten that memo. Shots rang out even as the gangbangers began running off in all directions; the presence of cops meant a short timeout in their game of killing.

Guns drawn, Kim and Velez jumped out of their squad car. They used the shelter of their opened doors to hunker behind and get the lay of the land—and of the carnage. Several bodies were bleeding out in the street.

From the shadows, they heard the staccato sound of approaching footsteps. Someone was running their way. To her left, Kim saw a presence take form. A skinny, wild-eyed kid wearing a red hoodie showed himself. In his right hand, she could see a gun.

Her partner saw the same thing. Staying low, Velez circled around the patrol car and took up a position roughly ten yards in front of the driver's side of the car. Kim wished she could wave him back, but it was too late. Vinnie was too gung-ho by half. She was the one who should be taking point. At least the rookie had known to position himself slightly to the right of Kim to keep clear of her direct line of fire.

"Drop the gun!" screamed Velez. "Drop it! Hit the ground! Now!"

For a moment, the gangbanger slowed, but then thought better of it and started to raise his gun. That was enough for Kim. She centered on his chest and fired. The banger should have been hit.

He should have dropped where he stood. But he was somehow untouched.

From the corner of her eye, Kim saw Vinnie falling to his knees and then toppling over. There had only been one shot. Her shot. But how could she have shot Vinnie? That couldn't be right. That was impossible.

"Vinnie!" she screamed.

Her partner would have to wait, though. The kid was turning his gun her way. As Kim raised her own gun, and focused her hologram sight on the banger, she shot and missed. With her target point blank, Kim fired a second time.

And missed.

The banger didn't. Kim never got off her third shot. The fire in her gut dropped her to the asphalt. She tried to right herself, but no longer had the strength to get up. From the ground she found herself staring at Vinnie. He wasn't moving.

Kim thought of Tina, her four-year-old, and Jason who was seven. Mommy wouldn't be coming home tonight. Mommy might never come home again. Before leaving for work Kim remembered she'd told each of her children she loved them. There was that at least, but it wasn't nearly enough.

She tried to slow the flow of blood coming out of her. Every second that passed was making her more lightheaded. I'm like the Little Dutch Boy, she thought, but I can't keep the dike from breaking. She lost consciousness as her blood filled the street.

◆◆◆

See the world, Cary Jones thought. That's what the army recruiter had told him. It had sounded so good coming out of the mouth of that slick recruiter in his dress uniform. Now, at the ripe old age of nineteen, Cary realized that just about anything would have sounded good to a kid who'd never been out of South Carolina. Hell, he'd barely been out of Gaffney. Growing up he'd thought of Gaffney as a shithole. But that was before he'd been deployed to Afghanistan. That whole damn country was a shithole.

The army said it was his job to train local militias in the proper use of firearms. The ragheads loved to shoot off weapons, but had little interest in doing anything else. At least half his trainees were high on kif. And even a kid from Gaffney could see that those he was training had no dog in the fight. Over the centuries, countless invaders had tried to make their claim to parts of this ancient land of warlords and fiefdoms. Eventually, the invaders all went away, always the worse for wear. The natives knew it was only a matter of time.

Those that Cary Jones was supposed to be training had the ultimate short-timer's attitude. Maybe that's why no one had showed up for training that morning. Why bother? Of course, it was possible there was some holiday going on. And it was damned hot, even by Afghanistan standards. The recruits might have come to their senses and said it was too hot to work. Or maybe they weren't in their senses, having gotten their hands on some great kif.

Or maybe they knew the shit was about to hit the fan.

When bullets were flying, or if danger even seemed imminent, the Afghan recruits were always noticeably absent. Earlier that day, Cary had reported the no-shows to his sergeant. It was enough for the regular guard to be doubled. Of course since his recruits hadn't shown up leaving him nothing to do, Cary had been assigned to that guard. Even worse, he'd been given picket duty. He was the first line of defense for the camp.

Cary didn't even want to think how hot and humid it was. Even the mangy local dogs were staying put. Everyone back home used to complain about the steamy, summer weather. Little did they know that compared to the weather in Afghanistan, Gaffney was heaven. Sure it got hot back home, but not hot like this. What was it that Grandma used to say? Then he remembered: "It's so hot the hens are laying boiled eggs."

Grandma was a big woman who didn't like the heat. She used to go to church carrying a big, white fan, and during the sermon she'd work that fan something fierce. Grandma was a Bible-thumper. Before being deployed, she'd prayed for him, quoting some biblical passage about his being a stranger in a strange land. Gran had sure been right about that. Cary felt like that guy in Ray Bradbury's *The Martian Chronicles* who was so far from home on that lonely and desolate planet. Afghanistan was his Mars, he decided. Cary wasn't much of a reader, but that had been a pretty cool book, at least compared to other books he'd been assigned in high school. When he'd arrived in Afghanistan he'd been shown around by a seasoned grunt who'd said, "This ain't quite the end of the world, but squint a little and you can see it from here."

Cary fought the torpor that came from the heat and tried to remain watchful. It was all he could do to raise his head. In the distance, where the winding road showed itself, he saw movement. Two figures were coming his way.

It might have been too hot for the dogs, thought Cary, but not for Ahmad. Cary didn't even need to raise his binos to make an ID on the kid. Ahmad had a way of carrying himself that separated him from the rest of the rat pack. And when he came "on a sales call," as this apparently was, he always wore his best Pashtun clothing. Sarge always told Cary and the other soldiers to not "engage" with the Afghan children, but Cary was an easy mark. Besides, to Cary's thinking, kids were kids whether they were in Gaffney or Kabul. Ahmad separated himself from his peers, though. The other children begged for candy or gum, but not Ahmad. He was like a peddler of old, always trying to hawk one trinket or another. Cary was always buying one of Ahmad's so-called "priceless relics."

The kid's companion was much older. He had to be the grandfather Ahmad was always talking about. That was another thing about Ahmad. His English was better than anyone else's in the village because he was always trying to sell anything he could to the soldiers.

"I will bring my grandfather to meet you," Ahmad had said. "No one makes sandals like Grandfather. You will see. He will make you some."

Sandals, thought Cary. As if he needed, or would wear sandals in this place. With all the camel spiders and scorpions around, Cary didn't dare wear sandals, but he was always a sucker for Ahmad's sales pitch. The kid—he couldn't be more than twelve—could have made a fortune in the States selling used cars.

Ahmad and his grandfather continued their trek up the hill. "My American friend!" the boy shouted. "I have brought my grandfather to greet you!"

Cary wasn't listening though. Other sounds had his attention. A billowing cloud of dust and smoke signaled the approach of a vehicle. The moving cloud obscured the driver and his passengers, but Cary was pretty sure what was coming up the pass wasn't the Welcome Wagon.

"Get off the road!" Cary screamed, wildly gesturing for Ahmad and his grandfather to scatter.

Ahmad tugged hard at the hand of his grandfather, but the old man could only move so fast. Roaring up the incline, and emerging from its dust cloud, Cary saw a makeshift-armored Toyota 4Runner. He pivoted, sprinting towards the fortified sentry post. As he vaulted behind a cement barricade, he heard the sound of bullets striking all around him, but it was the blast that rained debris down on him that really got his attention.

Shit. They had an RPG, and the sky was on fire.

From a kneeling position, Cary raised his eyes above the cement barricade. The mujahideen were firing away from every open window in the 4Runner. It was time for Cary to return the favor. He scoped on the driver's head and fired.

The windshield should have shattered. The driver's brains should have splattered all over the rest of the mujahideen. But Cary's round somehow went right—far right—opening up a red bloom that began coloring the robe of Ahmad's grandfather. The old man staggered, then fell to the ground.

Ahmad's wail was louder than the gunfire. His cry of pain and betrayal filled the air. Cary's barricade couldn't shield him from that raw anguish. Nothing could. Cary peered over the cement wall, but wished he hadn't. Ahmad was staring at him. Tears were pouring down his anguished face. The boy knew that Cary had fired the round that killed his grandfather. Cary knew that as well, although he didn't know how in the hell that had happened.

# 1
## STRAHAN THE SECOND

**K**endrick Strahan put a mint in his mouth and started sucking on it. He didn't want Lutz to suspect he'd been drinking. Most of all, he didn't want Lutz and his goon, Thursby, to know he was scared to be in their presence. When bad guys wear badges, though, it's tough to not be scared.

Shit, thought Strahan. How had it come to this? There had been a time when the world was his oyster. He had gone to Phillips Academy friggin' prep school in Andover, for God's sake. John Hancock hadn't only signed his famous signature on the Declaration of Independence. He'd also been a signer of the prep school's Act of Incorporation in 1780.

Everything had been easy for him at Andover. He'd been one of the school's top jocks, the tough kid from Providence. It didn't matter that Strahan didn't come from money like most of the preppies. His protection racket had offered him all the spending money he needed. He'd been well-paid to look out for little Tim Knapp, or "Timmy," as the kids called him. Knapp had even pulled strings to get Strahan into Harvard. But too much partying, and not enough studying, had gotten Strahan bounced out of the university during his sophomore year.

9

Is that where everything went south? No, Strahan thought, but that was when he started circling around the porcelain bowl. He'd stayed afloat long enough to get his degree from Granite State College in Concord, a school with a one-hundred percent acceptance rate. It was safe to say he was the only Andover alum to ever get a degree from Granite State College.

Strahan's redemption should have been the Secret Service. His nickname there had been "Harvard," which he'd secretly liked. It was a reminder of when he'd been Daedalus on an upward ascent. He'd held a job there for almost a decade before screwing up in grand style, and the Department of the Treasury had given him his walking papers.

That was when Knapp had come into the picture again. The years had been kind to him. He had grown out of being the skinny, frightened kid at Andover. Money and a gilded path do wonders for confidence. After graduating from Harvard and then going to the Wharton School for his MBA, Knapp had gone into the family business. Under several manufacturing labels, the Knapp family was a major arms dealer known as Arbalest, or the Arbalest Corporation. If it shot or exploded, there was a good chance that the Knapp family made it. James Bond's license to kill was nothing compared to the Knapp's. Six years ago, Strahan had signed on to work for the family business. He was a lobbyist for the Knapp family and their gun rights advocacy.

There, thought Strahan. He had pinpointed the time when he'd sold his soul. Thirty pieces had been his going rate as well.

Officially, Strahan worked as vice president of operations for the Gun Safety Institute. It was a bullshit title for a bullshit organization. The last thing the Gun Safety Institute was interested in was safety. Hiding behind the moral rectitude of the Second Amendment, the Gun Safety Institute did everything it could to promote the "rights" of gun owners in America. Not so long ago, their lobbying positions would have seemed extreme, but now America was a place where "open carry" laws and "stand your ground" legislation ruled. Even school shootings—more like massacres—weren't enough carnage to make the lobbying group reconsider its position. Armed guards, they said, were the answers.

To protect their interests, the Gun Safety Institute was a free spender. Legal bribery was the lay of the land in Washington DC. There was a reason that more than 15,000 lobbyists plied their trade in and around K Street near the halls of power. Strahan was one of those hustlers. At some level, he knew his success and that of other lobbyists was the very thing that threatened democracy. But Strahan couldn't walk away from all the money, and especially the perks, that came with his job. On a daily basis, he and his staff schemed to put more and more deadly weapons into the hands of more and more dangerous people worldwide. When he'd been in the Secret Service, Strahan had been disdainful of organizations like the NRA and the Gun Safety Institute. Their promulgation of guns and gun rights had made his job tougher and the world more perilous. And since then, he had only made things worse.

Strahan's sales territory was mostly five-star restaurants with top-shelf liquor and pole dance clubs preferred by the "Family Values" types. If Strahan did his job properly, enough of those politicos would set aside their sin meters for sex and coke, compliments of the "Institute." What the politicos didn't know was that Strahan's job also extended to documenting their activities and gathering sordid secrets. Funny how Strahan rarely had to use them, though. Once bought, their politicians stayed bought.

Around DC it was known that Strahan generously "lobbied" for tips, rumors, and rumors of rumors. The power of his payola had allowed Strahan to get wind of the Arbalest lawsuit just two days after it was filed under a court-mandated protective seal.

It was that lawsuit that Strahan needed to derail, especially before it gained steam. That, and bribery money owed, explained why he was in Libertyville, Illinois. Strahan only met out of necessity with the "dark side" of the Chicago Police Department's Fraternal Order of Police. Officially, Tom Lutz was retired from the CPD and its leadership, but in many ways, the former deputy chief now wielded more power than he had when wearing a badge. At Lutz's beck and call was Officer Ron Thursby. Judging by Thursby's "Incredible Hulk" muscles and patches of acne, he likely ingested a steady diet of steroids. Steroids and sociopathy were never a good combination.

Strahan took a few deep breaths. It was show time.

He was all smiles and waves entering the Libertyville Gun Club, an establishment that most of its customers had taken to calling "Bull's-eye" probably because of the huge bull's-eye situated at the entrance to the club and used as its logo. Heidi, the buxom, blond receptionist, greeted him by name. Strahan wasn't surprised. He'd hosted a number of events at the club, wining and dining police personnel from half a dozen Midwestern and Northeastern states. If you were a purchasing agent, or had anything to do with procuring weapons, Strahan wanted to be your friend. The new police force, just like a domestic army, needed to be outfitted. Assault vehicles, urban warfare weaponry, laser optics, specialized robotics equipment, and so-called "smart weapons" had become requirements for America's new and improved police army. Given the laws of capitalism, every time a bullet was fired, someone made money, and lots of bullets were being fired.

"It's so good to see you, Mr. Strahan," Heidi said, leaning forward to give him a good view of some cosmetic surgeon's handiwork.

"Good to see you. Kendrick please," he replied, with a smile and a wink.

Most of those who went to Bull's-eye only saw what was out in the open. That was vast enough. There were shooting ranges, a billiards room, a gymnasium, an indoor basketball court, and an Olympic-sized pool. Arbalest and similar corporate citizens had helped to pay for the complex. Supposedly, it had been built for "Chicago's finest," even though the club was open to the public—or at least some of it was. Most club regulars had no idea how big the building actually was and how many recesses it had.

Heidi buzzed Strahan through a door that was marked "Authorized Personnel Only." It was a starting point to get to what Lutz called "the Vault." Strahan thought a better name would be "the Serpent's Lair." As he walked through the door and down the hallway towards the private elevator, Strahan thought about the masons and slaves that had built the secret passageways and hidden rooms in the labyrinth. He wondered if there was any truth to the stories that "the help" never lived long enough to tell tales of all their furtive building.

Strahan took an elevator up to the second floor and waited for the door to open. That it eventually did open meant that someone was monitoring his movements and allowing him access to the Vault. Strahan had sponsored a party during his last visit to the Vault. He had made sure his special visitors were treated to the best in booze and broads. And after the party, there had been an uptick in the sales of Arbalest products.

He had to walk down another hallway before coming to the entry door of the Vault. From inside, a deadbolt was deactivated, allowing Strahan to open the door. The interior of the Vault looked like a massive man cave. The room had a bar and two huge big screen televisions. Antique weapons lined the walls, including muskets, flintlocks, and Civil War swords. For good measure, there were some exotic animal heads on the walls too, including a Cape buffalo, a lion, and a cougar. The adult playpen had video games and old-school pinball games; there were several playing tables for pool, foosball, and air hockey. When a cover was added to it, the pool table also functioned as Lutz's desk.

Lutz was sitting behind that desk. Lounging nearby was Thursby.

"If it isn't Strahan the Second," said Lutz.

Thursby nodded and smiled for his boss; he scowled at Strahan.

Lutz had taken to calling him "Strahan the Second." From what Strahan could determine, there were two reasons for that. Lutz had disdain for the moneyed set, for those individuals called "junior" or those with numbers after their name. Lutz was also amused by Strahan's paying lip service to the Second Amendment while selling Arbalest products at events held in the Vault.

"*Gentlemen,*" Strahan responded, making his greeting sound like a dubious proposition and daring a smirk of his own. He wasn't the only phony in the room.

Strahan approached Lutz and casually placed a bag on his desk. It looked like any athletic bag, but inside it was filled with hundred dollar bills. Lutz opened the bag and riffled though some of the packets of Benjamins.

"Beware of geeks that bear gifts," said Lutz.

It wasn't the first time Strahan had brought him bribe money, and it wasn't the first time Lutz had made his geeks comment. Still, it got a wolf smile out of Thursby. Lutz's muscle was openly packing heat, something only a cop whose workplace was a shooting range could get away with. Of course, in Thursby's holster there wasn't the usual 9 mm automatic preferred by most cops; he went old-school with a long barrel .357 magnum. The huge weapon actually appeared small in comparison to his mutant looking oversized body. Strahan often wanted to ask Thursby if he had been raised near a nuclear power plant.

"I wouldn't be bearing—gifts—if you'd get an offshore account," said Strahan. "In fact, I really wish you'd do that. These days, moving money is more and more problematic."

"You hear that, Ron?" said Lutz. "It's problematic."

"That's a shame," growled Thursby.

"I'm just saying it would be easier all around," said Strahan.

"Not easier for me," said Lutz. "I trust bankers even less than I do lobbyists. And so do the people that work for me. I guess I hang around with unenlightened sorts. We didn't go to prep school like you and your boss. I hear you guys were real close."

Lutz made the statement while gesturing with a limp wrist.

Strahan didn't even pretend to be amused. "You want to compare humble pie? I grew up in South Providence. My way to Andover was through a scholarship. And afterward, like you, I wore a badge for a lot of years."

"That's right," said Lutz, "I forgot that Strahan the Second was a real G-Man."

"He looks like a deliveryman to me," said Thursby.

"And today I'm delivering information as well as dropping off your motivation money."

"Our *commission*," said Lutz, "which we certainly earned. There's no way you could have unloaded all of those worthless ECW's without our help."

"I wouldn't call them worthless," said Strahan, but he didn't object very forcefully; in truth the Arbalest electrical conductive weapons weren't the best.

Lutz held up his hand to stop Strahan from saying anything else. "I got a tee time in an hour," he said. "Let's cut to the chase."

"You need to hear about a sensitive matter," Strahan said, giving a side glance to Thursby. "I think it's a matter best kept to the two of us."

"Whatever you got to say in front of me, you can say in front of Ronny," said Lutz.

Strahan nodded. He considered the best way to approach the subject. The last thing Strahan wanted to do was to excite these men out of fear of them acting hastily. "Forewarned is forearmed," he started.

"Damn, I wish I'd gone to Phillips Exeter," said Lutz, interrupting him. "Is that your way of telling me some shyster is trying to get us in his sights?"

Strahan unsuccessfully tried to hide the surprise on his face.

Lutz continued: "Do you think you're the only one, Mr. Strahan the Second, who has people at the Chicago Federal courthouse on your payroll? I heard about that lawsuit within an hour of it being *sealed*." He used air quotes to show his disdain. "In fact, I was surprised you didn't show up here yesterday."

"I had other appointments," said Strahan. He didn't add that word of the lawsuit had only reached him late yesterday.

"Uh-huh," said an unconvinced Lutz. "Well, here's the latest newsflash for you. This Angus Moore hasn't only been filing lawsuits. He's been calling around asking questions. And today he called me. He was asking about any payments I might have received from Arbalest."

Lutz looked at Strahan, his glance suddenly probing. "You heard from this Moore guy yet?"

"I have not," said Strahan, "though I expect I will shortly."

"As I understand it," said Lutz, "he's named you in quite a few places in this lawsuit of his."

"Shit," said Strahan. His source hadn't known the particulars in the lawsuit.

"As in deep doo-doo," said Lutz.

Thursby smiled at his witticism.

"We can't overreact," said Strahan.

Lutz lifted his hands palm out and looked befuddled for Thursby. "Do I look like I'm overreacting?"

Thursby shook his head. The movement looked somehow strange because his overly muscled frame seemed to have eliminated his neck.

"Because at this point, that shyster is just fishing for anything he can find," said Strahan. "He wants to muddy the waters."

"Muddy waters aren't good for fishing," said Lutz.

"No, they're not," agreed Thursby.

"What I'm saying is that he's using scare tactics."

"I can see how that might work with all those wrongful deaths of Sight-Clops being cited, along with product liability and knowingly distributing a defective and dangerous product."

"Ninety-nine out of a hundred of these cases are settled out of court," said Strahan.

"And what about that one in a hundred?"

"That's not going to happen."

"Did Knapp assure you of that?"

Knapp had not assured him of that. Arbalest had pulled Sight-Clops from the market, but said they had done so only because of the introduction of Sight-Clops' successor, the new and improved Eye-Clops.

"It's the price of doing business," said Strahan.

Lutz read through his dissembling. "One in a hundred odds suddenly doesn't seem that great," he said, "if we end up on the wrong side of those odds. And even if Arbalest wins the case, the last thing we need is to be scrutinized by the Feds."

"The Feds haven't even signed on yet," Strahan said, "and they might not."

"I told you I heard stories about the Sight-Clops being hinky two summers back," said Lutz. "Some shooters said it was sighting *way* off the target."

"There might have been a glitch in a few models," admitted Strahan.

"What you call a glitch, this lawyer is calling murder."

"Theatrics are part of the legal game."

"Game or not," said Lutz, "I don't like being a pawn."

"We could be"—Strahan searched for the word—"proactive, without being reckless. I have a guy who has worked for me before. He's good, as in real good, but you'd never know it by looking at him. He's like the ultimate whiz kid, as in electronics wizard. Through him we can know what the lawyer and his firm are up to and figure out the best way to proceed."

"It sounds like you better get your guy on this," said Lutz.

"There's one complication," said Strahan. "I'll need you to front the money."

"And why is that?"

"For the time being, Arbalest is asking for an accounting of all my expenses. I am afraid there will be a short period of time where you won't be getting 'commissions.'"

"Sounds like Arbalest is getting ready for a trial," said Lutz.

Strahan shook his head and said, "They're just being cautious. I am sure in a few months things will be back to normal."

The normally quiet Thursby spoke up: "They better be."

This time it was Lutz who nodded, while looking Strahan up and down. For a moment, Strahan understood what a mouse must think when confronted by a huge feral cat.

"What's your guy's name and how do we contact him?" asked Lutz.

"He calls himself Ivanhoe," said Strahan.

# 2
# FOLLOW YOUR BLISS

When he was a high school senior, Ivan Verloc's counselor had advised him to "Follow your bliss."

That had proved to be remarkably good advice. At the time, Ivan's bliss was voyeurism. Now, almost seven years later, he still hadn't outgrown that fixation, although his deviations were now much more wide-ranging.

When he was in his early teens, Ivan had gotten the reputation of being good with computers. By the time he was a sophomore, he was bringing home more money than either of his parents. Of course, Ivan didn't just fix the machines. He improved them with some special touches of his own. No one ever found his add-ons. Ivan made his client's computers his own surveillance devices. He especially liked fixing the computers of his female clients. Most of the laptops had cameras, and Ivan used those cameras for his own personal peep shows. He also monitored emails and Skype. As a young man, Ivan got a hell of an education. Early on, he learned a particular treasure: that everyone had secrets.

What turned him on most were strong women. He loved how they acted behind closed doors. After watching his world history teacher in action, Ivan went from an indifferent student to one that was completely engaged in her classroom. Only he knew the real Miss Wagner and how she made men grovel. She told them what to do, and they did it. In one of his favorite bits of footage, Miss Wagner was fully nude, except for spiked heels, demonstrating her favorite sex positions to one of her many cougar catches. For almost an hour, she schooled her young, eager partner with the same demanding voice she used in class to emphasize important teaching moments.

After that show, Ivan was always able to make lessons about the signing of the Magna Carta or the Treaty of Versailles seem much more interesting as he visualized Miss Wagner in spiked heels, fully nude, holding a whip.

And then there was Mrs. Barnes, who lived three doors down from his family's house in a typical suburban Ohio town. Mrs. Barnes had three children and volunteered much of her free time at her church where she also taught Sunday school. To look at Mrs. Barnes, you would have thought she was just another church lady carrying twenty extra pounds while juggling all the activities of her children. Luckily for Ivan, Mrs. Barnes liked to carry her laptop and tablet—the ones he specially doctored—around just about everywhere. That allowed Ivan an up close and personal look at the surprising number of individuals she hooked up with, including the pastor of the church, as well the female director of the choir, who she seemed to favor.

Follow your bliss, Ivan remembered. Oh, he had.

And he was following his bliss right now with a number of employees at the Bergman-Deketomis Law Firm, starting with Angus Moore. If it had an electronic pulse, Ivan followed it. He was monitoring the phone traffic, emails, Instagram and Facebook accounts, and Twitter comments of those employees most closely associated with the Arbalest and Sight-Clops case. Most of those in Ivan's sights had home security systems that were supposed to be looking out for bad guys. What they had done, without knowing it, was to supply Ivan with cameras into their personal lives.

For almost three months now, Ivan had been doing his monitoring. What he'd learned first and foremost was that Angus Moore was a working machine. From dawn until well into the night, Moore spent almost all his time building his case. Ivan's employers had hired him with the hope that he might find dirt on Moore. Good luck, thought Ivan. Moore was a Boy Scout, or at least seemed that way. He wasn't sleeping around, or hitting the bottle, or spending time on porn sites. The guy's only shortcoming, so far as Ivan could find, was that he was so consumed by the case he was working on that he wasn't able to have much family time.

But truth be told, Ivan was a bit annoyed with old Angus. With his nose to the grindstone, the man was not interesting. Kendrick Strahan usually provided more interesting targets. Five years ago, another client had electronically introduced Strahan to Ivan. There was a Florida congressman who was making things difficult for the lobbyist. All Ivan had to do was introduce some kiddie porn on the congressman's personal computer, and just like that Strahan's problem disappeared. At that time the two of them had never met in person. Ivan preferred it that way. He wasn't one for face-to-face if it could be avoided.

In fact, the less his clients knew about him, the happier he was. When he'd gotten into the shady side of surveillance, Ivan had carefully buried any information about where he lived and what he did. Since the people who employed him were not exactly ethical sorts, he knew they'd gladly throw him to the wolves if it would save their asses from trouble. That's why he had all kinds of safe-guards in place. That was also why he made sure he had dirt on whoever employed him. To them he was Ivanhoe. They didn't get the joke, but Ivan didn't care. Ivanhoe was a really oldie, moldy book about knights and things. But this Ivan, millennial Ivan, was a "ho" for money.

And even though Kendrick Strahan was pretending to be his employer on the Angus Moore and Bergman-Deketomis case, Ivan knew he was fronting for a union thug named Tom Lutz, a former bigwig with the Chicago Police Department. The irony of his situation was enough to make Ivan smile. Officially, he was working for the cops. Lutz was especially interested in big, boring Angus's bloodhound act when it came to the trail of bribery surrounding Sight-Clops. The bloodhound was getting even closer to Lutz.

Ivan finished up with an electronic sound file that he'd intercepted off of Angus Moore's cell phone while he'd been talking with Mike Bixby, a lieutenant with the Evansville Police Department. Bixby had attended the latest soirée inside the Vault. Apparently, the goings-on were such that Bixby stayed for only fifteen minutes, which was still long enough for him to describe what was happening at the gathering, as well as to confirm that Lutz and Strahan had been in attendance.

Yes, bit by bit, boring old Angus was making his case. By the time he was through, Arbalest would be waving a white flag, and the Feds would be handing out jail time to Strahan, Lutz, and other bribe-takers.

Ten minutes later, Ivan's private cell phone rang. He used the phone to make calls, but not receive them. The readout didn't tell him anything about the caller, but instead said *Private Caller*. It's probably a wrong number, Ivan thought, but answered it anyway.

"Ivan?" said the voice. "Or should I say Ivanhoe?"

Instead of being freaked out, Ivan played it cool. "How are you doing, Tom?"

During Ivan's illegal monitoring, he had heard Tom Lutz's voice enough times to know it very well.

Lutz played it cool as well, acting like the two of them were good friends. "Oh, you're good Ivan. Our mutual friend swore by you, but I think we both know not to believe much of what he says. I must admit though, you are everything he advertised and more."

"I'm glad to know you're pleased."

"The more information you've provided us," said Lutz, "the clearer it's become that this situation must be dealt with."

"I can understand that."

"Anyway, I guess it's time you packed up your shop and closed down operations"—there was a long pause—"unless . . ."

"Unless what?"

"Have you ever considered venturing outside the world of electronics?"

"What I like about electronics is the lucrative nature of the work."

"I understand other work can be quite lucrative as well. That is if it's done professionally, with no loose ends."

After two more minutes of cryptic discussion, the deal was struck.

# 3
# DRIVING MISS DAISY DUKES

**"C**an I fix you some eggs?"

Gina Romano pretended not to hear the too cheerful voice of her boyfriend, Bryan. She burrowed a little deeper into her prized 1,500 thread count Egyptian bed sheets. Gina didn't think of the sheets as being an indulgence, as sleep was a precious commodity for a lawyer who usually worked at least eighty hours a week.

Bryan Penn tossed aside the sheets. It was unlikely he'd noticed how comfortable they were. Sleeping outdoors atop leaves would have been more than fine for him. With one barely opened eye, Gina watched as he threw on sweatpants and a well-worn blue T-shirt touting the Blue Mantas, a local minor league baseball team. The veterinarian brimmed with energy every morning, on full tilt as soon as he opened his eyes. He was also blind to the fact that not everyone rolled out of bed as spirited as a golden retriever puppy.

And like a puppy, Bryan was not easily rebuffed. Coming around to her side of the bed, he crouched down and said,

"Scrambled or over easy, beautiful? And do you want an English muffin or toast?"

"Scrambled, and no bread," she grumbled, pulling the covers over her head.

Gina was the porcupine to his puppy, but luckily Bryan didn't seem to notice her quills. He was Viking blonde, with tousled hair and a beard. Her friends called him a hunk, but Gina had never been one for pretty boys. What scared Gina was that Bryan actually seemed to be a good guy. And what was even scarier was that after a year of dating, he seemed all the more smitten with Gina. Her mother had always said if something seemed too good to be true, it probably was.

Of course, her mother was about the last person in the world Gina should be modeling herself after. Getting far away from her family had been the best thing Gina had ever done for herself. Fifteen years ago, she had fled the Northeast and started a new life in Florida working for the Bergman-Deketomis Law Firm. Since then, she had become a partner and one of the firm's top litigators. Lots of people reinvented themselves in the Sunshine State—or at least they attempted a good veneer.

A shower was a must, Gina decided. The night before, she'd had makeup sex with Bryan. They'd made up a few times. That was another thing for Gina to be suspicious about. How was it that her love life with Bryan kept getting better? Last night had proved so enjoyable that it took Gina a moment to even remember what they'd been fighting about. Oh, yeah. They'd had words over Jennifer.

Jennifer was Bryan's other woman. She was older, a bleached blond, or maybe it would be more accurate to call her a faded canary yellow. Whatever the color, Bryan loved his "classic" 1970 Chevy C-10 truck with its factory V-8. Others weren't as enamored with Jennifer's looks, especially Gina's homeowner's association. The gated community had rules about where its residents and guests could park. If Jennifer had been a Maserati, they probably wouldn't have cared as much, but she was a rusting old truck with a lot of hard miles on her.

As Gina began showering, she thought about their argument from the night before. The two of them had watched a movie, and before going to bed Gina had made the mistake of saying, "The HOA doesn't like you leaving your junker on the street. How about parking it in the garage?"

"Junker?" he'd said. "Jennifer is a classic."

Gina had decided to do a play on "yo mama" jokes. "Yo, Jennifer is so ugly," she said, "Hello Kitty said goodbye to her."

To his credit, Bryan had laughed. But then he'd made some crack about how the people in glass houses that lived inside of gated communities shouldn't throw rocks or make judgments about those who couldn't afford to live inside their walls.

The *pièce de résistance* though had been his feminine French voice with which he'd summed up: "Let them eat cake."

That had been enough to set Gina off. She liked to blame her temper on her genetic makeup. Her father was Sicilian, and her mother was descended from Spanish Sephardic Jews. But Gina knew her short fuse wasn't only a function of her DNA.

"Don't you dare call me an elitist," she had told Bryan. "Nothing has ever been given to me. As a girl who plays in a boy's club, I think I know a little bit about discrimination, and because of that I don't tolerate it in any form."

"Methinks the lady doth protest too much," said Bryan.

Gina responded in her angriest voice, "Methinks you ought to shove it, Dr. Doolittle. Maybe monkeys like to be talked to that way, but I don't."

She had regretted the words the moment they came out of her mouth, but pride and fear prevented her from taking them back. Gina had driven out other men in her life with similar outbursts. But instead of storming off, or responding in kind, Bryan had said, "Do you know how beautiful you are when you're angry?"

Gina, who argued for a living, could only stand there with her mouth open.

"And since you brought up the subject of monkeys," said Bryan, "have I ever told you how bonobos resolve their conflicts?"

"I don't think so," Gina said, trying to lose her edge.

Bryan took her in his arms. "They engage in a quick round of sex," he said. "And just like that, their problems get resolved. The human race could learn a lot from the bonobos."

"Quick round, you said?"

"It doesn't have to be quick."

Gina found herself smiling in the shower. It hadn't been quick. It had been perfect. She only allowed herself a short reverie, though. It was time to return to the real world. Work awaited her. She was a shark, even if there was a part of her that would have preferred being a bonobo.

She grabbed an outfit from her walk-in closet and quickly dressed. Her makeup was applied almost as quickly. She'd heard her eyes described as "cat-like," probably because of their green hue. Or maybe there was something feral about them. Most people assumed that collagen had been applied to her lips, but they were just naturally thick ("bee stung," one boyfriend had called them). The same people also assumed her curves and youthful face had been assisted by a cosmetic surgeon, although Gina had never gone under the knife. Her mother had made that mistake too many times, trying to physically please her father. Mother should have known that no surgery would prove enough. Gina touched the few lines that were beginning to show on her face. Then she remembered that Bryan liked to say the dents and rust on Jennifer showed her "character," and suddenly Gina was feeling a little more charitable about the old girl.

From downstairs, Bryan yelled, "Your food is getting cold."

◆◆◆

In addition to the scrambled eggs, Bryan had made her a rasher of bacon. He'd even warmed two corn tortillas, knowing Gina's love for any food in a tortilla.

"You really know a way to a woman's heart, don't you?" she said.

"I hope so, even though when it comes to you, sometimes the way seems maze-like."

Gina took a bite of his eggs. He'd sautéed onions and peppers and included them in the scramble. Gina offered up some appreciative sounds.

"I better take a shower and change," he said. "I'll be stopping by the studio."

Bryan was a regular on a local TV show called *The Jungles of Florida*. The show spotlighted a nearby exotic animal rescue sanctuary where "Dr. Bryan," as he was referred to on the show, volunteered his time as a vet. In fact, it was that sanctuary that had brought the couple together. Gina had attended a fundraiser dinner for the sanctuary and found herself seated at the head table next to him. The two of them had talked nonstop, with the only break in their conversation occurring when Bryan did an interview for the local news. What Gina noticed most during the interview was the way the attractive young female reporter swooned all over him.

After the segment, Bryan returned to Gina and said, "Where were we?"

"I think we left off with someone saying, 'Thank you so much for your time, Dr. Bryan,' said a breathless Gina, sounding remarkably like the reporter. 'I really enjoyed our talk.'"

"I'm not used to being interviewed solo," he admitted. "I'm invariably in the company of lions and tigers and bears."

"Oh my," said Gina.

"And Clara."

"Clara?" asked a suspicious Gina.

"Clara the cockatoo," he said.

"I'm so glad you clarified," she said.

Bryan groaned before saying, "Clara is a loudmouth and a show-off. When I'm in her company, I definitely play second fiddle, which is how I like it. On the show, the animals need to be center stage. I'm just the help."

At the time, Gina had wondered if "Dr. Bryan" could possibly be as sincere as he seemed. They'd been dating ever since the fundraiser. So why did she still have her doubts about his sincerity?

"A shower sounds like a good idea," she said. "You wouldn't want to disappoint your female fans."

"I'm only interested in one of my female fans."

"Is that so?"

"How about you stop by the clinic after work? We can have dinner and discuss more monkey business."

"Somehow I have this feeling you're not talking about bonobos again."

The couple kissed. It wasn't quite a bonobo send-off, but it was a pleasant smooch. Gina said, a little breathlessly, "I'll try and be there by seven."

Even though Bryan had his own house, he had keys and the security code to hers. Gina opened the garage door and climbed into her black Porsche Cayenne. She pushed the ignition button but nothing happened, so she hit it again. Gina checked to make sure the car was engaged in park. Then she checked the headlights. When they came on, she concluded that it wasn't a drained battery, but probably something in the electrical system.

At the moment, her $80,000 car was an expensive paperweight.

Gina tried to start it again. And then again Bryan opened the garage door to the sound of Sicilian cursing.

"*Vaffanculo! Testa di cazzo!*"

He was glad he didn't know the translation and for once was not on the receiving end of Gina's temper.

"Need a ride?" he asked.

She offered a terse nod of her head.

Bryan decided to push the envelope a little bit. "And you're not embarrassed to be seen riding around in Jennifer?"

Gina gritted her teeth and said nothing. A grinning Bryan went around and opened Jennifer's passenger door. "Your carriage awaits, Cinderella."

As much as she didn't want to laugh, Gina couldn't help it. She even decided to join in the fun. "Shows you what dem uppity clowns running dat house owner's 'sociation know," she said in her best cracker patois.

"Darling," said Bryan, "the blood rushes around in the right places when you go all redneck on me."

"Tell you what, Bry-Bob," she said, "later on I'll be bringing out my Daisy Dukes just for you."

That's when both of them lost it. Gina wasn't used to starting the day with laughter. Normally, she put on her game face along with her makeup. Maybe Bryan really was the guy for her, she thought, even though she kept trying to convince herself otherwise.

Gina knew she came with lots of baggage. And at least for now she also knew it was nice having someone to help her to carry it.

# 4

# JUNK-YARD DOGS AND POLAR BEARS

**S**ince it was the last Thursday of the month, "Show and Tell" was on the company docket. That was the name Gina gave to it. She loved Show and Tell, which was otherwise known as the "Company Monthly Meeting." While Gina knew that most people hated to go to work meetings, she figured that was because they didn't work for Bergman-Deketomis. The monthly partner/associates meetings were always edifying, and the characters assembled always made it fun. Hearing her peers talk invariably inspired Gina. It wasn't as if everyone sat around singing "Kumbaya," but there was a feeling of a higher calling to the gathering. You didn't work at Bergman-Deketomis if you weren't passionate. The law firm certainly had its causes. Cases were pursued to try and make the world a better place. That notion sounded funny to most, especially when put into the context of a law firm. Certainly, no one would mistake Bergman-Deketomis for The Salvation Army. They survived as a business through winning settlements, but at the same time they took on all sorts of cases that other law firms, as well as the government, wouldn't touch—cases that needed to be tried, but were typically avoided because of the costs associated with them, or the inherent difficulties of prevailing in court.

Gina thought of the many times she'd heard Nick Deketomis say, "All right, let's go tilt at another windmill." That was his rallying cry to the troops. It was his call for them to take on a good cause, if not what other firms would think was a good case. They had to buy into the impossible dream. In many ways, Deke *was* Don Quixote, the tarnished knight who kept fighting. Their names—Deke and Don Q—were even similar. Two years ago, Gina and some of the other partners had bought Deke a life-sized metal statue of Don Quixote, which was now proudly displayed in his office.

She smiled at the memory of their unveiling of that statue, before a dark thought came into her head: *And that makes me who? Dulcinea?*

Gina tried to squash her dark thoughts. Most of the time she kept those judgments under the surface, but they weren't as far under as she would have liked. She came from a dysfunctional family. No, "dysfunctional" wasn't a strong enough word. She had hated her father, had been dismayed by the behavior of her mother, and had felt sorry for her younger brother. That's why she needed the outlet of her work. That's why Show and Tell invariably made her feel better about her life. Working with amazing people made Gina proud of being with the firm. And there was another reason she liked the meetings. At one time the government would have referred to the Romano household she had grown up in as a nuclear family, but Gina had never thought of it as a family. Not all orphans are without parents.

Bergman-Deketomis was her only real family.

◆◆◆

Gina arrived five minutes before the meeting was due to begin. The law firm had a number of conference rooms. The one where they were meeting was referred to as the Aerie, or the "Bird's Nest," even though it was officially called the ninth floor conference room. Gina preferred the name, Aerie. The setting had the feel of some giant nest atop a cliff. You didn't need to see like an eagle to feel you had the vision of one. From the Aerie you could see over Spanish Trace and out to the Gulf of Mexico. There was a huge oak table in the Aerie that easily accommodated the fifty or so partners and associates that would be attending, but Gina made it a point of arriving early to get a place near the head of the table.

Martin Bergman, founder of Bergman-Deketomis, always sat at one head of the table. Usually Deke sat to his right, except on those formal occasions when each man would sit on opposite ends of the conference table. Gina claimed a seat just three down from the head of the table; a moment later she was joined by Cara Deketomis. Smiling, she asked Gina, "Do you mind if I sit next to you?"

"By all means," said Gina.

As Cara settled in Gina asked, "How are you feeling these days?"

Less than a year had passed since Cara had been hospitalized and almost died from side effects from taking Ranidol. Ironically, at the time her father was pursuing a case against Bekmeyer Pharmaceuticals, the makers of Ranidol. Cara hadn't at first disclosed to her father that she had been on Ranidol, and not wanting to advertise the fact that she was using birth control only revealed this when it finally became absolutely necessary for him to know. Like so many dads, Deke sometimes had a blind spot when it came to acknowledging his little girl was growing up. Or in the present case, this attractive blond woman was all grown up.

"I'm doing great," said Cara. "I'm in this long-term study that monitors the health of Ranidol users, and, so far, all my data has been encouraging."

"With all the hours you've been putting in here," Gina told her, "I figured you had to have a clean bill of health."

"Yes, you know the life of an associate."

"I know the life of a *female* associate," Gina said, "and now I know the life of a *female* partner. You will, too."

Despite the advances of women lawyers, the same glass ceiling that was found in business also existed in legal firms. Bergman-Deketomis was trying to be the exception to that rule, but women just didn't seem to get the same respect as their male colleagues.

"Now I'm beginning to understand what they say about Ginger Rogers," said Cara.

"What's that?" asked Gina.

"She did everything Fred Astaire did, but backwards and in high heels, and yet Fred got all the dancing credit."

Gina smiled and reached out a hand to the shoulder of her younger colleague. It was no secret that Deke had worked Cara harder than any of the other associates before her illness and was now doing the same thing again. He didn't want the appearance of favoritism.

"Learn from my mistakes," said Gina. "Leave time for a personal life."

"Mistakes?" said Cara. "Bryan is a hunk."

"Life in the jungle can be fun," Gina admitted.

"I hear his show is being syndicated. Is that true?"

Gina nodded. "Right now it's being shown in a number of test markets. And they're trying to get Bryan to agree to travel out of the country so they can film him with different species in exotic locations."

"What does he think about that?"

"He's sort of torn. His practice is stretched thin as it is, especially with the new clinic. And going out of the country means we'll have even less time together."

"I hope the two of you can work it out," said Cara.

"I do too," said Gina.

And she really did, Gina thought. That surprised her. And it also made her feel vulnerable. She hated the idea of being dependent on someone else for her happiness.

Martin Bergman and Nick Deketomis walked through the door together at three o'clock exactly. Those outside the firm thought the two men were the odd couple. Bergman projected the tough, worldly grandfather role. He was the cynicism countering Deke's optimism. Bergman was Jewish and old enough to have experienced some of Florida's entrenched anti-Semitism firsthand. Deke was the outgoing Greek; Bergman was more reserved, more intellectual. But the sum of the two men had proved to be far more than their individual parts. They complemented each other perfectly.

Gina watched them as they took their seats. They had worked together so long now that their movements looked like those of synchronized swimmers. Each knew their routine. The Bergman-Deketomis building was the largest edifice in Spanish Trace, with the top six floors of the building taken up by the law firm. Here in the Aerie, Gina felt as if she could see the whole world. It was an overcast day in the Sunshine State. Low, gray clouds hung over Spanish Trace and extended out to the Gulf of Mexico.

Deke gestured for Martin to open the meeting.

"Are we done yet?" growled Bergman, drawing laughs from all those assembled. "I need a smoke."

He looked down to his index and middle finger which were holding the remains of a chewed but not lit cigar. "This building has my name on it," he said, "and yet the only place I can smoke is on the balcony upstairs."

"Diana says you can't even smoke there," said Deke, drawing even more laughter.

Diana was Bergman's longtime administrative assistant.

"Evil woman," said Martin.

"She loves you," said Angus Moore, "and is trying to keep you alive to see your eightieth birthday. The doctor told her that won't happen if she doesn't stop you from smoking."

"I keep telling her it's my special *imports* that are keeping me alive," Martin replied.

"But let's move away from the topic of Cohiba cigars and talk about something that is far more important than my smoke-saturated old body. Got a call from a friend who told me that the law firm of Peterson and Price in Cincinnati closed their doors last week after defaulting on a seventy million dollar loan that they accepted from a Wall Street school of sharks operating a high risk mezzanine fund."

Bergman appeared to take a bite out of his cigar and then continued with a slight chuckle, "There's a new trend developing where investment finance groups on Wall Street want to own law firms that have regularly sued them and their corporate pals over the years." His chuckle grew into a full belly laugh.

"Three weeks ago a couple of the prickly predators came to our office and made a proposal to me and Deke that you all will appreciate. They wanted us to accept one hundred and fifty million dollars in a nonrecourse arrangement that had interest and points at close to twenty two percent. Their pitch was that we could use the money to begin building Bergman, Deketomis law firms all over America and become the Walmart of lawyering."

Deke joined in, saying, "I'll point out, gang, that the conversation didn't end well. Let me see if I remember all the details. I believe it started out with Martin making them one of his creative counter offers. It involved a suggestion that would have required the shorter character of the two to place his head up the butt of his partner and carry him on his shoulders out the front door of our building into oncoming traffic. And to add more drama to the moment he pointed out that we could actually buy both of them and the entire mezzanine fund they were managing if we had any desire to do business with junk-yard dogs."

As the laughter in the room subsided Martin added, "Please wait until Deke and I are six feet under before anyone in this room seriously considers any kind of partnership with a pack of Wall Street body snatchers that are trying to sink their grubby claws into law firms, lawyers, and the people we are supposed to represent."

Deke added, "Let talk about a case that's going to cost a group of Wall Streeters a bunch of money before it's all over."

◆◆◆

As Deke talked about his toxic pollution case against DuPont, the room grew transfixed. Gina knew that whenever the firm used focus groups or mock juries, the participants invariably commented that what they liked about Deke was his passion and sincerity. That meant when he worked a courtroom, Deke could just be himself. Deke's southern accent was homey and without affect. Gina often thought that it was amazing how he'd grown up mostly on the streets and managed to become this person she so admired today. Gina saw something in the way Deke worked a courtroom that reminded her of an Atticus Finch.

Before she even took a job with the firm, Gina learned that *To Kill a Mocking Bird* influenced Deke as much as it did her. From the start this helped to establish a strong bond between the two.

Gina had always been curious about the author. Not surprisingly, Harper Lee's father was an attorney. Not only that, but he had defended two black men accused of murder. Gina felt even more kinship with Lee when she'd learned that her mother was mentally ill, most likely with severe bipolar disorder, which resulted in her being mentally and emotionally absent for her daughter.

Been there and done that, thought Gina.

Deke wove the parts of the DuPont story together. "We have documentation that proves DuPont poisoned the drinking water of seventy thousand people living along the Ohio River," he said. "Carol Morris and her team are gathering all sorts of solid data showing the spiking cancer rates."

Carol was the senior investigator for the firm. Always polite and pleasant, and the picture of a loving, older aunt, she was able to get information out of even the most reluctant people. And Carol also had an unparalleled confederation of resources in and out of law enforcement that she called upon when needed.

"Because of DuPont's run-off," continued Deke, "we have already established that the groundwater in five riverside communities was made toxic and that virtually anyone who drank from those community water facilities for more than a year has hugely elevated chances for getting cancer, thyroid disease, and lifelong ulcerative colitis. Everyone here knows my philosophy: shoot someone with a gun, it's murder; kill someone with toxic chemicals, and it's still murder."

Deke opened up his briefcase and pulled out a familiar looking item, an old frying pan. He held up the pan for everyone in the room.

"Exhibit A," he said, "a nonstick frying pan. It doesn't look like a killing machine does it? It's not even like one of those heavy iron skillets you sure don't want to get hit over the head with. But this frying pan is a lot deadlier than one made with iron. That's because making its nonstick surface comes with a terrible price, namely perfluorooctanoic acid, or C-8 as it is called by DuPont scientists.

"I am sorry to say this, but I can confidently tell everyone in this room that there are traces of C-8 in your blood. That is because C-8 persists in the environment for at least two million years, if not indefinitely. DuPont let that evil genie out of the bottle.

And they kept manufacturing C-8 even after they positively knew it could cause kidney and testicular cancer. In heavy doses, like those released into the Ohio River, C-8 has ravaged like the Four Horsemen of the Apocalypse. Even remote areas of the world aren't safe from its predation. Researchers in the Arctic have found C-8 in the livers of polar bears. There really is no escaping it, is there? And all because it was more *convenient* to use a frying pan that didn't require butter or oil. Had we known, like DuPont, that such convenience could kill us, I doubt very much we would have signed on."

"It's too bad we couldn't have a polar bear on the jury," said Martin.

—◆◆◆—

Four other lawyers spoke. They were all fact situations where a corporation chose not to obey the law because it was not cost-effective. There were ongoing cases involving everything from blood thinners causing fatal bleeding, to BPA hazards in everything from juice boxes to milk bottles, to the use of nanotechnology causing cancers at the molecular level, and banks washing money for terrorists.

Angus Moore was the last lawyer to speak. Deke had personally recruited Angus, just as he had Gina. Most of the other lawyers in the firm had come to Bergman-Deketomis through more traditional routes. It was easy to see why Deke had wanted Angus, thought Gina. She had more trouble in figuring out why he'd wanted her. Last year, Deke had paid Gina the highest possible compliment by asking her to represent him as his criminal defense lawyer on a murder case in which his far-right enemies had conspired to bring him down. Winning that case had been Gina's proudest moment as a lawyer.

Much like Deke, Angus was eminently likable. People called him a gentle giant. Gina thought if Hollywood was looking to remake *Mr. Smith Goes to Washington*, Angus would make a great

Jimmy Stewart, except for the fact that he was much more muscular than the actor. She had heard Angus played Division I football in college, but not from him. Unlike most jocks, Angus didn't dwell on his former glory days. Almost all the personal effects in his office were from his family life; there weren't any mementos from his football days. And unlike most other college football players, Angus hadn't gone to fat. If anything, he'd gone the opposite way, probably because of all the triathlete training he enjoyed doing. Right now, because he was in the middle of a case, Angus barely had time for his half hour daily cardio and weight training in the Bergman-Deketomis workout facilities. He'd convinced Gina to join him in working out a few times, but trying to keep up with him had been impossible.

"As everyone knows," said Angus, "gun control legislation in this country is all but dead. It has been more than twenty years since the Brady Bill, the last piece of significant legislation to pass through Congress, was signed into law. And since that time, the Brady Bill has been weakened and undermined at every turn.

"The NRA and the Gun Control Institute have bought Congress lock, stock, and gun barrel. They have stretched the boundaries of the Second Amendment and lobby against anything they believe infringes upon it. That has resulted in weapons manufacturers basically doing anything they want. These manufacturers have presumed they are either above the law, or are absolved by the law. In most cases they are right, but what the Arbalest Corporation has done can't even be protected by their very expansive interpretation of the Second Amendment.

"Four years ago, Arbalest brought Sight-Clops on the market. The Sight-Clops was supposed to be the latest and greatest hologram gunsight. All you had to do was get a bead on the target and pull the trigger. Gun enthusiasts ate it up. Everyone swore it did its job perfectly. Of course, shooters are just like anyone else. They prefer to do their shooting from the inside of an air-conditioned shooting range, or in the great outdoors on perfect weather days when there is little humidity. Maybe that's why the Sight-Clops defect didn't show itself right away. This defect even varied from product to product. But on hot, humid days some Sight-Clops malfunction in a way that has too often proved fatal. The Sight-Clops set up the shooter to fail. According to our information, the shooter was locked onto a target, but after pulling the trigger that round could end up five to ten degrees away from its intended target."

"That's rigged even more than the gun sights at a carnival," said Ned "Threepio" Williams.

Ned, who had recently been named a partner at the firm, was assisting Angus on the case. Even though he was approaching forty, Ned was still carded every time he was in a bar. Like Threepio from *Star Wars*, Ned spoke a number of languages. And his recall was about as good as Threepio's as well.

"As most of you know," said Angus, "some months back we submitted a letter to the Department of Justice asking the US federal government to use the information we had gathered from the person we believe is a credible whistle-blower to file a False Claims case against Arbalest, the manufacturer of Sight-Clops. In our letter, we asserted that Arbalest had scammed both state and federal governments out of hundreds of millions of dollars. We said the evidence of their culpability was overwhelming, and their conduct rose to a level of clear criminality."

"And let me take a wild guess at what's happened since," said Deke. "To quote from the movie *Cool Hand Luke*, 'What we've got here is failure to communicate.'"

"Pretty much," said Angus. "Getting anything out of the DOJ has been like pulling teeth."

"Who are you going through?" asked Deke.

"Assistant US Attorney Eva Trench has been assigned to our case," said Angus.

"We call her 'Stonewall Trench,'" admitted Ned.

Martin made a disparaging sound. "We've had dealings with her before," he said. "She's in the Fraud Division of DC. Main Justice, right?"

At the nods of Angus and Ned, Martin shook his head. "AUSA Trench is a remnant from Holder's Department of Justice. During his tenure, it should have been called the Department of Expediency. Holder never met a whistle-blower he liked, and Trench is probably of the same mind. The DOJ allowed Wall Street banks to steal trillions of dollars from the American economy in 2008, and in the end, not one of those bankers spent time in jail."

Deke added sarcastically, "You know what a fan I am of Justice. Their attitude is consistent when it comes to criminal corporations; no soul to save, nobody to incarcerate. Good luck with your dealings with them, Angus."

"Be that as it may," said Angus, "after our filing, Justice requested we bring them our whistle-blower, a forty-two year old male named Robert Diaz. We met with Trench in her office. Diaz worked for Arbalest for almost fifteen years. He claims that he brought his concerns about Sight-Clops early and often to upper management. Diaz even wrote a report saying that the gunsight calibration could be off by as much as half a degree every ten yards given certain weather conditions. Being a good employee is what got Diaz fired. After his dismissal though, Arbalest claims Diaz stole patent secrets. Naturally, they've threatened to press charges against him.

"At the time of our meeting with AUSA Trench, she seemed to be impressed with Diaz's testimony, but in retrospect I realize she was trolling for any and all information she could get. During the meeting she got us on a speakerphone call with investigators from the FBI, US Treasury, Department of Defense, and the Office of Inspector General. All of those agencies had read our complaint and asked us questions."

"So much for a sealed brief," said Martin.

"We can be sure that by now Arbalest knows every detail in the brief," said Deke.

Whistle-blower cases like this one were required to remain sealed from the public eye for a minimum of sixty days while the DOJ considered whether or not they would prosecute. The good news was that if the DOJ failed to do its job, a private law firm could step in and prosecute the case on its own. That was the crossroad the firm was facing.

"We've waited more than four months to hear back from the DOJ," said Angus. "Despite all my prodding, they've regularly requested time extensions to make their decision, and they claim that they are still reviewing the documents, emails, and recordings that we submitted."

"Thus, a perfect demonstration of stonewalling," said Ned.

"You know they say that laws are like sausage—it's better not to see them being made," said Angus. "I guess that makes the DOJ the biggest sausage maker of all. Clearly, it's extremely political, with huge egos and big personalities clashing over just about everything. Thrown into that stew are politicians and partisan politics. All of that might be contributing to Trench's lack of enthusiasm. Or maybe she doesn't think this is a case worthy of her AUSA status."

"So it's time we start making noise about their brain paralysis," said Martin.

"Exactly what I intend to do. I'm filing new motions with the court next week focusing on all the endless delays by the DOJ."

"How solid is your whistle-blower?" asked Deke.

"I won't say he doesn't have barnacles," said Angus. "But Robert Diaz stepped forward when others weren't willing to. He did what he knew was right in order to save lives."

"Tell us about these barnacles," said Gina.

"He has two ex-wives," said Angus. "Neither would call him a model husband, as he wasn't faithful to either. In addition to his skirt chasing, Robert has racked up some substantial debts, mostly through his ex-wives. In his own way, the guy is a romantic. He's still looking for true love. While he is a bit rough around the edges, Robert is no lowlife."

"Will he hang in there when things get ugly?" asked Gina.

In whistle-blower cases, it wasn't a matter of *if* things got ugly; it was only a matter of *when*.

"He stuck his neck out on the job," said Angus, "and Arbalest responded by blaming the messenger. They chopped his head off instead of pulling their defective product. And then they threatened to bring him up on charges. Instead of backing down, Robert became a whistle-blower. He wasn't thinking about a payday. He wasn't thinking about revenge. He spoke up because he couldn't stand the idea of a product he was associated with killing innocent people."

Angus's passion rose as he spoke. "I think we should speak up for those same reasons. Diaz was a senior quality control supervisor at Arbalest. He is not some tinfoil hat freak hustling the DOJ, and they know that. What Justice doesn't know is that they haven't been given everything pertinent to our case. I'm holding one particular card close to my vest that I thought it best not to disclose for fear of the information ending up in the wrong hands."

"Arbalest is one of Capitol Hill's favorite sugar daddies," said Ned.

"So your case is good," asked Deke, "and your whistle-blower is reasonably solid, but Trench is noticeably dragging her feet?"

"She is," said Angus.

"My guess is that Trench's boss is encouraging her to move at a snail's pace," said Deke.

Angus' brow furrowed. "Why?"

"Get your program here," said Martin, acting like he was a ballgame hawker. "Get your program and read all about the players."

Deke translated Martin's ballgame parlance. "US Attorney Abe Castillo was an Obama appointee whose legal roots stemmed from being an in-house counsel for three different defense contractors. Castillo was sponsored for his job by Senator Ric Grant of Illinois."

Gina connected the dots: "Which happens to be where the corporate headquarters of Arbalest is located."

Deke nodded. "Still, I'm not sure Justice thinks it can steer clear of all the potential bad publicity this case would bring them. It seems to me they're taking a huge risk by not joining us going forward with this. And does Senator Grant really want to be associated with the friendly fire deaths of innocent American soldiers, police officers, and civilians?"

"We don't need the DC bureaucrats dragging us down anyway," said Angus. "We've got a good case without them."

"A good and *expensive* case," said Martin. "I suppose I don't need to remind everyone that whistle-blower cases tried without federal involvement traditionally have a pitiful success rate. And why is that? It's because political roadblocks inevitably develop in the course of pursuing these cases, and without the Feds bulldozing these obstacles out of the way, everything usually comes to a big standstill."

"This case has massive ramifications," said Angus. "In our sights are defense contractors, the gun lobby, and all the people they bribe, such as lawmakers and police union bosses. Their recklessness has wounded and killed people, so with or without the government's help I believe it's our duty to go forward with this case."

The conference room fell silent while those present absorbed Angus's words. At last, Deke spoke up. "Well said, Angus."

Gina couldn't help smiling, knowing how much her friend and mentor relished taking on the really tough cases, especially when they had the high moral ground. Martin Bergman was ever the pragmatist though.

"When you take on the gun lobby Angus," he said, "you better expect them to come out with all their man toys blazing. As we take this on, make sure our balls don't get bigger than our brains. My biggest fear is that as these multinational giant corporations continue to suck up political and economic power, they'll become not only 'too big to fail' but 'too big to prosecute.' I am so old, I dream in black and white. However, some truths never change. You can be sure that criminal corporations able to wield that kind of power aren't afraid at all of using criminal conduct as a means to their ends. How far they'll go, I don't know, but it should scare the hell out of us just a little bit."

Martin stopped talking for long enough to look woefully at his still unlit cigar, and then continued speaking. "These days, the odds are stacked against whistle-blowers. Think about what happened to Assange. Granted, he's a schmuck, but forced incarceration, even if it is in a cushy embassy, is a little much—well, I digress. In regards to your case, Angus, it seems to me that when the DOJ is waffling on a case that looks like a slam dunk, something's rotten and usually opportunity awaits. But you'll need to tread carefully."

Waving his cigar to the room, Martin concluded by saying, "Common wisdom is that you don't poke a snake with a stick. Be aware that what we're doing is poking a stick into a nest of vipers."

# 5
## ONE LAST TOAST

**S**how and Tell had concluded at a little after five, but Gina's workday continued on. At six-thirty, she was still behind her desk working on getting out a brief on a Title VII sex discrimination case. The problem was the firm's printing department. Gina had been put on hold yet again by one of the tech support people. Her filed brief had been rejected by a judge because it did not follow the federal appellate rules on formatting, namely, the heading on one of the brief's fifty pages was inconsistent with the court rules. A $2.2 million case had been thrown back at her over that single page. Because of that, she needed the entire brief reformatted and reprinted, and she needed it yesterday.

Gina couldn't help thinking about the conversation she'd had earlier with Cara. Most working women did have to be Ginger Rogers, she thought, dancing backward and in high heels. There was no way one of the male partners would have been put on hold for this long. They would have raised hell. But if Gina did the same, she'd probably be called a "ball buster." She was doing her best to keep her temper in check, even in this exercise of futility.

One stupid, insignificant, formatting error, she thought. More and more, Gina was beginning to think the law was more about form than substance. She recalled how the brief from New England Patriots' quarterback Tom Brady, defending his actions in Deflategate, had been thrown out by a court clerk because it was not printed on the precise shade of white paper required.

The law was supposed to be about shades of grey, not about the frigging shade of white paper.

And now, she had to jump through another stupid hoop. Somewhere, sometime, bean counters and bureaucrats had won the war and now enforced its rules.

According to her phone, she'd been put on hold by the printer guy eleven minutes and twenty-eight seconds ago. "Hello," said Gina. "Hello?"

But neither the printer guy, nor the universe, was apparently listening. Gina's phone display went blank and she realized that she had been disconnected.

"Shit!" she yelled.

She slammed the phone into its cradle just as Angus tentatively poked his head into her large corner office. "Is it safe to enter?" he asked.

"It will be after I have a few minutes to come unglued," she said.

"Take your time with that," said Angus.

Gina waved for him to take a chair, and then she got the printer guy on the phone. Calmly, but firmly, she said, "If you put me on hold again, I will write you up to your supervisor and mention that your inaction and/or indifference might have cost this firm more than two million dollars. Can you hear me now?"

Suddenly, the printer guy was more than accommodating, and the problem with the incorrectly formatted page was resolved. When Gina hung up the phone, Angus nodded his approval.

"You have such a sweet side," he said with a wry smile.

"It sometimes goes unnoticed. Can you imagine?"

"You got a minute to talk?"

"For you, I've got at least two minutes. What's up?"

"What do you think about helping me on the Arbalest case?" he asked.

Gina didn't immediately answer. "I thought Ned was your trusty second," she finally said.

"He is. But Deke wants Ned's help in the DuPont wars. And there was one area in particular where I know you'd be the perfect confederate in this case."

Instead of asking him where that area was, Gina said, "When you took on the Arbalest case, I was disappointed that you didn't ask me to be second."

Angus nodded. "I seriously considered asking you, but the biggest reason I went with Ned is his way with languages. The Arbalest case is going to go international, and Ned can use his German, Spanish, French, and whatever else he speaks."

That made sense, thought Gina, but she still had the sense that something else had factored into his decision.

"You should know I took a semester of Latin," she said.

"If we get a case in Vatican City I'll remember that," he said.

Then Angus decided to come completely clean with her. "I knew that in the initial stages of this Arbalest case, Ned and I would have to spend a lot of time together, and we have. We've traveled together, eaten together, and spent a lot of late nights together. If the two of us had done that, Gina, I am not sure I could have trusted myself. In case you don't know it, you are and will always be my 'what if?'"

Although Angus was ten years older than Gina, when she had first come to the firm the two of them became lovers for a short time. No one ever knew about that. At the time, Angus was recently divorced from Darcy, his college sweetheart. But Gina and Angus had both realized a workplace romance just wouldn't jive. Their time together was short but sweet, and the two of them actually came away from their split liking the other even more.

Angus continued talking. "You know how it is when you start a big case. I've barely seen my wife and child these past three months. And I've seen you and Bryan together. The two of you have a good thing. On my own end, I think I was afraid of the prospect of having to spend all that time with you. Or maybe I was afraid of finding out that you just looked at our time together as a fling."

"Never," said Gina. "And thank you for your explanation, as well as saving a place in your heart for me."

Being Angus's "what if" meant more to Gina than she could say. A one in a million guy like Angus actually held her in esteem. A part of him even loved her. That kind of validation gave her hope that she had somehow surmounted her upbringing.

"And now that you've got me all dewy-eyed," said Gina, "why is it that you think I'm so invaluable to your case?"

"I need someone to go toe-to-toe with AUSA Trench."

"So you want a catfight?"

"This isn't about gender," Angus answered. "This is about the two of us playing tag team on her, with you being the good cop and me being the bad cop."

"Why do you get to be the bad cop?"

"Because I'm older," he said, "and I've already presented myself to her as the heavy. Listen, Trench has a history of settling important cases like this one for chump change. She gets to pad her resume and claim victory, while at the same time giving the so-called losers not much more than a slap on the wrist. It's win–win for Trench. So in the future, when she decides to run for the Senate, Trench will be able to portray herself as being tough on crime, while at the same time she'll be collecting big contributions to her campaign coffers from those individuals and companies that essentially got free passes and no jail time."

"So what's my role as good cop?" asked Gina.

"You are going to be a righteous talking point," he said. "And I'll need you to elegantly deliver a threat of sorts. Nobody can do an elegant threat like you can."

"You really know how to sweet talk a girl," said Gina. "So what elegant threat am I going to make to an already hostile AUSA?"

"The threat will reference something I'm working on. Right now, I'm following a lead that I'm hoping will force the Justice Department into actually prosecuting some white-collar criminals. Justice needs to be concerned that I will embarrass them all the way up to the top if they engineer a quick settlement for pennies, and then Bergman-Deketomis recovers hundreds of millions of dollars against Arbalest in state and federal courts all over America under a simple defective product theory."

"Can you tell me more about the lead you have?" asked Gina.

"I will when I have more proof. For now, though, I'm hoping you'll settle for a drink."

"You buying?" she asked.

"I'm hoping to prevail upon the charity of the prettiest bartender in Spanish Trace."

"How do you know my bar is stocked?"

"Because the other day when you opened a filing cabinet I noticed an unopened bottle of Scotch that, if I'm not mistaken, you were given last Christmas. And while it's a fine bottle of Scotch, I think it has aged long enough."

Gina went and retrieved the bottle and then found two water glasses. She handed Angus the bottle of Scotch and let him open it. He poured two fingers worth into each glass.

"I think I was saving this bottle for some courtroom victory," she said, "but this is even better."

Each of them raised a glass. Angus surprised Gina with his toast:

> *Here's to the prettiest, here's to the wittiest,*
> *Here's to the truest of all who are true,*
> *Here's to the neatest one, here's to the sweetest one,*
> *Here's to them all wrapped in one—here's to you.*

Gina found herself wiping away a tear as they touched glasses.

# 6

## DARK WAS THE NIGHT

Even though Gina and Angus both had plans for the night—Gina had her dinner date with Bryan, and Angus had a night of going through whistle-blower paperwork—neither hurried to finish their drinks.

"Didn't I see Bryan drop you off this morning?" asked Angus.

"Bryan was enjoying chauffeuring me so much I am surprised he wasn't honking Jennifer's horn and flashing her lights to draw even more attention to us."

"Jennifer?" asked Bryan.

"That's what he calls that old work truck of his. It's a 1970 model, and Bryan tells me Jennifer was the most popular girl's name that year. Whenever I suggest to Bryan that Jennifer is long in the tooth, he takes umbrage. And this morning when my car wouldn't start he took particular pleasure in giving me a ride."

"Should we offer a toast to Jennifer?"

"Let's not," said Gina.

Angus hid his smile behind his upturned glass. "So how are you getting home?" he asked.

"I am going to take an Uber over to Bryan's clinic," Gina said. "From there we'll be going out to dinner."

"How about I give you a ride?"

"I gladly accept," she said, "unless your ride is an old Chevy truck. That I only do for true love."

◆◆◆

Angus pulled his Lincoln Navigator out of the parking garage. His oversized frame fit perfectly in the oversized vehicle. Gina happily sunk into the vehicle's plush leather seats and closed her eyes. Both lawyers hadn't been able to leave work without taking home over-stuffed briefcases, but working nights and weekends wasn't anything new to them.

Gina wasn't surprised when she heard music coming from the speakers. She remembered Angus and his eclectic musical taste. He liked everything from hip-hop to jazz. When Gina had commented on that, Angus had merely said, "I get my best ideas from great music."

The unusual blues Angus was playing now connected with Gina's mood. The singer was picking and projecting something that touched her. His humming and moaning tapped into a feeling of loss, both sad and beautiful. The two of them listened in silence as both were transported into the mood and sentiment of what was being communicated. When the song concluded, both of them sat silently. The music deserved respectful pause.

"What was that?" Gina finally asked.

"That was Blind Willie Johnson singing, *Dark Was the Night, Cold Was the Ground*."

"When he was strumming that guitar, it felt like he was reaching deep inside of me."

"Most people who hear it react the same way," said Angus. "I'm not sure if it's blues or a spiritual. I only know it's something unique. I bet you even the extraterrestrials can feel its power."

Gina turned her head. "What are you talking about?"

"I'm talking about the Voyager probe," he said. "Back in the '70s, Carl Sagan and a bunch of scientists were told they had to succinctly sum up our planet and people in sounds and music. Can you imagine how daunting a task that would be? So they collected all sorts of insects and animal sounds. And they included laughter. I'm glad they did that. And they offered up 'hello' in scores of languages. The scientists were also smart enough to include the universal language: music. *Dark Was the Night, Cold Was the Ground,* was one of their selections."

"They chose well," said Gina.

"The last I heard," said Angus, "the Voyager probe exited our galaxy. It's headed for some star that's about forty thousand years away. Blind Willie is now singing for the universe."

"Play it again," said Gina.

Angus was happy to comply.

"Researchers say Blind Willie wasn't born blind," said Angus, "but became that way because of an evil stepmother."

"That sounds like the beginning of a fairy tale," said Gina.

"Supposedly, Willie's father caught his wife in bed with another man. And his wife, Willie's stepmother, threw lye during their fight. The loss of Willie's eyesight was collateral damage."

Gina thought about her own shitty upbringing. At least she'd come out of it with intact eyesight. In fact, maybe her eyes were too wide open.

"Why don't you pull up right there," she said, pointing out an open spot on the street near Bryan's clinic.

Angus steered his Navigator into the space. The parking lot of Bryan's clinic was about half full with cars even though it was almost eight. The exotic exterior jungle motif was striking. It was an unusual looking building that had been Bryan's dream, but the costs for construction had been a nightmare.

Gina unbuckled her seatbelt and opened the passenger door. The back of the Navigator suddenly lit up. Someone must have pulled up directly behind them with their brights on. Glancing over her shoulder, Gina tried to stare down the driver. *Asshole*, she thought, but didn't say it. The presence of Angus always tempered her cursing. She had one foot out of the car when she turned to thank Angus, but didn't get the chance. The Navigator's interior lights dimmed, and then with a squeal of tires the SUV rocketed away from the curb and into traffic. Gina's door flew open.

"Hey!" she shouted.

Cars around them honked their horns, annoyed by Angus's erratic driving, or startled by Gina's open front door. She pulled her leg into the vehicle and turned to Angus.

"What the hell . . ." she started to say, but stopped when she saw Angus looking around bewildered.

"I'm not in control of the car!" he shouted.

The steering wheel seemed to be turning on its own and his braking was having no effect. Angus tried to shift the car out of drive, but couldn't. He took his eyes off the road, looking Gina's way. As his SUV moved in and out of traffic, her door continued to swing one way and then another.

Fighting to sound calm, he said, "Gina, you need to make sure your door doesn't close all the way. Right now it's the only exit. All the other doors and windows are locked and not responding."

Wide-eyed, Gina nodded to show she had heard. At that moment, the SUV began slaloming side to side. The cascading movement almost caused the door to close. As it came towards her, Gina grabbed her briefcase and braced it under her feet, angling it so that part of it hung out the door. As the slaloming continued, the door flew back and forth; its hinges squealing like a wounded animal as it bounced one way and then another.

Angus pushed and pulled everything within his reach, trying to bring the car to a stop. Nothing was working. It was almost as if the car was possessed. And now the evil spirit possessing it began acting out even more. The car's high beams went on, then its hazard signal. What was worse was the Navigator was picking up speed. And now the headlights were going on and off, a signal to the cars ahead to pull aside.

The wind whipped at Gina through her opened door. She didn't know what to do. "Angus!" she yelled.

The ram from behind sent them careening.

"Son of a bitch!" screamed Gina.

Their SUV straightened out on its own. Angus looked through the rear view mirror. Lights were right on their tail.

"We've somehow been hijacked by the car behind us," said Angus. "Your only chance of getting out of here alive is to jump!"

"*Our* only chance, you mean."

"I'm locked in," said Angus. "They even have control over my safety belt."

Gina reached down to her purse and pulled out a folded knife. With a flick of her wrist the three-inch blade popped out. She leaned over and awkwardly began cutting at Angus's seatbelt.

"Gina, let me do that . . . and get ready to jump."

Angus quickly cut through the restraint, even as their ride grew more perilous. The Navigator's speedometer continued to climb, going from seventy-five, to eighty, to ninety miles an hour. The bright lights behind them stayed right on their tail. Gina turned around and shaded her eyes, trying to see who was in it. At the wheel was an unkempt man who was maybe twenty-five. His face was obscured because of the cap he was wearing.

Gina was better able to see the passenger, probably because his face was aglow from the laptop or tablet he was holding. The passenger had a mop of curly hair that reminded her of Harpo Marx, save that his hair was darker. He looked innocuous, like any another millennial in casual garb. The only thing out of the ordinary was the wide smile covering his face as he set about killing them.

"He's taking us to the General Forrest Bridge," said Angus. "That's where this drive is going to end. He'll have to slow us down just before the hill and the curve leading up to the bridge. If he has us going more than forty-five or fifty, we'd turn over. The curve is where you'll have to jump."

"That's where *we'll* jump."

His eye was on the speedometer. Their vehicle was slowing down on their approach to the bridge as he'd known it would have to. The Navigator was now on the shoulder.

"Now!" he said, grabbing Gina in his arms.

"No!" screamed Gina.

She was afraid to be hurled out of the moving car. They were still going too fast. There was no way she would survive. But Angus didn't listen. He rallied every ounce of strength and focus in his powerful frame, knowing he would have to throw Gina onto the roadway shoulder and clear of the moving cars. There was a confluence of time and space, while everything seemed to slow down as she was being catapulted from the speeding vehicle. Before hitting the asphalt, Gina was sure Angus yelled something. It sounded like "Bull's-eye," but it might have been, "Don't die," or it could have even been, "Goodbye."

She landed on the outer reaches of the shoulder, far enough away from the road to be safe from any traffic. But you don't exit from a car that's going fifty miles an hour without suffering the consequences. She rolled and rolled, going over asphalt, to grass, to scrub, leaving parts of her skin everywhere behind her. And then her leg caught on something, but that wasn't enough to stop her. It was enough to shatter it, though, as she continued on her roller-coaster nightmare.

As best as Gina could figure it, her body came to a stop at the same time Angus was taking his last breath. Even in her dazed state, she was able to make the connection with what almost sounded like a sonic boom. Angus was right about the Navigator's final destination. It was the General Forrest Bridge. That terrible sound of impact told her just how fast the SUV must have been going when it slammed into a pillar.

"Angus!" Gina cried knowing he was gone. Her voice sounded strange to her ears. It was almost as if someone else was speaking. Gina fought off shock. It would have been easy just to lie there, but she couldn't do that. Gina was aware enough to realize that she had to find a way to move if she wanted to live.

Blood was everywhere, but the worst of the bleeding was occurring in the vicinity of what looked like a seriously mangled leg. Her greatest fear was that her femoral artery had been severed.

No one would find her this far from the road, Gina knew. She could hear the traffic. It was close, probably no more than twenty-five yards away, but if she was to be seen, Gina would have to get back to the road.

She couldn't walk. Even crawling felt all but impossible. But that was her only option.

"Don't worry Angus," she said as she clawed her way through dirt, "I'm not giving up." Gina pulled herself forward. "Shit," she moaned. "Shit." But as much as it hurt she wasn't going to stop.

Her fingers gripped the ground, and even knowing more pain was coming, they pulled. "They don't know what is coming after them, Angus." She imagined herself in the galley on a ship, pulling and pulling again. That was how she advanced. "It will be ugly, Angus, real ugly." She heard the drums, and Gina crossed more ground to their beat, her screams joining in with the pounding in her temples. "They don't know what's going to come after them, but they will. They'll see." Her good leg pushed off, and pushed off again. Gina's blood greased her path.

She fought through the pain and occupied her mind with the thought that the real Gina Romano was just waiting for something like this. She'd been in hiding all this time. But she's coming out. And she won't be pretty.

Somehow, Gina had made it to the road. She raised herself to one knee and began flagging down the passing cars.

# 7

# A MANSION BUILT ON BONES

**A** text message ordered Kendrick Strahan to Tim Knapp's Lake Geneva, Wisconsin, home and included his itinerary. There was no explanation other than the directive.

Despite that, Strahan had a good idea of why Knapp wanted to see him, and that was reason enough for Strahan to not be looking forward to the visit. At least Knapp had sent the company plane for him. That streamlined his travels from DC. The nearest major airport to Knapp's home was Chicago's Midway. A driver was waiting there to take him the hundred miles to "the Arbors." At one time, the homestead had been referred to as the "Arbalest Arbors," but sometime in the last half-century the corporate nomenclature had been lost.

Someone hadn't wanted the trail of blood, he thought.

Like many nineteenth century tycoons, the Knapp family had bought a summer retreat right on the shores of the lake. They joined other families with names like Swift, Wrigley, and Sears. While those other captains of industry had long ago left the area, the Knapp family had held on. Four generations of Knapps had called the Arbors home. Each generation had added to the mansion. It was now the crown jewel of Lake Geneva. Knapp had himself some impressive digs.

When Strahan had first visited the Arbors, he and Tim Knapp were at Andover. Back then, Tim had done everything he could to try and impress Strahan. It was almost as if they had reversed positions, with the poor kid from Providence acting like the privileged one. That kind of hospitality had expired long ago. Strahan was the hired help now. The past was buried. He suspected Knapp hadn't provided him the private plane and chauffeur treatment out of courtesy, but rather out of expediency. Or maybe Knapp didn't want Strahan to have documentation showing they were having the meeting.

No matter what the reason was, Strahan decided he might as well enjoy his ride in a Rolls-Royce. The chauffeur's name tag identified him as Geoffrey. Strahan had tried to engage Geoffrey in several conversations, but the man had proved to be terribly tight-lipped. Maybe he was under orders to not engage with Strahan. Or maybe he didn't like riffraff in "his" car.

At least the Rolls came with a stocked bar. There was even an ice bucket. Strahan picked up the tongs, dropped two cubes in his glass, and poured himself a more than generous amount of Pappy Van Winkle's Family Reserve.

Geoffrey's disapproving visage could be seen in the rear view mirror. Strahan lifted his glass and saluted him. Then he took a drink, voiced his approval of its contents, and smacked his lips loud enough for Geoffrey to hear even through the glass partition that separated them.

Left to himself and to his drink, Strahan had time to think about his life. His wife, Patty, had left him five years ago. She'd stuck it out with him after his Secret Service washout, but said "the rot" from his new work was too much to bear. Patty said that being a lobbyist changed Strahan. He wasn't sure that was true. "The rot," as she called it, had probably always been in him. His job had just allowed it—encouraged it—to spread and escape. Still, if necessary, he'd use his failed marriage and blame it on the job to try and manipulate Knapp. There was no plan B for Strahan. He needed to hold onto his job however he could.

The Rolls came to a stop at a private road and an electronic gate. When Strahan was a kid, there had been a guard at the entrance who manually opened and closed the barricade. That gatekeeper was a victim of technology. Geoffrey punched in a code, and the security gate opened. Most people were only afforded a view of the back of the house from the lake. That was impressive enough, but nothing compared to the expanse of the front view.

The Knapp family had adopted the crossbow as its family crest. Amidst the fine woodwork in the front of the house, the first arbalest could be seen. Some artisan had carved it into the wood long ago. It wasn't quite in keeping with the current logo of the Arbalest Corporation, but that too had evolved over the last century. Nowadays, they stamped the image of an ancient crossbow on almost all of the company's weapons of war. It had become a ubiquitous image, at least to those familiar with weaponry.

Of course Tim Knapp and his family who lived in their mansion on Lake Geneva never talked about the business. Jessica, Tim's wife, was busy being a mother, at least until the last two of her four children reached prep school age. At age ten, each of them would be shipped away, which would allow Jessica more time for Pilates, golf, and her many Junior League projects. And Knapp served with distinction on a dozen or so boards, all of them far away from any killing fields, or mean streets.

Without a word, Geoffrey opened the door for Strahan. At least, the driver was consistent. Geoffrey motioned for Strahan to proceed toward the house. The two men climbed the steps, and then Geoffrey opened the door. Strahan had seen the grand entrance before, which saved him from having his mouth drop open. It really was a grand entrance, with the kind of elaborate wood and stonework usually only seen in the castles of royalty. A huge chandelier lit up the entrance and offered a perspective of just how high the ceilings were. In the distance, at the far end of the house, windows opened out to the expanse of Lake Geneva. If the water hadn't been so choppy, Strahan would have thought it was a masterpiece still life painting.

Geoffrey didn't lead Strahan far. Knapp was waiting for him in a den, or office, or a room that the family probably referred to with some quaint name. Unfortunately, Knapp wasn't alone. That bastard, Quentin Carter, was sitting with him. Carter liked to claim he was the Knapp "family lawyer." That folksy title was far removed from what Carter really was. Mobsters need their consigliere. That's the kind of counsel he was. To look at him, you wouldn't know what a slippery snake he was. Carter was small, effete looking, and presented himself in Savile Row suits. Strahan typically referred to him as the tiny avatar created mostly to carry out the company's dirty work.

Neither Carter nor Knapp got to their feet when he stepped into the room. There was a third chair near to where they were sitting, one not nearly as nice as their plush leather chairs which could have easily served as monarch's thrones.

"Don't get up, gentlemen," said Strahan, although he was well-aware that neither was so inclined. Strahan crossed the room and sat in the empty chair. His vantage point was lower than the other two men; he hated being forced to look up to Carter and assumed the lawyer had engineered this disadvantage. In their previous meetings, Carter never hid his disdain for Strahan.

"I assume you've already had your refreshment in the drive over," said Carter.

Strahan knew the lawyer's observation was more an attack than a nicety, but he still pretended to be amused. "I don't need a drink, thank you," he said.

"Crash into any buildings lately?" asked the lawyer.

It hadn't been buildings Strahan had crashed into, but he didn't correct Carter. His job with the Secret Service had come to a "crashing end" when he'd lost control of his $150,000 specially equipped company vehicle and plowed into a White House barricade. The .19 he blew on the drunk-meter closed the deal.

"Not lately," said Strahan. "I know that's a hazard in your line of work with all your ambulance-chasing quality of lawyering."

"Why don't both of you shut up?" said Knapp.

Strahan hid his surprise. Knapp was usually mild-mannered. Somehow he seemed to have grown a pair.

"There's a reason you were summoned here, Kendrick," said Knapp. He nodded to his lawyer so that his mouthpiece could speak on that matter.

"In light of recent developments," the lawyer said, "we have been reviewing our potential corporate liability both internally and externally."

"Explain that in English," said Strahan.

"I assume you are aware of the False Claims lawsuit being brought against Arbalest in Chicago Federal Court by the firm of Bergman-Deketomis," said Carter.

Strahan nodded.

"The lawsuit contends product liability for the Sight-Clops instrument. It also alleges our illegally bribing officials in law enforcement and the military, as well as civilian contractors. There is the suggestion that these bribes were not only monetary in nature, but that lavish gifts were given ranging from tickets to professional sporting events, to the services of professional escorts. It is also alleged that parties were held which rivaled those in Sodom and Gomorrah, where there was all manner of illegal drugs and activities going on. All of that is bad enough. The charges are serious enough that Arbalest is doing its own internal investigation, as you know. But something has happened that we need to know we are clear of: Angus Moore, the lead attorney for Bergman-Deketomis, recently died under suspicious circumstances."

"I told Carter that you never would have plotted, or condoned, or had any part in such an action," said Knapp. "But now I need to hear from you. Do we have any exposure in this area?"

Strahan looked at Knapp's anxious eyes. It was almost funny, thought Strahan. Knapp's company was responsible for the deaths of thousands, or more likely hundreds of thousands of people, but he desperately wanted to make sure his hands were clean of this one death.

"If you think I set up, or sanctioned, that lawyer's death," said Strahan, "then I'm here to tell you that I'm innocent."

"Are you saying you had nothing to do with Moore's death?" asked Carter.

Strahan turned away from Knapp. It was easier to look at the lawyer. "Like I said, I don't know anything about that death. I read the lawyer might have been drinking. There's also the suggestion that he and his passenger might have been diddling around behind the wheel, which could explain the reckless driving that witnesses reported seeing."

As forceful as Strahan tried to make his words, and as much as he wanted to believe them, he knew that it was more than a coincidence that the lawyer had died after he'd given Ivan's name to Lutz and company. Strahan wasn't a lawyer, but he wondered if that involved him as a conspirator in a crime. No, not a crime, a murder.

He turned to his old companion hoping that he believed him, but Knapp wasn't even meeting his eyes. At some level, Knapp knew Strahan was lying. The lawyer knew that as well.

"If this lawsuit proceeds," said Carter, "there will be allegations of your involvement in all sorts of illegalities."

Strahan didn't like the idea of his being hung out to dry. "Then maybe you should make sure it doesn't proceed," he said.

"You brought this on yourself," Carter said.

"Did I?" asked Strahan. "Just how exactly am I supposed to go about lobbying politicians and union leaders and purchasing agents, all of whom have their hands out and their zippers down, wanting something for something? This whole thing I'm asked to do is a pig in a prom dress, and everyone here knows that."

"Kendrick," said Knapp.

"All this time I've been left to my own devices to make sure Arbalest's weapons keep selling. Why weren't any questions being asked of me before? My job was to make sure those orders kept coming in, and no one cared if what I was selling was defective, or not up to par. As long as my numbers were good everything was fine. That's why you gave me that discretionary fund, so that I could make things happen."

"And that's why you no longer have a discretionary fund," said Carter. "As far as I'm concerned, you're lucky to still have a job."

There was a reason for his continued employment, thought Strahan. If the lawsuit proceeded, Arbalest would happily sacrifice him to the Feds, or whoever was doing the investigation. Strahan would be the company fall guy. He was sure that behind the scenes, the company was already distancing themselves from anything illegal that he might have done. The best they could hope for was that Strahan would fall on his own sword.

That wouldn't come without a big price, thought Strahan, but apparently that negotiation would have to wait for another day.

"I think that concludes our business," said the mouthpiece.

The door opened. Geoffrey must have somehow been summoned. He was there to escort Strahan to the car.

Strahan stood up. His only immediate goal was to see if he could finish the rest of the bottle of the 10-year-aged Old Rip Van Winkle by the time they arrived at Midway.

Geoffrey and Strahan walked out to the car. The chauffeur silently opened the door, and Strahan took a seat. Even before the Rolls began to move, Strahan set about filling his glass.

A man needs his goals, thought Strahan, taking his first of many sips.

By the time they arrived in Chicago, the bottle was empty, and Strahan wasn't feeling any pain.

# 8
# THE HOVERING OF ANGELS AND VULTURES

"I dream of Gina with the light brown hair, borne, like a vapor on the summer air."

Bryan and that silly song of his, thought Gina. It was his version of Stephen Foster's "Jeannie with the Light Brown Hair." Of course, he changed Jeannie to Gina. And she liked to remind him that her hair was more of a sexy, deep brunette than it was light brown. That never stopped his singing though.

"I long for Gina with the day dawn smile, radiant in gladness, warm with winning guile."

It was Bryan's way of serenading her, she knew, but how he'd glommed on to the standard, Gina didn't know. "Jeannie" wasn't nearly as famous as other Foster creations like "Oh, Susanna," or "Camptown Races," or even "Beautiful Dreamer," but Bryan seemed to have settled upon it as "their" song. Maybe Bryan liked it because it was a "courting" song back in the nineteenth century. It was time Bryan came into the twenty-first century.

Gina tried to tell him that, but something seemed to be preventing her from getting the words out. She knew this was very strange, but she couldn't quite get why. Eventually, Bryan stopped singing. It sounded like he was choking up. But why did he sound so sad?

She couldn't quite open her eyes, but even through her eyelids Gina knew it was daytime. Where was she? This couldn't be her bedroom, nor was it Bryan's.

Open your eyes. Gina tried that command on herself. It went from her brain to her eyes, but it was easier thought than done. She struggled and fought for her body to comply. All she had to do was open her eyes. Why was that so difficult? It was like lifting a heavy weight beyond her strength. But she wasn't going to let that stop her.

Damn it, *open sesame*, she thought, straining with all of her might. Almost imperceptibly, lifting up just far enough for her to see, Gina's eyes opened slightly.

What was that tube coming out of her arm? And was that an IV drip?

She stared at an elevated leg and tried to make sense of it. The way the leg was suspended, with all the hardware attached to it, made it almost look like a modern sculpture. The disembodied leg was an interesting touch. But was it really disembodied?

In the background, she could hear sucking sounds. It sounded like Darth Vader, she thought. Through her fog, Gina realized it was her own breathing.

That's why her throat hurt so much. She was on a respirator. Gina panicked. She wanted to flee, but nothing worked, not her hands, nor her legs, nor her head. She couldn't quell her fear.

Around her, alarms began going off.

"What's wrong with me?" she thought, and then the eyes she'd worked so hard to open closed, and the light gave way to darkness.

The alarm went silent just as Bryan, Deke, and Cara turned the corner, and then the three of them realized the sound must have been coming from inside the room as Dr. Bray talked to three nurses just outside of Gina's hospital room. Although the doctor as a rule projected a cool, composed persona, at the moment he was looking edgy and severe. Whatever he was saying was enough to make the nurses scatter in different directions.

"No," said Bryan, reacting to the doctor's body language.

He ran down the hall, followed closely behind by Deke and Cara. "What's wrong?" Bryan called. "I was here just ten minutes ago, and she was fine."

It took a moment for Dr. Bray to make sense of the interruption and understand what Bryan was saying. He lifted a hand to calm Bryan down, and then spoke to him reassuringly. While the gray-haired doctor's bedside manner was sparing and methodical, he had the reputation of being an outstanding doctor. "Everything's fine," he said. "Apparently, Gina didn't like being in an induced coma, and she had a little bit of an awakening. With the amount of anesthesia she's receiving, that was surprising. I am guessing she is a very strong-willed individual."

Bryan's nods and Cara's tears confirmed that prognosis.

"Her waking up is a good sign," said the doctor, "but I made the call to increase her anesthesia so as to keep her condition stabilized. For now, she needs to recover from her blood loss and shattered leg."

Gina had been in her induced coma for two days. When she'd been brought in, the doctors hadn't been sure if she would live or not.

Bryan asked, "How much longer will you keep her under?"

"Based on what I saw with that head injury, my best guess is two more days," he said.

"Can she hear us?" asked Deke. "Can she understand what we're saying?"

"If we were monitoring her brain activity, you would see Gina responding to the stimuli of your presence," he said. "Does that mean she understands the essence of what you're communicating? That's probably a stretch. But there's no question that she's comforted by the presence of loved ones. I can only encourage all of you to keep doing what you're doing. Continue talking to her. Read to her. Hold her hand."

"I was singing to her," Bryan admitted. "I'm not sure if it was a song she likes much."

"If you were singing it," said Cara, "I'm sure she loved it."

"Knowing Gina," Bryan said, "she probably hated it so much that she decided it was time to wake up and walk out."

"Can you really blame her?" asked Deke.

There had been a lot of tears over the last two days. It was nice to see a few smiles for a change.

◆◆◆

As the Gina vigil continued, her friends took turns spending time with her. After Cara had found out that Gina's favorite book was *To Kill a Mockingbird*, she downloaded a copy and began reading it aloud to her.

As Bryan quietly entered the room, Cara was reading from the book. "'We know all men are not created equal in the sense some people would have us believe —some people are smarter than others, some people have more opportunity because they're born with it, some men make more money than others, some ladies make better cakes than others—some people are born gifted beyond the normal scope of men.

"'But there is one way in this country in which all men are created equal—there is one human institution that makes a pauper the equal of a Rockefeller, the stupid man the equal of an Einstein, and the ignorant man the equal of any college president. That institution, gentlemen, is a court.'"

Cara looked up from her tablet and smiled at Bryan. "Gina could have written those lines," she said. "I know how much she believed in people having the opportunity to have their day in court."

He nodded. "The law is like a holy vocation for her. She is as passionate about her job as I am about mine.'

"Don't ever tell my dad this, Bryan, but when I was a senior in college it was actually Gina who sold me on the idea that I wanted to be a lawyer."

Bryan pulled a chair close to the two women and settled into it to hear the story.

"It was the first day of a major trial," said Cara, "and because I'd talked about the possibility of practicing law, my dad had suggested I watch the goings-on. The drug company that Dad was suing rolled out at least a dozen lawyers, all of them impeccably clad and probably each a Harvard Law graduate. There wasn't a female on their team, and there was barely a female in the courtroom.

"One of the defendant's lawyers intercepted Gina as she was approaching the plaintiff's table. It was clear he was looking for an excuse to flirt. He said, 'You're lucky we're not deposing a bunch of Third World Indian doctors today like we did in our last case.' Gina looked puzzled and said, 'Excuse me?' That's when the lawyer, in his uppity, cultured Boston accent, said, 'You're the court reporter, aren't you?'

"Gina shook her head and told him, 'No, and I'm not barefoot, and I'm not pregnant.' Then she smiled sweetly, and as if explaining to a two-year-old, pointed to an area in front of the bench and said, 'Let me help you with this. In a big boy courtroom like this, the court reporter, he or she, sits over there.' Then she pointed to the plaintiff's table. 'And I'll be sitting over there. I'm one of the plaintiff's lawyers. There are only two of us, but for the next two weeks, we will be the ones humiliating you and your dirtbag client while the court reporter who, again, sits over there, will be the one documenting all the fun.' And then Gina passed by the lawyer, and joined my father at the plaintiff's table.

"Over the course of the trial, she did a brilliant opening and a powerful closing, tormenting them just like she said she would. That week, she was the last best hope for the widow of a forty-five-year-old man who died from a stroke four days after he began using a drug that was supposed to be the newest breakthrough in controlling diabetes. After I watched Gina in court, and after I saw that passion, I wanted to be her."

◆◆◆

Instead of reading for Gina, Bryan preferred talking to her as if she was fully alert. He hoped it calmed her as much as it did him. In the aftermath of her accident, Gina looked like she had been through a war.

"Gina, sometimes I wonder if vet offices shouldn't come with confessionals," said Bryan. "Today was a good example. This mother, and her adult son who was maybe twenty, brought in their pug. The dog was behaving oddly and presenting with unusual symptoms, including a reddish-yellow coloring around his mouth. While the mother was alarmed, the young man was doing his best to downplay the pug's condition. Finally, the kid came clean. He admitted the pug had eaten his stash of marijuana, something he had been forbidden from having inside the house. What's more, since the pug had acted like he had a case of the munchies, the boy had given him a bag of Cheetos."

He stopped talking when another man entered the room. The newcomer was about five foot ten, with dark hair and eyes. He looked to be in his early thirties. There was something familiar looking about him, but Bryan couldn't quite place it.

"Geez!" said the man. "My God, Gina. You really look like shit."

Bryan couldn't help but feel offended by the man's words. What if at some level Gina was hearing them?

"She's been through a terrible car accident," said Bryan. "What's your excuse?"

The man stiffened, clearly not enjoying being on the receiving end of Bryan's rebuff. "I'm Peter," he said, "Gina's brother."

Gina had confided to Bryan about Peter's miserable upbringing and how she'd been charged with helping to raise her younger brother.

"Oh," said Bryan, and then recovered enough to offer his hand. "I'm Bryan."

Peter warily shook the other man's hand and said, "Are you Gina's boyfriend *du jour*?"

"We've been going together for more than a year," said Bryan, trying to hide his disappointment that Gina hadn't told her brother about their relationship.

"Do you have a key to Gina's place then?" Peter asked.

Bryan wasn't sure how to answer the question, or even if he should, but he finally said, "I do."

"That's a relief," Peter said. "I just got in town, and I know Gina would want me to stay at her place rather than a hotel. If you give me the key, I'll make a copy for you."

"I wouldn't feel right about doing that without Gina's approval," said Bryan.

"Like I said, I'm her brother."

"And like I said, I wouldn't feel right doing that. Tomorrow, the doctor is hoping to bring Gina out of her induced coma. I don't know what condition she'll be in then, but maybe we'll be able to ask her about the key. That's only maybe, though. She might be overwhelmed."

"I can assure you it wouldn't be any big deal to her," said Peter. "If the two of you have been going together as long as you say, you must have heard about me."

Bryan loved Gina, but he detested entitled people. His first impression of Peter Romano was that he was a bona fide asshole.

"I've heard of you," Bryan said, but purposely didn't elaborate. "Did you rent a car?"

Peter shook his head. "I thought I would borrow Gina's while I was in town since she won't be able to use it."

"And how long are you going to be in town?"

"My plans are open. It's kind of dependent on how Gina is."

More than ever, Bryan hoped Gina's recovery would be swift. "I can give you a ride to a nearby hotel," he said.

"I'm afraid that's not going to work," said Peter. "When I saw the news about Gina's accident I took off in a hurry and mistakenly left my credit cards at home."

"That's alright," said Bryan, "I'll pay for your room."

Peter reluctantly nodded. His body language suggested it was the least Bryan could do for him.

◆◆◆

Bryan refused to leave Gina's room until someone else came to visit, even though Peter didn't seem to think that was necessary.

"You said she's in a coma, right?" he asked.

"An induced coma," said Bryan.

"That means she doesn't know if anyone is here or not."

"You might be right," said Bryan.

The two of them said little after that, although every few minutes Peter offered up an impatient sigh as he paced around the room. Since Bryan didn't feel comfortable speaking to Gina in front of Peter, he spent his time holding her hand. Still, the appearance of Martin Bergman was a relief to both of them.

Bryan had met Martin on several social occasions and shook his hand.

"How is she?" asked Martin.

Before Bryan could answer, Peter interrupted. "You're Gina's boss, right? We met once. I'm her brother, Peter. Remember me?"

Although Martin acknowledged knowing the young man, his smile was initially guarded and grew increasingly so when Peter tried to get Martin to vouch for him and endorse his idea of having a key to Gina's place.

Refusing to get involved, Martin said, "I think you should appreciate Bryan's looking out for your sister's interest." Then he patted the younger man on his shoulder and moved by him, walking over to Gina's bedside.

"My poor girl," he said, reaching for her hand.

"I guess there's no point hanging around here any longer," said Peter.

Bryan ignored him and pointed out to Martin the TV remote in case he wanted to turn it on while he sat with Gina.

"Good idea," said Martin. "I've got just the show to get Gina better on my watch."

The older man took the remote and turned on the TV and did a little channel surfing. His choice of shows surprised Bryan. Martin selected Fox News.

Winking at Bryan, Martin offered an explanation. "Gina hates this televised box of butts. This will help her rally."

◆◆◆

When Bryan pulled Jennifer up to the passenger loading zone at the hospital, Peter unsuccessfully tried to hide the smile on his face. As much as Gina teased him about Jennifer, Bryan knew it was all a joke. Gina wasn't one to put on airs. Her smile was never superior, as was her brother's at that moment.

"Quite the chick magnet, huh?" said Peter.

"It's a work vehicle."

"Are you in construction?"

"I'm a vet."

Peter looked surprised. "And this is a work vehicle?"

"I have patients that weigh a lot. And sometimes I haul a thousand pounds or more of monkey chow, dog kibble, bird feed, and medical supplies. That doesn't take into account the seven hundred and fifty pound alligators I occasionally have to transport."

Peter's smirk was gone. He seemed to be reconsidering Bryan and the relationship he apparently had with Gina. "So, do you think you're Mr. Right for my sister?"

"I think so Dr. Phil."

"Are you good for her?"

"I think we're good for each other."

"Has Gina told you about our wonderful parents and upbringing?"

"She's told me a few things."

"Now I remember," said Peter. "Gina called me a few months ago. At the time, she said she was dating a real animal whisperer. I didn't expect she'd still be with the same guy."

Bryan smiled at Gina's description of him. Being an animal whisperer wasn't something he called himself. Still, people liked to comment on how good he was with animals.

"It's probably a good thing that you're a vet," said Peter.

"Why is that?"

"I know my sister. She can be every inch a wild animal, the kind I'm not even sure an animal whisperer can take on."

"Maybe your sister has changed from when you knew her."

"Are you sure you're a vet?"

"I'm sure. Why do you ask?"

"A vet would know a leopard can't change its spots."

Two minutes later Bryan pulled into the parking lot of a Motel 6. "Really?" said Peter.

"Really," said Bryan.

# 9
# A TIME FOR TARDY JUSTICE

The only reason the waiting room at the hospital wasn't overflowing with employees from Bergman–Deketomis was because of a memo sent out by Deke. He requested that all staff refrain from visiting until Gina's doctor and/or Gina deemed it appropriate. Of course, Deke exempted himself from his own memo.

He and Bryan waited together for hours. In the late morning, a few hours into their wait, they were joined by Peter. So far there had been two updates on Gina's condition delivered by Portia Ridge, RN. Nurse Ridge was Dr. Bray's go-between and would have made a good drill instructor. She was an imposing figure in starched scrubs, a no-nonsense woman of color who wasn't about to put up with fools or anyone wasting her time. Nurse Ridge told them when Gina was removed from the anesthesia and life support and later confirmed the patient was conscious and that Dr. Bray was running tests on her.

"When will we be able to talk to her?" Deke asked.

Nurse Ridge stared him down and said, "You may talk to her *when* and *if* the doctor says you can."

Another hour passed until Nurse Ridge reappeared. "Please come with me, Mr. Deketomis and Dr. Penn. Dr. Bray is ready for you."

"What about me?" Peter asked. "Does Gina know I've been waiting here?"

Without answering, Nurse Ridge turned around and began walking away. Deke and Bryan hurried to catch up with her.

Behind them Peter yelled, "Ask Gina if it's okay for you to give me a key to her house."

◆◆◆

"Five minutes," said Dr. Bray, who was standing outside the door to Gina's room. "That's as much time as I'm giving the two of you, and the only reason you're getting that long is because of Gina's being so *insistent*. When she initially awakened, Gina didn't remember what had occurred, but then everything started coming back to her. That's when we were forced to restrain her. Even with her leg in traction, she was trying to get out of bed. It was only after I sedated her that she calmed down enough to start insisting that she be able to talk to the two of you. I suspect she's holding on to consciousness now only because of that."

"Me first," said Bryan.

Deke nodded as Bryan walked by him and into Gina's room. Her eyes instantly bored into his. They were wild, afraid. Bryan wondered if they were the eyes of a mad woman. Then he noticed how Gina was trussed up and how frightened she was. Bryan hurried to her bedside, and then, as gently as possible, worked his hands under her restraints and cupped her trembling left hand between his.

"I was so afraid," Bryan said.

"You didn't leave me," Gina said.

"Of course I didn't leave you. I have been here every day. A lot of us have been. Every night the nurses have had to kick me out. But I always came back the next morning, and I stayed here for as long as they let me."

Gina's eyes weren't as wild looking now. His presence reassured her, but it seemed as if she was trying to remember something.

"Did I hear you singing?" she asked.

Bryan started laughing. "I did sing for you. I serenaded you with 'Gina with the Light Brown Hair.'"

"I don't have light brown hair."

"I know," he said.

"I don't have any hair now, do I?" she asked.

"Hair grows back," he said.

"I'm a mess," said Gina.

"In a few months this will all be behind you," said Bryan, "and you will be as beautiful as you were."

With a sad shake of her head, Gina said, "I don't think it will ever be behind me." Then she added, "I need to talk to Deke now."

—◆◆◆—

Deke hated hospitals. He hated the sights and the sounds, but most of all he hated the smell. All the chemicals in the world couldn't mask the odor of death and dying. The scent from flower arrangements, he thought, only made everything worse.

He walked up to Gina, a phony smile on his face, but she immediately put an end to his masquerade. "Angus is dead, isn't he?" she asked. "I kept asking the doctor that, but he never answered my question."

"We lost Angus," Deke consoled.

A tear rolled down her cheek, but Gina refused to give in to grief. This wasn't the time. She had something important to say.

"He was murdered," Gina said.

"You're certain?" asked Deke.

"Yes," she said.

Her voice was getting weaker. She was finally letting the sedation take effect.

"Okay," said Deke.

"He saved me," said Gina.

"I wouldn't have expected anything less of him."

"I am going to find them," she vowed. "I won't let them live."

Deke nodded, as if what she was saying was the most reasonable thing he'd ever heard. He didn't try to calm her or change the subject. All he said was, "I want to help."

That was enough for Gina. She closed her eyes and nodded off.

◆◆◆

Dr. Bray caught Deke on his way out. The doctor wanted to know what Gina had said.

"She was asleep by the time I got into the room," Deke told him, and he then excused himself.

Deke took the stairway to avoid people. It would be easy to discount what Gina had said. She was doped up, in critical condition, and had undergone brain trauma. Notwithstanding all this, he was absolutely sure she was telling the truth.

He also knew she was serious about wanting to find and kill Angus's murderers. Deke had been just as serious telling her he wanted to be part of that. For years, Deke and Martin had been afraid something like this would happen. That their enemies would decide it wasn't enough to combat them in the courtroom. Now they'd taken the battle to them, and a member of the firm's family had been murdered.

For some reason, Deke kept remembering this course on criminal justice he'd taken long ago in law school. Professor Hodges had been an old dinosaur who was overly fond of quoting long dead English poets. One of his favorite rhymes, which the class was forced to hear on several occasions, was from John Dryden:

> *Murder may pass unpunished for a time,*
> *But tardy justice will o'ertake the crime.*

This time Deke wasn't going to wait on tardy justice. He was an officer of the court, but he wasn't going to be a servant to statutory or common laws. Hammurabi had called for an "eye for an eye." Sometimes the old laws superseded all others. This was personal. This was family. And because of that, Deke was determined to practice the oldest law of all: the law of vengeance.

# 10
# MUTUALLY ARMED DESTRUCTION

**"A**re you still in Florida, Ivanhoe?"

Ivan didn't immediately answer, even though he'd been expecting Lutz to contact him after the car crash. He wasn't in Florida, but didn't want to volunteer that information. As far as he was aware, Lutz knew next to nothing about him and he wanted to keep it that way. He had actually returned to his home in Ohio that was about an hour away from where he had grown up. Of course, not even his parents knew he lived there. No one did. There was nothing special looking about his house and no one would have ever guessed about the interior "home improvements." The house was on a lot that was almost two-thirds of an acre, allowing Ivan privacy from his neighbors.

"This is a secure line," Lutz told him.

"There is no such thing as a secure line," said Ivan.

"You didn't answer my question," said Lutz.

"You still owe me for the job."

Lutz had paid half in advance; he still owed the other half for the work that had been done. "That's not happening, Ivanhoe. Our agreement was based on no loose ends. You left loose ends."

Ivan knew Lutz was talking about Gina Romano. He had planned carefully and decided not to abort the attack when she unexpectedly turned up in Angus Moore's car.

"I thought that particular loose end would only make things look that much more copacetic."

"Is copacetic another word for making matters a lot shittier than they were?"

When Lutz had approached Ivan about doing "wet work," he'd jumped at the opportunity. Ivan had always imagined going gangster. In fact, Ivan had collected quite an arsenal of weapons. His favorite pastime was playing violent video games. If there wasn't a lot of blood, along with shootings and explosions, Ivan didn't want to have anything to do with it.

He'd been proud of figuring out a way of killing the lawyer without anyone knowing it was a hit. Ivan had spent hundreds of hours planning everything out to make it look like an accident. It was pure luck that Gina Romano had lived, even though he was sort of glad she had. The woman was his kind of sexy. She'd caught his eye right away among all the Bergman-Deketomis legal eagles.

"All right," said Ivan. "Let's forget what you owe me."

"What we owe you?" said Lutz. "I am afraid you owe us, Ivanhoe."

"It's too bad you have buyer's remorse."

"You're the one who's going to have remorse unless we come to a new understanding."

"You don't think I walked into the job blind, do you, Lutz? I always make it a point to know who I'm doing business with. You think I didn't know who Strahan was in bed with? I have some great conversations between the two of you."

"Talk is cheap, Ivanhoe. It can be interpreted so many different ways. I like something more tangible. I've got something I think you'd like too. It's a picture. How about giving me an email address where I can send it?"

Ivan gave him the address. It was only a few seconds later that his server told him something was in his mail box. He opened the file and saw the picture of Toffey. It was clearly an "after" photo. You could see that Toffey's brains had been blown out.

"We knew there was no way we could get near a smart guy like you, Ivanhoe," said Lutz. "But your little helper was another matter. All we had to do was plant a tracking device on him. You sure kept that meth head busy. Listen carefully, and see if I got this right. Dressed up, he didn't look as much like a junkie. And you had him looking like he worked for alarm companies and fumigators. He was always scouting out locations and systems for you. That was smart of you. He was the one in the public eye while you remained concealed. He planted your bugs and cameras. And when he wasn't doing your bidding the two of you liked playing cards and video games. But you couldn't have a witness to what you did, could you Ivanhoe?"

"What is it you want?"

"We need to meet face-to-face, Ivanhoe. We need to restructure our agreement. I'd like you to come visit me in Chicago."

"That's not going to happen."

"We're in business. I'm talking about a business deal. I know you have conversations and evidence that put my hand in a cookie jar, and worse. Now I've got something on you."

"If I hang, you hang," said Ivan. "I've set up some fail-safe measures. If something happens to me, the dirt I have on you will surface. That's a promise."

"I expected as much," said Lutz. "We're like the US and Russia. Each side has mutually assured destruction. That's why it's to our benefit to keep our relationship going, and that's why I'd like you to come to Chicago tomorrow."

"Not Chicago," said Ivan. "That's your home field."

"Where then?"

Ivan thought about it. "We'll meet at Fort Wayne. Be in that city at two o'clock. That's when you'll hear from me. I'll call you with where we'll meet."

"Call me at this number," said Lutz, and recited the number.

"Got it," said Ivanhoe.

Lutz clicked off, and Ivan found himself staring at the picture of Toffey. He'd found Toffey early on during his surveillance of the law firm. Ivan was skateboarding around Spanish Trace, getting a lay of the land. People never gave him a second look. To all appearances, he was just another high school kid with a skateboard. No one would ever have guessed he was almost twenty-five. In fact, if it wasn't for Ivan's hair he probably wouldn't have been noticed at all. Old people liked to say his white man's 'fro was like Peter Frampton's when he was a rocker. Ivan wasn't really a vain sort, but he did like his hair. There was something Samson-like about it. He felt it gave him strength.

Ivan knew he needed a helper for his work and had been looking for the right person. Not far from his rundown motel was a 7-Eleven where Ivan got his groceries, which always included lots of candy. At least twice a day he also went for his Big Gulp fix. He'd been leaving the convenience store when Toffey called out, "Got any spare change?"

Toffey was a tweaker. Ivan knew that with one glance. But that didn't rule him out of Ivan's employment pool. Ivan fronted him the change and then some, handing over a five dollar bill. As they sucked on their Big Gulps, Ivan got to hear about Toffey's life. Ivan looked young for his years, whereas Toffey looked old. As it turned out, both were the same age. Toffey was definitely looking for work, or more to the point, was looking for money to pay for product.

Ivan started Toffey out slow, but bit by bit he proved himself. The best way to get Toffey to do the job right was by supplying him with product after the completion of the task. He could stay on task when he knew a reward was imminent.

Ivan knew the guy wasn't like so-called normal people. He didn't think like they did, or feel like they did. Ivan was aware enough to know there was something missing in him, something that made it impossible to relate to others. That made him similar to a meth-head, he thought. The desire to use meth blurred any notions of right and wrong. That's why Toffey was fine with being the driver, even as Ivan had commandeered the big lawyer's Lincoln and driven him to his death. Ivan promised the junkie some very special product when they were done. That's what the guy was fixated on.

They drove to a remote spot where Ivan had left his rental. And then it was like the two of them were having a late-night picnic on a blanket that Ivan spread out. Toffey grabbed the baggie of meth Ivan provided and then took a huge hit from his grubby glass pipe. He moved deep with the dopamine flood in Tweaker Nirvana. In an unusual moment of compassion, Ivan waited until the tweaker took a second hit before he unloaded a 9mm slug into Toffey's brain—he died with a smile on his face, and Ivan dragged him over to the hole he'd dug earlier.

Being a gangster wasn't as much fun as Ivan had thought it would be. It was better in the video games.

After he deleted Toffey's file he began preparing for his next day's meeting.

# 11
## SHEEP SHEARING

Ivan called Lutz at two o'clock exactly. "I'm at the Botanical Conservancy at 1100 South Calhoun Street. Don't go inside the exhibit. You'll find me outside in the back behind their southwest lawn."

"We should be there in about ten minutes," said Lutz.

It was closer to fifteen minutes later when Lutz came at Ivan from one direction, and Thursby approached him from another. Each of the men was scouting the area. Like sharks, they narrowed the space with each pass.

When Lutz got closer to Ivan he said, "Interesting place to meet, Ivanhoe."

"You ought to see the inside. There are three separate areas, all of them climate-controlled with different collections. Each area has a different landscape. One is seasonal, one is tropical, and the last is a desert."

"Geez, I don't want to miss any of that."

"Around us there's something special as well."

"And what's that?"

"I've set up hidden cameras that are live-streaming now. You know those incriminating audiotapes I told you about? If something happens to me, everything gets sent out. That will happen at midnight unless I intervene."

"I thought you were already *copacetic*," said Lutz, throwing Ivan's word from the day before back at him, "with our mutually assured destruction."

"You can't be too careful."

Thursby silently came up behind Ivan. For a big man, he moved very quietly.

"You need to return to Florida right away," said Lutz. "We need eyes and ears on the firm."

"I don't work for free."

"No, you work for us. We're here to remind you of that. I'm giving you five thousand in expense money and you're lucky to be getting that. Florida has the death penalty on the books. That's what you're looking at. It's in your interest to get us everything on the firm you can. We need to be kept up-to-date on their game plan."

"You could have told me that over the phone."

"But we wouldn't have been able to do this over the phone."

Lutz signaled Thursby. With his left arm, the man grabbed Ivan and lifted him from the ground. From the corner of his eye, Ivan could see him reaching into his coat. Ivan was terrified he was pulling out a gun, but that wasn't what was in the thug's hand. "You're an amateur, Ivanhoe," said Lutz. "You think someone who saw all that big hair once, wouldn't take notice if they saw it again?"

Ivan's arms were pinned against the rock-hard body of his attacker. He tried kicking with his legs, but didn't get anywhere.

"I don't think it's a good idea to struggle right now," said Lutz. "In fact I wouldn't even say anything except maybe, 'Baaahh.'" In Thursby's right hand was a pair of battery-operated clippers.

"Now where are those cameras of yours?" asked Lutz. "I'm thinking we should all be smiling and waving so that later you can enjoy the show."

Ivan went limp in Thursby's arm, but that didn't make his shearing any less painful as the clippers raked across Ivan's scalp; it felt as if the goon was pulling his hair out at the roots. As brutal as the shearing was, it was over quickly. A military barber probably couldn't have cut his hair as quickly.

"Are we clear on who is calling the shots here?" asked Lutz.

The shorn Ivan nodded. Thursby opened his muscled arm and Ivan fell to the ground. The big man stood over him and stared. Ivan wanted to curse him out, but was afraid of provoking 'roid rage.

"What?" he asked.

"You going to tip your barber?"

Lutz started laughing riotously, tossed the envelope of expense money in Ivan's lap, and then the two men walked off. Ivan reached for a lock of his sheared hair, studied it wistfully, and then tossed it aside.

# 12
## CRIME AND PUNISHMENT AND THERAPY

**D**eke hadn't been alone with Gina since she'd been brought out of her induced coma. He was responsible for that. On the occasions he'd visited, Deke had known others would be there. With the passage of time, Gina could have come to the conclusion that she'd been dreaming or hallucinating. Even if she remembered what they'd talked about, by now she might have decided vigilante justice wasn't something she could be a part of. It would be easy to blame her loose words on her being in shock or on the drugs.

That would be best for Gina, Deke thought, but not for him.

Deke had started his career as a prosecutor who firmly believed that people who planned and engineered the murder of other people should die, preferably in the electric chair rather than by "humane" lethal injection. He had testified in front of the Florida legislature about the need for a death penalty for predators who raped small children.

That wasn't lip service. That was Deke to the core.

Martin always thought it funny that Deke had the reputation of being a bleeding-heart liberal. He told anyone who would listen that Deke was more like "hanging" Judge Roy Bean than Justice Ruth Bader Ginsburg. Deke had earned his reputation as a liberal from his frequent appearances on national radio and television, where typically the issues discussed were civil rights, women's rights, freedom of the press, and questions of liability. When it came to issues of law and order, crime and punishment, and the death penalty, Deke returned to his persona as the angry prosecutor. He was proud that he had convicted murderers and succeeded in getting death-penalty verdicts. According to Deke, he never lost a minute's sleep putting a killer on death row. Heinous crimes, in his view, needed to be met with unblinking justice.

If Angus Moore was murdered, his killers needed to be dealt that same fate. For Deke, that was black and white. And if the state or the Feds wouldn't see to that justice, Deke was willing to take the law into his own hands. Since the accident, Deke had used the firm's investigators, especially Carol Morris, to run a shadow investigation into the death of Angus. Carol and her team were still gathering facts.

The Spanish Trace police hadn't yet ruled on the cause of death, but their initial take on it seemed to preclude murder. They had determined that both Angus and Gina were drinking and thought that might explain his erratic driving. There was also speculation that Angus had been "showing off" for his lady friend. Another theory put forth was that Angus and Gina had been fighting, which could explain the reckless driving, as well as Gina's being thrown from the car. It could also explain the suicide of Angus. If he assumed Gina had died after being thrown from the car, and thought he was culpable, Angus might have decided to end his own life. That would explain his plowing into a bridge support while going over a hundred miles an hour. At that speed he also might have just lost control.

Carol Morris's investigation, though, was revealing plenty of discrepancies in the various theories put forth by the police. That was why Deke was here today. He had questions for Gina. Carol had already talked to her twice, but hadn't come away satisfied with her answers.

"I don't think she's being totally forthcoming," Carol had told Deke, "even though I'm not sure why that is."

It was possible, Carol thought, that Gina had a form of PTSD. Another possibility was memory impairment due to a brain injury. Gina was, after all, undergoing extensive cognition therapy. At first, Dr. Bray had said Gina dove into her physical and mental therapy at full speed. But in the last two days the doctor had told Deke that Gina hadn't been as cooperative. She was impatient, he said, and was demanding to go home.

"Hey," said Deke, standing at the entrance to Gina's opened door.

She was carefully applying ointment to the "road rash" that covered most of her body. As Gina looked up, Deke was glad to see the happy recognition in her eyes. She waved him in and said, "Good timing. Big Nurse that terrorizes me every day just left. If you close the door behind you, we might actually be undisturbed for a few minutes."

"Big Nurse?" asked Deke as he took a bedside seat. "Sounds like you're making friends fast around here."

"Believe me," said Gina, "she lives up to that name. The psych ward would be preferable to having to undergo all of her neurological tests and so-called brain therapy."

"And on top of that," said Gina, "today I really started shedding. I'm like a snake losing its skin. Everything on me itches."

"You're looking better," said Deke.

That was a white lie. Gina was at the point in her recovery where her body was displaying the trials she'd endured. Her extensive bruising ran the gamut of colors from eggplant purple to banana yellow. And then there was also her "shedding," as Gina referred to it.

"If you really think I'm looking better," Gina said, "you better sue the doctor that did your Lasik surgery."

Deke smiled. He thought it was a good sign that Gina's self-deprecating humor had returned.

"Did I mention I'm going stir-crazy?" said Gina.

"I kind of figured that out."

"You need to get me out of here."

"I'll smuggle you a cake with a nail file in it," he said.

Gina gave him a "not amused" look. Deke decided to forego the humor. "You almost died a week ago. Like it or not, you need this recovery time."

"If you want me to be a good patient during this enforced captivity," said Gina, "I'll need some quid pro quo."

"What do you want?"

"You need to make me lead attorney on Sight-Clops and Arbalest."

"That's impossible."

"It's not impossible. I can get up to speed while I'm recovering here."

"Ned is the logical one to take over for Angus."

"No he's not," said Gina. "Before he died, Angus asked me to come aboard. He wanted me to, in his words, 'go toe to toe with AUSA Trench.' He also admitted that he should have brought me in the case even earlier. So I'm not the only one who is asking. Angus is asking as well."

"You're too close to the case," said Deke.

"We're all too close to it," she said. "But I'm the only one who *needs* to be close to it."

Deke picked up on her emphasis. "And why is that?"

"If we want *justice* for Angus," she said, "it will require our asking probing questions. As the lead attorney in this case, it would be my job to ask those kinds of questions. It would be expected. No one would think anything of it. Nor would anyone ever question any fishing expedition I might undertake. That's pretty much the norm. However, if I wasn't the lead attorney, my asking too many questions would raise red flags. We don't want those kinds of *suspicions*. It would be counterproductive to our *goals*."

With each emphasized word, Gina revealed the subtext of her conversation. She clearly hadn't forgotten the discussion they'd had in private.

"I'll have to think about it," said Deke.

"Don't try placating me. You know I'm right. You know it's the best way to go. This isn't something you can do yourself, especially with the demands of the DuPont case. Clearly you need an insider. That's the only way we can work on this together."

Her argument was a forceful one. Deke was sure she'd probably practiced it in her mind for the last day or two. But it was up to him to point out the flaws in her case.

"You're not well enough to take on that kind of workload," he said.

"You know what will make me well?"

"What?"

"The Arbalest case," she said. "Let me guess: since Angus died no one has done any work on it."

"You're right," said Deke. "We've been doing things like making sure his wife was taken care of and seeing that his daughter was able to get the best adolescent counseling available. And we've been trying to help you, even if you haven't noticed."

"I've noticed," said Gina, her voice low. "But Angus was murdered, Deke. And I was almost murdered as well. That's not something I will ever be able to forgive or forget."

Playing the role of devil's advocate, Deke said, "Nothing you've said to Carol, or the Spanish Trace police, makes them believe a murder took place."

"Detective Jenkins is investigating the case," she said, spitting out his name. "I don't have to tell you he couldn't find his asshole with a flashlight."

The year before, Jenkins and his ilk had presumed Deke was guilty of murder in their rush to judgment.

"What about Carol?" he asked.

"The answers I gave her might not have been as complete as they otherwise could have been," said Gina.

"And why is that?"

"We can't involve her in a conspiracy that could land all of us in prison if it goes bad. This needs to be our risk alone."

"But we're going to need Carol and her investigators unknowingly helping us in this. I want you to tell her everything you remember, and don't hold back on your suspicions. It's critical that we get all our findings right. We have to be sure that the party in our crosshairs is guilty."

Gina nodded. "Suddenly," she said, "I'm remembering a few things that Carol will want to hear."

"Good," said Deke. "We need to go by the book in the early stages of this investigation. In that way nothing looks out of the ordinary."

"Understood," said Gina. Then she asked, "Have you decided yet?"

"Decided what?"

"To have me head up the Arbalest case."

"I can now understand all those reports I've been getting saying that you're driving your doctor and the nurses crazy."

"You can't wait on this, Deke," she said. "I am sure the bad guys thought that killing Angus might put an end to our case. At the least, they knew it would buy them more time. They knew we would be in disarray and assumed it would be a long time, if ever, until we picked up the pieces. The bad guys will be using that time to destroy evidence, as well as go even deeper underground.

"Angus told me this was the rare case in which he could proceed in all sorts of ways. One of those ways was to go forward with our whistle-blower's claim, with or without Justice on our side. He also pointed out that we could pursue a traditional defective product case against Arbalest and sue them individually for every case where it caused a wrongful death or injury. What excited Angus most, though, was the possibility of getting jail time for the sorts that don't usually get it.

"You heard him in the monthly meeting. He said he was working on getting some evidence. Later, he said the same thing to me. I suspect it was his pushing on this that got him killed."

"I'll pass on that information to Carol and her team," said Deke, "And I'll warn them at the same time."

"Warn?" she said. "I want to pursue whatever Angus was looking into. That's why you need to let me read through his notes. I want to retrace his steps and find out where he was applying the heat. And then I want to add additional pressure. I want to provoke our enemies."

Deke knew when he was beaten. "All right," he said, raising his hands to surrender. "You've got the case."

# 13

## WHO GUARDS THE GUARDS?

The next day Angus's notes, along with printouts from his case files that filled a dozen boxes, were brought to Gina. She was also given the access codes to his private computer work files, along with the shared files that could be accessed by partners.

All of those things she had pretty much expected. What Gina wasn't expecting was Bennie Stokes. After Bennie delivered everything to Gina, he didn't leave. Instead, he informed her that he was now her bodyguard.

"No offense," Gina said, "but I didn't ask for a bodyguard, and I don't want one."

"I'll be just outside if you need me," said Bennie.

Gina immediately dialed Deke's private line. "What's the idea?"

"If you want Arbalest," he said, "it comes with Bennie. And I'm not talking about just while you're in the hospital. Bennie will be assigned to you for as long as you work this case."

"That's ridiculous!"

"It's nonnegotiable," said Deke, and ended their conversation.

Gina chafed at the idea of being assigned a bodyguard. It wasn't that she didn't like Bennie; it was just that she didn't like encumbrances in general. She knew Bennie was involved in the firm's security, but hadn't interacted with him much over the years. He was an imposing figure to be sure, a man of size and stature. There was also no mistaking his Native American ancestry. The two feathers weaved into a single braid of his long, black hair made it that much more obvious. He was definitely someone you'd want on your side in a fight, but that didn't mean she had to be keen about his watching over her. Still, if they were going to be spending time together, it only made sense for Gina to know more about him.

"Bennie," she called, "if you don't mind I'd like to have a little chat."

The big man took several steps into the hospital room and stood there.

"Please come and sit down next to me," she said. "I promise I won't bite."

He did as Gina asked, although his large frame barely fit in the chair.

"It must be awfully boring for you out there," Gina said.

"I don't mind the quiet," he said.

"What I'm saying is that you should feel free to take breaks whenever it suits you. And you should feel free to eat lunch away from the hospital. No one likes hospital food."

"I'll be bringing my own food, Ms. Romano," he said, "just like I did today."

"Call me Gina," she said. "I just want you to know, Bennie, that you don't have to stay out front like a, like a . . ."

"Like a cigar store Indian?"

Gina laughed. She was glad her imposing looking bodyguard had a good sense of humor.

"Like it or not, Gina, Deke has put you in my charge. He says bad people might want to hurt you. I'm not going to let them do that."

His sincerity worked better than any argument could, and Gina decided to learn more about this gentle giant. "I think we came to the firm at about the same time, didn't we Bennie?"

"I think we did," he said. "But I've actually been an employee for a lot longer than you. I started working for Bergman-Deketomis when I was thirteen."

"When you were thirteen?" She couldn't hide the surprise in her voice.

Bennie nodded. "I met Deke when I was twelve. All my life I'd lived on the Big Cypress Reservation with my grandmother, Holata. She was the one who got our tribe to retain Bergman-Deketomis in our suit against the sugar industry. They'd been dumping all their byproducts illegally on the res for more than half a century. Gran knew that kind of dumping was creating a real witches' brew. Deke proved in court just how toxic those byproducts were. He showed how poison had leeched into the groundwater and called it the Seminole Nation's very own 'Love Canal.'" Unfortunately for my grandmother, Deke was right about everything he alleged. Gran had been drinking that poisoned water for her entire life, and it pretty much rotted out her kidneys and liver. She died when I was thirteen. And that's when Deke hired me."

Bennie's smile told Gina there was more to the story.

"He put me on the company payroll," he explained, "and said I was being hired to be a good student. Bergman-Deketomis paid for me to go to boarding school. They were prepared to pay for college as well, but I was a pretty fair football player and got a scholarship."

"Did you start working for the firm right after college?"

"Not right after," said Bennie. "I always wanted to be in law enforcement, but things didn't quite turn out the way I hoped."

"Oh?"

"Before I got accepted into the police academy," he said, "I made sure my hair and feathers were okay with them. It's a cultural thing, as well as a spiritual thing. And the feathers were relics; I never really knew my father, but he made sure the feathers passed down to me, just like he had gotten them from his father.

"There was this one instructor, though, who kept making a big thing about my hair and the feathers. 'Squaw,' he called me and 'Featherhead.' When he learned I was Seminole, he referred to me as 'Semi-hole.' And of course, there was 'Tonto,' and 'Chief,' and 'Radish.'

"His favorite name though was 'Tiger Lily.'"

"Why was that his favorite?"

"Because he could tell it was my least favorite," said Bennie. Then he explained, "Tiger Lily was the Indian princess character in *Peter Pan*."

"What an asshole," said Gina.

"We were doing takedown and restraint training," he said, "when the instructor told our class that he would demonstrate his hold on Tiger Lily."

"I'm betting that hold didn't go very well."

"Not for him," Bennie said. "I think his arm ended up about as shattered as that leg of yours. The entire incident was written up as a training accident, but I was asked to withdraw from the academy."

"So that's when you started working for the firm?"

Bennie shook his head. "After getting bounced from the academy, I felt so sorry for myself that I moved back to the res. Granny's old double-wide was there, so I took up residence in it. Then one day, I got this unexpected visitor. Deke showed up. He didn't lecture me, but he didn't hide his disappointment either. 'Your grandmother was a great woman,' he said. 'She loved you more than anything. How do you think she'd feel if she thought you had given up?'"

"Sounds like he pushed you in the right direction," Gina said.

"The firm has paid for a lot of security training for me over the years," he said.

"And I bet none of the instructors called you 'Tiger Lily.'"

Bennie seemed to think that was funny.

"One other question," said Gina, "because I know it's something the nurses are going to be asking me: are you married?"

"I am," he said. "I have a good woman, and I have four good reasons under the age of eight to never want to jeopardize my relationship."

◆◆◆

Later that afternoon, Bennie extended his sizable arm and stopped Gina's brother Peter from walking into her room. "Name and business?" he asked.

"Geez," he said, "what is this, the Inquisition?"

"He's fine, Bennie," Gina yelled. "That's my brother, Peter."

Bennie lowered his arm and extended his hand. "Nice to meet you," he said.

"Yeah," said Peter, doing a fist bump on Bennie's fingers while walking by.

Shaking his head, he sat down next to Gina. "What's that?" he said, speaking loud enough for Bennie to hear.

Embarrassed, Gina said, "You mean 'who is that?' His name is Bennie Stokes and he's kindly watching out for me."

"He's some kind of guard?"

Gina nodded. Peter seemed to think the whole idea was funny. "Why do you need a guard?"

"Because Angus was murdered, Peter. And Deke decided it would be a good precaution for me to have a bodyguard."

Peter was three years younger than Gina, though for all intents and purposes, she had raised him. Their relationship seemed to be more mother and son than sister and brother. In the past Gina had always been the one to help Peter out of tough situations. This was the first time that Peter had come to help her. He'd put everything aside when he heard about Gina's crash. Gina had been touched by that. Still, Peter was Peter.

"Your Cayenne is all fixed now," he said, jingling its keys. "They let me sign for your debit card which they had on file. And speaking of debit cards, how about giving me the pin number to yours?"

"Why do you need it?" asked Gina.

"Because like I told your boyfriend, Tarzan, I brought very little money with me. When I heard about your accident, I took off in such a rush I never realized I didn't have my wallet and credit cards."

It was clear neither Bryan nor Peter had come away with a good first impression of the other. "Is Sara sending your wallet?" Gina asked.

"She promised she would, but when I called today she said it had slipped her mind."

"It's probably tough on her with you being away."

"I'm glad you're as sympathetic as you are," he said. "That means you won't mind giving me your pin number."

Her brother was absolutely single-minded when he wanted something. "Zero, eight, one, two," Gina said.

"Hey, that's my birthday: August twelfth."

"I know."

◆◆◆

Trying to get up to speed with all of Angus's work was a daunting task. As Deke had suspected, Gina wasn't able to concentrate with her usual single-mindedness. Part of that stemmed from the pain medications she was being prescribed. And then there was also her secondary search. Gina wasn't only hunting down information; she was also looking for potential suspects in his murder.

It was midafternoon when she heard Bryan's voice out in the hallway talking to Bennie. The two men had met before at functions held by Bergman-Deketomis, and each had taken an instant liking to one another.

When Bryan walked in the room he took notice of all the boxes, as well as the paperwork spread over Gina's hospital bed.

"What's going on?" he asked.

"I've taken over Angus's Arbalest case," she said.

"So that explains Bennie?"

Gina nodded.

Bryan took a seat and sighed. "This is crazy. The only thing you should be thinking about is your total and complete rehabilitation. Instead, you've already taken what's a crazy schedule and essentially redoubled your work."

"It's what I wanted, Bryan. I had to beg Deke for it."

He shook his head. "Here I thought you were lucky enough to have escaped brain damage. Now I'm not so sure."

"It was always there," said Gina. "I was just glad you never noticed before."

She reached for his hand. That was as much of an apology as she could offer. Bryan accepted her act of contrition and her hand.

"How are you going to manage this?" he asked.

"I'll be going home in a few days," she said. "For a time, I'll set it up as my office. I'll have help, I promise. Yes, I will be super busy, but I think we should make lemonade out of lemons."

"And how will we do that?"

"You've been putting off doing that filming in Australia and New Zealand. Why don't you go ahead and make those arrangements? We can both be busy on different continents."

"I don't like the idea of not being around for you."

"Peter says he'll be there for me."

Bryan looked skeptical. "If that's the case," he said, "he'll have to give up his barstool at Snooki's. He's already become a regular there."

"And how would you know that?"

"I stopped by and had a beer with a few friends last night," he said. "That's when I saw Peter and noticed how familiar he was with the place and the people there."

"I'm glad to hear that Peter's making friends," Gina said. "When we were kids, we knew to not have friends over. We were afraid they might catch our father in one of his *moods*. No one suspected what was going on behind the walls of our beautiful Georgian home." Gina felt a need to justify Peter's character defects.

"I'm listening if you want to unburden yourself."

"I wish it was that easy," she said. In the past, Gina had merely told Bryan that she'd had a "Dickens-like" childhood. "My father was a sadist, and his favorite target was my mother. She was his punching bag. They had quite the sick relationship. After he beat her, mother would self-medicate until she was oblivious to his behavior. Usually that went on for days at a time. Of course, by doing that, she threw out any responsibility for raising us. Peter and I were Dad's secondary targets. It's one thing to let yourself be hit, but it's another when you don't intervene on behalf of your children. I can never forgive my mother for doing nothing to save us from what was going on."

"So, out of your own necessity," said Bryan, "you became strong."

Gina nodded. "My father had the power, though. He was the investment banker. 'Eddie' Edward Romano bought everyone in Ridgewood's goodwill through all his donations. His *generous* contributions shielded him from the world seeing what he really was."

She thought about Angus and revenge. That wasn't something she could talk about with Bryan, but she could talk about another plot that occurred at another time.

"Peter was ten when he broke his arm. I don't remember what Peter supposedly did. I only remember the glee in Dad's face when he snapped his son's arm. Of course, my mother and father told the doctor that Peter's 'accident' happened while he was playing. When Peter came home and I saw him in his cast, I decided my father had to die. That's when I hatched up my murder plot. I was a thirteen-year-old girl who methodically tried to think of the best way to murder Eddie Romano.

"What I came up with wasn't bad. There was this stairway that led up to our bedrooms on the second floor. We could always hear Father marching up that stairway. That short, squat, creep would always be drunk and would sound like a winded wildebeest. My idea was for Peter to meet him at the bend on the stairway. There, he could drop a noose over Dad's neck. We knew that when the old man was drunk he often didn't notice what was going on around him. Once the noose was around his neck, I told Peter I'd do the rest. From above, I'd pull the knot tight. One end of the rope would be looped over the railing. Holding that end of the rope, all that I had to do was jump out from the landing. I had actually done the calculations. I was pretty sure my weight, and the speed of my fall, would be enough to hang the old man.

"All that was left was for the deed itself. I constructed a noose and did some trial runs with Peter, practicing for the murder. And then I picked a day that was supposed to be *the* day. When we heard his car pulling into the driveway, I directed Peter to his spot. But that's when little brother got cold feet. I suppose I should be grateful he did."

"You only suppose?"

She nodded. "There's a part of me that wishes we had done it."

"Wow, I'm betting that's not a story you tell everyone."

"You're the first, but what it should tell you is that I'm damaged, and Peter's probably even more so."

"I have a different takeaway," he said.

"And what's that?"

"I'm glad you didn't have a handgun around the house."

"Aren't you afraid that a troubled sociopath didn't fall too far from the tree?"

"No," he said, "We're all human, and humans are always a little messy."

◆◆◆

Carol stopped by to see Gina at just before five. Bennie wouldn't let her in the room without first giving her a big hug. The two of them often worked together on investigations for the firm.

"Oh Gina," Carol said, looking around at all the boxes. "You're not doing our sex a favor. Men already think we shouldn't take more than two days off after childbirth. With you getting back to work so soon, you're just reinforcing that."

"I'm doing it for Angus," said Gina. "And your own dark circles are telling me you're doing the same."

"Evidence tends to get lost," Carol admitted, "if you don't get to it early on. And unfortunately, the Spanish Trace Police Department needs a refresher course in securing evidence. I know they're short on staff and are dealing with limited resources, but I sort of blew a gasket when I learned that what was left of Angus's Navigator was being stored out in the open at Barancus Auto Salvage. I suppose our local police thought that since it was already a wreck, it was okay to leave it unprotected and unmonitored. When they let us collect it for testing, it was pouring rain, which contaminated the evidence that much more."

"During Deke's trial, I found too many instances of sloppiness like that," said Gina. "It's hard to tell if they're incompetent or indifferent. I always likened them to that man who was asked, 'Are you ignorant, or are you apathetic?' To which he responded, 'I don't know and I don't care.'"

Gina had heard Deke tell that story in a courtroom. He was a lot better in the telling than she was, but both women laughed anyway. On occasion, each sought out the other at the male-dominated Bergman-Deketomis firm just so that they could compare notes about how women were faring in the world of lawyering. After a few rounds of screams, cussing, and laughter, both usually left those conversations aggravated, but motivated.

"What did the car tell you?" asked Gina.

"We're still documenting our forensic investigation of it," said Carol, "but we're fairly certain the vehicle's electronic system was compromised. We also believe an accelerant was planted in several areas of the car. That would explain the fire that engulfed the car upon impact and why it burned so long and so violently."

"Someone wanted to destroy the evidence."

"And unfortunately for us, they mostly succeeded. What we're trying to do now is to see if there might be CCTV footage that can help us. You don't electronically commandeer a car without some serious tinkering. We suspect that work was done at Angus's house. During the month before the accident, the Moores had a construction team putting on an addition to their house. Because of that, Angus parked on the street in an area where anyone could have sabotaged his car pretty much undisturbed. Neither Angus nor his neighbors had security cameras, but we've been gathering footage from nearby streets hoping we can find a pattern of a car that doesn't belong in the area making late night visits."

If it was there, Gina knew Carol would find it.

"Look for a young white male," said Gina, "with a full head of curly brown hair."

"What age would you guesstimate?"

"I'm thinking late teens," said Gina. "I only got a glimpse of him, and I remember being surprised at how young he was. The light from the laptop was what illuminated his face, and I remember thinking, 'He's just a kid.' The only memorable thing about him though was that big mop of curly hair. It extended up and out and down to his shoulders."

Carol jotted down some notes. Then she asked, "Have you been able to remember anything else since we last talked?"

Gina nodded. "There's one image that keeps coming back to me. It's been haunting me. Angus was trying to throw me clear of the moving car. That required enormous strength on his part. He essentially had to lift me with his arms, make sure he timed his throw with a door that kept opening and closing and make sure I landed on the shoulder of the road so I would not be hit by the car behind us."

She felt her heart pounding. Just recollecting the story resulted in Gina's reliving her panic and terror.

"I was out of my head," said Gina, her voice cracking, "but somehow Angus kept it all together. He yelled something just as he was releasing me. I sensed what he cried out was important because he made a great effort to be heard over the wind and the chaos. Even now I can hear him, and that's why it's so frustrating. I know Angus was trying to tell me something. But I'm not certain what it was. I can see him yelling. His mouth is opening and closing. He's saying two syllables, I'm sure of that. But what he is saying is still eluding me."

"What do you think he's saying?"

"I want to believe it's 'Bye-bye,' but I don't think that's it. And it might also have been, 'Don't die.'"

Gina opened and closed her mouth, trying to match it with her memory of Angus doing the same.

"Or it could have been 'bull's-eye,' or 'bull's lie,' or maybe 'blue spy.'

Carol wrote down every possibility. "It sounds like the last syllable ended in 'eye.'"

Gina tentatively nodded and said, "That's what I'm seeing. That's what I'm hearing."

"You did great," said Carol, touching Gina's shoulder. "I'll follow up."

"I hope it's a better clue than rosebud," said Gina.

# 14
## IT'S A LONG WAY TO THE TOP

After two weeks in the hospital, Dr. Bray finally relented to Gina's insistence on being allowed to go home. That Gina was using her hospital room as an auxiliary law office might have had something to do with his decision. In addition to her security team led by her big Indian friend, she had lawyers and paralegals coming and going. And every day she stayed in the hospital resulted in more paperwork and clutter from the case so it had become more difficult for staff to get in and out of her room.

Bennie made all the arrangements for Gina's relocation. For the time being, Gina decided she would live and work out of her living room, which was on the first floor. In a week's time, she was supposed to be getting a walking cast, which would give her the option of navigating the stairs and returning to her upstairs bedroom.

Under Bennie's watchful supervision everything was packed up. And then it was Bennie who wheeled Gina out of the hospital, lifting her up into the passenger seat of his Ford F-150. The two of them even celebrated Gina's release by stopping to have two carne asada burritos. When they arrived at Gina's house, the last of her belongings from the hospital were being unloaded. Even her comfortable queen bed had been brought down from the master bedroom to the living room. And it was upon that bed that Bennie carefully deposited Gina.

"If you don't mind," said Bennie, "I need to walk the house and the nearby grounds. And later I'll need to get the names and descriptions of your neighbors so I can pass them on to the other guards."

"I was sort of hoping we could eliminate my security detail," Gina said. "After all, this is a gated community."

Bennie seemed to find that amusing. "Those gates won't even slow down anyone who wants to get in here."

Both of them turned to see Peter yawning and making his way down the stairs. "I was wondering what all the noise was about."

"I'll be back from my tour of the grounds shortly," Bennie said.

"Thanks," said Gina, and then turned her head toward Peter. "It's half past one," she said. "Isn't that a little late to be getting up?"

"Not if you didn't get to bed until around four in the morning."

Gina patted a spot on her bed. "Sit down, Peter," she said. "We need to talk."

"I've got a headache."

"Sit down," Gina said, but much more forcefully than before.

Acting like the wronged party, Peter sulkily took a seat on Gina's bed.

"I hope you know how much I appreciate you coming to help me, but don't you think it's time you went home? You've been away from Sara for almost two weeks. I'm sure she misses you terribly."

"I am afraid, big sister, that you're wrong about that."

For some reason, Peter was choked up. He cradled his chin in his hands and refused to meet Gina's eyes.

"I have neither a waiting wife nor a home to return to. It's not a pretty story, and I don't like telling it, which is why I've been avoiding this moment. As you probably know, Sara has wanted children from the first. Because of that, we decided to let nature take its course."

Gina had never spent much time with Sara. She was an attractive woman and a successful real estate agent, but, like Gina, Sara was used to playing the "mother" role with Peter. Maybe that was why the two women never seemed to hit it off. Peter only needed one mother in his life.

"We'd been married for two years, and Sara hadn't gotten pregnant. On a couple of occasions she'd gotten worked up over that, so unbeknownst to her I went to have my boys checked."

Peter offered up another sigh. "Long sob story short," he said, "I'm shooting blanks. My guys barely swim. My doctor said there was no way they would get to the deep end of the pool. Their motility, he said, was virtually nonexistent. After I digested that bit of news, I tried to think of how I was going to break it to Sara. Before I did that, though, she came to me with some news of her own: she was pregnant."

"I'm so sorry, Peter," said Gina.

"That's two of us," he said. "As you can imagine, I almost lost it when she told me she was pregnant. But I decided to play it cool. There was this part of me that wanted to know who the father was. That's when things went from terrible to truly awful. Her partner in crime was my partner in real life, Kumar Singh."

Gina's grades and test scores could have gotten her into any university in the country, but she'd stayed in New Jersey and gone to Rutgers in order to be a parent to Peter during his time in high school. Instead of making friends in the dorms or joining a sorority, Gina had gotten an apartment halfway between Rutgers and the Ridgewood "house of horrors." Peter had spent every weekend in her apartment. Even when he went to Columbia, Gina had limited her law school choices to institutions that allowed her an easy commute to see her brother. She'd first heard Peter mention Kumar's name after the two of them became friends in college. Afterward, they'd gone on to get their MBAs at the Samuel Curtis Johnson Graduate School of Management at Cornell University. From there, they had started their own struggling hedge fund.

Gina couldn't imagine how it felt being betrayed by your best friend and your wife. "How terrible," she said. "I wish you had told me."

"I was too embarrassed to tell you," he said. "And it only gets worse. It was my inheritance that got our hedge fund going. Kumar had put us in a position where we were betting the house on what he thought was a foolproof derivative formula. Guess what, it wasn't. I lost all my money, and our clients got hosed."

Gina and Peter's mother had died of a drug overdose. Two years later, the same month Gina was graduating from law school, her father died. It was "his present" to her, Gina told Peter. Edward Romano left a sizable estate to his children, but Gina had refused to accept a penny of "blood money," thus making Peter the sole beneficiary.

"You don't have any savings?" asked Gina.

"You see before you a poor man," he said. "With your indulgence, I'm here to start a new life. Once again, it's you and me against the world."

Gina gave her little brother a hug. "We'll get through this," she said. "We always have."

◆◆◆

A formal funeral service had already been held for Angus, but he hadn't yet had his "send-off" by his family and closest friends. Now that Gina was up and about, and enough time had passed for the shock of their friend's death to settle in, Deke went to visit with Angus's widow, Cathy.

"I'm here for your blessing," said Deke. "The firm wants to hold a celebration of life for Angus."

"What took you so long to ask?" said Cathy.

She had even suggested that right after the celebration might be a good time for her husband's cremated remains to be spread at sea at Carson's Cove. Whenever they had free time, Cathy and Angus liked taking out the boat to "their" spot. The two of them enjoyed snorkeling and scuba diving. Most of all, they enjoyed puttering about just spending time together. That's why Angus had told Cathy that even after he died it would be nice to return one last time to Carson's Cove and have some of his ashes spread there.

As for the rest of his remains, the two had agreed to have their ashes mingled in an urn and then spread in the gardens outside of the chapel in North Carolina where they were married.

"It's a beautiful spot," Cathy told Deke. "The moment we saw it, each of us knew that was where we had to be married. When Alicia is older I'll take her on a pilgrimage there and show her where her daddy and I were married, and I'll let her see the place where one day I'll want her to spread our ashes."

Deke and Cathy agreed that the celebration of Angus's life would start with a dockside party at the Spanish Trace Yacht Club. Afterward, a more intimate party would board the 120-foot company yacht the *Jean Louise* for the twenty-minute sail to the cove. And in his perfect spot the waters of the gulf would receive some of Angus' precious ashes.

As soon as Gina heard when the ceremonies would take place, she couldn't help but think the timing was propitious. The celebration of his life coincided with the same date her hard cast was to be replaced with a walking cast. By then, she was sick of using crutches, or worse, of being carried around by Bennie. She prided herself on being independent and hated having to rely on Bryan and Peter to do all her errands for her. A walking cast would mean mobility, even though Dr. Bray cautioned her to take it easy at first.

◆◆◆

The ceremony, Gina realized, would be her first real outing since the car crash. And even though she'd had many visitors in the hospital, most of those at Bergman-Deketomis hadn't seen her in weeks. After being fitted with a walking cast, Gina managed to walk upstairs to her bathroom. Normally Gina spent very little time applying makeup, but today she lingered and did her best to cover up the bruising and redness that could still be seen over much of her body. It was a shame she couldn't wear a veil, à la Marlene Dietrich. Dressing for the ceremony was also a challenge; she had to get her formfitting black dress over her cast. During the last month Gina had gone from a hospital gown to T-shirts and shorts. She hadn't worn a dress and wouldn't have for anyone other than Angus. She was going to look good for him one last time.

When Gina came downstairs and did her reveal, Bryan started whistling. "You look great," he told her.

"I'll need those lies on a frequent basis tonight," she said.

Even Peter seemed to think she looked good too. After a moment's careful scrutiny, he gave her a thumbs up.

A few minutes later, Bennie joined their party. He smiled when he saw her, but she headed off his compliments. "I feel terrible that you have to work because of me, Bennie. I know that you should be relaxed and celebrating Angus's life like everyone else at the firm, and I tried to convince Deke to assign me a different security arrangement so you could enjoy yourself, but he wouldn't listen."

"Actually," said Bennie, "he did end up listening to you. Today he called me to say I had the shift off, but I had to refuse."

"Why?" Gina asked.

"It's easy to control security when you're in one spot," said Bennie, "but tonight you'll be in multiple spots and interacting with hundreds of people, many of them strangers. You think I'd let anyone else have your back?"

"I am sure no one will be out to get me tonight, Bennie," she said.

"I don't want to take that chance. And don't worry about me not saying goodbye to our friend. I'll multitask!"

That brought a smile to Gina's face. Bennie was good at doing that for her. "Thanks," she said. "And truth be told, I'm grateful that you'll be watching out for me."

"And so am I," said Bryan. "I never would have agreed on leaving the country and going to Australia and New Zealand if I hadn't known that you and your crew were seeing to Gina's safety."

"We'll keep her safe while you're gone," promised Bennie, "but as for tonight, I might need your help."

"What can I do?" asked Bryan.

"I am one of those people who should never get on a boat," Bennie said. "Even though I already took some Dramamine, in case I get seasick you're going to have to look out for Gina."

◆◆◆

As they approached the Spanish Trace Yacht Club, they could hear the music from bagpipes playing "My Bonnie Lies over the Ocean." Angus had been proud of his Scottish ancestry, and on one occasion he had even participated in Florida's version of the Highland games where he'd competed in such events as the caber toss, haggis hurling, and the stone put. The tartan kilt he wore had been in his family for three generations.

They drove around the yacht club looking for a parking space. "Even the disabled parking spots are filled," Bennie said as he pulled into temporary parking. He turned his head around and looked at Peter. "I don't want your sister to have to walk far, so it's best if the two of us get out here. That means you'll need to take my truck and park it wherever you can find a space."

"And here I thought I was an invited guest," said Peter, "not a valet."

"My God . . . I'll do it," said Bryan.

"I'm just kidding," said Peter, even though it didn't sound as if he was.

Bryan helped Gina down from her seat. She had brought her crutches along as a precaution, and Bryan took them from her to carry. Bennie joined the two of them, but motioned with his hand for them to wait. After scanning the area, Bennie's nod told them to proceed forward.

Gina had been told that four hundred guests were expected at the celebration. Because the yacht club didn't have a meeting room to accommodate those numbers, they had set up a huge canopy on their grounds. From inside the overhang, they could see a vocalist and four kilted bagpipers. The musicians were starting up a new song, and the strains of their music and the singer's words sounded familiar to Gina.

"That can't be," she said.

But it was. "'Ridin' down the highway,' sang the singer, 'goin' to a show.'"

Behind the vocalist, the pipers played.

"That's AC/DC's 'It's a Long Way to the Top,'" Gina said.

"Yes, it is," said Bryan.

She wiped tears away from her eyes and said, "I forgot there were bagpipers playing in that song."

"That's what makes it so unique," said Bryan.

There had been a part of Gina dreading this night. Yes, it was being called a celebration of life, but it was still a final farewell to Angus. Now, though, all her reservations disappeared. She was at the right place, doing the right thing, and if Angus had scripted a sendoff Gina knew in her heart this was the music he would have chosen, complete with bagpipers.

"It's a long way to the top," the vocalist sang, "if you wanna rock 'n' roll."

"Bryan," said Gina, "I want to dance."

# 15
## SPILLED ASHES AND SPILLED SECRETS

It really was a celebration of life, thought Gina. She had always thought bagpipers only played at funerals, and that their repertoire was limited, but in addition to playing traditional Scottish songs these pipers played such standards as "Ode to Joy," Pharrel Williams' "Happy," and rock classics that included "Don't Stop Believin'," "We Will Rock You," and "Smoke on the Water."

On big screens in half a dozen locations around the yacht club were picture memories documenting Angus's full, if too short, life. Between breaks in the music, different speakers offered up stories about him. There was no avoiding some tears, but most of the time there was laughter.

Gina was almost embarrassed by all the attention her coworkers were giving her. People lined up to hug her and ask how she was doing. No one seemed to notice how Bennie stayed close to her, or his extreme vigilance.

About an hour into the party, Bennie whispered something to Gina and Bryan, and the two of them followed him over to where

Deke was talking with one of the firm's associates. Upon seeing an eye signal from Bennie, Deke excused himself and then joined the threesome.

"I might be overreacting," said Bennie, "and I don't want anyone looking that way, but on the far shore I've noticed a character who appears to be monitoring the goings-on here while pretending to fish."

"What's our fisherman look like?" asked Deke.

"Young," said Bennie. "He might still be in high school."

"Does he have long, curly hair?" asked Gina.

"Short hair," said Bennie. "For the past half hour I haven't seen him cast a line. And the top of a sand bluff is not exactly a place anyone would be fishing. What he's pulled from there could be a directional mic. And it's hard to tell in the shadows, but I also think he has a night optics scope."

"I think it's time for you to go on your own fishing expedition," said Deke.

"I was thinking the same thing," said Bennie as he slipped away from the yacht club grounds.

◆◆◆

Ivan monitored the party from his vantage point as he thought to himself that the night had been pretty much a bust. He had counted on a few sets of loose lips, but all everyone seemed to be talking about was the dead lawyer. No one had even been speculating on his cause of death. In fact, just about everyone seemed to think the lawyer had died in some freak accident, which happened to be the current assessment of the Spanish Trace PD. Ivan hoped that would be the official verdict, even though he doubted the dead lawyer's firm would go along with that. Their investigators had done a much more thorough job than the police had. They had not only collected evidence at the crime scene, but had locked away the wreck so they could carefully examine it. Ivan knew that Morris woman already had come up with a working theory about an accelerant having been planted in multiple spots in the vehicle. In a confidential memo, or what was supposed to be a confidential memo, she had speculated that the only way the Navigator could have burned as hot and as furiously as it had was if some kind of accelerant was positioned in the front and rear of the vehicle.

Hell, thought Ivan. I should have billed the lawyer's family for his cremation.

The wake had started at dusk, and Ivan had been glad for the shadows. He liked doing his work in the dark. In another hour, family and friends would be leaving port to go and dump the lawyer's ashes. They wouldn't be going very far, and Ivan had scouted out a potential listening post over Carson's Cove, but he didn't think it would be worth his time going there.

He brought a night vision scope up to his eye and scanned the dance floor. There was a hot number shaking her stuff, and Ivan watched her in action. Her assuredness, and the way she took control of her partner and the dance floor around her somehow reminded him of his old history teacher, Miss Wagner. He wondered what Miss Wagner was doing these days. Ivan had heard she was no longer teaching. Everyone was always talking about how the lessons of a good teacher stayed with you for the rest of your life. Ivan was lucky to have been the recipient of some of those lifelong lessons.

Reluctantly, he turned the scope away from the dance floor and looked around the area. He had heard the sound of some small craft approaching him and thought it was just another boat docking in the harbor or some fisherman going out at night to try his luck. What he didn't expect to see was a Zodiac coming his way. It had to have been moored to the *Jean Louise*, Ivan thought, or else it wouldn't have been able to get on him so quickly.

As the Zodiac continued its approach, Ivan took the precaution of gathering his gear, which he stowed in his combination pack/bait box. He could leave behind the pole; Ivan had wiped it clean just minutes before. When the operator of the craft made his landing, there was no question that he had targeted him. As soon as Ivan saw the man's silhouette, he knew his pursuer had to be that hot lawyer's new bodyguard, the guy he thought of as Chief. No one else at the party was that big.

Instead of coming right at him, though, Chief was charging up the hill at a diagonal. The big man was a lot faster than Ivan would have expected, and his strategy had caught Ivan flat-footed. Because he'd delayed, there was actually a chance that Chief could beat him to the high ground.

Ivan adjusted by pushing off and upwards a few steps. His move forced Chief to go all in with his upward sprint. That's when Ivan pivoted and headed for low ground. It was almost like a cartoon, with the two characters racing opposite ways.

The sandy soil leading up the bluff had challenged Chief's big body. Getting footing was difficult, and as the ground had opened up beneath his feet his momentum had slowed. Ivan wasn't having those problems going the opposite way. As he moved downwards he used his skateboarding skills, running and sliding until reaching more level ground. When he looked back he saw that Bennie had reversed his field and was coming down the hill after him. With every step, though, the man's higher center of gravity was being challenged. For Ivan, it was like watching a tree fall over. Chief's fall, and his momentum, caused him to tumble down the hill. Ivan took advantage of his adversary's misfortune, running up the bluff as fast as he could. As he neared the top, Ivan paused to wave at his downed opponent.

It wasn't the smartest move, he realized. The bear of a man roared and then came after him again. Luckily for Ivan, he was far enough ahead to reach the sidewalk before Chief could get his hands on him. Once there, he hurriedly pulled his skateboard from his pack and then rocketed off. He was hell on wheels, and within seconds was out of sight.

◆◆◆

Bennie returned carrying a fishing pole. He made sure he wasn't contaminating the evidence by using a glove he'd fashioned from a trash bag. Deke was waiting for him near the boarding ramp to the *Jean Louise.*

"Catch anything?" Desk asked.

"A pole," said Bennie. "We'll have it dusted to see if there are any prints."

"Did you get a good look at him?" asked Deke.

"White kid," said Bennie, "probably around eighteen. I'd put him at five and a half feet and no more than a buck forty. He's got a military crew cut. And he's damned fast."

"Are you sure you haven't lost a step since your gridiron days?" teased Deke.

"I've probably lost two steps," said Bennie, "but I can still run a helluva lot faster than you ever could."

"It's my mouth that has to be fast, Bennie, only my mouth."

"You got no worries then, Deke."

"Gina is already onboard," said Deke. "She and Bryan decided to hole up ahead of everyone else. Now we're gathering up the others for Angus's last cruise."

"I'll see you inside," said Bennie, and began walking up the ramp.

◆◆◆

*Jean Louise* was referred to as the Bergman-Deketomis "company boat." It was actually Deke's 120-foot yacht that he made available along with its captain for employee weddings, birthdays, and anniversaries.

This would be its first funeral run.

There were around forty passengers aboard, a mixture of Angus's family, old friends, and his closest work friends. Most of the passengers were taking advantage of the balmy weather on deck, but Gina was resting her leg in the cabin along with Bennie, Bryan, and Cara.

"Was Jean Louise the name of Deke's mother?" asked Bryan.

Both Gina and Cara burst out laughing.

"My dad didn't really have a biological mother to speak of," said Cara. "She gave him up to foster care when he was ten. Over the course of eight years, he had eight different foster mothers. Then he aged out of the system."

"That doesn't sound like a storybook childhood."

"It wasn't," said Cara. "Maybe that's why my dad has been looking after lost kids all his life."

She thought about that for a moment, and then said, "Maybe in a way Jean Louise was his mother."

Cara turned to Gina. "Do you know I was reading that book to you just a few weeks ago? My dad told me it was your favorite one, just like it's his."

"What book?" Bryan asked. "And who is Jean Louise?"

"Everyone knows her as *Scout*," said Gina. "She's Atticus Finch's daughter and the narrator in the book *To Kill a Mockingbird*."

"And here I always thought her real name was Scout," said Bryan. "But then again I've only seen the movie. I've never read the book."

Deke and his wife, Teri, entered the cabin and walked over to join the group. The couple had been with Cathy and Alicia on the starboard deck, but had left them so that Angus's friends could have private time with them.

"We were just talking about you, Dad," said Cara.

"I wanted to know who this Jean Louise was," said Bryan.

"And whether mom should be jealous of her," said Cara.

Teri bared her teeth and looked fierce, making everyone laugh.

"I actually was going to name this ship 'Teri Time,'" said Deke, "but your mom insisted that I name her after something, or someone, that had to do with the law."

"You picked the next best name to 'Teri Time,'" said Gina.

"To Teri and Jean Louise," said Bryan, raising his glass.

Everyone but Bennie lifted a glass; since he wasn't drinking he raised his hand. "Here, here," said a slurred voice from the back of the cabin. Peter had slipped into the cabin and was helping himself to the open bar—again. Gina knew her brother was not a circumspect drinker. Whenever he drank too much he became chatty, but not in good way. There was always an edge to his words. Too late, Gina wished she had been more closely monitoring his drinking.

"Peter," said Gina. "I was hoping you'd come around. Why don't the two of us go out to the deck?"

"You mean the four of us?" he asked. "There's me and you, and your big shadow there. And let's not forget Tarzan. He doesn't go anywhere without his Jane either." Peter snickered. "I guess that makes me Cheetah."

"It sounds like you've had enough to drink, Peter."

"Ever the big sister," said Peter. "I think it's kind of funny that you have a bodyguard, big sister, especially since you were always my bodyguard."

"That's ancient history," said Gina, trying to change the subject.

Peter continued, undeterred. "It's nice to have an avenging angel for a sister. When I was thirteen, dear old Dad must have decided he didn't like the look on my face, or maybe he just needed to feel a little better about himself. So he cold-cocked me. Along with breaking my nose, he also managed to cut open my face. When I got to the hospital—silly me—I told everyone I had fallen down the stairs. By then the staff there was getting to know how clumsy I was, because they had to see on the charts how only a few years before I had *accidentally* broken my arm."

"No one wants to hear this, Peter," said Gina.

"Anyway," Peter said, speaking over his sister's objections, "Gina got home later that night. The future valedictorian of Ridgewood High was always busy doing school activities. She saw my stitches and my nose and didn't have to ask me what happened. That's when she did an about-face and stormed off. I ran after her. The only stop she made was in the hall closet where I kept my sports stuff. And then it was on to my father's room.

"My mother's room was as far away from my father's as our big house allowed. The two had their special relationship: Dad would beat up Mom, and then she would self-medicate. I don't know if Gina watched cop shows back then, but she kicked open the double doors to my father's room better than any badass cop ever did. Boom! The doors flew open and two naked women popped out from under the covers. It was one of those nights Father referred to as his 'ladies in waiting evening.' The two hookers knew to scatter, but dear old Dad wasn't as fast on the draw. He stayed in bed.

"'Gina!' he screamed, but she wasn't in the mood to listen. She came at him and swung my Louisville Slugger. And then my father did one thing right: he ducked. For a valedictorian, Gina had a great swing. She missed his head by less than inch, but took out most of the headboard.

"Then she came after my father again. For the fat, old, mean bastard that he was, Eddie Romano proved to be light on his feet.

Gina shattered lamps, vases, and mirrors as she tried to find the sweet spot on his head. And then fat Eddie was able to duck under one of her swings and managed to run out of the room. He and the hookers took refuge behind a locked bathroom door. I've always wished I could have seen them cowering.

"And after all that, Gina went to the door of the bathroom. You would have expected that she'd be huffing and puffing, but she was barely even breathing hard. And in an amazingly calm voice she said, 'If you ever touch Peter again, I will kill you.'

"I think the smartest thing Eddie ever did was to believe her threat. He never hit me again because he knew Gina would do just as she promised. That's why I find the idea of her having a body-guard funny. You're worried that someone might try and hurt her? I'd be more worried about Gina going after that someone."

Peter finished his rant. Absolute silence followed until Gina finally spoke.

"It's time you listened to me, Peter. And I would suggest you listen as well as Father did. I want you to put your drink down now and not have another drink while you are aboard this ship. And for the rest of tonight I expect you to speak only when spoken to, and when you do I expect you to respond graciously. "Tonight we are here to honor the memory of one of the best individuals I have had the good fortune to know. From this moment forward you will be respectful of the widow and her daughter and all the good people on this ship. If you can't do that, Peter, I will . . .'"

Everyone was afraid Gina would say the same thing she had to her father, but for Peter her threat was even worse.

" . . . stop being your sister."

Peter nodded to show he understood. Then he walked out of the cabin, but wasn't able to navigate a straight line.

Teri came over and draped her arms around Gina, pulling her close. "I'm sorry you had such an awful upbringing," she whispered. "But despite that, you turned out to be a remarkable person."

As others closed in on her to offer similar sentiments, Gina held up her hands. "I appreciate the group hug, everyone, but I'm okay. Please forgive Peter's airing of our family's dirty linen. These days Peter and I have a bit of a strained relationship because he's not sure if he should treat me as a sister or as the mother who raised him.

"Anyway, this isn't my night. I would ask you to please put the last five minutes behind you, and let's go out on the deck now and get ready to say goodbye to our good friend, Angus."

# 16
## WITHOUT JUSTICE

Three days after Angus's ashes were scattered, Martin Bergman received a phone call from Eva Trench at the Department of Justice. The firm had been pushing hard for Justice to make a decision as to whether they'd be joining them in their action against Arbalest. Justice's straddling of the fence had put Gina in a bind; she needed to know what the five-hundred-pound gorilla would do before proceeding with the case. At the moment, she was planning on how to proceed by employing two strategies: "with Justice" and "without Justice."

Eva Trench had been born and bred in Queens. As an undergrad she went to City College of New York before getting her degree from NYU. Afterward, she had gone to law school at Columbia. Her New York City roots could be heard in her every syllable.

"Mr. Bergman? Thank you for taking my call. As you know, we have been considering the merits of your Arbalest case for some time now. And while your brief makes some good points, we still came away unconvinced. Those in my office agreed with me when we unanimously decided to pass on Arbalest."

"It would have been nice if you had communicated that to us a month or two ago," said Martin, "instead of making us wait."

"Like I said, we spent a lot of time discussing the case's merits. Overall, though, we had to conclude it was a loser."

"That's an interesting conclusion," said Martin. "One day I would like to hear how that was reached."

"We'll have to talk," she said. "In the meantime, you got any idea what you're going to be doing now?"

For the moment, Martin decided he didn't want to tip his hand. He wanted to keep Trench talking. "I am sure whatever conclusion we reach," he said, "will be unanimous as well."

"If I were you," she said, "I'd drop it like a hot potato."

"And if I were you," said Martin, "I would have embraced this case knowing it was the right thing to do."

"Without us, it's doubtful you can win."

"Is that so?" said Martin. He had been practicing law for more than thirty years longer than Trench and hated being talked down to.

Trench didn't pick up on his sarcasm. "The odds are certainly against you," she said. "And since your lead attorney died in that DUI crash, pursuing the case becomes that much more problematic."

Martin bit the inside of his cheek. He resented Trench's bringing up the death of Angus, and worse, her presumption that he'd been drunk. His first impulse was to tell her what he thought of Justice and how it only liked picking the lowest of low-hanging fruit. He wanted to upbraid her for not taking action in a case where a corporation was selling a dangerously defective and murderous product while making taxpayers foot the bill. But instead of saying those things, he did his best to be deferential and charming.

"Ms. Trench, I'm so sorry to hear you will not be participating in our case against Arbalest. I'm sure working with Justice would have made a huge difference for us in the courtroom. But nonetheless, I think we'll try and plod on without your expertise."

"I'm afraid you'll be throwing good money after bad on this one, Mr. Bergman," she said, "but proceeding, of course, is your prerogative."

"Thank you," said Martin.

"But since you insist on continuing," Trench said, "I'll want to monitor the proceedings. Who will be the lead lawyer for your firm?"

Martin knew Trench was hedging her bet. Her "monitoring" would allow her to know which way the wind was blowing. The DOJ had been known to jump in on cases at the last minute where they "helped" settle multimillion-dollar actions after doing virtually no work and after initially refusing to help prosecute the case.

"Gina Romano will replace Angus Moore as lead counsel on the Arbalest case," said Martin.

"Gina Romano?" said Trench. "I don't know her."

"You will," Martin promised.

# 17
# WHISTLING A DIFFERENT TUNE

**M**artin delivered the news to Gina in person. Now that she had her walking cast, she was back working in the Bergman–Deketomis building. When she was told that Justice wasn't coming aboard their Arbalest case, Gina didn't even blink hard.

"Good," she said to Martin. "That means we can proceed in a hurry-up offense. I want our opposition off-balance and on their heels. I am going to see about scheduling everything as quickly as I can which will mean spending a lot of time in Chicago. Cara will be helping me with briefing and discovery requests."

"She'll like that," said Martin. "She's been chomping at the bit to be thrown into the fray."

"The first thing I want to do is to meet with our whistle-blower," said Gina. "I need to be comfortable with Robert Diaz and make sure he's the horse we want to ride. Since Ned's already met with him, I am going to ask him to try and get Diaz to fly down today or tomorrow."

"That is fast," said Martin.

"Put on your seatbelt," said Gina.

She regretted the words even as they came out of her mouth because it made her think of Angus. Her gut burned. In a way, she was glad it hurt. It was motivation for her to take that pain to others.

◆◆◆

Robert Diaz eyed Gina skeptically as she hobbled into the conference room where he was waiting. She returned the same look to him. Neither one of them, she was sure, was experiencing love at first sight.

"I'm Gina Romano."

"Are you my new attorney?"

"That remains to be seen," she said, and took a seat.

"No offense," said Diaz, "but I'm not sure about the idea of a lady attorney."

"Offense taken," said Gina. "And just so you know, I'm not convinced of the idea of having you as a client."

Diaz looked surprised. He was a middle-aged man of average height. His hair looked suspiciously dark; she guessed he was dying it to maintain a youthful appearance to keep up with the ladies. Diaz was carrying about fifteen extra pounds, but Gina could understand how some women might find him attractive.

"What are you talking about?" said Diaz.

"Mr. Diaz"—

"Rob," he said, already sounding conciliatory.

"Rob, you need to sell me on why this firm should spend another dime working on your case, especially as we have other potentially less problematic candidates waiting in the wings."

"But this is my case," he whined.

"This is a case against Arbalest," Gina said. "You came out as a whistle-blower against Arbalest. You did the right thing. But my firm does not have to make this a whistle-blower case. We have the option of handling this as a basic defective product civil case. That would give us plenty of clients besides you."

"Why would you do that?"

"Because I'm afraid you're a bit sketchy, Rob. You have the baggage of ex-wives and ex-girlfriends. It wouldn't take much to paint you as an opportunistic hustler looking for a big payday."

"Angus had no problem with me," he said. "He knew I did the right thing for the right reasons. I wasn't looking for a payday when I went to my bosses and said there were problems with Sight-Clops."

Gina allowed him a begrudging nod for his good deed.

"And after I was fired," he said, "I could have just said to hell with it. But because Sight-Clops was killing people, I dropped a dime. I wasn't looking to get rich. I didn't even know that was a possibility until after Angus contacted me."

"And is that what motivates you now?" asked Gina.

"I can't say the idea of a windfall wouldn't be nice," he said. "I'm kind of running on empty these days. Hell, I've been doing day labor jobs just to get by. But the money isn't the only thing. There should be consequences for innocent people getting shot for no reason."

"What if I were to tell you that testifying in this case might potentially put you in danger?"

"What kind of danger?"

"Angus Moore died under suspicious circumstances."

"I thought he had an automobile accident."

"It wasn't an accident," said Gina. "I was in the car right before it crashed."

"Are you saying he was murdered?"

"Yes, I am. That's not something the police believe, but I am convinced of it."

Diaz shook his head, not liking what he heard. Then he remembered something. "So that's why Angus wanted me to go there."

"Where did he want you to go?"

"He's got this hunting cabin in Montana. He was trying to get
me to go there before the trial. But I didn't like the idea of being
out in the wilderness all by myself."

Angus had recognized the dangers in this case, thought Gina,
but he'd kept forging ahead.

"That's why I need to know if you're all-in on this case, Rob.
We don't want your testimony to be timid or reluctant."

"You think I'm on someone's hit list?" he asked.

"If I had to guess, I doubt it. Any more deaths are sure to raise
red flags. But that doesn't mean those we're going up against won't
try and intimidate you or turn up the heat in ways I can't even
think of now. That's why I need to know if you are going to stand
firm—or if you're going to take a powder."

"I'm here," he said, "aren't I?"

Up until then, Gina had made a point of not shaking Diaz's
hand, and he had done the same. But now she extended her arm,
and the two of them shook hands vigorously.

Diaz said, "I hope you're this scary in court."

Ten minutes later, Ned, Carol, and Cara joined Gina and Diaz in
the conference room. Sitting outside the room, making sure they
wouldn't be disturbed, was Bennie.

Gina made introductions. Ned had already met with Diaz, and
Carol had talked to him over the phone. Diaz was quite happy,
though, to be introduced to Cara. He sucked in his gut and was all
smiles with the attractive younger associate.

Carol tried to get him to focus on something other than Cara's
backside. "Before we get down to the nuts and bolts of the meeting,"

she said, "I am wondering if Mr. Diaz will play a little game of word association with me?"

Diaz shrugged and nodded.

"While working at Arbalest," she said, "did you ever hear anyone reference 'blue sky'?"

Diaz thought about it, but then shook his head.

"What about 'bull's lie'?" she said.

"Never heard that one," he said.

"And finally," she said, "how about 'bull's-eye'?"

"Bull's-eye," he repeated. "That sort of sounds familiar, but I can't place it. Of course, testing with targets did occur at Arbalest. And I'm sure there was talk of hitting the bull's-eye. Maybe that's why it sounds familiar."

"Thank you," said Carol. She nodded to Gina signaling the floor was hers.

"Where are we with Madsen-Zimmer?" Gina asked Ned.

"They actually sounded pleased that we wanted to proceed with depositions ASAP," said Ned, "and they say they're good to go next week if we're serious. They agreed to move faster than the judge's standard scheduling order and waive any time limitations in us setting depos."

"In other words," said Gina, "they believe they are going to get a quick dismissal, and the less time we have to dig around, the better off they will be."

Ned nodded. "That's the way I see it, even if that's not how a defense counsel usually plays it. My suspicion is that these orders are coming directly from Arbalest's in-house counsel."

Everyone in the room recognized that the typical defense strategy was to drag by way of motion wars and to take every advantage of procedural delays during the discovery portion of the litigation. A long-drawn-out discovery period was like a private ATM for a team of defense lawyers all billing at a thousand dollars an hour.

"We have a new investigative lead on someone we need to talk to," said Cara. "Private Cary Jones was stationed in Afghanistan and claims Sight-Clops was responsible for his shooting and killing an Afghani civilian. Private Jones is scheduled to be discharged from the army next week."

"Where is he stationed now?"

Cara looked at her notes. "He's at Fort Bragg in North Carolina."

"You need to talk to him as soon as possible," said Gina. "Tomorrow isn't too soon. If you can avoid going through a judge advocate, that would streamline the process. Consider this a fact-finding expedition. Right after he's discharged, we'll make it a formal deposition."

"Will do," said Cara.

"Let's make this a blitzkrieg and benefit from their quick discovery strategy," said Gina. "Madsen-Zimmer won't expect that. They think that with all their lawyers they'll have an advantage in numbers. What they're going to find out is their having those numbers is only going to make them a lot less nimble than us."

She turned her attention to Diaz. "While we have you here, Rob, I think we should go over with you the names of those we have on our preliminary deposition list. Now is the time for you to provide us with the names of any other individuals that might corroborate your testimony, or help us with the case.

"Then I'd like you to tell us again in minute detail what happened when you reported the problems with Sight-Clops to upper management. I know you already did this with Angus, but we need to be specific with your timeline of events. We'll be comparing what you say to us with what you said to Angus. You're probably thinking that's a waste of time, as we've already taken down your account, but you're going to have to be very specific. If the lawyers at Madsen-Zimmer find any inconsistency in your account, they'll try and discredit you as being an unreliable witness. From our end, the more specific you are the better it is for us. Your testimony should help us identify memorandums and reports that Arbalest should have written up as a matter of course."

Diaz looked confused. "What do you mean?" he asked.

"It has been our experience," said Gina, "that the electronic and paper trails that should be there all too often magically disappear."

"You mean like that meeting where I spoke to the suits and to Knapp about Sight-Clops malfunctioning?"

"That's it exactly. There should certainly have been a written account of that meeting. From our end, we're going to demand they produce that file or paperwork."

"And from their end," said Ned, "they'll say that file was accidentally deleted or the paper account was inadvertently shredded."

"They do those kinds of things?" asked Diaz.

"That's just the leading edge of what they'll do," said Gina.

"I think I can refer you to one of those reports you're looking for," said Diaz.

Gina motioned for him to continue speaking.

"When I got fired," he said, "they marched me out of the building like I was some kind of criminal, and that upset some of my coworkers. I mean, it wasn't like I was the only one who knew about the problems with Sight-Clops. That first night I was fired I started hearing from my colleagues. They knew better than to call or email from work. Everyone said what a raw deal I got. They thought it was typical that management was blaming the messenger and not their product. And one of my friends even emailed to say that management was already aware that Sight-Clops was prone to malfunctioning when it was extremely hot and humid. He said a confidential report had been circulated which stated that."

"Who told you this?"

"I don't want to get him in trouble," said Diaz. "In fact he told me all of this on the QT."

"We need his name, Rob."

"The only reason he called was to make me feel better. But he also told me he couldn't get involved, especially with his being only six months away from retirement. He couldn't jeopardize that, he said."

"Now he's less than three months from retirement," said Gina, "and I promise if Arbalest tries to screw him out of his pension or benefits, we'll sue them big time."

"There has got to be some other way."

"I am beginning to see why Angus believed so much in you, Rob," said Gina. "In front of a room of skeptics, me among them, he insisted that you were a stand-up guy. I can appreciate how you're trying to protect a friend. But you're going to need to let us question your coworker. He can refuse to talk to us, but that will have to be his choice."

Diaz sighed. When he'd first caught sight of this lady lawyer walking into the room and giving him the stink eye, he'd wondered with all her bruises and scabs if she had been in a bar fight. Now he'd spent enough time with her to know she was a pit bull. Once she had her teeth on something, she wasn't going to let loose. There was no question about it. This Gina Romano scared him more than his ex-wives.

He gave up the name: "Merle Marcus."

# 18

# THE RELUCTANT LEPRECHAUN

Before flying into Chicago, Gina had Carol and her team research Merle Markus and a potential witness named Kim Knudsen. The lead on Knudsen had been uncovered before Angus's death in a random interview with two ex-police officers wanting to be hired as local investigators in Angus's case. Gina suspected that the lead was a long shot but worth pursuing.

Gina's plan was to introduce herself to both witnesses and give them the news that she would be deposing them in the near future. There were pros and cons to Gina making herself known this way. "Ambush interviews" sometimes created hostile witnesses. No one liked being told they had a future date on the hot seat. Still, it had been Gina's experience that sometimes you learned more in that initial meeting than you did from a long deposition.

Merle Marcus's background check had already revealed one surprising thing: he was an entertainer, the so-called "Marquis of Skokie." His site offered links to two YouTube video clips, one which showed him dressed up and speaking as Mark Twain—"The political and commercial morals of the United States are not merely food for laughter, they are an entire banquet." And in the other he was Tevye from *Fiddler on the Roof* —"You might say every one of us is a fiddler on the roof trying to scratch out a pleasant, simple tune without breaking his neck. It isn't easy."

"No, it's not," said Gina, clicking off before Merle could sing "If I Were a Rich Man." The Marquis of Skokie's website had already revealed to Gina what she needed to know. Tomorrow, Marcus had a six o'clock performance scheduled at the Sunrise Chateau. A quick Google search revealed that the Marquis was going to be performing at a nursing home.

It was a show, Gina decided, that she couldn't miss.

-◆◆◆-

Gina and Bennie's flight was due to land at Chicago's O'Hare Airport at four o'clock. Frequent travelers in and out of that airport liked to say they had gone from "full hair to no hair because of O'Hare." The weather conditions at and around there were often challenging. The "lake effect" of Lake Michigan resulted in many of O'Hare's annual 160,000 weather-related flight delays. The weather culprits included snow, wind, rain, fog, and thunderstorms. Luckily for Gina and Bennie, none of those were in the forecast. When the two of them had flown out of Spanish Trace it had been sunny and seventy-five. The forecast for when they were due to land in Chicago was for gray skies and a temperature of forty-five.

The three-hour flight was a chance for Gina to work. She had time to read the background report on Officer Kim Knudsen. Afterward, she compiled a list of questions that she hoped Knudsen would answer. Twenty months ago, in the line of duty, Knudsen had accidentally shot and killed her rookie partner, Vinnie Velez, while she herself had been shot by an assailant. Her abdominal injuries had kept her off the force for more than a year. Since her return though, she had been assigned only a part-time desk job. Gina wondered what Knudsen thought about being relegated to what was essentially office work. She probably didn't like it, but Gina was betting her husband and two children did.

The plan was to do the Knudsen "ambush" tomorrow morning right after she dropped her two kids off at school. Her youngest was in kindergarten; her oldest in third grade. According to their investigators, Knudsen wasn't scheduled to work. Afterward, Gina had a ten o'clock meeting with Robert Diaz. He had returned home to Chicago the day before and was supposed to be gathering up some old paperwork that might have some bearing on their case.

"Hey, counselor." The loud voice was right in her ear. "Earth to Gina."

Gina looked up from her work to see Bennie smiling at her. Even though they were both in first-class accommodations, his seat was barely big enough for him.

"Because of you," said Bennie, "our flight attendant looks like she's about to take no prisoners. You don't want to get us on the No Fly List, do you? Turn off your laptop and put it away. And like the lady said, 'Fasten your seatbelt and make sure your seat back and folding trays are in their upright positions.'"

Gina realized the plane was making its final approach to the airport. She quickly did as Bennie had advised.

"You'd make a great flight attendant," she said.

"Please be careful when opening the overhead bins," he said, "because *shift* happens."

"It surely does."

◆◆◆

Gina tried to send Bennie ahead to get their rental car, but he refused to leave her. The lawyer in Gina hated that her arguments were falling on deaf ears, but on a personal level she tried to hide the comfort she really felt.

The rental car, an Expedition big enough for Bennie, didn't take long to secure. Still, Gina was worried about their timing. If at all possible, she wanted to catch the Marquis of Skokie before his scheduled performance. Luckily for them, Marcus was performing in his hometown of Skokie which was only about fifteen miles from the airport. There was still the obstacle of rush hour traffic though.

"Don't worry," said Bennie, "we'll make it on time. You need to learn how to have Indian patience."

"And what is Indian patience?"

"Look at me. You see my 'no worries' attitude? When I say we'll make it to the Sunrise Chateau on time, all you need to do is have Indian patience and a little faith."

"Sunrise Chateau," Gina repeated, wrinkling her nose as if she sniffed something terrible. "How do these nursing homes come up with such awful names?"

"You'd rather go to a place called Wrinkled Wasteland?"

"That, or maybe Demented Cove."

Gina had to laugh. She loved that Bennie was becoming comfortable enough around her to relax.

◆◆◆

They arrived at Sunrise Chateau at half past five. Bennie pulled into the parking lot and picked a spot across from a van in the loading zone. The back doors of the van were open and a man wearing a green hat, green outfit, and pointy shoes, was piling speakers onto a moving cart.

"It's probably better if you stay in the car," said Gina. "I don't want to scare him."

"Don't you be going after his lucky charms," said Bennie in a brogue.

"How is it that I managed to get assigned the Seminole version of Jerry Seinfeld?" Gina asked.

"Lucky, I guess."

Gina opened the door, carefully got down from the Expedition, and then limped over to the van. At her approach, Marcus turned around. He was wearing a fake, red beard. On the front of his emerald green leprechaun outfit was a flashing shamrock; there was also a button that read, *Kiss Me, I'm Irish!*

"The Marquis of Skokie," said Gina, extending her hand. "I'm pleased to meet you."

They shook hands and he said, "The honor is mine, young lady."

"That's quite the outfit," said Gina. "Wasn't St. Patrick's Day two months ago?"

"I'll be singing to one of the residents," he said. "They assure me she's very Irish." In a confidential voice he added, "I don't think most of the seniors living here have any idea what month it is anyway. They're just glad to hear 'Danny Boy.'"

"Before the pipes start calling you," she said, "I'm hoping we can talk for a minute. My name is Gina Romano, and I'm with the law firm of Bergman-Deketomis. We are representing Robert Diaz in his whistle-blower suit. Here's my business card."

Suddenly, Irish eyes were definitely not smiling. Marcus took a step back. "Shit," he said.

Gina was still holding her business card out to him. With great reluctance, he took it between his thumb and forefinger, apparently afraid of it coming into contact with any other part of his body. "I told Rob I couldn't be involved in this."

"I just have a few questions for you, Mr. Marcus."

"In eleven weeks I retire," he said. "I have it figured out to the minute. Why do you think I have hung in there for nineteen years and forty-one weeks? My parents said I could never make it as an actor. 'Get your degree in something practical,' they told me. 'Get a real job.' I studied bookkeeping, and over time got my degree in accounting. But I only felt alive when I was on stage. When I was younger, I performed in all the big theatres in town. I had roles at the Cadillac Palace, the Ford Center, and Goodman Theatre.

"And now I'm wearing a fucking leprechaun outfit. What's a nice Jewish boy doing something like that? Do you think I don't know how ridiculous I look? I know. But it's a job. And I get to sing and act, which is a hell of a lot more than I can say about my day job. So I don't care that I'm wearing a neon shamrock. I stuck it out at Arbalest to get my benefits. I put in twenty soul-sucking years at the company store. And that's why I can't afford to lose my benefits now."

"Please hear me out, Mr. Marcus. If Arbalest makes a move to try and deny you your pension, or your benefits, I will represent you at no cost in court. And I can assure you if it ever came to that, which I think is highly unlikely, I would do my best to make Arbalest realize the costly error of their ways."

"I can't talk to you, lady," he said.

"You will talk to me," said Gina. "In fact, in the very near future I will be deposing you. But for now, we don't need to be tied up in legal formalities. My hope is that you can confirm what Mr. Diaz told us."

"Just wait eleven more weeks," he said. "We can talk then."

"We'll need to talk before then, but you won't be alone. I'll be deposing a number of individuals who work at Arbalest. The story of Sight-Clops and its fatal defects will come out long before you are deposed."

"I'm just an accountant," he said. "I'm not on the operations side. I don't deal with any of our products. My end of things is debits, credits, balance sheets, and profit and loss ledgers; things like that."

"Robert Diaz told us that shortly after he was fired you called him," said Gina. "Diaz said you claimed that management already knew that Sight-Clops was prone to malfunctioning in hot and humid conditions. Apparently you and other managers were privy to this information which was circulated in a confidential report."

"I wasn't supposed to get that report," Marcus said. "It came to me by mistake. If I'm lucky, no one even knows I got a copy."

"But you know better than to trust luck, don't you, Mr. Marcus? What is that line actors like to say when they're out of work? 'If it wasn't for bad luck, I wouldn't have any luck at all.'"

Marcus nodded.

"Because of that," Gina said, "I'm thinking that someone in your position probably made a copy of that report, especially someone who'd worked a job he hated for almost twenty years. Such a report might be looked at as an insurance policy. Am I right?"

She could see from his expression that she was right. Marcus was still looking for wiggle room though. "You're just speculating," he said.

"What I'm not speculating about is that you did commiserate with Robert Diaz. And during that conversation you referenced a report. Tomorrow I'll be meeting with Mr. Diaz, where we'll certainly be discussing this matter. You should know that because of what you told him, we will be asking Arbalest to provide us with a copy of that confidential memorandum."

Marcus scratched at his fake, red beard, which threatened to come off. "It's like what my mother always told me," he said. "No good deed goes unpunished."

After thinking about it for a moment he added, "I'll get you what you need."

◆◆◆

Gina and Bennie arrived at their hotel at a little after seven. Bennie had made sure the two of them had connecting rooms and had asked for those doors to be unlocked. As they started up the elevator to the fifteenth floor, Bennie said, "Are we going out for corned beef and cabbage, or are we eating in?"

"Not even the promise of a pot of gold will get me out of my room tonight," she said.

"Room service sounds good to me as well," said Bennie.

Gina wished she could take a nice, long bubble bath, but her cast made that pretty much impossible. However, she thought, there was something else to look forward to.

"Chicago is one of the test markets for the syndication of Bryan's show," she said. "He told me it would be airing at eight o'clock tonight."

"My kids are big fans of his," said Bennie.

"I'm kind of getting to be a fan myself."

The two of them got off on the fifteenth floor and walked down the hallway to their rooms. Bennie did a quick review of Gina's room, and then checked to make sure the door between their rooms was unlocked.

"When you decide what you want to eat," he said, "give me a call. I'll put in your room service order so that it gets delivered to my room."

Gina didn't want, or feel she needed that kind of special service. "That's not . . ."

He cut off her protest. "Humor me," and then he closed the doors between their rooms.

Gina hobbled over to the window. The lights of the Chicago skyline, along with the moon, put a shine to the waters of Lake Michigan. It was beautiful, but she couldn't completely appreciate the view. She never could when she was working.

Early in her legal career Gina had loved traveling. And she remembered how it had always seemed like a naughty pleasure to be able to order room service. But over the years that thrill had vanished. Solitary dining no longer had the appeal it once did. She looked at the menu selections and debated between a club sandwich and a New York steak sandwich, and after making her choice called Bennie.

"Has madam decided?" asked Bennie.

"I'd like the New York steak sandwich, rare."

"Madam has chosen well. Do you want the French fries, the sweet potato fries, or the baked potato with accompaniments?"

"I guess I'll try the sweet potato fries."

"And what kind of dressing do you want on your salad?"

"Bleu cheese, please," she said.

"I'll call it in," he said.

When Gina heard the knock at the connecting door she shouted, "Come in."

*The Jungles of Florida* had just started, and Bennie did his best to quickly deliver the food without interfering with Gina's viewing. He placed everything on a table and with a French accent said, "Bon appétit."

Gina called out her thanks as he closed the door. Using her hands, she ate the fries while watching Brian tell the story about Tristan the toco toucan. Tristan had somehow broken off almost five inches of his normally twenty-five-inch upper beak.

"Because a toucan's beak is so long—it makes up almost half of the bird's surface area—it isn't as solid as it looks," said Bryan. "In fact, its beak is made up of mostly air. That might explain how Tristan broke his bill. Still, without our help that broken beak would be a death sentence. Toucans depend on their oversized beaks for such things as cutting through fruit and appealing to the opposite sex. But perhaps the beak's most important use is for heat regulation. When it's hot, or when a toucan is expending lots of energy, it will release heat through its beak. Conversely, when the temperature is colder a toucan can block the flow of blood to its beak, retaining the heat in the body."

Over the course of the show, Tristan's journey to regain his beak was documented. After Bryan managed to get a mold showing the state of Tristan's broken beak, two college undergrads used that mold and a 3D printer to create a replacement toucan bill. The only problem with the replacement beak was that its color was too lackluster.

"Let's face it," said Bryan, holding up the replacement beak. "What lady toucan is going to want to have anything to do with this dull and uninspiring beak? Luckily for Tristan, Christina has just the solution."

Christina was a twenty-something modelesque artist. She was certainly as good for ratings as she was for Tristan. There were a number of close-up shots of Christina airbrushing Tristan's replacement beak. Most of those shots managed to catch Christina's backside, or a view of her bending forward in her mostly unbuttoned oxford shirt.

After the show's happy ending—Tristan's beak was restored to its full splendor and he flew off into the sunset—Gina called Bryan.

When he answered, Gina attempted to imitate Christina's breathless voice: "Do you think this will work, Dr. Bryan?"

"You saw the show?" he asked.

Gina continued in Christina mode: "Personally, I think Tristan's beak is popping, Dr. Bryan. There's no doubt in my mind it will be a chick magnet."

"I hope she's right."

"I need to learn how to bat my eyes like she did. And I must remember the beseeching way in which she said, 'Dr. Bryan.' I am sure you found that sexy."

"You are what I find sexy."

"Right answer, Dr. Bryan."

"And when can you carve out some time to see the doctor?" he asked. "I'll be leaving for Australia later this week."

What he didn't say, but was clearly on his mind, was that the two of them hadn't been intimate since the car crash.

"I'm still getting back on my feet," Gina said, "and I mean that both figuratively and literally. And I must admit I haven't exactly felt sexy with my cast and my bruises and scabs. Peter's moving in doesn't help either."

"So come over to my place."

"I will," said Gina. "But I'll need a little more time."

"Don't make me wait too long."

"Is that a threat?" she asked.

"No," he said, "It was a pitiful admission that I miss spending time with you and being together."

"I miss that too," she said.

"Get some beauty sleep," he said. "I love you."

"Me too," she said, and ended their call.

But Gina didn't sleep. She felt out of sorts. Would Bryan have told Christina to get some beauty sleep? She doubted it.

On her nightstand was a radio, and on impulse Gina turned it on. An announcer said, "You're listening to WCPT, bringing progressive radio to Chicago." And then she heard an edgy rendition of the classic song "Ring of Fire," which apparently was the same name for a talk show being hosted by Sam Seder and Robert F. Kennedy, Jr.

"You hear that Trump plans to shut down the Department of Education?" said Seder. "Yeah, he plans to do that by renaming it Trump University."

"You're not going to keep telling those agonizingly bad Trump jokes are you?" asked Kennedy.

"Not me," said Seder. "But while we're on the subject, how do you know you're reading a Donald Trump book?"

"Tell me," said a cooperative Kennedy.

"It begins and ends with Chapter Eleven."

Gina clicked off. Normally she would have enjoyed the banter of the two men, but she was still unsettled after talking with Bryan. Gina knew she was to blame for their lack of intimacy, and she also knew that she hadn't been completely honest with her boyfriend. There was another reason she'd kept him at arm's distance and was still pushing him away.

It is hard to love a man, when your heart is filled with hate. And it is hard to love when you are consumed by the dark thoughts of planning a murder.

# 19
## REAL LIFE MONSTERS OF THE MIDWAY

"**T**hat's the car," said Bennie. "It matches with the make and license plate number." He was comparing the vehicle to the information that had been provided to them by the Bergman-Deketomis investigators.

Kim Knudsen's baby blue Ford Mustang was parked in her driveway. She and her schoolteacher husband lived in Edison Park, a low crime neighborhood that was home to many Chicago cops.

"Now I've just got to get her to open the door," said Gina.

"You should have brought a copy of *The Watchtower*," he said.

"I'll try my best smile instead," said Gina. "She's more likely to open the door to a solitary woman than she is to both of us, so I'm going to need you to stay here."

"Good luck," he said.

Gina crossed the street and then hobbled up the walkway to a one-story brick ranch home. She rang the doorbell and waited.

Although she couldn't hear anything from inside the house, Gina was sure she was being scrutinized through the door's peephole. The door was finally opened by an unsmiling woman, who stayed behind the safety of her screen door while eyeing Gina.

"Ms. Knudsen?"

The woman at the door looked much older than the pictures of Officer Knudsen that Gina had been provided by the Bergman-Deketomis investigators; it was clear just how much her ordeal had aged her.

"Who are you?"

"I'm Gina Romano. I'd like to ask you a few questions if you don't mind."

"You're a bloodsucker?"

"I'm a lawyer with Bergman-Deketomis."

"Same thing," the woman said.

"I'm on your side," said Gina.

"No one is on my side."

"My firm is going up against Arbalest. We are collecting evidence that will show the Sight-Clops gunsight was defective."

"I'm not supposed to say anything without my union representative present."

Gina decided to take her best shot with the limited information she had about Knudsen. "Is that the same union representative who advised you to say nothing during your shooting review and disciplinary hearings? Are you satisfied with the end result of that advice? The Chicago Police Department interpreted your silence as a tacit admission of guilt in the death of your partner Officer Velez."

The mention of Velez's name broke apart Knudsen's mask, revealing for just a moment the extent of her suffering. But then she regained her stolid front.

"I have been specifically advised to say nothing about the death of Officer Velez as that might impact my standing as a CPD officer."

The door began to close and Gina spoke faster and louder. "We are finding other people like you who have suffered because of Arbalest's defective product. Plenty of people have been killed and wounded. You are not at fault for Officer Velez's death."

"I was the one who shot him." Her voice was muted by the partially closed door and by the pain that came with her admission.

"We're going to show that during hot and humid conditions, the Sight-Clops' targeting was a disaster waiting to happen. And what's worse, Arbalest apparently knew this."

"I can't do this," Knudsen said. "I can't open up old wounds."

"I'd like to hear from you about what happened that night."

The door began to close again. "Good luck with your case," said Knudsen.

"I'm going to leave you my card," said Gina. "Like it or not, you'll be hearing from me soon, and next time it won't be only the two of us talking. I intend to depose you."

The front door shut and Gina heard the sounds of a dead bolt closing. She put one card in the screen and the other under the front door mat that said Welcome.

◆◆◆

Gina joined Bennie back in the SUV. "Not a long conversation," he said.

"I don't blame her. She's been through hell. She's haunted by the death of her partner and her guilt. And she's been warned not to talk to people like me. She wants to believe she's innocent. That's a far cry from feeling not guilty."

Gina's cell phone began ringing. She looked at the display. Robert Diaz was calling. "Good morning, Robert."

"Shit!" yelled Diaz. "Are you fucking kidding me?"

Gina could hear road noise over the phone and yelled to be heard. "Robert! Robert!"

"That bastard just played bumper cars with me on the damn freeway! And now he's riding my ass!"

"Who did that to you?"

"A cop!" yelled Diaz. "He's in a CPD squad car. I'm pretty sure he's the same guy who was following me yesterday, but not in a squad car. Today he's been on my tail for at least the last mile."

"Where are you?"

"I'm in the Chicago Loop, closing in on the end of the Ike."

"The what?"

"The Dwight D. Eisenhower Expressway!" yelled a frantic Diaz. "I'm afraid to get off the Ike onto a side street. I think that's what this guy wants."

By that time Gina had brought up a map of Chicago on her phone and was trying to locate Diaz's location.

"Do not pull over even if he flashes you," said Gina. "Turn west on the 290. That will keep you on a highway. You want to make sure there are plenty of eyes around you at all times. Stand by, and I'll give you the address where I want you to go. Does your car have GPS?"

"Yeah, yeah, give me the address!"

Gina tried to remain calm as she focused on her best option.

"Proceed to 4901 West Cermak Road. That's in Cicero, Illinois. We will meet up with you there."

Diaz repeated the address as Bennie entered it into their own Expedition's GPS.

"The bastard is enjoying this," said Diaz. "He's got one arm out the window. It's like the arm of one of those bodybuilders. And when he sees me looking at him through my rearview mirror he lifts his thumb and forefinger towards me like he is aiming a gun."

"Listen to me," said Gina. "I want you to obey every traffic law. I want you to drive as slowly and carefully as your grandmother. Don't give him any excuse to pull you over for anything, including talking on a cell phone while operating a vehicle. And if he does flash you, pretend you don't see. We're on the way!"

Diaz dropped his phone on the seat next to him, but they could still hear him cursing.

"So where are we going?" asked Bennie. He was flooring the accelerator, and they were weaving in and out of traffic.

The GPS told them they were a little more than seven miles from their destination.

"Since he's got a dirty Chicago cop on his tail," she said, "we don't want to involve the CPD. Cicero has its own police department that's autonomous from CPD. I'm betting little brother won't look too fondly on big brother horning in on his territory."

"We're going to the Cicero police station?"

"You got a better idea?"

Bennie had increased their speed to numbers Gina had never seen as a driver or a passenger. She found herself kicking at an imaginary brake on the floorboard and leaning into the turns as Bennie maneuvered the SUV through heavy traffic.

◆◆◆

It was Lutz who had sicced Thursby on Diaz. Technically, Thursby worked at the thirteenth precinct on the South Side of Chicago, but he was on "special assignment" to Lutz. It had proved to be a much more profitable duty than his police job. According to Lutz, Diaz was a threat to their gravy train.

"I think the suspect will need to be 'tased,'" Lutz told Thursby.

"Understood," Thursby had said.

Thursby had two conductive electrical weapons (CEW). One of them had been issued by the department. The second, which was only brought out on occasions like this, had special modifications. When used, it was designed to deliver a shock that would induce heart failure. Thursby figured with the way he had been playing a little cat and mouse game with the victim, it was likely this Diaz guy was probably halfway to that heart attack already.

"Where are you going, dead man driving?" mused Thursby.

By this time, he had thought the presence of a CPD cruiser on his tail would have resulted in Diaz's exiting from the Ike, but now his mouse was trying to move over to get on Interstate 290 going west. That wasn't in keeping with Thursby's plans. He didn't want Diaz driving outside of Chicago's city limits.

Thursby lit him up, but didn't turn on the siren. Instead of pulling over, Diaz picked up speed and got on the 290.

—◆◆◆—

"He's got his light bars flashing," said Diaz. "He's pissed. He's signaling for me to pull over."

"Keep driving," said Gina. "In fact, get in the right lane and slow down to fifty. We're trying to catch up with you."

"What's in Cicero?" asked Diaz.

"A cop shop," she said. "It's only a couple of blocks over from the 290. You know there are plenty of cameras at police stations. Don't stop until you get there. When you pull into a space I want you to have your sleeves rolled up, with both yours arms out the window and your hands exposed."

"That's the best plan you got?"

"You'll be safe if you do that."

Gina sounded absolutely certain of what she was saying and tried not to think about the video images she'd seen of Chicago cops shooting unarmed suspects.

"And we'll be there right after you. In fact, if you want I'll call the Cicero station right now and tell them to be expecting you."

"No," said Diaz. "Stay on the line with me. And if anything goes down, I want you recording it."

"I'll do that," Gina promised.

"Shit!" screamed Diaz.

"What?"

"That asshole just bumped me again! My car almost spun out of the lane!"

"How far are you from the Cicero exit?"

"About half a mile."

"When you get off the freeway," she said, "if you think your life is in danger, don't stop for lights or stop signs. Just keep on driving until you get to the police station."

"I think the bastard is going to hit me again. He's speeding . . . shit!"

Over the phone they could hear the sound of a collision. "Rob? Are you okay? Talk to me!"

"You need to sue this son of a bitch for assault!"

"One case at a time. But for now you need to focus on what I'm telling you to do."

"I don't want to die in Cicero," said Diaz. "My father told me nothing good ever came out of Cicero. He said that Al Capone went to Cicero to try and escape the Chicago PD. And now I'm doing the same."

"You're doing great, Rob."

"I'm scared shitless. Here comes the exit. Where are you?"

"No more than a minute behind you."

"Don't be late for the party."

◆◆◆

As Bennie turned the Expedition into the parking lot of the Cic-ero Police Department, Gina said, "We'll do it like we agreed. That means no heroics. He's got a gun and you don't."

There was no time for Bennie to argue, even though they hadn't "agreed" to anything. Gina had told him to play the cam-eraman, though he would have preferred to skip the lights and camera and go directly to the action.

They both jumped out of the Expedition. A very big man had his very large gun pointed at Robert Diaz. He was in a shooter's stance. Diaz was yelling, "I am unarmed! I am unarmed!"

"Officer!" yelled Gina. She was walking as fast as she could, even with the encumbrance of her cast. "My name is Gina Romano. I am Mr. Diaz's attorney of record. He is the individual that you have your gun trained on. As you can hear, and as you can see, my client is unarmed. At this moment I am on the line with WCPT. They are broadcasting our conversation live. Is there anything you would like to say over the air?"

Thursby holstered his .357 Magnum and got out of his shooter's stance. He stood up to his full height and tried to stare down Gina, but the war of eyeballs didn't work to his advantage. Under her unre-lenting gaze, he looked away, but not before spitting on the ground.

"Officer," she said, "since you're driving a Chicago police car, isn't Cicero out of your jurisdiction?"

Gina motioned for Bennie to film his police car. As Bennie fol-lowed her lead, the two men glared at one another. The tinderbox was ready to go off. Gina was hoping someone would emerge from the tiny police station at any moment, but soon realized instead that she might be on her own. "That's my co-counsel filming our inter-action, officer," Gina said, trying to avert a fight. "We will be logging this in as evidence. Now, would you please answer my question regarding being out of your jurisdiction?"

"The violations occurred in Chicago," he said. "And despite my very visible attempts to pull the offender over, your client refused and forced me to follow him here."

"You're in street clothes," said Gina. "Where's your uniform, officer? I'll need your name and badge number."

Thursby didn't answer.

Gina continued: "Did you identify yourself as a police officer to my client? You see, Mr. Diaz and I agreed to meet at the Cicero Police Department to discuss any complaint you might have against him. Of course, I was shocked to see your gun drawn and pointed at him even though he was sitting in his car with his hands in clear view. My client did everything he could to show you he was unarmed and no threat."

"I observed your client driving erratically on the Ike," he said. "It was there I first tried to pull him over. I noticed him illegally talking on his cell phone while driving. His unlawful flight certainly gave me grounds to proceed as I did."

"Did you inform your dispatch that you were chasing a fugitive?"

"I didn't see the need. In fact, before you intervened, counselor, you will be happy to know I had already decided to let your client off with a verbal warning. Have a good one."

Thursby turned around, covered the ground to get to his cruiser, and got inside. Gina limped over to his window, Bennie right behind her. "You still haven't identified yourself to me, officer."

He shook his head and placed a hand over his ear as if pantomiming he couldn't hear. Then he backed out fast enough to lay tire on the ground, pausing only to call out, "Have a good day, Ms. Romano."

It was clear he remembered her name.

# 20
# NEAR–DEATH EXPERIENCE AND TRUE LOVE

"Lady," said Diaz, "you got some brass balls."

"I'll take that as a compliment," said Gina.

"That goon wanted to kill me. That goon would've killed me. I mean you see a cop's flashers and you pull over, right? And that's what I would have done. And something tells me if I had, I wouldn't be alive now."

"And that's why you need to come with us, Rob. Someone has targeted you. And if that someone can get the cops to go after you, then you're not safe from anyone. You're going to have to fly to Florida with us today."

He shook his head. "I can't."

"You can and you will. I told you what happened to Angus. And now you had your own near-death experience."

"I'm in love," he said.

Bennie made an exasperated sound akin to a steam whistle and then said, "Do you want me to hit him over the head and carry him through the airport terminal?"

"I am talking about true love," said Diaz. "When 'Officer Steroids' had his cannon pointed at me, all I could think about was her. And I thought how unfair it was that I'd finally found love, and the woman I wanted to spend the rest of my days with, and how I was going to die."

"And what's to stop you from having that same thought tomorrow when someone else shows up and puts a hit on you?" asked Bennie. "If you want to live, it's time to get out of town with no delays. And that includes love."

Surprisingly, Gina was more sympathetic than Bennie. Diaz's talk of what had gone through his head when he thought he was going to die had reminded her of what she had felt during her last ride with Angus. Like Diaz, she had been thinking that death had called at a time that was most unfair. She had thought of Bryan and how against all odds she might have a chance for happiness and love.

"Do you think you can talk your lady friend into flying out of Chicago today?" Gina asked. "And you can't sugarcoat what that will entail. She needs to know the two of you are going into hiding. That means for the next month or two neither one of you can be making calls, or sending out emails, or even going out in public. You'll also be assigned a security detail. Someone from our firm will be staying close to you."

"Will we be in Florida?" Diaz asked.

"Yes," said Gina.

"Can you set us up at a beach house?"

Gina looked at Bennie. He shrugged his shoulders and then reluctantly nodded. "I guess for at least the first few days we can put them up at that beachside B&B where the firm sometimes stashes witnesses before a trial."

"Is Louis okay with staying there with them?"

Louis was Bennie's younger brother who also worked security for Bergman-Deketomis. "After I talk to him, he will be."

Diaz had been closely following every word of their conversation. "You can deliver all of that from your end?"

"This isn't a vacation, Rob," said Gina. "The whole purpose of getting you out of town is to protect you from some very bad people."

"That might be," he said, "but what my sweetie is going to hear is a trip to Florida and a stay at the ocean."

"Make the call and sell her," said Bennie. "We need to get moving. Tell her she has to be packed and ready within the hour."

# 21
# A SOLDIER'S STORY

As much as Cara Deketomis loved working for her father's law firm, the life of an associate wasn't easy. Bergman-Deketomis believed in a "sink or swim" philosophy for its associate lawyers, even if you were the daughter of one of the firm's founders. There was no guidebook on how to proceed. She'd been sent to North Carolina on a "fact-finding" mission to talk to one particular soldier. No one had advised her as to how she was to accomplish this task. Everyone at the firm just expected her to get it done correctly.

What Cara hadn't expected was how immense Fort Bragg was. She'd had no clue that its boundaries consisted of two hundred-fifty square miles and extended into four separate North Carolina counties. It wasn't only the size of the place that was daunting. There was somewhere in the neighborhood of forty thousand active duty personnel stationed there, and that number could go up to fifty thousand depending on what was happening around the world.

Fact-finding, thought Cara? Fort Bragg, she now knew, was the largest military base in the world. Among those that called it home were Delta Force, the 3rd Special Forces Group, the Joint Special Forces Command, the Joint Special Operations Command, and the John F. Kennedy Special Warfare Center and School.

And she was expected to find and talk to one soldier. She might as well try to find a needle in a haystack while she was at it.

Gina had tried making calls, but Fort Bragg seemed to be set up to rebuff inquiries like hers. She wasn't family of the soldier, nor was she on army business. Because what information she had on Cary Jones was scant, it was hard to bluff her way through. She tried going through the switchboard, but that got her nowhere. After that she tried to find a way past the gatekeepers by attempting to work through visitor information, newcomer services, the soldier support center, on-post housing, and the reception company services.

The bureaucracy was overwhelming and it also kept Cara out. She needed to find a way to outflank that wall of paperwork and regulations.

Cara did an internet search of restaurants, looking for a micro-brewery-type restaurant in Fayetteville. Good beer and good burgers, Cara reasoned, were sure draws for soldiers. Her search area excluded Bragg Boulevard. In her short time in Fayetteville, Cara had discovered that hookers worked that street 24/7. The Hooah House on Sycamore Dairy Road though looked promising for her purposes.

◆◆◆

Cara had brought business attire for the trip, but now she tried to make it look more casual. She didn't want to appear older and more mature than her twenty-four years. She wore her blond hair down and shucked her jacket. The minimal makeup she'd been wearing was now enhanced, particularly around her eyes. When she set out for the Hooah House, Cara looked every inch the attractive young woman that she was.

The brewery/restaurant wasn't exactly a sports bar, but it was a place that catered to males and the military. Team USA was its target market. There was a bar section as well as a restaurant section. Cara chose to sit in the bar section. There was a good late afternoon crowd, but Cara was able to get a table of her own. The big screen televisions were tuned into different sporting events, mostly baseball and basketball. That didn't stop most of the viewers from taking notice of Cara sitting alone.

The beer list was daunting, and Cara was nowhere near finishing reading the menu when a petite brunette server with a pony tail and a name tag identifying her as *Britt* came up to her.

"Y'all want something to drink?" Britt asked with a thick southern accent and a smile.

Unlike most Floridians, Cara had a bit of a southern accent herself because of having been born and raised in the Panhandle, but it wasn't anywhere close to Britt's.

"I was trying to figure out what beer to order," Cara said, "but I'm afraid it would take me all day to read your beer list."

"What kind of beer do you usually drink?" asked the server.

"I like lighter beers."

"Then I'd recommend our 'Blonde Bomber,'" she said. "We brew it on the premises."

"Sounds good to me," said Cara.

When the beer arrived, Cara took a long swallow. It was good, and besides, she needed the liquid courage. When she'd come up with her plan, it had seemed reasonable to her. But now that she was acting out her plan, it seemed stupid. There was probably some easy way for her to contact Cary Jones that didn't involve wishful thinking and a cock and bull story. She took another swallow of her beer.

I am not going to cry in my beer, she thought.

"You picked a beer that matches your hair, ma'am," a voice said.

A soldier in camos was standing next to her table.

Cara looked up at the soldier and smiled, and then looked back at her beer. "You're right," she said. "I just hope my beer doesn't have split ends."

She and the soldier shared a laugh.

"Are you waiting for anyone, ma'am?" he asked.

"No, I'm not," said Cara. "Would you like to join me?"

"I certainly would, ma'am."

"Please don't call me ma'am," she said. "It makes me feel old. My name is Cara."

"I'm Jesse," he said.

Suddenly, Jesse wasn't alone. Two other men in camos had come up behind him. "And I'm Bobby," said one of them. "Darrel," said the other.

"Well Jesse, Bobby, and Darrel," said Cara, "I'd be pleased if all of you would join me."

The soldiers didn't need to be asked twice.

◆◆◆

Playing the "damsel in distress" might not have been the most professional way of getting word to Cary Jones, but the three soldiers helped her navigate through military obstacles that would have left most civilians in the lurch.

Cara told the soldiers that she was a "friend of a friend" of someone who knew Cary from Gaffney and had been entrusted to pass on a message to him. Of course, she had lost his email address and had hoped ("silly me") to be able to enter Fort Bragg where she could ask around for him. That plan, she admitted, had been stopped at the entrance gate, where she'd been turned around along with her vehicle.

The soldiers asked her questions about Cary, and she answered with what little information she could provide.

While Cara bought the soldiers beers, they made calls on her behalf to other soldiers on base. By the time Jesse, Bobby, and Darrel were finishing their third round, Cary Jones had been located, and the number to his cell phone was triumphantly handed over to Cara.

Cara signaled Britt that it was time for another round. She was still nursing her first beer. "You gentlemen have been such a big help," she said, "that drinks are going to be on my tab all night, as long as you promise to take a cab home."

"You're not leaving, are you?" asked Jesse.

"For now," she said, "I'm just excusing myself to call Cary."

"And you really don't have a boyfriend?" asked Darrel.

"I really don't have time for a boyfriend," said Cara. "My work keeps me very busy."

"'Lady Lawyer,'" said Bobby, "we agree with your stipulation to avail ourselves of alternative transportation in lieu of driving ourselves in exchange for continued libation on this eve."

▸◆◆◆◂

When Cary Jones answered his phone, his voice wasn't what Cara expected. He was soft-spoken and sounded diffident, nothing like the three testosterone-driven males with whom she had been drinking.

"Since Jones is such a common surname," said Cara, "I want to make sure you're the same Cary Jones who grew up in Gaffney and recently returned from Afghanistan."

"Well," he said, "I did grow up in Gaffney, and I did just return from Afghanistan. What else do you want to know?"

Cara asked him a few more questions and made sure she had the right soldier. When she was satisfied she had found her man, Cara had to come clean.

"I am sure you are wondering what this is all about Mr. Jones. I know earlier you heard from other soldiers that a friend of a friend of yours from Gaffney wanted to talk with you, but I am afraid that's not the case. I apologize for using that false story to track you down."

"It didn't quite sound right," he said. "Or as we might say in Gaffney: Don't piss on my leg and tell me it's raining."

"I promise not to do that to your leg. I am a lawyer, Mr. Jones, and I'm hoping you'll agree to meet with me. I'd like to ask you a few questions."

"What kind of questions?"

"I'd like to discuss what happened to you in Afghanistan. I should mention that my firm is suing Arbalest. They are the weapons manufacturer that made Sight-Clops. We're pretty sure that Sight-Clops is a defective product, and its use has resulted in many deaths and injuries."

From his end of the phone Cara heard a loud exhalation of breath. "Mr. Jones?" she asked.

"Cary," he said. "You are the first person to ever call me Mr. Jones."

"Cary," she said, "it sounded as if you had a strong reaction to what I just said."

"I told everyone my gunsight was off. I said it had to be way off. But no one believed me."

"I believe you," said Cara.

"Thank you," he whispered.

"I'd like to talk about what you experienced."

"I don't know if that would be good," he said. "Everyone tells me I need to put what happened behind me."

"I imagine that's a lot easier said than done."

He didn't answer, but Cara knew his silence spoke plenty.

"I'm not much of a philosopher, Cary, but I have always tried to follow a little bit of advice my mom gave me every time I was unwilling to let loose of all the things that used to make me angry. She had a quote she borrowed that said: 'For every minute you hold your anger inside, you give up 60 seconds of piece of mind.'"

Jones broke his silence. "Your mom sounds like a smart lady."

"I think so too," said Cara.

"I don't think the brass would want me talking about what happened."

"Not even to an old friend of an old friend from Gaffney?" she asked.

She made him laugh, even though he sounded out of practice. "Have you ever even been to Gaffney?" he asked.

"The only time I've been in South Carolina was when I went to Myrtle Beach on spring break with some college friends a few years ago."

"Did all of you act silly?"

"I am pretty certain that we did, if I remember correctly."

"How old were you?"

Cara thought about it. "I think I was nineteen."

She heard something that approximated a laugh or a grunt from his end of the line. "What?" she asked.

"I shot and killed a man when I was nineteen while on spring break in Afghanistan. Now I'm twenty years old and I feel like an old man. I should have been getting silly in a place like Myrtle Beach or Fort Lauderdale."

"Look," said Cara, "I'm up here from Spanish Trace. I don't know Fayetteville other than avoiding Bragg Boulevard. How about we meet up? If you don't want to talk about Afghanistan, that's fine. I promise I won't push you. All you'll be doing is spending a little time with a friend of a friend from Gaffney."

"I'm off-duty tomorrow until zero thirteen hundred hours," he said.

"As it happens," she said, "so am I."

◆◆◆

They had agreed to meet at a restaurant called the Waffle Spot at "zero nine hundred hours." Military time notwithstanding, Cara arrived fifteen minutes early. Despite her being overly punctual, Cary was already there waiting out front.

She knew who he was without ever having seen a picture of him. Maybe it was the way he was looking at her, as if trying to identify someone he only knew by voice. Perhaps it was his forlorn look that gave him away. Or she might have been clued in by the bags under his eyes that advertised his hard service. Or maybe it was just that this soldier reminded Cara of her brother, Andy. The last time she'd seen Andy, Cara had been surprised at how much he'd grown up. He'd deferred going to college to have the opportunity of working with at-risk children from the Middle East, but in the fall he would be starting up at the University of Florida.

"Cary?" she asked.

"Cara?" he said.

The two of them shook hands. "It's probably good we're by ourselves," said Cara. "Our names are just too similar. We'd have to listen closely to see if someone was saying 'Cara' or 'Cary.'"

Cary nodded. He had a hard time looking at Cara for more than a second or two. It was clear that it had been some time since he was in the company of a pretty, young woman.

"Are you hungry?" Cara asked.

When he nodded, Cara decided to take up both sides of the conversation. Soon enough she was sure Cary would find his confidence, and with it, his voice. She would see to that.

"I was so glad you picked a place with waffles," she said. Cara focused on putting him at ease. She knew she needed to be less lawyer and more everyday Cara.

"When I was a girl I always looked forward to Sundays because that was the day we'd go out for waffles. Usually we went after church. And I always wanted a pile of whipped cream on my waffles. There was this one server who would make faces in the whipped cream using blueberries and strawberries."

Cary was nodding and smiling as he opened the door for Cara. Since returning from Afghanistan he had been trying to reconnect with America, but without much success. Maybe eating waffles with a pretty girl would help him find his way back.

—◆◆◆—

Cara and Cary were on their third cup of coffee. The breakfast crowd was gone and the lunch crowd was beginning to trickle in. Cara hadn't yet asked him a single question about Afghanistan, although it seemed as if they'd talked about almost everything but that.

"You really do need to meet Andy," said Cara. "The two of you are just about the same age. If you visit Florida I'll make sure he shows you around."

"I'd appreciate that," said Cary.

"Do you know what you want to do when you get out?"

He shrugged. "I'm not sure. For three years I've had someone else telling me what to do. I kind of have this dream of getting back to nature and decompressing for a few months from everything I've been through."

"I can understand your wanting to do that."

Cary reached into his pocket, pulled out several coins, and placed them in front of Cara. The coins weren't elaborately decorated, although there was some Arabic script on each.

"Ahmad sold me these coins," said Cary. "They don't look like much, do they? That's because image-making is forbidden by Islam.

"Two and three times a week he would come and try to sell me something. I bought a Soviet soldier's cap and some medals, even though I didn't want to hear the story of how they had been obtained. The Afghanis didn't care that the Soviets were a superpower, just as they don't care that we're one. They sent them packing, and soon they'll send us packing."

Cara nodded to show she was listening.

"Ahmad was always selling me things for 'Mrs. Cary.' He couldn't believe I didn't have a wife or girlfriend back home. Over time, he got me to buy lapis lazuli jewelry, jingle chains with beads, and jewelry boxes. Everything came with a story. That's what I liked most, hearing his stories."

Cary cleared his throat and looked away for a few seconds. "After I shot his grandfather," he said, "Ahmad never came back. The army gave some settlement to his family. I wish I had a settlement, and I'm not talking money. I told my superiors that the gunsight was defective. I said that I had absolutely locked on to my target. And that target was nowhere near the heart of an Afghan grandfather."

"I know you've been beating yourself up ever since that happened," said Cara. "But it wasn't your fault. You were told to trust your equipment and trust what your eyes told you. You didn't do anything wrong."

"You should have seen the way Ahmad looked at me. His eyes still follow me. I can't escape them. I never got to tell him how sorry I was. I never got the chance to say it was a terrible accident. I hope more than anything that you're right about it not being my fault, but I still feel there's blood on my hands."

"I am so sorry, Cary," she said.

"You and me both," he said.

# 22
## COPS' CLUB

The day had not begun well for Gina Romano. When she awakened, she couldn't find her cell phone. That had put her in full panic mode. Her cell phone was essentially her life. She used it to take notes and make recordings. It woke her in the morning and played gentle music at night. All of her contacts were on her phone.

Peter called her cell number from various spots around the house, but they hadn't heard the familiar ring tone. Then she and Peter had searched the house, but came up empty.

For once, her younger brother was the voice of reason. "Your phone didn't get up and walk away," he said. "And since you made calls on it last night, and you didn't go out, we know it has to be somewhere in the house."

Then Peter had stepped up for her big time and said, "You go to work. I promise I'll turn the house upside down looking for your phone. And I promise I'll find it."

When her desk phone rang she was hoping to see Peter's name on the display, but it was Carol.

"We've got the name of that cop and that led us to Bull's-eye."

Gina's day suddenly improved. "Back it up," she said. "You linked our bad cop with bull's-eye?"

"Officer Ron Thursby," said Carol, "works out of the thirteenth precinct. That's on the South Side. He's got quite a reputation there, but for the past eighteen months he has been on special assignment, or more accurately, union business. His boss is former Chicago cop and deputy chief Tom Lutz, who now heads up the CPD union."

"What's the bull's-eye connection?" asked Gina.

"Lutz works out of Libertyville Gun Club," said Carol. "The place was built as a shooting range for Chicago cops, but most of its facilities are also open to the public. In addition to being an indoor and outdoor shooting range, it has a gym, a pool, and workout facilities. There's also a meeting hall for union business. Corporate money contributed to the building of Libertyville. Among those corporate donors was Arbalest."

"Angus referenced Libertyville," said Gina. "He suspected there was collusion going on between Arbalest and the CPD union. Angus also said that lots of questionable parties were thrown in what he referred to as Libertyville's 'private facilities.'"

"I guess in his reports Angus didn't call Libertyville by its cop name," said Carol.

Gina finally made the connection. She was angry at herself that it had taken her this long to figure it out. "The cops call it Bull's-eye!"

"Bingo," said Carol. "Out front of the club there is this display, a big slab of marble or granite, where some sculptor carved out a bull's-eye."

"Can we put this Thursby or Lutz anywhere in Florida around the time Angus died?"

"I knew you'd ask me so I already have my team looking into that now."

Gina took a moment to respond. Angus's face was seared into her memory. It had taken all his strength to try and toss her clear of the moving vehicle. Up until now, she hadn't been sure what his last words had been. From essentially beyond the grave, he had yelled, "bull's-eye." She returned to the present. "Great job, Carol. Tell me when you know more."

Ten minutes later she got another wonderful call. "Hey, Sis," said Peter, "Do you sleepwalk?"

"I don't think so."

"Then why was your phone jammed under that mattress of yours?"

"You found my phone under the mattress?"

"It was pushed about two feet in."

"How strange."

"I'm thinking the alarm went off, and you reacted by pushing your phone under the mattress."

"I have no recollection of that."

"That's why I asked about your sleepwalking."

"When I see you, I'm giving you a big hug," she said.

Peter was not one who enjoyed hugs from his big sister. "How about you promise *not* to hug me if I bring your phone to work?"

"Deal! You are a lifesaver!"

# 23
## I KNOW IT WHEN I SEE IT

In most cases, the legal system moves at a glacial pace, but Madsen-Zimmer continued to be a cooperative participant in Gina's hurry-up game. Gina was now even more certain that someone high-up in Arbalest was giving them no choice but to speed things along.

Her suspicion was that Quentin Carter himself was calling the shots. Carter had the ear of Arbalest's owner Tim Knapp. Usually the only time that lawyers for the defendant worked this quickly was if they were being ordered to, or if they were confident of a dismissal. Gina wondered if she was missing something. She knew the case inside out from both sides of the argument. In her own mind she had prepared a case that would withstand any motion Madsen-Zimmer could present for dismissal. Was it possible Madsen-Zimmer had some rabbit ready to pull out of a hat?

It was always hard for a trial lawyer to not be paranoid.

The day after Madsen-Zimmer submitted its filed brief to Seventh District Court's Judge Lyn Sanders asking for a dismissal of Robert Diaz's case against Arbalest, Gina and her team met in a conference room and began pouring through the paperwork. The substance of Madsen-Zimmer's brief was that the suit should be dismissed because Arbalest was a critically important contractor to the US government and therefore immune from punishment.

For Gina, the Madsen-Zimmer brief was oddly anticlimactic. Although the Madsen-Zimmer team had managed to come up with thirty different reasons to dismiss the Robert Diaz whistle-blower suit, Gina couldn't help but think that their arguments and the precedents they cited were overly basic and routine. Judging by the sounds her team was making as they went through the same paperwork, those were their thoughts as well.

Madsen-Zimmer's first defense was to deny that anything improper had ever taken place on the part of Arbalest. That was followed by the argument that, yes, something criminal might have occurred, but the statute of limitations had run out, and the case against them should be dismissed. From there, they argued that even if Arbalest was involved in any wrongdoing, Diaz was not the proper party to bring a claim against them.

"Let's see," said Ned. "They start with, 'My client is innocent.' And then they segue to, 'And even if my client is guilty, the game is over because no one caught us soon enough.' And then they go to my favorite: 'Even if you have a case, your whistle-blower can't bring a claim against his old company because he participated in the crime too. He was a criminal right along with us.'"

"I love the way they try to imply that they are above the law," said Cara, "and that our suing Arbalest would put the safety of all America at risk."

"More and more defense contractors are trying to use that one," said Ned. "Their claim is that since they are working for the government and doing their best to keep America safe, they should get a pass when they screw up. I call it the 'Old Glory' defense."

"I wonder if all those dead people they left behind would agree they were doing their best?" asked Cara.

"Their families sure don't," Ned answered, "but Arbalest contends that the government wanted a gunsight, and that's what they provided them. Their contention is that's the sum of their contract, and that there is nothing in it that says Sight-Clops had to actually work correctly."

"Look at paragraph fifteen," said Gina. "They might as well have submitted as evidence a Monopoly 'Get out of Jail' card. On the one hand they're admitting Arbalest might have been wrong in accepting taxpayer money, but then they say because the federal government knew the gunsight was defective and bought it anyway, the company is not liable."

"Madsen-Zimmer's defense is to throw everything against the wall," said Ned, "and see what sticks. Unfortunately, we've seen those tactics work with some judges."

"What do you know about Judge Sanders?" asked Cara.

"She has a reputation for being fair," said Gina.

"If that's the case," said Ned, "she'll have to allow our suit to go forward. I'm certainly not seeing anything compelling in these arguments. But you never know what's going on behind-the-scenes."

Ned turned to Cara. "They say there are two kinds of lawyers; lawyers who know the law, and lawyers who know the judge."

"Should we really be worried about that kind of collusion with a federal judge?" asked Cara.

"If she were a state court judge, I'd be far more concerned," said Gina. "Nothing I've heard about Judge Sanders would ever lead me to the conclusion that she is anything but ethical."

"But does she know bullshit when she sees or smells it?" asked Ned. He turned to Cara: "What do you call a lawyer who spent more time doing political favors than trying cases?"

"I don't know," answered Cara.

"Your Honor," said Ned.

"Any other thoughts on their brief?" asked Gina.

"I am surprised it seems so . . . boilerplate," said Ned. "Especially since it's signed by Charles Zimmer. You would think when one of the founding partners puts his name on a document, it should wow you.

"I guess I was also expecting something better from a dozen of silk-stocking lawyers all billing at a thousand dollars an hour." Ned turned to Cara and asked, "What's the difference between a wealthy corporate lawyer and a poor corporate lawyer?"

Cara shook her head.

"A poor corporate lawyer makes your case drag on for years," said Ned. "A wealthy corporate lawyer makes it drag on for decades."

"Years ago, I attended a legal conference," said Gina, "where Charles Zimmer was one of the presenters in a course that discussed strategies for keeping bank executives out of prison after a jury conviction. That might be the long game Zimmer is playing with this brief. His firm's job might be more focused on keeping upper management out of prison by signaling all the defenses they could conceivably use if the DOJ started rattling sabers about a criminal case."

"Same old, same old," said Ned. "If you wear an Armani suit and have an army of Wall Street lawyers, you walk."

Ned had spent five years working as a serious crimes prosecutor in Miami. He had put plenty of drug dealers and violent criminals behind bars, but had always been astonished at how the system was so unwilling to imprison white-collar criminals.

"Before seeing this brief," said Gina, "I would have guessed Madsen-Zimmer was counting on a dismissal. Now I don't think that is their hope. What I'm reading tells me Madsen-Zimmer wants to make sure this case never goes to trial.

"Still, I want us to respond to this brief like it's our backs that are against the wall and not theirs. I want our response to be cogent and compelling. In fact, I want to blow them out of the water right from the get-go. I also don't want to give them time to breathe. I want our response on Judge Sanders' desk in two days."

"You're kidding?" said Ned.

Gina shook her head. "I don't want to let up the heat, even for a moment. And so far Judge Sanders has been fine with the fast pace."

"Lie to me and say we'll be done by midnight," Ned said, "so that I can tell my wife that's what you said."

"We'll be done by midnight," said Gina.

"Can we meet back here in thirty minutes?" Ned asked. "I'm going to have to call my wife and clear today's schedule."

"Me too," said Cara, then added, "What I meant to say is that I have to call my friend and cancel our movie date."

"I'll see everyone back here in thirty minutes," said Gina. "And I'll bring Rachel back to help us."

Rachel Frank was a paralegal who was great at researching briefs and was an expert at making order out of legalese chaos.

As Ned and Cara walked out of the conference room, he began telling her another lawyer joke. He'd worked as a lawyer long enough to have heard them all.

———◆◆◆———

Ned and Cara weren't the only ones who had to make explanatory calls. Gina had tentatively said she could attend Bryan's *hooroo* party—hooroo was apparently an Australian way of saying "good-bye"—beginning at six that night. Writing the brief meant Gina wouldn't be able to attend.

"G'day, mate," said Gina.

"That remains to be seen," said Bryan. "Getting a midday call from you makes me suspicious that I'm about to be stood up."

"I'll pretend you didn't say that," said Gina. "The main reason for this call is to confirm our dinner date at the Blue Planet tomorrow night at seven o'clock."

"I can't wait," said Bryan.

"And as my bon voyage present to you," said Gina, "I expect you to order their surf and turf."

Planet Blue was Spanish Trace's best restaurant, and their surf and turf consisted of bacon wrapped lobster and wagyu beef. It was as decadent as it was costly.

"You really don't have to," said Bryan.

"I do," said Gina. Her tone suddenly changed, becoming higher and more apologetic. "Especially since I won't be able to make it tonight."

"I knew it."

"I'm sorry," Gina said. "My team is writing an important brief, and I can't skip out and make them do the work."

"I think I liked it better when you were in the hospital," Bryan said. "At least I got to see you there."

"You know how important this case is to me," said Gina, "and you know I warned you about how busy I am going to be over the next few weeks. Isn't that why you thought it made sense to go to Australia now?"

"I'm still disappointed you won't be able to make my hooroo party."

"I'll make it up to you tomorrow night."

After their dinner at the Blue Planet, the plan was for Gina to stay over at Bryan's house. At dawn she'd be giving him a ride to the airport, and he'd begin the first leg of his journey to Australia.

"I like the sound of that," he said. "Can you elaborate on that topic, though? I mean it has been so long since we've had sex that I've forgotten who ties up who."

"Why do I get the feeling you're trying to work my apology into phone sex?"

"I am deeply offended," he said. "But if you talk dirty to me, I'll forgive you."

Gina faked a little heavy breathing, and then in an entirely too seductive whisper said, "You want some freedom of speech dirty talk? In 1964, in the obscenity case of *Jacobellis v. Ohio*, US Supreme Court Justice Potter Stewart wrote about why the material in question was not obscene, and because of that he believed it was protected under freedom of speech."

She paused long enough to loudly fake a groan; her breathing grew faster and more primal, and in the homestretch her whispering became that much more frantic: "When it came to hardcore pornography, Justice Stewart said that he really couldn't define it, but he wrote, 'I know it when I see it.'"

Gina's story and her rapid breathing, came to a sudden stop.

"That's talking dirty to me?" said Bryan.

"It is until tomorrow night," and then whispered, "Bye, baby."

# 24
## BUNGLE IN THE JUNGLE

Whenever the two Stokes brothers were together, people took notice. Louis Stokes wasn't quite the beheomoth Bennie was—the younger brother was probably two inches shorter and forty pounds lighter—but he was still an imposing figure. People sometimes mistook Bennie and Louis for one another. Their faces were certainly similar, and both wore their dark hair long, but Louis didn't have feathers in his hair. Louis was also more given to smiling even though it was Bennie's wry humor that made people laugh.

It was the younger of the two brothers who was heading up the Robert Diaz security team. Earlier that morning, Louis had called Gina and asked if he could meet with her and discuss a "situation."

Bennie preceded Louis into Gina's office. Unsmiling, he taunted, "I hope this guy doesn't give you any grief. I'll be glad to throw him out if he does."

"It won't come to that," said Louis, "lucky for you."

The two brothers did a little more jawing back and forth.

When the big man took a seat, Gina asked, "What can I do for you, Louis?"

He looked away, not meeting her eyes. "I am afraid we're going to need to find new accommodations for Mr. Diaz and Ms. Reinhart."

"Why is that? I thought Rob was happy where we situated him."

"He is," said Louis. "But he and Miss Honey are loud."

"Loud," repeated Gina.

"They are *loud*," said Louis, "four or five times a day. And at night they are especially *loud*. Mr. and Mrs. Terry say it's so loud they can't sleep."

"Who are Mr. and Mrs. Terry?"

"They own the B&B," said Louis. "To be honest, I can't really blame them. Everyone on my team can't help but notice the loudness."

Maybe Rob Diaz really had found his true love, thought Gina. "Thank you, Louis. Tell you what; I'm going to find alternative accommodations for Mr. Diaz and Ms. Reinhart. Just have them packed and ready to go within the hour."

"Thank you, Ms. Romano," he said.

Gina thought for a minute, and then called Martin Bergman. The founding partner's house was one of the largest in Spanish Trace. It was fenced in, and had a state-of-the-art security system. No one could approach it without setting off lights, and beyond a certain point alarms were triggered. Gina had heard Martin say his house was like a fortress, and probably more secure than any residence other than the White House.

"Martin?" said Gina. "Is that guest house of yours currently being used?"

◄◆◆►

The lawyers at Bergman-Deketomis were used to multitasking and working several cases at the same time. Because the Arbalest case had been all-consuming, Gina had fallen behind on her other cases. She knew this week would be spent playing catch-up with other work, and perhaps the next week as well, depending on how quickly Judge Sanders responded to the Madsen-Zimmer motion to dismiss their case.

Peter called Gina's cell at midday. Even though she hadn't gotten home until one the night before, Peter still hadn't been in. She wondered if he had already found a girlfriend. Making friends with the opposite sex had always been a talent of his. If he was dating already, Gina wasn't sure what she thought of that. He was still married, after all.

"Hey, little brother," said Gina.

"Hey to you," said Peter. "You've been working such long hours our paths haven't crossed."

"You've been putting in some late hours yourself," said Gina, fishing to get a few answers as to what her brother had been up to.

"That's why I thought we should spend a little time together. And you did say you owed me for finding your phone. How about taking your *poor*—and unfortunately that word pretty much describes my current economic state—brother to dinner tonight?"

"Having dinner with you sounds great," said Gina, "but I'm not sure if tonight works for me."

"I'm sure even Clarence Darrow rested on occasion," he said.

"It's not that," said Gina. "It's just that Bryan and I have plans. He's leaving for Australia in the morning."

"Well, I wouldn't want to be the third wheel," Peter said.

Gina could hear the hurt in his voice. "You wouldn't be," she said. "And you're welcome to join us if you want."

"Are you sure? Because I was hoping to get your thoughts on a business decision I was considering."

"Then join us," said Gina. "We're meeting up at seven at the Blue Planet."

"I won't be intruding?"

"Of course you won't."

"Okay, I'll see you there tonight."

After Peter hung up, Gina found herself staring at her phone. In any given conversation she knew exactly what to say, but not to her younger brother. Old habits die hard. She had always looked after Peter, and couldn't help doing it still. Gina almost considered calling Peter back and telling him she'd take him out to dinner the following night. That's what she should have told him, Gina knew. After all, this was supposed to be Bryan's bon voyage dinner. But instead of calling Peter, Gina decided to text Bryan.

"I am not canceling tonight," she wrote. "I am looking forward to tonight! But I made the mistake of inviting Peter to join us. Please forgive me! Please tell me everything is fine. XXOO!!"

Gina sent the message and grimaced. She knew Bryan wasn't exactly enamored with Peter. He hadn't approved of his behavior while Gina was hospitalized, and hadn't liked Peter's drunken monologue on the *Jean Louise*. Peter's living in her house was also a bone of contention. It certainly hadn't helped her and Bryan's, of late, nonexistent sex life.

Bryan didn't immediately respond to her text. Even when he was with patients, Bryan was usually good about getting right back to her. Maybe he was in surgery, she thought.

Or maybe he was just pissed.

Five minutes after she sent her text, the sound of a doorbell ringing told Gina she had received a text. She opened her display and saw Bryan had responded.

"Since I am going to have to put up with your brother," he wrote, "I WILL be ordering the surf and turf. XXOO. Promise me, though, he won't be coming with us to my house."

Gina sighed in relief. It was a good thing she had a forgiving boyfriend. She texted back, "I PROMISE!!!!!"

◆◆◆

When her phone alarm went off, Gina could barely believe it. She had hardly put a dent in her deferred work, but there was no way she was going to be late for dinner. There were at least fifty items on her to-do list that she hadn't tended to. Among them was to call Cathy. Gina didn't want Angus's widow to feel abandoned. It was important for Cathy to know how Angus was so near and dear to all of their hearts. Gina wished she could tell Cathy the rest of the story, the story that only she and Deke were privy to. The hunt for the killer of Angus was ongoing; so was their pursuit of paybacks.

Gina went to the restroom to tidy up. She gave herself a critical look in the large mirror. There were bags under her eyes that Gina did her best to cover up. The bruising from the accident, she was happy to see, had almost completely vanished. It was the same with her road rash; her daily ministrations of vitamin E oil and coconut oil had helped restore her skin to its former luster. Gina reapplied some lipstick, and added a hint of perfume.

I'm almost all the way back, Gina thought. She was actually feeling a little nervous. Before the car crash, she and Bryan had found a wonderful rhythm with one another both personally and physically. Was she ready to get back into the saddle? Was she ready to resume their increasingly-bonded relationship?

"Anticipation," whispered Gina, and then began humming the Carly Simon oldie.

◆◆◆

Bryan hadn't been able to find a big enough space for Jennifer anywhere near the Blue Planet. Luckily, he had arrived early, so it was no big deal that he had to park a few blocks away. As he stepped onto the crosswalk, though, Bryan saw a familiar figure standing on the opposite corner. Peter was talking to a young man. At Bryan's approach, the young man took off in the opposite direction.

"Who's your friend?" Bryan asked.

"Friend?" asked Peter. "Oh, that guy? He was panhandling in Florida's Panhandle."

The two men began walking toward the restaurant together. "I'm afraid we're getting more and more panhandlers in Spanish Trace," said Bryan.

"That's actually a good sign," said Peter.

"Begging is a good sign?"

"Spanish Trace is attracting more and more wealth. Beggars aren't stupid. They don't set up shop in poor areas. They go where the money is."

"It sounds like you should be a spokesperson for the Trump administration," said Bryan. Then, trying to make his point like a spin doctor might, Bryan spoke with the pompous assurance of a talking head: "If you're seeing a lot more beggars, and you are, then that's a very good thing."

Peter wasn't amused. "Did you ever stop to think I might know what I'm talking about? I have an MBA, and I'm a Chartered Financial Analyst."

"I'm sorry," said Bryan, but his apology wasn't exactly what Peter wanted to hear: "I guess you do know about begging."

The two men walked in silence the rest of the way to the Blue Planet.

—◆◆◆—

Gina sat at a window table looking out at the water. When she had first moved to Spanish Trace, she never imagined that one day she would think of it as home. The beauty of the place had overwhelmed her right away. She was used to New Jersey after all, and compared to that, Spanish Trace seemed like some wonderfully exotic world with vibrant tropical colors. The city was small enough—fewer than sixty thousand residents—to be intimate. But it was also large enough to support several museums, a botanical garden, and several art festivals.

To most outsiders, Spanish Trace had the reputation of being a navy town. Certainly the presence of one of the largest US naval air stations spoke to a military presence, but the city was now much more than that. Maybe that's why so many high profile individuals were calling Spanish Trace home, including actors, musicians, writers, scientists, and athletes.

And nowadays, even she called it home. Gina's main complaint about her adopted home was that she wished there were more young urban professionals. The infrastructure for Spanish Trace seemed more accommodating to the old than to the up-and-coming. Gina also didn't like the threat of hurricanes. Every hurricane season seemed to bring more storms with more violent damage. For a woman who had been referred to since law school as "Hurricane Gina," she still hated hurricanes.

Gina looked away from the water and saw Bryan and Peter enter the restaurant at the same time. Neither was smiling, which she took as a bad sign. She stood up and waved them over to the table.

—◆◆◆—

Great food and great service tends to smooth over most things, and the Blue Planet delivered on both. The wine hadn't hurt either. Gina and Peter were both working on their third glass, but when she tried to pour another glass for Bryan he declined.

"I think I've had my limit," he said. "Last night my coworkers decided dinner wasn't enough, and all of us ended up at Snooki's."

"Where you had a drink or two," said Gina.

"Or three or four," Bryan admitted. "My coworkers seemed to think I needed some drinking practice if I hoped to fit in Oz."

"Hobnobbing doesn't hurt in Spanish Trace either," said Peter. "In fact, I've been meeting a lot of potential clients in the local drinking establishments."

"What clients are you talking about?" asked Bryan.

"That's what I wanted to talk to my sister about," said Peter to Gina. "I've been thinking about opening a wealth management office in Spanish Trace."

Like the protective big sister she was, Gina pretended to be happy for her brother, smiling and saying, "Oh, Peter."

Bryan was less agreeable. As far as he was concerned, Peter had stayed in town too long already. "What about your business in Connecticut? And didn't Gina tell me a few months ago that your wife was pregnant?"

"Thank you for being so circumspect," said Peter to Gina, "in not spreading my sad tale." Then he turned to Bryan and said, "I had a business and I had a wife, until my business partner and my wife decided to make a more perfect union together with each other. After I was ruled out as being the biological father of my wife's imminent baby, I put spouse, home, and business in the rearview mirror."

"Sorry," said Bryan. "I didn't know."

"It's all for the best," said Peter. "And Spanish Trace looks like the perfect place to start over. There's certainly no shortage of old people with money here. I've been looking for potential office sites."

"I've seen some good business rentals available," said Bryan.

"But you didn't go the rental route yourself, did you?" asked Peter.

"No, I didn't. We bought and built."

"That must have cost a fortune. You built in the high-rent district."

"It wasn't cheap," Bryan admitted.

"I should say. You must be in debt up to your eyeballs."

"Maybe not quite that high," said Bryan, clearly looking uncomfortable with the subject matter.

He was glad when Peter suddenly seemed distracted. "Look at the time," he said, and then reached for his cell phone. "Geez," said Peter, "I forgot to charge my cell. Can I borrow yours for just a minute, Bryan? I promised a potential client that I'd get back to him."

"No problem," said Bryan, handing Peter his phone.

"I'll make my call out on the balcony," he said, excusing himself from the table.

As he walked away, Bryan extended a hand to Gina and said, "Alone, at last."

Gina took his hand into hers, but their alone time didn't last. The maître d' came hurrying toward their table. "Dr. Penn, we have a caller from Australia on the line asking for you."

"How did the caller know you were here?" asked Gina.

"Probably my work. They knew we were dining here and must have told the caller," Bryan said, getting to his feet leaving Gina alone at the table until Peter rejoined her.

"What gives?" her brother asked. "I saw Bryan take off."

"Someone from Australia called the restaurant looking for Bryan."

"Maybe it's the same person who just emailed him," said Peter, handing over Bryan's phone to his sister.

Like many people, Bryan had his phone synced to his email. Gina could see that someone had sent Bryan an email with the subject matter: *Emergency message from the Land Down Under!*

"I better open this in case it's something Bryan needs to know about now," said Gina.

She clicked onto the link and a picture appeared along with a message. When she'd been growing up, Gina had heard such pictures referred to as, "beaver shots." There was a written message that came with the graphic picture that read: *If you need a work testimonial, Doc, I can vouch that you took great care of my down under. And I will swear by your bedside manner.* The text was signed, *T.*

"What is it?" asked Peter.

Gina shook her head. She didn't know what to say. The wonderful meal that only a moment before had warmed her stomach, now felt like lead. She was tempted to toss the phone on the table, but Pandora's box, not to mention T's, had already been opened. Gina clicked on a link to a video file that had come with the text. The first thing she heard was the music to Jethro Tull's song "Bungle in the Jungle." Bryan's television show opened with the same music, but not with the footage she was seeing. A familiar looking woman was naked and positioned with her hands and knees on a bed. The camera followed the contours of the woman's body, pausing to take in her curves. Then the camera pulled back to show a smiling Bryan, as he approached the woman from behind.

Without warning, Gina's food came out. She tried to contain her vomit but her revulsion brought up more than just her food; it brought back the terrible memories of her youth.

Red-faced and utterly humiliated, she grabbed a napkin and wiped at her lips. "I'm so sorry," she said, her words directed at the diners around her.

She handed Peter her credit card and said, "Pay. Give a big tip to whoever cleans up. And tell Bryan to get his own ride to the airport."

Head lowered, eyes averted, and her mortification absolute, Gina limped her way out of the restaurant.

# 25
## GUNS DON'T KILL

**G**ina knew that Bryan had warned her, in his own way—when she'd been in Chicago he had told her, "Don't make me wait too long." He'd been pushing for intimacy for the last month, but she had put him off. Gina had her reasons for needing a time-out: she hadn't felt pretty with her body bruised and covered with scabs, and her leg in a cast.

And she needed time to recover from Angus's death. His murder had unsettled her; plotting revenge and making love were too contradictory for her to reconcile, and she had known better than to try.

Gradually, though, she'd been healing. Her libido had been coming around. But he hadn't been willing to wait.

Scott, one of Bennie's security team, walked her to the car. Gina was glad a bodyguard had been stationed outside the restaurant. That made it much easier to explain what she wanted done.

"Tonight," Gina said, "instead of patrolling my house I want you stationed at the security gate. There is a good chance my former boyfriend Bryan might try and get in. He knows the entry code, and with it he might try to illegally enter. If you see him, he needs to be told that he no longer has access rights and will be arrested if he trespasses."

"I'm going to need to run this by Bennie," Scott said.

"Yes, please do that," Gina said, "but don't call him for five minutes. From my car I'll get hold of Bennie and tell him what I want done."

⬧⬧⬧

Gina was a little less tight-lipped providing Bennie with information, but not much. She told him that she and Bryan were no longer a couple, and that he was no longer an approved visitor at either her home or work. Bennie promised Gina that he would contact the rest of her security detail with the news.

"Bryan will be leaving for Australia in the morning," said Gina, "and should be there for the next two weeks. I imagine by the time he returns we'll both have put this behind us." She hoped Bennie believed that lie.

Step by methodic step, Gina tried to eliminate Bryan from her life. She blocked all his numbers from having access to her cell phone. Then she worked the controls of her laptop to reroute any email from Bryan to go directly to her spam box and at work she would have I.T. do the same thing; hopefully all his future emails would go directly to trash.

Bryan's emails weren't the only things of his going to trash; Gina went through her house and removed all mementos that might remind her of him. It was a painful cleansing. It was also,

Gina told herself, a necessary exorcism. While ridding herself of her demons, Gina suddenly remembered where she had seen the "other" woman. "T" was a bartender at Snooki's. The timing of her email suddenly made sense; Bryan had ended up at Snooki's the night before. By the sound of it, he'd closed the bar. But that was apparently only the beginning of his night out. Bryan must have gone to her home. What was *T's* name? Tammy, Gina remembered. The bartender was an extremely attractive brunette. Bryan had apparently thought so as well.

Peter came home about an hour after Gina and saw how she had spent her time ridding herself of any reminders of Bryan. For once, their roles were reversed. In the past it had always fallen to Gina to comfort him.

"I'm sorry," he said. "I feel your pain and know it hurts like hell."

"It was about time I moved on anyway," said Gina. "Bryan was a fling that I held on to for too long."

"I told Bryan you had gotten sick when he came back to the table. And, of course, he couldn't help but see that you had been sick. I told him that you wouldn't be available to drive him to the airport in the morning."

"I'm sure that's no big deal to him. In fact, I know just the person he should ask."

"He wanted to come over and see you tonight, but I discouraged him."

"If he had come over," said Gina, "an armed guard would have discouraged him."

"Anyway, he said he'd call."

Good luck in getting me on the line, thought Gina.

"When I was talking with him," said Peter, "I don't think he had any idea what happened."

"As soon as he tries to call me," said Gina, "he'll see her call. And then he'll add two and two together, which adds up to around a thirty-eight double D."

"I'm here for you," said Peter. "It's like old times."

"Yeah," said Gina, "it's just like the good old days."

She couldn't contain the bitterness in her voice.

-◆◆◆-

Gina took some of the heavy duty medication that had been prescribed to her after the crash. It was just enough to knock her out.

She awoke at nine, three hours later than when she usually got up. By now, Gina knew Bryan was on his way to Australia. She was glad that for the next two weeks he was going to be ten thousand miles away from her. That wasn't far enough, she thought, but at least it was a start.

Gina called work to say she would be coming in late. The medication and the hangover from the breakup had left Gina feeling groggy. She knew her detractors liked to refer to her as an "iron maiden," as if feelings were something foreign to her. Gina wished they were right. But even when she was hurting, she *did* have an iron will. That would see her through the early, difficult days of the breakup.

Work would help as well, just as schoolwork had. Growing up, Gina had never settled for anything less than an "A." Studying saved her from having to interact with her parents. Work would save her from thoughts of Bryan. Or at least that was her plan.

There was a part of her, though, that knew she had pushed him away, right up until the night before last. If Gina had gone to Bryan's hooroo celebration, he probably wouldn't have strayed. She had yet to meet a male saint. Her reluctance to be with him after the accident couldn't have been easy for him to accept, especially after the way they had connected on so many levels. Gina remembered the last night the two of them had made love at Bryan's place; it had occurred just a few days before the car crash.

He had invited her to his house for a home-cooked dinner, and over the course of the evening they had gotten progressively sillier. They ate in his backyard where he had a picnic table. Whether by neglect, or by design, Bryan's backyard really did look like a jungle. It was overgrown with foliage that included birds of paradise, fan palms, and banana trees. In that green setting, he had serenaded her with his harmonica, playing "That's Amore." Gina supposed he had learned that song in honor of her Italian heritage.

Whatever the reason, his up-tempo playing had awakened all the special needs animals that were living in cages in his backyard. Gina had never heard "That's Amore" played to the accompaniment of grunts and whines and howls and growls. Probably no one had ever heard such a chorus. And what was loudest was her laughter. How she had laughed. Gina would miss that.

And she would miss Dr. Doolittle. But he was dead to her now.

◆◆◆

Gina looked up to see who was knocking at her door. Carol smiled at her and asked, "Got a minute?"

"For you," Gina replied, "of course."

As Carol took a seat, Gina considered telling her about Bryan, but then she became resolute about not opening that door. At work Gina was determined to remain dry-eyed, and the only way that would be possible was not to talk about him.

"I know you've been waiting to hear about our timeline investigation of Ron Thursby and Tom Lutz," Carol said. "From what we can determine, though, neither of those men could have been in Florida at the time of Angus's death. It would appear that neither left Chicago during the dates in question."

"You're sure of this?"

"Ninety-nine percent sure," said Carol. "It isn't as if we have access to their desk calendars. But we do have witnesses that put them in Chicago, and there's no record of them being on any airline manifests at any airports near Spanish Trace around the time of his death."

"Our whistle-blower believes Thursby meant him serious harm."

"He's probably right," said Carol. "Thursby's jacket is full of charges of excessive force. Everyone knows he's juiced on steroids, which makes him highly unstable."

Gina remembered her encounter with the man and how she had willed herself to not be intimidated by him. It was a miracle she'd managed not to shake.

"Lutz is even more dangerous than Thursby, though," said Carol. "He's smart. He knows where the bodies are buried. Angus was right to direct you to Bull's-eye. Bit by bit we're learning about a lot of bad things that went on behind those doors. Unfortunately, the goings-on seem to be mostly sealed by a police confessional. All we have so far are rumors of business deals being conducted through the use of blow and prostitutes the same rumors say the shooting hall is a front for illegal weapons and drug trafficking."

"How do we connect Arbalest with that?" asked Gina.

"Angus's file shows that he was interested in an Arbalest lobbyist named Kendrick Strahan. For several years, Strahan has been chummy with Lutz. Strahan claims that during that time he regularly paid cash to rent out the Bull's-eye meeting room. While some of those gatherings appear to be legit, we suspect most of the *rental* payments went into Lutz's pocket. In return for that bribe money, Lutz helped Strahan push Arbalest products to the Chicago Police Department, as well as the police departments of other cities throughout the Midwest."

"You can get me a report documenting this?" asked Gina.

"We're working on that now," said Carol, "but before we dot our i's and cross our t's I wanted to give you this heads-up."

"I appreciate it," said Gina. "And while you're here, I'm wondering if you can tell me why Officer Thursby was chasing down my whistle-blower."

"Lutz might have decided it was in his best interests to put an end to your Arbalest case by ridding himself of Diaz."

"If at first you don't succeed," said Gina, "try, try again." Then she explained, "I am wondering if it was Lutz who put the hit on Angus."

"I don't have any information telling me that," said Carol. "All I can say is that Lutz is dirty, even though he has managed to shield himself from any incriminating charges."

"Thank you," said Gina, "and please thank your team."

"I'll do that. How is your Arbalest case going?"

"We're waiting on a judge to tell us if she's dismissed our case or if it's going forward."

"That must not be easy."

"It's torture," Gina said. "I am sure we answered every point of the defendant's motion to dismiss, and by the merits of our arguments we showed why the case should proceed. But in the end it comes down to what the judge decides. And of course every day I have to wait is another day I second-guess myself. Should I have been slower in responding to their motion? Should I have beefed up our arguments? Should I be worried about some bias the judge might have? Could I have done something to better position ourselves in this action?"

"Don't beat yourself up too much," said Carol, before she excused herself.

That seemed like good advice, Gina thought. But she also knew it was advice she would find impossible to follow.

—◆◆◆—

The only thing that seemed to help Gina avoid self-recrimination was work and workouts. Being hospitalized and then having to wear a cast had gotten in the way of her fitness. Now she punished herself to get back into shape. The cast was no longer an excuse to not do cardio. She limped along in the treadmill, rode the recumbent bicycle, rowed on the rower, and even did the elliptical. Anger drove her. She wanted to be ready for the courtroom. She wanted to be ready to do what was needed to Angus's murderer. And she wanted to regain her smoking body for life after Bryan.

No one interrupted Gina during her punishing workouts in the Bergman-Deketomis gym. But even Gina's sweaty, stern face wasn't enough to stop Cara from breaching her sanctuary. The young associate came barging into Gina's private space waving a piece of paper, causing Gina to reluctantly interrupt her routine.

Cara couldn't contain the excitement in her voice. "This just arrived from Judge Sanders," she said, and then read the two words Gina had been waiting for: "Motion Denied."

That was enough for Gina. The case against Arbalest would proceed. She pumped her right arm; that was the extent of her physical display. Right away she segued into all business.

"I need you, Ned and Rachel in the conference room in fifteen minutes," she said.

—◆◆◆—

The three lawyers and Rachel all gathered in the allotted time. The paralegal nodded to Gina to show she was ready to begin her note-taking.

"Let's not allow Madsen-Zimmer time to breathe," said Gina. "The game clock starts now. So far they've let us dictate the pace. I want depositions to begin in ten days or less."

"You think they'll allow that?" asked Ned.

"They didn't get a quick dismissal at this stage," said Gina, "so I'm thinking Tim Knapp himself may be giving them orders to rush this to either another shot at dismissal or a quick resolution. By their thinking, the sooner we start with depositions, the less time it will allow us for discovery. And even if Arbalest wants nothing more than this case to disappear, they still won't think about settling until they see how the depositions go. Being as we are now on the topic of depositions, I say Kendrick Strahan should be placed at the top of our list."

"What about Diaz?" Ned asked.

"Obviously, we want to put off his deposition as long as possible," Gina said. "To use a boxing term, what we'll want to do first is pound at Arbalest's midsection. Each person we depose will add to that pounding. By the time they take a deposition of Diaz, we'll have him loaded up with enough information to knock them to the mat."

"What are your thoughts about deposing Merle Marcus?" Cara asked.

"I don't want to offer up his name right away," said Gina. "Let's wait until we're already in the midst of depositions before revealing his name. Suspecting that we have other potential whistleblowers waiting in the wings will help edge Madsen-Zimmer closer to 'panic attack' mode. We'll give them just enough information to feed that suspicion."

"I think Kim Knudsen should be high on our list," Ned said.

"Agreed," said Gina. "I am hoping my meet and greet with her might have provided her the wake-up call she needed to rally her courage to stand up to Arbalest. Any positive little thing we get from her will help us. If our facts are accurate we have an experienced patrol cop with an expert shooting rating who somehow hits her partner in the back even though he was standing as much as five feet to the right of her target."

"Tell me the fix wasn't in on the shooting," said Ned. "Given those facts, how could CPD's internal affairs come to their conclusion that Knudsen's shooting was a case of 'human error'?"

"We'll at least hear what Officer Knudsen thinks of that conclusion," said Gina. "We'll also see what she thinks about CPD's chain of evidence custody and learn how the Sight-Clops she used in the shooting ended up in the hands of Arbalest first before making its way to an internal investigation team."

"That sounds like evidence tampering to me," said Cara.

"Our little bird is learning to fly," said Ned, "as well as being skeptical."

"What's even worse," Cara said, "is the betrayal Officer Knudsen must have felt when her own department turned on her."

"You're right," said Ned. "Our investigation shows CPD used a rape defense on one of their own. When in doubt, blame the victim."

"Let's be sure to cover that in the deposition," Gina said. "In CPD's official report they ignored Officer Knudsen's repeated claims that her firearm malfunctioned and instead suggested that her story was merely a form of denial."

"Guns don't kill people," said Ned, quoting from an old and vilified NRA ad campaign, "people kill people."

That seems to be their position," said Gina. But they've added to the equation. Now even defective guns don't kill. That's the altar Officer Knudsen was sacrificed upon. CPD concluded that she persisted in believing her weapon was at fault so as to not be overcome by the guilt of killing her partner."

"We have to spend more time on that one," said Ned.

"Normally," said Gina, "we should spend days deposing everyone involved with the department's failure to secure a legitimate chain of custody. And we would question the giant leap in reaching conclusions by the department's second-rate report on the shooting. But with the facts we have, our best approach is to throw plenty of marbles on the floor and see if they have a way to pick them up. Better to find out now."

As the day wore on, the lawyers continued to discuss which individuals they wanted to depose, and in what order, while at the same time making notes for their investigators to look into. One of the first rules of law is to not ask questions when you are not sure of the answers. Before depositions kicked in, they had to make sure of all the answers.

"What about Cary Jones?" Cara asked. "I think his is a very compelling story."

"The problem I see with deposing him," said Ned, "is that there is no way the army would agree to handing over his M4 carbine and the Sight-Clops attached to it."

"And because Private Jones is still in the army," said Gina, "a Judge Advocate General might insist upon being involved. We wouldn't want to have to work through a third party."

Cara couldn't hide her disappointment. "I've heard Cary's story," she said. "Everyone in this room would be moved by what he has gone through because of that Sight-Clops piece of junk."

"Then let's go ahead and introduce that story," said Gina. "I want you to write up Private Jones' account of what happened and have him sign an affidavit saying he agrees with your write-up. We can supply that affidavit to Madsen-Zimmer and say that we might, or might not, be deposing Private Jones. That might push them to depose him, and we can control his story better on cross-exam."

Cara nodded her approval. "That works for me."

"Who else is on your deposition list?" asked Gina.

"I think we need to go after Paul Long," Ned said. "He was the Arbalest supervisor to both Diaz and Marcus. We know he got the same incriminating memo that Marcus did. And he would have been present when Diaz warned higher-ups about Sight-Clops."

"Agreed," said Gina. "Let's try and make Mr. Long as uncomfortable as possible. I'm guessing Madsen-Zimmer has no idea of the documents Diaz and Marcus have provided us, and I'd be surprised if they don't flat-out lie during discovery by telling us no such documents ever existed. The more big lies we catch them in, the more zeroes in the settlement."

"You think they're going to lie about documents that they know exist?" said Cara, sounding truly appalled.

Ned said, "Your dad has told you there is no Santa Claus or Easter Bunny, hasn't he?"

"We have to assume the worst," said Gina. "And that's why we should tie-in every discovery request to documents we have in our hands. Every time Madsen-Zimmer tells us those documents don't exist, we'll put that supposed nonexistent piece of paper up on a big screen during depositions and have their own employees read them word for word."

"I think we should put Sal Ricci on our list," Ned said.

"Who is he?" asked Cara.

"He's the CPD gunsmith who installed the Sight-Clops on Officer Knudsen's firearm. Ricci is likely the one who turned over the Sight-Clops to Arbalest for *testing*. I'm thinking he must be on their payroll one way or the other. And even if he's not, Ricci's job requires him to repair and replace firearms and accessories to firearms. You can count on the fact that Officer Knudsen was not the only one at CPD who had problems with Sight-Clops."

"I think we should also consider Betsy Mackey," said Cara.

It was Ned's turn to blank on who she was: "I don't remember her."

"Diaz said she was the secretary taking down notes when he spoke out against the Sight-Clops," Cara said. "You know how Gina is always saying you don't go after the big fish until you catch the little fish? I am hoping Betsy's testimony can put Tim Knapp's fingerprints all over this disaster."

"I'm flattered when you quote me," Gina claimed, "especially when I say something that makes sense."

"So you want to put Knapp on the depo list?" Ned asked.

"I do," Gina said, "especially since we know Madsen-Zimmer will try to make sure that depo never happens. They will fight desperately to avoid having him testify under oath. As part of discovery, though, we should be asking for any communications between Tim Knapp and any Arbalest employee regarding an internal investigation about abuses, complaints, or problems related to the Arbalest product Sight-Clops."

"You think that's going to get us anywhere?" asked Ned. "Madsen-Zimmer will simply argue that Knapp, in his position as CEO is privy to trade secrets and government secrets that will need to be protected. Because of that they will try to stop the deposition."

"I expect them to do that," Gina answered. "But nothing gets the other side's attention more than a shot right at their heart." Except, she darkly thought, murder. That was a topic she wanted to explore, even if in a roundabout way. "What do you think of the idea of taking an early depo of Tom Lutz and Ron Thursby?"

"That's a long shot," Ned responded. "First, they will lawyer up if they haven't already. Secondly, they are not directly involved with the manufacturing of Sight-Clops. Also, you can count on the fact that there is no way their private lawyers will cooperate with the rocket depo schedule we have now. They will only slow things down."

Gina didn't have a good response to that. She couldn't say that she was running a parallel investigation into the murder of Angus Moore and wanted to have the chance of putting Lutz and Thursby on the hot seat sooner rather than later. She couldn't come out and say that violent revenge, along with winning the Arbalest case, was her real motivation.

# 26
## "WHAT DO YOU MEAN, WE?"

Lutz looked at the display on his cell phone. For the third time that morning, Strahan the Second was calling him. Lutz had barely listened to the last two messages Strahan had left for him. The man liked to go on and on. But Lutz decided he'd left Strahan hanging long enough. Besides, he didn't want to have to sift through another message.

"What is it?" Lutz asked.

"You're there," said Strahan, clearly relieved. "Why didn't you call back? I've been trying to reach you all morning."

"I've been busy."

"I wouldn't have called if it wasn't important. *We're* in trouble."

"What do you mean *we*, white man?"

It was one of Lutz's favorite jokes. Just the punch line was enough for most people, but not Strahan. Maybe they didn't tell those kinds of jokes at Andover.

Like some shrill old woman, Strahan said, "What are you talking about?"

"The Lone Ranger and Tonto are surrounded by five thousand screaming braves," Lutz said. "It's clear the end has come, so the Lone

Ranger says to Tonto, 'It looks like we won't survive this one, old friend.' And Tonto replies, 'What do you mean *we*, white man?'"

"That's very funny," said Strahan. "Did you know I've been served?"

"I think you mentioned that nine or ten times in your messages."

"Have you been served?"

"No, I haven't," said Lutz. "And even if I had been, I wouldn't be running around like a chicken with its head cut off."

"I am going to be deposed by that law firm I told you about, the one with the lawyer that died."

Lutz wondered if Strahan was recording their conversation and responded accordingly. "I don't remember you mentioning that," he said.

Strahan just kept on talking. "I tried calling Tim Knapp, but he's not taking my calls. His snake for a lawyer, a bastard named Carter, said Arbalest would be providing me a lawyer to prepare for the deposition. He said this lawyer would hold my hand through the whole thing and that I shouldn't worry. As soon as that S.O.B. said those words, I knew it was time to start worrying. Carter is selling me down the river. I'm going to be Arbalest's sacrificial lamb."

"Is that so?"

"We need to do something."

Lutz considered saying for a second time, "'What do you mean *we*, white man?'" It was a classic, after all. But you don't throw pearls before swine, even Andover swine.

"Maybe you should refuse the company lawyer," said Lutz, "and get your own mouthpiece."

"Maybe I should cut a deal," said Strahan.

Lutz didn't like what he was hearing, but he didn't rise up to take the bait. "Maybe you shouldn't panic. You sound like a guilty man. That's why you need to talk this out with a lawyer you trust, if there is such a thing. I am sure he'll calm you down. I am sure he'll tell you this law firm and their deposition is nothing more than a fishing expedition. And when faced with that, all you have to do is tell them, 'Go fish.'"

Strahan's breathing was no longer as loud over the phone. Lutz continued to talk, doing his best to sound like the voice of reason.

"You're a lobbyist for Christ's sake," said Lutz. "What lobbyist doesn't cut a few corners? What lobbyist doesn't have a slush fund? You play in a dirty and rigged game. You didn't write those rules."

"I sure didn't. I just played the hand I got."

"Get that lawyer as soon as you can," said Lutz. "You'll feel better after you talk to him."

"I'll do that," said Strahan.

After one or two more "attaboys," Strahan hung up. Then it was Lutz's turn to make a call. Without identifying himself he said, "What do you got?"

Lutz listened for a minute before saying, "So, by following the money all they've been able to get is smoke and not fire?"

Whatever was said apparently satisfied Lutz. "For the moment then, we're not on the big-game list?"

Lutz listened some more until he said, "All right, Ivanhoe. Keep me informed."

The nerd was his insurance policy, thought Lutz. As long as he was monitoring Bergman-Deketomis, Lutz didn't have to worry about what the law firm was doing. And if things got too close to them, they could pin everything on a dead Ivanhoe.

Lutz looked over at Thursby. He was sacked out on the sofa. "Hey," he called, "I hate to interrupt your beauty sleep, but I need you for something."

# 27
# QUICK DRAW

The day after Judge Sanders informed both sides that the trial was to proceed, Gina had subpoenas served on Kendrick Strahan, Officer Kim Knudsen, gunsmith Sal Ricci, Private Cary Jones, Merle Marcus, Betsy Mackey, Paul Long, and Arbalest CEO Tim Knapp. As if that wasn't enough to keep Madsen-Zimmer busy, Gina's team also requested they provide them with a long list of remarkably specific documents pertaining to Sight-Clops.

In the days since, little in the way of those documents had been produced. Gina was sure that either the Arbalest paper shredders, or those of Madsen-Zimmer, or both, were working overtime. Perhaps for that reason Madsen-Zimmer still wasn't objecting to the idea of a fast-paced discovery schedule and had agreed to proceed with most, but not all, of the depositions within the next two weeks. The line in the sand for Madsen-Zimmer was the deposition of Tim Knapp. To prevent this, they gathered affidavits from highly paid experts claiming that testimony by Knapp created a real and present danger to Arbalest as an irreplaceable military contractor to the United States government and that such a deposition could adversely affect national security.

Because of this, before the depositions could take place, Judge Sanders asked to hear from both sides regarding whether Tim Knapp should be deposed.

Gina flew to Chicago for the oral arguments. Madsen–Zimmer sent five lawyers and a curveball. One of their lawyers was a former lover. Aiding in Arbalest's defense was Zack Templeton. Gina had dated Templeton during her days at Rutgers. At the time, he was a great poseur, playing the role of a left-wing radical with a full beard and ponytail. Even though Gina was several years younger than Templeton, she had soon concluded then that he was a fraud with the depth of a reality show TV actor. She had planned to end their relationship, but Templeton finished it before she did. He opted out by saying he was "enamored" of another first-year law student.

Templeton, Gina knew, was supposed to be a distraction. But the truth is she found the Madsen–Zimmer ploy laughable. Did Madsen–Zimmer think all Templeton had to do was bat his eyes to get her flustered? Did they believe she had been pining for Templeton all this time? After all, it had been a long time since she'd been a beginning law student.

"Gina!" said Templeton, opening his arms to give her a hug.

Her response wasn't vindictive or planned, even if it seemed so. Without thinking, Gina responded by calling Templeton the nickname by which the third-year female law students referred to him.

"Quick Draw," she said.

The "official" explanation that came with the nickname was that Templeton resembled the cartoon character Quick Draw McGraw. But everyone knew that wasn't the real explanation.

Templeton slunk back to his side.

Even behind black robes, Judge Sanders looked like a well-put-together woman in her mid-sixties. Her white hair was stylishly coiffed. As Gina had suspected, the judge wasn't one to let matters drag out. She asked questions and quickly ended any answers that dragged on. In fewer than forty minutes, Judge Sanders heard arguments on the Knapp deposition. Gina hammered at her points.

"This isn't about us trying to find out about Arbalest trade secrets," stressed Gina. "Our deposition of CEO and owner Tim Knapp won't stray into any top secret governmental areas. We won't be asking about proprietary formulas or marketing strategies or sales projections. What this is about is Sight-Clops, and nothing else. We want to know what Mr. Knapp knew and when he knew it. On President Harry Truman's Oval Office desk was a thirteen-inch sign that read: 'The Buck Stops Here.' We need to talk to Mr. Knapp to find out where that Arbalest buck did stop."

Both sides offered up legal precedents that they believed supported their positions. Judge Sanders listened and occasionally asked questions. When the judge was satisfied that she'd heard enough, she said, "Thank you for your input. Over the course of the next week, I will consider the merits of your arguments and inform you of my decision."

The judge's deferral wasn't a surprise to either side. In most cases like these, the judge didn't make an immediate decision. Often the answer came in the form of a written opinion.

Still, Gina came away thinking it had been a very good day for the law firm of Bergman-Deketomis.

◆◆◆

From his listening post, Ivan Verloc was having trouble staying awake. Lawyers were a different breed, he thought. They could talk all day in what sounded to him to be a different language. No matter how small the point, they argued about it.

At the moment the Bergman-Deketomis lawyers were playacting in order to get ready for their depositions. One person played lawyer, and one played witness. Everything the lawyer did was open to critique, from the questions asked to the pacing of the questions and the tone of voice used.

Ivan concluded that his own home team might be in for a wicked few days ahead. After jotting down some notes for Lutz, he decided to tune into a different listening channel. What was Kendrick Strahan up to?

He'd put the listening device on Strahan's phone more than a year ago. Ivan was proud of the special bug he'd constructed. It didn't require Strahan to make or receive calls for him to listen. The bug was voice-activated. Whenever Strahan talked, it recorded. That was how Ivan had gotten the goods on Lutz and Thursby.

Ivan listened in, but Strahan wasn't talking. He checked Strahan's log and saw that nothing had been recorded for the last twenty-four hours. Strange, Ivan thought. He decided to listen in to what had last been said.

At the first sounds of the gasping and thrashing around, Ivan realized he hadn't gone back far enough. Either that, Ivan thought, or he'd gone too far. Hearing those sounds made the hair rise on Ivan's arms. It sounded like someone was dying.

Ivan found a spot earlier in the digital recording. By the sounds of it, Strahan had been awakened from a sound sleep.

"Hey! What the hell are . . ."

Strahan hadn't gotten the chance to finish his question. Those were his last words, but not the last words that were recorded.

"Hush!" said a familiar voice. "Just relax."

Ivan was guessing that Thursby put Strahan in a sleeper hold. The cop knew about forensics. He knew how to stage a crime scene to tell the story he wanted. And because of that, he made sure Strahan was still alive when he pulled his body up the ladder and put his neck into the noose. Strahan's garret must have been prepared earlier for him, no doubt while he was asleep.

"Go for it," said an encouraging Thursby. "Try and get that noose off."

For a moment Ivan couldn't understand why Thursby would be cheering on Strahan's struggles. What a sick fuck, he thought. But then the motive became clear: Strahan's fingerprints and DNA would be all over the rope. Merciful executioners made sure the victim's neck snapped when coming down. Thursby had not been merciful.

Ivan listened to Strahan's choking and thrashing about. And then it became too grisly even for him to listen to any longer. Those final gurgles were sickening. And Ivan sure didn't want to hear the man's death rattle.

Hearing lawyers prepare their case, Ivan thought, was preferable to listening to Strahan's hanging, although he knew he was completely capable of strangling another human being if money was right.

# 28
## A MEETING OF MINDS

**W**ord of Kendrick Strahan's death reached Gina and her team just as they were about to leave for the day. A neighbor had detected an unpleasant odor. The preliminary report was that Strahan must have been hanging in his apartment for at least three days.

Washington, DC police were conducting an investigation into Strahan's death, even though they said it appeared to have been a suicide.

"The cynic in me says that Arbalest can't help but be delighted with this turn of events," said Ned.

Gina couldn't argue. Strahan's timely death was the best piece of news Madsen-Zimmer could have hoped for.

"We're going to have to reshuffle the order of the depositions," said Gina. "And we'll need to reexamine those questions earmarked for Strahan to see if they can be asked of others on our list."

But not today, Gina decided. She could see everyone was tired. "Enough is enough," she said. "After all, tomorrow is another day."

As everyone gathered up their paperwork, Gina realized that she'd been quoting Scarlett O'Hara from *Gone with the Wind*.

Tired "goodbyes" and "see you in the morning" were uttered. Her team had been at the office for thirteen hours. One long day might not have been too hard, but they'd been putting in longer hours for more than a week straight, including weekends.

Things had been made worse by Bryan. After being shut down by the Bergman-Deketomis switchboard, and exhausting his own efforts to contact Gina by phone, text, and email, he'd convinced two of their mutual friends to call Gina and speak on his behalf. The friends said that Bryan was desperate to talk to Gina and was willing to do whatever it took to make things right between them. Gina had done her best to not blame the messengers. They had been duped by Bryan, just as she had been duped. From them, she learned that Bryan said the Australian shoot was going well, even though he claimed to be desperately upset about not being able to communicate with her.

"It's one of those things," Gina had told the two callers and had pretended that she might get in touch with Bryan.

But that wasn't going to happen. The ache in her heart notwithstanding, Bryan was out of her life. It had all happened for the best. Or at least that's what she tried to tell herself. Arbalest and searching out Angus's killer was taking up every waking minute of every day. Had she not broken up with Bryan, it was possible the stronger sense of her connection with him might have subdued her personal jihad to avenge the murder of Angus. So without Bryan now, there were no excuses to keep her from focusing in.

Gina trudged down to her car. Her shadow today was Steve. She was glad he wasn't a talkative sort. Gina felt all talked out.

It had been a grey day in Spanish Trace; the clouds had never lifted, but instead had sat heavily along the coast. The haze had seemed to infect her entire team. Or maybe it was just the string of long days.

There had been one piece of good news, though. Gina's doctor had said it was likely her walking cast could come off in the next few days. If that was the case, she would start the depositions unencumbered. She even visualized herself wearing heels. No, she decided, not heels but boots, as in Nancy Sinatra. The kind of boots made for walking all over the opposition.

"Thanks, Steve," she said.

"Will you be stopping for food, Ms. Romano?"

"No, I'll be going straight home tonight."

"I'll follow you there," he said.

Dinner would be canned soup, thought Gina, followed by sleep.

◆◆◆

During the drive to her home, Gina used her car's voice command system to call Deke's cell. She knew he was in the middle of his DuPont trial and was surprised to hear how animated he sounded on the phone.

"Good day?" asked Gina.

"Great day," said Deke. "DuPont's lawyers have been trying to do their three monkeys imitation—'see no evil, hear no evil, speak no evil'—but today those monkeys came home to roost."

Gina didn't bother telling Deke he was mixing his metaphors. When he got excited, Deke tended to do that.

"After DuPont's lawyers said that no one at the company was aware of the toxicity of perfluorooctanoic acid—or C-8, as it's internally called—" Deke told her, "I paraded three former employees in front of the jury. They all testified that the dangers of C-8 were well-known inside the company, and in fact it was considered so toxic that DuPont's managers warned their employees that C-8 was shown to cause cancer."

Even though there was no jury in the vicinity to hear him, Deke's voice was becoming loud with indignation. "Before this trial is over, I'm hoping to get my hands on one of those memos that went around warning employees about the poison in the local water supply. I know that memo is squirreled away somewhere. But even if it doesn't turn up, I've got plenty to work with. You know the game; their lawyers are doing the Nuremberg thing of "I know nothing," and then day after day we're coming in right behind them showing what DuPont knew and when they knew it. I just wish we had been able to bring this case ten years ago. Think of how much cancer could have been prevented."

"Better to look at it from the perspective of how much cancer you are preventing now," Gina said.

"Isn't that the truth?" he said. "Now that the world knows about the hazards of C-8, there's another interesting development. Prosecutors in the Netherlands are taking a look at DuPont's pollution in their backyard. They've been sitting in court watching the death tolls mount from C-8 exposure."

"It sounds like you might be inflicting more than a little pain," she said. "But I recall a certain lawyer who once warned me, 'When you're trying to wrestle big bulls to the ground, you better watch out for their horns.'"

"Whoever told you that was one smart cowboy."

"Speaking of which," Gina said, "there's been a new development in our case. Kendrick Strahan was found hanging from a rope."

"He was the dirty lobbyist who worked for Arbalest, right?"

"That's the one."

"I get the feeling you don't think he killed himself."

"He worked for the Gun Safety Institute, and you're telling me he suddenly developed a conscience?"

"GSI is not exactly Habitat for Humanity."

"No, they're not."

"You think this has a tie-in with our situation?"

"That thought crossed my mind."

"Are you getting closer to finding our person or persons?"

"I'm not sure," she said. "Of course, now that Strahan is dead there's one less individual on my list."

"Before we proceed, we'll need to be one hundred percent certain."

"That's my feeling as well."

"Great minds think alike," said Deke.

Gina didn't tell him that twisted minds thought alike as well.

# 29
## MISSING THE TARGET, HITTING THE TARGET

**O**n a sunny Tuesday at just after nine in the morning, Gina, Bennie, Cara, Ned, Carol, Rachel, and two additional paralegals landed at Chicago's O'Hare Airport. Two drivers in large SUVs were waiting for the Bergman-Deketomis contingent. The first deposition was scheduled for ten o'clock.

Half an hour later, the SUVs pulled up in front of a modern, blue-colored glass skyscraper that was across from Chicago's lakefront. An express elevator took the group up to the thirty-third floor. Gina's walking cast had been removed the day before, and it felt like a weight had been lifted from her. Her limp was almost undetectable and her dressy pants outfit hid the temporary atrophy that had developed in her leg.

One of Madsen-Zimmer's male paralegals came out of his office to greet them, as well as to provide an escort. He bypassed Gina and Carol in order to shake Ned Williams' hand first, assuming he was lead counsel.

The reception area showcased Madsen-Zimmer's spectacular view. Grant Park, with its many fountains and huge plaza was in the foreground, and Lake Michigan offered a huge blue backdrop. Gina liked the exterior view much more than the interior one. Madsen-Zimmer showcased the firm's success with ultramodern furniture made up mostly of stainless steel and glass. Everything was sleek, geometric, and cold; that coldness extended throughout the interior, even to the artwork. There were no paintings of sunrises or sunsets and no portraits of individuals. Instead, there were modern takes on city skylines and displays of buildings at night with a few lit offices—black and white images of anonymity amidst the masses.

The paralegal escorted them to a conference room where an I.T. team was already waiting. The room was set up with digital video cameras and a screen. A stenographer and videographer were both tending to their equipment in preparation for the proceedings. Bottled water, coffee, and soft drinks were available at a table near the door.

As if magically summoned, the Madsen-Zimmer legal team showed itself. In a game of numbers, they easily could have claimed victory. This time, Zack Templeton merely wooed Gina with his eyes, but didn't get too close; the nickname of "Quick Draw" was clearly something he didn't want known. Charles Zimmer was among the lawyers. Gina resisted asking him if he was still working to keep bank executives from spending any time in jail. Zimmer pretended to be an avuncular sort, putting his arm around Gina and telling her a few stories of the interior design costs associated with his firm's new digs.

"You'll have to show me your etchings another time," said Gina, slipping out of his patronizing arm. "But since we're working with a seven-hour time clock that I assume is already ticking, I think we had better proceed. Is your team ready to go?"

Each of the law firms had agreed to a seven-hour deposition window for the first two days. Gina's pushing along the proceedings wasn't merely an opening gambit; she wanted the maximum amount of time to ask questions. The game clock wasn't going to beat her. On too many occasions, she'd seen other lawyers beginning to get to the heart of the matter just as their time ran out.

Both law firms took up positions on the opposite sides of a steel conference table polished to a high gloss. Gina made sure to take her seat directly across from Paul Long, the morning's first witness. Long's lips were already dry; he kept nervously licking them without effect. And while he was being sworn in, he did a lot more licking.

Gina pulled some paperwork from a thick file and placed it on the table. As Cara had promised, the Cary Jones affidavit had made for compelling reading, but what was even more germane to their case was the paperwork provided by Diaz and Marcus that showed Arbalest was aware of what happened to the soldier all the while they continued to pretend there were no problems with Sight-Clops.

"Do you recognize the name of Private Cary Jones?" Gina asked.

"No."

"What about Officer Kim Knudsen?"

Long shook his head, and Gina asked him to respond verbally. "No, I never heard that name," he said.

Gina held up copies of Merle Marcus's emailed documents and signaled the AV guy to show the exhibits on the large video screen set up in the room. "Were you aware that Arbalest had in their possession the files of both individuals I just asked you about as part of their internal investigation of Sight-Clops?"

Zimmer objected. "We are unaware of those documents you are referring to and question their validity."

"First of all, Mr. Zimmer, I didn't ask you that question. I asked your witness. Secondly, if you believe that you are going to make obstructionist objections and comments throughout this deposition, then we should go ahead and get the judge on the phone right now. You know the rules. I ask questions, you object if you want, and the judge rules later on whether to strike the question. So, I'll ask the witness again: Mr. Long, did you know the document you now have in front of you was in the possession of Arbalest?"

"I know nothing about this document. No one has ever shown it to me."

"Mr. Long, just to be clear, no one at Arbalest ever told you that we had requested this exact document in discovery and that we were told it never existed? Is this the first time you've heard that?"

"Objection!" Zimmer was on the edge of shouting. Gina noticed his red face and early hints of a sweaty brow and knew she had a fun day ahead.

"Mr. Long, since you have never seen this document, did anyone at Arbalest share with you what is written on page ten there on the screen. . . . Let's read it together: *There have been a number of reports from the field that show that under certain conditions Sight-Clops has failed to perform as expected.*'

"Is that the first time you have seen those words, Mr. Long?"

"Yes it is, but just like everyone else who worked on Sight-Clops, I have total faith in the product, and I'm proud to be an Arbalest employee. We always operate at the best of our ability."

Neither Long's body language, nor his words, came across as convincing. He had clearly been coached to parrot company PR pabulum.

"And since you are a proud employee," said Gina, "what is it that you do at Arbalest?"

"I'm an engineer," he said.

"Then you would know of a former employee named Robert Diaz, correct?"

"Yes," Long said.

"Did Mr. Diaz ever bring up with you his suspicions that Sight-Clops had serious flaws?"

"I don't recall."

"So you may have discussed that?"

"We discussed Arbalest products as part of our job. I can't be expected to remember every conversation I ever had."

"I am not asking you to remember every conversation you ever had, Mr. Long," said Gina. "But I am asking you to recall one particular conversation. Were you at the meeting which took place last October ninth in the Arbalest second-floor conference room where Mr. Diaz brought up his concerns about Sight-Clops and was subsequently fired?"

"Yes, I was there."

"Was the owner of Arbalest, Tim Knapp, also there?"

Zimmer knew what was coming. "Ms. Romano, I may need to take a quick break at this time."

Gina fired back, "No, the only breaks we will take are the ones set out in the agreed order. That's about an hour and a half from now. Otherwise, I will ask the court reporter to get the judge on the phone and I will make an argument that your conduct has moved from protecting your witness to witness tampering. Now Mr. Long, was Tim Knapp at that meeting? Yes or no."

Paul Long looked from one lawyer to the other, unsure what to do. Zimmer looked as if he was on the same hot seat as the witness. Gina knew the opposing lawyer was likely calculating the risks of being sanctioned if he continued his excessive attempts to obstruct the flow of the deposition.

"Yes," Long finally answered.

Gina didn't hide her smile. It had just become more likely that she could get a favorable ruling from the judge about the need for Tim Knapp's depo. He was now in her sights.

And she wouldn't be doing her aiming with a Sight-Clops.

Gina started her next round of questions.

—◆◆◆—

No one on the Madsen-Zimmer side expected Gina to finish up with the witness as soon as she did. An early lunch was agreed upon, and at one o'clock both sides resumed the deposition proceedings.

"Lean and mean" was how the Bergman-Deketomis team had practiced for the depositions. For the afternoon session, Gina took the seat next to Ned Williams. She had learned a lot of her depo strategy under the tutelage of Nick Deketomis. Deke was one for using baseball analogies; he likened the use of lawyers doing depositions to pitchers throwing fastballs. According to Deke, you started the game with a pitcher who was good at smoking the opposition. Then, mid-game, it was always good to change pitchers as a way to offer up a different look and feel.

"First you come at them high and fast," Deke liked to say, "and then you bring in a reliever and challenge them with off-speed pitches."

Deke also seemed to think it was good to have "lefty on lefty," and "righty on righty" matchups. That translated to women lawyers talking to women witnesses and male lawyers talking to male witnesses. Of course, there were plenty of exceptions to his pitching strategies; what it came down to was getting the right matchup. The best game plan was figuring out your lineup ahead of time and matching up strengths against perceived weaknesses.

Ned, Gina had decided, was the right person to question CPD locksmith Sal Ricci, who clearly prided himself as being a "tough guy." Ricci wore blue-collar garb to his deposition—steel toe boots and an industrial uniform-type shirt and pants. His shirt had a patch with the name *Sal* written on it, and his shirtsleeves were rolled up to reveal two old-school blue tattoos. On his right arm was a coiled snake with the words, *Don't Tread on Me*; on his left arm was an inked blue-metal gun. Above the gun were the words: *I miss my Ex . . .* Beneath it was written *. . . But my aim is improving.*

Ricci was fifty-four, but looked older. He was sworn in for the record and loudly chewed on a piece of gum while waiting for the questioning to begin.

"Good afternoon, Mr. Ricci," said Ned. "For the record, I'd like you to confirm that you're employed at the CPD Libertyville shooting range, known by most as Bull's-eye."

"Correct," he said.

"How long have you worked there?"

"I've been there since it was built."

"So you've been there for five years?"

"If you say so."

"But you've been employed by CPD for twenty-five years?"

"That sounds about right."

"Where were you working before Libertyville?"

"For most of the time I was at Southside."

"Southside is the older shooting hall for CPD personnel, is that right?

"Yes," he said.

"And I understand as part of your job you repair and rebuild firearms, is that also correct?"

"Yeah."

"Have you installed Arbalest gunsights onto weapons at the club?"

"Yeah," said Ricci. It looked as if he was about to say more, but a glance from Templeton was enough to remind him that he was supposed to keep his answers short.

"Tell me about your relationship," Ned said, "with police union president Tom Lutz."

Ricci shifted his arms and frowned. "What do you mean by *relationship?*"

"Mr. Lutz works in the same location as you, correct?"

"Yes," he said.

"Is he your boss?"

"I'm employed by CPD," said Ricci, "not by the union."

"But as union president, I imagine Mr. Lutz wants all CPD officers to be properly trained and armed. Is that so?"

"I guess."

"And isn't it also part of your job to train officers in how to handle their firearms?"

"Yes," he said.

"And did Mr. Lutz encourage you to replace all CPD gunsights with the Arbalest gunsight known as Sight-Clops?"

"Yes."

"I understand that in addition to training CPD officers as to how to use the Sight-Clops," said Ned, "you also traveled to other cities where you demonstrated the use of that product. Is that true?"

"Yes."

"Why did you do that?"

"Like you said, I demonstrated."

"But who was asking you to do this?"

"You ever hear of something called the Brotherhood of Blue? Cops are cops. We help each other out. We share things."

"So you shared things, as you called it, with police departments and purchasing agents throughout the Midwest?"

"Yes."

"Where you demonstrated the Sight-Clops?"

"That wasn't all I demonstrated."

"Yes, you demonstrated a number of Arbalest products, did you not?"

"I guess so."

"Yes or no, Mr. Ricci?"

"Yes."

"When you demonstrated the Sight-Clops product, Mr. Ricci, did you mention to potential buyers that the gunsight doesn't work properly in hot, muggy weather?"

"It was my experience that they worked just fine," said Ricci.

"Are you saying that's always been your experience?"

Ricci looked over to the Madsen-Zimmer lawyers. When they didn't help him, he shrugged and said, "We never had any problems here."

"You work inside of an air-conditioned building," Ned said. "But the summer before last, you did an outdoors demonstration in Naperville where I understand things didn't go so well. Can you tell me what happened?"

"One of the sights was off," said Ricci.

"On the day in question, it was ninety degrees and very humid, wasn't it?"

"It was hot," said Ricci. "That's about all I can say for sure."

"Tell me what happened with the Sight-Clops that didn't function properly."

"The shooter missed."

"Did the shooter miss by an inch? Or two inches?"

"He missed the target."

"He completely missed the target?"

"That's what I said."

"At what distance was he shooting?"

"Around ten yards."

"So we're talking a distance of only thirty feet?"

"Yes."

"How big was the target?"

"Thirteen inches by eighteen inches."

Ned approximated that size with his hands. Then he asked, "And was the shooter experienced?"

"He seemed to know what he was doing."

"Was he a law enforcement officer?"

"Yes."

"And I understand he was an expert marksman, is that true?"

"I couldn't say for sure."

"And what did this officer tell you after he missed the target?"

"He said the sight was way off."

Ned nodded. Then he came with a different off-speed pitch. Gina had coached him to introduce the names of Lutz and Thursby in his deposition.

"Was CPD Officer Ron Thursby with you on that occasion?"

"I couldn't tell you for sure."

"But Officer Thursby was frequently at your side when you did these demonstrations and met with purchasing agents?"

"Yes," Ricci said.

"In what capacity did he serve?"

"He demonstrated products."

"Arbalest products?"

"Yes."

"Did you notice if Mr. Lutz ever gave Mr. Thursby a bag of cash to take with him when he met with—"

Before Ned could finish his sentence, both Templeton and Zimmer were on their feet. Zimmer spoke first: "Objection! Mr.

Ricci, I'm instructing you to *not* answer that question! This lawyer is being abusive and is trying to suggest that you participated in criminal activity. You have every right not to answer."

Ned pretended to be surprised by their vehemence. "I'm sorry I must have stepped on some sensitive toes there. Now, if you two will take your seats, I'll be happy to withdraw the question. At the same time, that question isn't just going to go away. Sooner or later in this proceeding, it will be addressed."

"What will also be addressed is your conduct," said Templeton.

"So, Mr. Templeton," said Ned. "What's the going price for a corporate lawyer's false outrage? I'm guessing about ten thousand dollars a day, right?"

"Do you have any more questions for the witness?" Zimmer asked.

"You're only looking at the very tip of a big iceberg my friend." Ned replied.

◆◆◆

Ned's questions branched out. He questioned Ricci's relationship with Arbalest and then brought up the death of Vinnie Velez. Specifically, he asked about the Sight-Clops gunsight on Officer Knudsen's gun.

"Now you personally installed the Sight-Clops on both Officer Velez's department issued handgun, as well as on Officer Knudsen's gun?"

"Yes," said Ricci.

"And according to what we know, those gunsights were installed just ten days before the fatal shooting."

"That sounds right," said Ricci.

"And you properly installed both of their gunsights?"

"Yes," said Ricci.

"Then how do you explain the fatal shooting of Officer Velez?"

"The ruling was that it was human error."

"How is it that you received Officer Knudsen's gun and gunsight after the Velez shooting?"

"I guess someone thought it was my job to test it."

"But you took this weapon and gunsight and turned them over to Arbalest rather than leaving them in an CPD evidence locker?"

"They're set up to do all sorts of testing."

"You've worked around law enforcement for decades, and you never thought giving them the firearm and gunsight would potentially taint the chain of evidence in a homicide investigation?!"

For the next half an hour, an incredulous Ned tried to make sense of the "fox being put in charge of the henhouse." Through different avenues, he continued to press Ricci as to how a gun and gunsight involved in a fatal shooting had gone missing from police custody only to end up in the hands of the very people who manufactured it. Despite numerous objections, the Madsen-Zimmer lawyers couldn't stop the bleeding, but it was Ricci who put an end to his deposition.

"Mr. Ricci," Ned asked, "how many handguns do you personally own?"

"Somewhere between forty and fifty," said Ricci.

Ned lowered his voice and slowed his pace. "Now I want you to think real hard. If we went and looked right now, how many of your guns would have a Sight-Clops sight attached to them?"

Ricci got to his feet and stared Ned down. "Come by my house, shyster, and I'll show you my guns up close and personal." Then he stormed out of the room.

Behind him, Ned yelled, "Is that none? Is your final answer, sir, that you do *not* have a Sight-Clops on even one of your own guns?"

# 30
## SHARED TEARS

Even though Deke was working his own case a thousand miles away, to Gina, Ned, and Cara, it almost felt as if he was the fourth lawyer in the room with them. The lawyers had learned their jobs under Deke. It was under his catechism that they had become trial lawyers.

"If you want to be a trial lawyer that's a force of good in this world," Deke often said, "if you want to be a trial lawyer who succeeds, then you need to have the character and strength to stand your ground even when you are surrounded by those who reject and even hate what you stand for."

From anyone else but Deke that would have sounded like lip service, but he had practiced what he had preached all his career and had built his practice around attorneys with similar beliefs.

Gina and Ned would have had trouble working at a firm like Madsen-Zimmer because they needed their causes; they needed to believe in something besides living for billable hours. Deke made every effort to build his firm with lawyers driven by a healthy conscience. He would often ask his young trial attorneys how it would make them feel to have a job in a corporate defense firm where they would be asked to use their skills to prevent widows and orphans from being compensated after reckless corporate conduct killed "Daddy." That's what drove them to succeed far more than a paycheck. For the Madsen-Zimmer lawyers, it was all about the Benjamins and the lifestyle that came with them. It didn't matter that they were representing businesses like Arbalest. Their lawyers bought into a lifestyle of hobnobbing with the rich and powerful, being members of country clubs, dining at posh restaurants, and sending their children to private schools. They practiced the kind of law that enriched them financially, but all too often left them morally bankrupt.

On the second day of depositions, the body language of the opposing lawyers revealed much; the Bergman-Deketomis team had a bounce to their step and looked eager to continue; the Madsen-Zimmer lawyers came in tired and dragging. Gina suspected they had strategized until late in what was referred to as a regroup session, which was a postmortem of the first day's depositions designed to better prepare the team for the proceedings of the next day. Good luck, thought Gina. She couldn't wait to send them and their battle plan running for the hills, as she and her team would most definitely continue pulling threads to see what might unravel.

Before the deposing formally began, Charles Zimmer asked to go on the record. Gina knew what he was about to say, but allowed it anyway. With patriarchal gravitas, Zimmer bemoaned the "unprofessional" and "acrimonious" conduct of the Bergman-Deketomis legal team from the day before, and he said because of that they might be seeking sanctions. As one, the Madsen-Zimmer side nodded in sanctimonious disapproval even though at the time they did not know that would be the highpoint of the day for them.

Betsy Mackey was the first witness sworn in. She had worked at Arbalest for four decades doing secretarial work. Her first boss had been Gordon Knapp, grandfather to Tim Knapp.

When Carol Morris had done her background check on Betsy, she'd learned that her retirement was imminent and that having a short timer's attitude had loosened her tongue. Betsy was of the opinion that "Timmy" was not nearly the man that "Mr. Gordon," or Timmy's father, "Mr. Lyndon," was. In fact, Betsy was heard to say that Mr. Gordon and Mr. Lyndon would never have cut employee benefits as Timmy had, especially when Arbalest was recording record profits. She also disapproved of Timmy's moving much of Arbalest's manufacturing offshore.

When the videographer and stenographer signaled they were ready to go, Gina smiled and began. She knew Madsen-Zimmer expected her to be as aggressive and dogged as she'd been the day before. They had worked out a system among themselves to try and interrupt her fast pace and throw off her rhythm. But the lawyer they expected, the devil in heels, didn't show herself. Overnight, she had been replaced by an angel.

"Good morning, Mrs. Mackey," she said. "Before we begin I'd like to say that I love your dress. It's so nice to see such vibrant floral colors in such a boring sterile environment."

"Thank you," she said, her smile contrasting with the glower of Charles Zimmer who'd just heard his precious interior design slammed.

Gina continued: "I promise I will make this as painless as possible, Mrs. Mackey. In fact, I doubt our talk will take us much longer than it would if we were to sit down and have a cup of coffee together."

Looks passed between the Madsen-Zimmer lawyers. This wasn't going as they had expected. They had thought Gina would try and relentlessly grill the older woman in the hopes of wearing her down.

"That sounds fine," Betsy said.

Gina continued to present a persona that was so sweet that sugar wouldn't melt in her mouth. "And I want you to stop me right away if you have any questions about anything. I don't want you to think I'm out to confuse you, or trying to trick you into saying something you might regret. Does that sound okay with you, Mrs. Mackey?"

"That sounds fine with me, dear. And why don't you call me Betsy?"

Templeton bit his lip. He had coached the witness to be wary of the opposing lawyers. But he hadn't expected one of those lawyers to try to kill his witness with kindness.

"Thank you, Betsy. I'd like to start by asking you about your job. You've worked for Arbalest for a long time."

"Forty years in February," she said.

"It's rare these days to see such loyalty in the workplace," said Gina. "What is it you do for Arbalest?"

"I started as personal secretary to Mr. Gordon," she said.

"That is Gordon Knapp, correct?"

"Yes," Betsy said. "I worked for four years until he retired, and then I worked for Mr. Lyndon. I worked for Mr. Lyndon for more than twenty years," she said.

"And you were his personal secretary as well?"

"I was, but the workplace changed. With the advent of computers, I became an administrative assistant, and my work responsibilities expanded."

"After Lyndon Knapp retired, did you become Tim Knapp's personal secretary?"

"Yes and no," Betsy said. "Mr. Timmy usually telecommutes most days during the workweek. Of course, I was always there to help him with anything he might need."

"What about on those days that Mr. Tim Knapp did come in. Did you do his secretarial work?"

"Yes," said Betsy.

"And did that work include taking notes during office meetings?"

"It did," she said. "When I was hired by Mr. Gordon, I could do shorthand at one hundred and eighty words per minute. Even now, I can still do one hundred and fifty. Not bad for a woman my age, is it?"

"That's more than impressive," said Gina. "I wish I had your skills. Sometimes, I look at my own notes that I've scrawled down and I can't make heads from tails. But I'm curious if you were doing your shorthand last October ninth in the Arbalest boardroom when Robert Diaz spoke about problems associated with the Sight-Clops gunsight."

"I can't confirm that particular date," Betsy said, "but I do remember Rob talking about the Sight-Clops."

"Later that same day," Gina said, "Robert Diaz was fired and had an armed guard escort him from the building. Do you remember that?"

Betsy sighed and nodded. "I sure do."

"Did you like Mr. Diaz?"

"Everybody liked Rob," said a smiling Betsy. "He was a flirt. He always pretended to serenade me. And he always brought me candy. He did it just to be nice to an old lady. He knew I loved chocolate."

"I love chocolate too. I'm wondering, do you remember what he said about the Sight-Clops before he was fired?"

"He said that when it was very hot and humid, the gunsight would not work properly. He said people had died because of that."

"You seem to remember that very distinctly," Gina said.

Templeton intervened: "Just ask her questions, Ms. Romano. We don't need your side comments."

Gina continued as if Templeton were not even in the room. "How is it that you seem to vividly remember that conversation?"

"I think I sort of perked up when I heard Rob talking about Sight-Clops. You see, I made this association with the cyclops. You remember that Kirk Douglas film where he played Ulysses?"

"I'm afraid I missed that one," said Gina.

"It's a good one," said Betsy. "I saw it when I was a teenager. And what stuck with me most was this monster, this cyclops, who ate Ulysses' men. I had nightmares for days. And so, when I heard the name Sight-Clops, I thought cyclops."

Gina looked across the table at Templeton. He was in hell.

"Well," said Gina, "I sure hope you won't have any nightmares from this deposition."

"I won't," said Betsy. "We're not done already, are we?"

Gina nodded and said, "I told you it would be like having a cup of coffee. But I want to thank you for spending time with me."

"Oh, it was my pleasure, dear. It was like me talking to my youngest daughter. I bet the two of you would get along famously."

One of Madsen-Zimmer's paralegals stood up to escort the witness out of the room. The rest of their team did their best not to look at one another. They knew how much Gina had accomplished in such a short time. Through Betsy's testimony, Gina had been able to link Robert Diaz's expressing his reservations of Sight-Clops in the presence of Tim Knapp. She had landed the big fish that she wanted.

Judge Sanders still hadn't ruled as to whether Tim Knapp could be deposed, but now Betsy Mackey had opened the front door for Bergman-Deketomis to do just that. Madsen-Zimmer's worst nightmare of having Arbalest CEO Tim Knapp placed under oath was now not just looking possible, but inevitable.

"If it's all right with you," said Gina, speaking to those across the table, "we'd like a break now."

"Fine with us," said Zimmer.

"Let's make it an extended break," she said, "since we are so far ahead of schedule. We'll use that time to send written and video copies of Mrs. Mackey's testimony to Judge Sanders."

Zimmer didn't like what Gina said any more than he'd liked what had occurred. He stomped out of the room. Behind him, almost in lockstep, the Madsen–Zimmer team followed.

◆◆◆

Carol joined Gina and the rest of her team at the Starbuck's in the Madsen–Zimmer building. Gina couldn't help but notice how many texts and calls Carol had received that morning. She handed Gina a piece of paper.

"What's this?" Gina asked.

Carol shook her head, put her finger up to her lips, and pointed to the page. On it she had written, *Your phone might be bugged. I'd like to borrow it for the next fifteen minutes and have it checked out.*

A numb Gina handed over her phone. Her eyes asked Carol to provide more of an explanation.

Carol took out a notepad and began writing. *I've had this feeling that something wasn't right with our building's security. It was a bunch of little things. So I ordered a sweep above and beyond our monthly electronic counter-surveillance. Most offices were clean, but not yours. That's where two bugs were found.*

Gina motioned for the pen. Carol gave it to her and she wrote, *Were the bugs removed?*

Carol shook her head and then wrote her response. *We are hoping to be able to follow the surveillance devices back to the operator.*

Gina nodded her approval.

*If your cell phone is bugged,* wrote Carol, *we'll be doing the same thing—trying to catch the spook. For the short-term you'll just have to watch what you say.*

Gina nodded again. Then she reached for the pen and wrote, *What about my home?*

Carol retrieved the pen and started scribbling. *We will be expanding our sweeps to employee cars and residences. My gut feeling is that's where we'll find even more bugs.*

As Carol walked away with the cell phone, Gina couldn't help but feel a sense of violation. She felt something else, though, something almost hopeful.

Maybe they had a lead on Angus's murderer.

Ten minutes before her deposition with Officer Kim Knudsen was scheduled to take place, Carol returned with Gina's cell phone. Her nod was all Gina needed to see. There was a bug on her phone. For now, there was nothing Gina could do about that. She needed to focus on her deposition.

Carol and her team had provided Gina with lots of biographical information on Knudsen. And her short face-to-face with the officer had provided Gina with what she believed was a good feel for Knudsen. Gina liked to go into depositions with a "read" on the witness. That understanding, she was convinced, made the difference between a good deposition and a bad deposition. Any lawyer could ask questions, but few could properly connect with the true agendas of most witnesses.

The lawyers of Madsen-Zimmer had no idea which lawyer would be confronting them: the hard as nails, fast-talking, fire-breathing harpy that had intimidated Paul Long or the sweet and kindly soul that had charmed Betsy Mackey. For them, it was a troubling kind of multiple-front lawyering.

What they weren't expecting was the thoughtful and introspective Gina Romano.

It was Zack Templeton who escorted Officer Knudsen down the long hallway that led to the conference room. Gina sensed trouble within the ranks when she heard Knudsen raising her voice at Templeton as the two approached. There was no doubt in Gina's mind that Templeton had been offering advice to the officer every step of the way, and that advice was not being well-accepted.

Gina wasn't surprised about that. Kim Knudsen was one of the good ones. She was a loving mother and wife and cared about her department and her city, even though the system had treated her so poorly. Gina was betting Officer Knudsen's resentment also extended to Arbalest.

It was there, on that pool of resentment, that Gina needed to focus. Her job had already made Officer Knudsen an experienced witness. And lawyers from Madsen-Zimmer would have tried to coach her even more. Gina was experienced in dealing with potentially hostile witnesses. She was aware Knudsen could shut down many of her inquiries. But Gina was counting on her being able to convince Knudsen they were both on the same side.

"Officer Knudsen," said Gina, "I would like to thank you for your service to your community. At the best of times, you are asked to do an impossible job under impossible circumstances. And at the worst of times, I know, terrible things can happen. I've read your file cover to cover a dozen times. I have a pretty good idea what you have been through since the accident, and I am so sorry. This morning, I'm going to have to ask you about some difficult and no doubt painful issues regarding the loss of your friend and partner in the line of duty."

"Are you going to ask questions, Ms. Romano," Templeton asked, "or are you going to continue with this warm and fuzzy Oprah routine?"

Templeton wasn't looking at the witness when he made his remark; he didn't see, as Gina did, Officer Knudsen's angry glare at Templeton as he spoke and the slight hint of tears welling up in her eyes. Gina was always astounded by what she referred to as

247 / Mike Papantonio

"corporate defense compassion atrophy." Thankfully for her purposes, that compassion atrophy had already begun playing itself out.

Gina took a deep breath and shook her head with genuine disgust. "I am sorry if Mr. Templeton thinks I have crossed his distorted line of acceptable friendliness. But with his permission, I'm ready to proceed with my line of questioning."

Templeton waved his hand for her to continue.

"Officer Knudsen," said Gina, "I understand your father was also a Chicago police officer, is that right?"

"Yes, he was." Knudsen couldn't hide her pride in her father's service.

"And did he teach you to shoot a gun?"

"Yes, he did. He was a good teacher."

"I am sure that he was. You became a great shot. At the police academy, you were the second-highest scored marksmen in your class, is that right?"

"Yes," said the officer.

"And you won two statewide handgun shooting competitions, is that right?"

"Yes, but that was a while ago."

Gina kept pressing. "It actually wasn't that long ago, Officer Knudsen. In fact, you won the last competition just one month before your partner was tragically shot and killed."

"Under the advice of my union representative," she said, her tone unmistakably hostile toward someone, maybe everyone, "that's not something I am supposed to talk about."

Instead of pushing, Gina retreated. "All right, for now we'll put the shooting aside. Still, it's my understanding that you were assigned to train other police officers with handguns. Is that correct?"

"Yes," she said.

"And for how many years did you do this?"

"Five years," Knudsen said.

"And this involved target shooting?"

"Yes," she said.

"And how far away were these targets?"

"The distance ranged from ten yards to fifty yards."

"Officer Knudsen, did anyone make you aware of the fact that in yesterday's deposition my colleague talked to Sal Ricci?"

Gina thought she detected a look of distaste passing over Knudsen's face.

"You're supposed to be deposing today's witness, not talking about yesterday's witness," said Templeton.

"Don't you think Officer Knudsen has a right to hear that during one of Sal Ricci's shooting demonstrations, on a hot and humid day, an expert shot equipped with a Sight-Clops gunsight missed the target from ten yards away?"

Though all the Madsen-Zimmer lawyers raised their voices to shout their objections, Gina's voice was heard by Knudsen over all their noise. That's all she really wanted to accomplish.

"He missed?" Officer Knudsen asked.

"Completely," said Gina. "And there are dozens of verified examples showing how Sight-Clops directed the round far from where the target was centered. Did your union representative share that information with you, Officer Knudsen?"

"The witness has already told you that she doesn't want to discuss her own shooting without her union rep present," said Templeton. "Because of that, we object to this entire line of questioning. Let's move on."

Knudsen ignored Templeton and responded with an unmistakable edge in her voice, "The ballistics report showed Vinnie was only twenty feet from me."

"Your gunsight gave you a false read, didn't it, Kim?" said Gina.

With Zimmer on one side of her, and Templeton on the other, the Madsen-Zimmer lawyers tried to get control over what was happening, but the train had left the station.

"I told everyone it was the gunsight," she said. "But no one listened to me. They said I just panicked. They told me I was in denial."

"Had you ever used your Sight-Clops before during hot and humid conditions?" asked Gina.

"No," she said.

Gina signaled the AV operator. On the room's big screen, a list of names appeared. The operator scrolled down to the bottom of the list. "Officer Knudsen, this is a list of one hundred and sixty-three names, and counting, that we have gathered so far."

The officer studied the screen, confused by the scrolling names.

"I'd like to ask you if you know any of these people," Gina asked, "aside from Officer Velez."

After looking at the names for a minute, Knudsen said, "I don't recognize any of the other names."

"The list you see," said Gina, "includes people who have been killed or wounded as a result of faulty Sight-Clops gunsights. Has anyone from Arbalest ever shown you a list like this?"

"Objection!" Templeton shouted. "Are you questioning the witness or are you giving another one of your touching speeches?"

"Let's call it a speech, Mr. Templeton," said Gina. "And when you hear the rest of it in trial, you're going to love the ending."

# 31
# BURNING DOWN THE HOUSE

**W**ith the two days of depositions concluded, Gina thought she'd have the rest of the week to catch her breath. In the weeks to come, her team and Madsen–Zimmer's would find dates for her to depose Merle Marcus. If Gina prevailed with Judge Sanders, she would also be able to add Tim Knapp to the deposition list. Of course, if that was the case, it was likely that Madsen–Zimmer would drag their heels as long as possible before allowing the deposition to take place.

What Gina couldn't have known was that the Arbalest case was anything but done for the week.

The Bergman–Deketomis contingent leaving Chicago was slightly smaller than the one when they'd arrived. In fifteen minutes, the last of their team would be at the airport on their way home after a grueling couple of days in the Windy City.

Gina wished that Carol hadn't left and felt frustrated that she couldn't ask her friend about all the important questions kicking around in her head. She also couldn't talk to her coworkers about her phone being bugged, or even warn them to avoid speaking about certain topics. Everyone needed to act and sound natural to avoid scaring off whoever might be listening. Gina doubted whether Madsen-Zimmer had any involvement in the bugging. They'd been caught flat-footed too many times during the depositions, she thought, for them to have been privy to any of Bergman-Deketomis's strategizing about the case.

One of the biggest questions on Gina's mind was how long the bugs had been in place. She had to assume the worst and guessed they'd been around a month or more. What had she said, Gina wondered, that could damage her personally or professionally? Of most concern to Gina were her conversations with Deke. Her only solace was that ever since she'd voiced her need for vengeance in the hospital, she and Deke had been guarded in what they said to one another. In fact, in thinking back to their cryptic conversations, Gina couldn't help but think they must have sounded like mobsters afraid that Big Brother was recording them. At least on that end, she felt secure.

By this time, Carol would have told Deke and Martin about the surveillance. Knowing Carol, Gina was sure she would limit those in the know. In fact, she'd probably come up with some fabrication explaining why the firm needed access to certain Bergman-Deketomis's offices as well as to the cars and homes of several key employees.

Bennie interrupted Gina's musing. "Everyone says you hit a home run," he said. "So why is it that you're scowling?"

"I'm half Sicilian," Gina said, "and half Spanish Sephardic Jew, so if I'm not planning a vendetta, I'm probably feeling guilty."

"Which is it?"

"Half and half at the moment," said Gina.

"I'll be glad to get home," said Bennie.

Gina wished she could be as enthusiastic, but at the moment her home didn't feel like her castle. Someone had invaded her office and her privacy, and Gina wouldn't be surprised if they'd done the same to her home. How could she be expected to relax in a bugged home?

Her cell phone began vibrating. After Carol returned it to her, Gina had put it on vibrate mode during the deposition and had forgotten to put it back on to ring. Gina looked at the display and then motioned for everyone in the van to be quiet. Someone was calling from Judge Sanders' office.

"Ms. Romano," said a male voice, "this is Hunter Joseph, the clerk at Judge Sanders' office. Are you still in Chicago?"

"I am," Gina said.

"I know this is last minute notice," he said, "but we just had an opening on our court docket. Would it be possible for you to meet with Judge Sanders and representatives from Madsen-Zimmer in her chambers tomorrow morning at nine o'clock? The judge has come to a decision in regard to your deposition request."

—◆◆◆—

When Gina finished with the call she said, "Ned? Bennie?"

Both men looked at her. "Each of you will need to make two calls. The first will be to your wives. You're going to have to tell them that there has been a change in plans and you won't be coming home tonight."

"What's up?" asked Ned.

"We'll be meeting with Judge Sanders in her chambers tomorrow morning to get her decision as to whether we can depose Knapp."

"Yes!" said Ned. "I knew we'd hear from her sooner rather than later. I'm betting this morning sealed the deal."

"Let's not count our chickens before they hatch," said Gina.

"What's the second call we need to make?" asked Bennie.

"I am going to give you my credit card number, and each of you will be calling a florist. I want you to order the kind of arrangement which will not only get you forgiven by your wives, but will get you open arms when you arrive home."

"Ah," said Cara. "That's sweet. What about me?"

"I didn't think you had a boyfriend," said Gina. "And besides, you and Rachel will be flying home as planned."

"Who needs a boyfriend?" said Cara. "I was going to order the flowers for me."

Bennie, Ned, and Gina were on their way back to the same hotel they'd just checked out of that morning, when Gina received her second phone call relating to Arbalest. "This is Angela King calling from the Department of Justice on behalf of Assistant United States Attorney Eva Trench," a woman said. "AUSA Trench would like to know if Gina Romano is available to talk."

Eerie, thought Gina. First, the call from the offices of the Seventh District Judge, and now the Department of Justice was calling.

"This is Gina, and I am available to talk now."

A moment later, Trench was on the line. Her Brooklyn accent was as thick as Gina had been told.

"Ms. Romano, this is AUSA Trench. Thank you for taking my call."

"My pleasure," said Gina.

"I understand you have been upsetting the Arbalest applecart these past two days," said Trench.

Justice seemed to be unusually well-informed, thought Gina.

"I'm glad to hear you're paying attention," she said, "even if it does seem belated."

"Oh, we've always believed the case had possibilities," said Trench, with more than a touch of defensiveness.

"That's news to me," said Gina. "We have a few more depos ahead of us that you're welcome to sit in on. That should really convince you that our case has . . . what did you call it . . . 'possibilities?'"

"Before I do that," said Trench, "why don't the two of us have a talk? What are you doing tomorrow afternoon at two?"

It was perfect timing, thought Gina. The flight from Chicago to Washington, DC, would take about two hours. If the Bergman-Deketomis company plane was available, it might even take less.

"It just so happens I'm staying over in Chicago tonight," said Gina, "and should be able to make it to DC by two."

"Who would have known?"

*You,* Gina wanted to say, but didn't.

◆◆◆

There was a men's clothing shop off the lobby in their hotel and Ned went to pick up a new dress shirt, socks, and underclothing. Gina always overpacked with "just in case" clothes and didn't need to get a new outfit.

Bennie and Gina went ahead while Ned shopped. On the drive over, Bennie had once more arranged to have a connecting room with her.

"I hope you don't mind room service again, Bennie," she said.

"Mind?" he said. "Last night, I had shrimp scampi and filet mignon. Guess what I'm having tonight?"

"I'm thinking surf and turf again."

"You got it," he said. "When you know what you want, just call me with your order."

"You don't have to be my taster, Bennie."

"I probably should taste your food," he said. "Let's not forget we're in Chicago, home of Officer Thursby and Boss Lutz. The sooner we get out of here, the happier I'll be. But in the meantime my job is to make sure you continue breathing properly."

"Thanks, Bennie."

For the second night in a row, Bennie checked Gina's room. By the time he finished, she had her order ready.

"You can call in our orders whenever you're hungry, Bennie," she said. "All I want is a bowl of the clam chowder and a Caesar salad."

"That's all?"

"I'm not that hungry."

"You've been losing weight," he said.

"I doubt it," Gina said, although she had noticed her clothes weren't as tight.

"Why don't you have one of those molten lava cakes?"

"It sounds like something you can personally recommend."

"It was delicious," Bennie admitted.

"Okay," laughed Gina. "I'll have a molten lava cake as well."

"À la mode?" he asked. "Vanilla ice cream goes perfectly with it."

Gina raised her arms and surrendered. "Okay," she said, "with vanilla ice cream."

––◆◆◆––

Bennie knocked on the connecting door before he opened it and delivered Gina her food. During the time the door between their rooms was open, she was treated to the aroma of Bennie's shrimp and steak. The scent made her remember the meal she'd had with Peter and Bryan at the Blue Planet.

She abruptly terminated her stroll down memory lane. Gina couldn't afford that distraction. Tomorrow she needed to be at the top of her game.

It wasn't easy to put aside her feelings, but she'd had a whole lifetime of training doing just that. And even though she was now less hungry than she had been before, she was afraid Bennie might take notice of what she had or had not eaten. Because of that, Gina ate everything on her tray.

Later, she would wonder if the molten lava cake was as good as Bennie said it was. Even though Gina ate all of it, she couldn't recall its taste.

◆◆◆

In Judge Sanders' chambers the next morning, Charles Zimmer was the sole representative from his firm. It felt odd, thought Gina, to not be facing down a throng of lawyers. Zimmer knew the time for showmanship and bluster had passed. Now he was holding out all his hopes on this ruling. Keeping Knapp out of the hot seat was the best possible outcome he could hope for.

In the privacy of her chambers, Judge Sanders had replaced her black robes for the comfort of a pantsuit the color of robin's-egg blue. Many judges maintained legal formalities even in their chambers. It was Gina's experience that the less confident judges filled their chambers with law books and legal trappings. Judge Sanders had pictures of her children and grandchildren. The artwork of her grandchildren could be seen in various spots around the room.

The judge spoke calmly. She had written out her decision, but didn't refer to her notes. Instead, she began explaining her decision in a way a lawyer might talk to a jury rather than a judge talking to lawyers in chambers. It was clear she had struggled with her decision and had an appreciation for how important it was.

"Today," she said, "one party will leave unhappy. That can't be helped.

"As lawyers, we have all used depictions of Lady Justice's images to make our point with juries. We've all heard the argument about how her left hand holds a set of scales. It is upon these scales that she must weigh the merits of the case. When a case like yours is brought before me, I can't help but imagine those scales. I consider the merits of your arguments and the weight they carry, and I put that weight on the scale item by item. Sometimes the scales easily tilt one way; sometimes there is a stasis, with the smallest of separations in the weight. This was one of those slight tilts."

The judge took off her glasses and with a cloth cleaned them. "I did my weighing, and although I sometimes worry about abusive discovery gone wild, I don't see that here. In this case, I have concluded that Arbalest owner and CEO Tim Knapp must comply with discovery and disclose those documents that have been requested. I will carefully examine all of the documents Mr. Knapp will be questioned about and will disallow any of them if I find national security interests, or trade secrets, need protection.

"In addition to complying with discovery requests served on Mr. Knapp, he will also be required to make himself available to be deposed by the plaintiff's attorneys. The contents of that deposition will be sealed until I have had the time to carry out an in-camera review. Ms. Romano, please draw up that order and forward it to me for my approval."

In the world of legal jargon, what had just happened to Madsen–Zimmer and Arbalest was called "being burned down." As the judge announced her decision, Zimmer's distressed expression epitomized the embodiment of the phrase.

As they exited the chambers, Ned hummed a triumphant refrain of the Talking Heads classic, "Burning Down the House."

From the courthouse lobby, with Bennie standing guard and scowling so as to discourage anyone from entering their space, Gina and Ned shared a cell phone and excitedly called Deke with the news.

"Don't settle cheap," said Deke, "and don't settle easy."

"We're going to see Eva Trench now," Gina said.

"That will give Madsen-Zimmer and Arbalest time to sweat," Ned said.

"Give my congratulations all around!" said Deke.

After the call, Ned could be seen looking all around. "What are you looking for?" Gina asked.

"Somewhere," Ned said, "not too far from here, I imagine Charles Zimmer is on the phone with Quentin Carter or maybe even Tim Knapp. I can't imagine they're having a pleasant conversation."

"We have a plane to catch," said Gina.

Bennie led interference for them, walking just ahead of the two. He made a short call to the driver as they walked. "We're on our way."

Out front a driver was waiting for them. As they were getting into the car Gina's phone rang. "Guess who?" she asked Ned.

"Could it be Charles Zimmer?"

Gina sent the call to her voice mail. "Let him sweat for awhile."

# 32

# LADY JUSTICE AND THE FAT LADY

Gina returned Zimmer's call as they were being driven to the airport.

"You haven't left the courthouse already, have you, Ms. Romano?"

"As a matter of fact I have, Mr. Zimmer. We have a big depo to get ready for, don't we?"

"Is there any way you can turn that car of yours around?" he asked. "I think if the two of us put our heads together, we could come to a possible resolution in our little dispute."

"If you consider our dispute *little*," said Gina, "then I doubt we have anything to talk about."

"What I meant to convey is that I don't think our differences are insurmountable."

The subtext of what Zimmer was saying was that he'd talked to Knapp and was told to settle the case. Gina knew Knapp was afraid to go into a deposition not knowing what cards she was holding, and if he perjured himself in this particular case he would likely spend time in jail—his tailored Brioni suit and one-percenter status notwithstanding. It was even possible he might be black-balled by the Lake Geneva Country Club set.

"I'm not ready to talk numbers with you," she said, "seeing as my information is incomplete."

"We won't try and shortchange you on the numbers," Zimmer said. "We'll use tried-and-true formularies and come up with a settlement you think is fair."

"That's not the information I'm talking about," said Gina. "My colleague, Angus Moore, was murdered. Our investigators are trying to determine whether Arbalest knew anything at all about that murder. I need to hear from Mr. Knapp that no one from Arbalest was in any way involved. Obviously, that is a conversation you probably want to have in private rather than in open court."

"Even though I am only the messenger in all of this," said Zimmer, "I want you to know that you have my complete attention, Ms. Romano. As soon as we finish talking, I will call Mr. Knapp and tell him everything you've said. I think it would be extremely beneficial for the two of you to have a face-to-face. If you turn your car around, I could arrange that meeting as early as this afternoon."

"That won't work for me," said Gina. "I have a two o'clock meeting with the Department of Justice. Ms. Trench apparently has something she wants to talk about."

"Shit," said Zimmer, not even trying to hide his unhappiness. "You know that once the feds get involved, any settlement becomes virtually impossible."

"I think we can assume their involvement is a done deal," said Gina, "but if Arbalest is willing to fully cooperate, I can minimize the Fed's involvement to little more than purely money interests."

"I can assure you that my client wants to satisfy all your concerns," he said, "as well as conclude a settlement as soon as possible. Would you consider flying back to Chicago for a dinner meeting tonight?"

"No," said Gina. "I will be flying home tonight. However, if you and Mr. Knapp want to fly to DC today, I'd be glad to talk to the two of you over a late afternoon cup of coffee."

"I'd like co-counsel along," said Zimmer. "And I am sure Mr. Knapp would want his longtime family counselor, Quentin Carter."

"That's fine with me as long as your co-counsel isn't Zack Templeton," said Gina. "He needs to have his midlife crisis on his own time, not mine. I'm pretty sure Tim Knapp would understand how unprofessional it was for you to bring in Templeton. The truth is by doing that it ended up making it that much more difficult for us to be civil towards you. Don't you agree?"

"I apologize, Ms. Romano," said Zimmer. "In retrospect I can see our efforts were misguided. Mr. Templeton will stay home. Will four-thirty work for you?"

"We'll confirm the time and place in the next hour," said Gina.

◆◆◆

This wasn't Gina's first time visiting the Department of Justice, but she had never been summoned by an AUSA on such short notice. As ironic as it might seem, Trench and Justice now needed to be involved in the approval of any settlement, despite the fact that months earlier she had said the DOJ didn't want to handle the "loser" case. Such bureaucratic regulations defied logic, but Gina would deal with them. Angus had wanted Gina to "handle" Trench; this was her chance to do exactly that for him.

Surprisingly, it was Ned who brought that up during their flight. "All along," he said, "Angus wanted you to deal with Trench. He told me he was going to try to get you on board with the case. He also said you should have been working with us from the first. I don't know why he didn't approach you."

Gina did know why, but would never tell.

"Anyway," said Ned, "I'm thinking you should go at Trench mano a mano."

"Before he died, Angus told me he wanted me to be the good cop to his bad cop against Trench," she said," but I don't see that happening today."

◆◆◆

Their driver let them out a block from Justice, and the three of them walked along Pennsylvania Avenue.

"This area of city and federal buildings is called the Federal Triangle," said Gina. "Justice is a trapezoidal lot amidst the triangle. Detractors say it should have been an octagonal shape, like a STOP sign."

Bennie read the wording on the building: "Robert F. Kennedy Department of Justice Building."

"Robert F. Kennedy was an attorney general," said Ned.

"I might have grown up on the res," Bennie said, "but that doesn't mean I'm not acquainted with Robert Kennedy and his big brother. Gran told us kids that the Kennedy brothers were the only two white men, aside from Nick Deketomis, who ever gave a damn about people like her."

"I wonder what the Kennedy brothers would think of how justice works in this country now," said Gina.

Before entering the grounds, the three of them walked around like tourists, looking at the neoclassical building with its art deco elements and ten-foot marble statues.

Finally, Gina looked at her watch and said, "I guess I better go through security."

"Typical overachiever "A" student," said Ned. "You always have to be early."

The two men hugged her goodbye. Bennie refused to leave until he saw Gina pass through screening and processing and enter the building.

As Gina passed beyond the security checkpoint, a young African-American woman approached her. "Ms. Romano," she said, "I'm Haley. AUSA Trench asked me to escort you to her office."

"Are you an intern?" asked Gina.

"I am," said Haley.

"Where are you going to school?"

"Delaware State University," she said. "I'll bet you never heard of it."

"I haven't," admitted Gina.

"Go Hornets," Haley said. "It's a good college and had a tuition I could afford."

"I went to law school at Rutgers," said Gina, "another state school."

"And now you're a lawyer?"

Nodding, she said, "I work for one of the best law firms in the country. So if you don't get into an Ivy League law school, that doesn't mean it's the end of the road for you."

"That's good to know, especially since just about everyone working here came out of some Ivy school. What kind of law do you practice?"

"I'm a trial lawyer," said Gina. "Usually, I am involved in mass torts. But last year I defended my boss in a murder trial."

"No way!"

"Way," she said and smiled.

"That's cool," said Haley. "By the way, I can play tour guide if you want. They made me learn a lot of things about this building."

"Where are we standing now?" asked Gina, looking up at the high expanse.

"It's called the Grand Hall," said Haley.

"Since we have a little time to kill," said Gina, "take me on the scenic route."

Haley did as asked, pointing out mosaics, limestone figures, murals, and art deco plaster reliefs. The two of them stopped to admire one particular statue.

"Hello beautiful," said Gina, speaking to the artwork. Then she turned to Haley and said, "Just this morning, I was in chambers with a circuit court judge who talked about Lady Justice."

"She's called the 'Spirit of Justice,'" Haley said. "She was made out of cast aluminum in the thirties, which explains some of her art deco elements."

"She's not wearing a blindfold," observed Gina.

"Most people notice she's not wearing much else either," Haley said, referring to how the young woman's toga had slipped off her shoulder, revealing one of her breasts.

"You're probably too young to have ever heard about the great cover-up," said Gina.

"What's that?"

"No one ever seemed to think anything about the Spirit of Justice's state of undress," said Gina, "that is until 2002 when the office of US Attorney General Tom Ashcroft arranged for drapes to cover her up."

"You're kidding?"

Gina shook her head. "It was quite the kerfuffle. I was in law school at the time."

Their walk to the offices of AUSA Eva Trench took them another ten minutes. From the street, it was hard to get a perspective of how large the Justice building was; but once inside you experienced its enormity.

"Spread out over these seven floors," said Haley, "there's almost one and a quarter million square feet. Luckily, we're almost at the end of our walk."

"I was about to ask for an oxygen mask," Gina said.

Trench's outer offices were grey and austere. Kafka could have easily written about them. Gina checked the time; it was fifteen minutes past when their appointment had been scheduled.

"Ms. Romano," said the receptionist, "AUSA Trench will see you now."

Gina was buzzed through a security door, which gained her admittance to Trench's offices. The room wasn't overly large, or maybe Trench's oversized desk just made it seem that way.

"Sorry to have kept you waiting," said Trench. "The AG was asking me for an update on a case I'm working."

Gina didn't believe a word of it; her skepticism showed itself in her reluctant smile. The two women shook hands; they were about the same height and had similar coloring. Trench was a dozen years older and carried herself with the kind of swagger usually seen on men in their twenties.

"Have a seat," she said.

Gina took a chair and faced her, waiting to hear what Trench had to say. The AUSA pursed her already thin lips, where only a narrow band of red lipstick that looked more like a facial gash could be seen.

"We've decided we want to be more active in the Arbalest whistle-blower case," said Trench.

"What prompted your change of heart? It wasn't very long ago that you categorized our case as a 'loser' to my boss Martin Bergman."

"We revisited the merits of it."

"I find your timing"—Gina let the word hang there—"impeccable."

"Is that so?" Trench said, offering up the words with a Brooklyn-accented disinterest.

"I am sure it won't come as a surprise to you that Arbalest wants to settle with us."

"You know what they say about how it's not over until the fat lady sings," said Trench. "I don't hear her singing yet, do you?"

"I don't much like opera," said Gina, "or operatic intrigue."

"That's surprising," said Trench, "with a name like Romano."

"I also don't like extortion," said Gina.

"There are rules," Trench said. "Let me remind you of those rules. In a whistle-blower case the DOJ has to authorize a minimum threshold amount for the settlement. And in case you forgot, we're also the ones who determine the percentage of money your whistle-blower is entitled to if the case does settle. Now, if you're going to tell me that your whistle-blower is entitled to the maximum amount of thirty percent of the settlement, I'll take that into consideration, or I might not. The truth is I have all the authority and you have none."

Trench leaned back in her chair, offering a much too large self-satisfied smirk.

"Is this the time when I am supposed to back off and play all nice?" Gina asked. "Because if it is, I'm sorry, I completely missed my cue. And as you must have heard, my firm is never inclined to run scared, Ms. Trench. If I'm going to do any running, it will be out of this office. And you wouldn't want me to do that because your office wouldn't get any credit for settling this case, and the government wouldn't get any settlement money. And we're talking about millions and millions of dollars.

"Do you think I moved fast this past month pushing this case to where it is now? Just wait and see what I can accomplish by next month after I abandon the DOJ and my efforts on this whistle-blower avenue all together. The message that Arbalest will get from that is to pay less attention to the importance of any DOJ settlement and more attention to all of the defective product lawsuits I will file across the country. They will understand that if they don't deal with me, they will never get closure on this litigation.

"In a week's time, I'll have filed a dozen independent defective gunsight product liability lawsuits from California to New York. And in one year's time, I'll have filed hundreds more. I will work around the clock, and you'll read about my successes. Not a month will go by where I don't get some multimillion dollar jury verdict. That kind of success won't go unnoticed. In other words, Ms. Trench, both you and I know this might be a better mass tort case than a whistle-blower case.

"Rest assured, though, it will be my goal to tell every reporter who asks about those cases that the DOJ, and you personally, passed on the chance to handle this case yourselves."

With barely contained fury Trench said, "Those are very big moves, Ms. Romano."

"Yes, well here's my first big move." Gina placed onto Trench's desk a copy of the first product liability lawsuit that would be filed.

The AUSA looked at the lawsuit paperwork and then back at Gina.

"Both of us know this can't end well for you, Ms. Trench." Gina had always suspected Trench had backed away from the

Sight-Clops case because of political influence. Now she was all but certain the fix had been put in by one particular senator from Illinois, which happened to be where Arbalest's corporate headquarters were located.

But now Trench could feel the shifting wind; above everything else, she was a realist. "So," Trench said, "Let's talk about what it is you expect out of this department."

Gina placed her list of what she expected on Trench's desk. At the top was her requirement that she have unencumbered authority to settle for an amount she determined to be appropriate. Next on the list was that her client Robert Diaz receive 30 percent of that settlement. Third was a demand that Arbalest be sanctioned with a monetary penalty to be determined by the DOJ along with a press release exposing the civil violations the company had committed.

All the items listed below these were simply boilerplate. There was a signature line for Trench, and she signed the document without any hesitation. There were no kind good-byes or niceties exchanged as Gina put the document in her briefcase and made her exit.

# 33
## LOOK MOM,
## NO BLOOD ON MY HANDS

Gina suspected that Ned's choice of a small deli meet-up was a reflection of his warped sense of humor, as it was located between Ford's Theatre and the International Spy Museum. By this time, Carol had probably managed to warn Ned his phone might be bugged. Assassination and spycraft, thought Gina. This case had it all.

Ned and Bennie had moved two tables together, which took up much of the delicatessen. On those tables were coffees, beverages, and a few of the deli's appetizers.

Four men in suits consulted for a moment out front before entering. This wasn't the kind of establishment where they typically met for power lunches and dinners. Gina was sure the foursome had flown in on the Arbalest company jet. As Bennie stood up to vacate his space, Gina handed him her purse. "If you don't mind, Bennie," she said, "I'd like you to watch this."

"And this, please," said Ned, passing him his cell phone.

Bennie took the items without comment and stationed himself near the front of the restaurant.

It was Zimmer who made the introductions, but from that point on Quentin Carter did the speaking for Arbalest.

"Thank you for meeting with us Ms. Romano and Mr. Williams," Carter said. "Mr. Zimmer has expressed to us your concerns, which prompted us to want to meet with you as soon as possible."

Carter looked around the two tables and beyond, making sure no one was listening. "As I understand it," he said, "before the terms of any settlement can be discussed, you want assurance that no one at Arbalest was involved in any way with the murder of your colleague, Angus Moore."

Gina nodded.

"I am sure it will come as a surprise to you," said Carter, "that when Mr. Knapp and I heard about Mr. Moore's death, we were naturally concerned. Even when early reports suggested Mr. Moore had died in an auto accident, Mr. Knapp and I wanted to be assured that was all there was to it. Because of that, we summoned Kendrick Strahan to Mr. Knapp's house in Lake Geneva only two days after Mr. Moore's death.

"Strahan, as I am sure you know, was a lobbyist in the employ of Arbalest. More than that, at one time Strahan was a personal friend of Mr. Knapp's."

At a nod from Carter, Knapp began to speak. He was a middle-aged man of fair complexion. His face was remarkably free of wrinkles, which made him look younger than he was, but also gave his features a look of only being partially formed.

"I knew Ken from our time at boarding school," said Knapp. "He was a star athlete back then. Ken was a smart guy; he was on scholarship, but still was always looking for shortcuts. Others always wrote his papers, including me, and if he could copy or cheat he would. Ken liked to party as well. He had a smuggling ring which brought in booze and grass to school.

"Ultimately, those habits and proclivities caught up with him. Ken was later expelled from Harvard, although over time he did get his degree from another college. When he was in his mid-twenties, he got a job with the US Treasury working for the Secret Service. He put in more than ten years before self-destructing there. That's when he called me begging for a job. I thought he might be good for marketing, especially with his background in law enforcement. I offered him a position with the Gun Control Institute, which is essentially a lobbying arm of Arbalest.

"By most accounts, Ken was an effective lobbyist. There is no question that sales increased under his direction. Because of that, Ken was essentially given free rein. In retrospect, it's clear he needed more oversight. I am also of the opinion that I did him no favors by making him a lobbyist. We are now aware that position brought out the worst in him."

"Are you suggesting that Strahan murdered Angus," asked Gina, "or ordered his murder?"

Carter and Knapp had an ocular consultation. It was the lawyer who ultimately spoke. "Mr. Knapp doesn't think Mr. Strahan would ever have knowingly condoned murder. I am not so sure. When Angus Moore started asking questions about bribe money being paid to politicians and purchasing agents, Mr. Strahan became noticeably agitated and nervous."

"So when you heard about Angus's death," said Gina, "you had Strahan come to Mr. Knapp's Wisconsin home where the two of you interviewed him?"

"That's correct," said Carter. "I took notes at that meeting and will be happy to provide them to you."

"For now, give me the gist of the conversation."

"Strahan was hiding something from us. That was apparent to me. Mr. Knapp asked him outright if he was involved in Mr. Moore's death. Strahan said he had nothing to do with it."

"Did you believe him?"

"No," said Carter. "I was certain he knew more than he was telling us. Mr. Knapp had the same impression."

"But the two of you were willing to leave it at that?" asked Gina.

"We put Mr. Strahan on notice that there would be an audit of his department," said Carter, "and we pulled the plug on his sizable discretionary fund."

"What have your findings revealed?"

"Unfortunately it has become clear that Mr. Strahan was handing out bribes," said Carter, "or what he liked to call 'pay for play.' We also have evidence that Strahan frequently rented out the Libertyville Shooting Club for the kinds of parties Arbalest would never have condoned."

"But conveniently for you," said Gina, "Strahan died."

"I wouldn't call it convenient," said Carter. "I know Mr. Knapp doesn't call it convenient. I would much rather have Mr. Strahan here to answer your questions. But because he is not, Mr. Knapp will commit to providing whatever your firm needs to satisfy itself that no one at Arbalest, with the possible exception of Mr. Strahan, had anything to do with Mr. Moore's death. To help you in that endeavor, you are welcome to do a forensic accounting of Arbalest and the Gun Control Institute.

"As I mentioned, we are already doing our own investigation, and what we've already found is more than disturbing. Because Mr. Strahan's friendship with Mr. Knapp was well-known, he was able to bypass standard protocols. Special exceptions were made for him, and because of that, he was able to promote projects that Mr. Knapp knew nothing about."

"Ken and his shortcuts," said Knapp, shaking his head.

"Mr. Strahan convinced accounting that Mr. Knapp was okay with setting up a distribution account where his substantial sales commissions were funneled into what he called 'marketing expenditures.' That money, along with his purported rental expenditures for Libertyville, provided him with a huge slush account."

"I would never condone murder," said Tim Knapp. "I couldn't live with bloody hands."

It was a strange admission from the CEO of one of the world's largest small-weapons manufacturers, but Gina actually believed him.

She turned to Ned and nodded.

"If things check out as you say they will," Ned said, "and we will turn over every stone making sure they do, we will be asking for a settlement of five hundred million dollars."

Zimmer opened his mouth, ready to vent his outrage; Carter silenced him with his index finger.

"As well as a separate fifty million dollar settlement," said Gina, "providing for a V.A. Wounded Soldiers Fund in Angus's name. That donation needs to be separate from the whistle-blower settlement so that the DOJ doesn't benefit from it at all."

"Will Arbalest be allowed to use this donation as P.R.?" asked Carter. "After what you've been putting us through, we could use some good publicity."

"That's fine," said Gina.

Carter turned to Knapp and got a small nod.

"Nothing we've heard today would preclude a deal," said Carter.

# 34
## NO TRACKS

The scientific name for the cockroach order is *Blattodea*, which derives from the Latin word *blatt* and essentially means "an insect that shuns light."

Like cockroaches, Ivan Verloc preferred the darkness. And also like cockroaches, Ivan was sensitive to any disturbances in his environment. Ivan hadn't been born with the long, flexible antennae of cockroaches, but he was attuned, just like they were, to seen and unseen threats.

And like a cockroach, Ivan was adept at disappearing. In fact, that's what he was doing. He was shutting down his entire Bergman–Deketomis operation. Every dark tunnel he'd bored, every back door that he'd explored, was being closed. And what he couldn't shut down he made every attempt to camouflage so that he would leave behind very few traces of where he had been and what he had done. It was likely he was being overly cautious, but he was okay with that.

His special phone rang, and Ivan debated whether he should talk to Lutz. Then he decided it was time to have a last conversation.

"What's the matter, Ivanhoe?" said Lutz. "I haven't heard from you in days. Don't you love me anymore?"

"You mean like Strahan loved you?"

"Poor guy committed suicide."

"Really?" said Ivan. And then over the phone he played his recording of Strahan's last minute on the planet, down to his final choked gurgle.

"That's now part of your file," said Ivan. "Remember our talk about mutually assured destruction? With all I got on you, you're looking at a life sentence."

"And where do two murders put you, Ivanhoe?"

"Far from here, that's where," he said. "I'm shutting down operations. This will be the last time we talk."

"You don't want to get on my bad side, Ivanhoe. I need my mole to keep working."

"Your mole has found another hole. Almost overnight, the people at that law firm have become more guarded in what they're saying. I get the sense they're afraid Big Brother is listening in."

"You're being paranoid. Why don't you put on your big-boy pants and tell me what's going on?"

Ivan released the phone from his hand like it was a mic drop.

From his end of the line Lutz heard the loud impact followed by the faint words, "Elvis has left the building."

# 35
## FOUL HENRY

Gina pretended to celebrate along with Ned and Bennie on the flight home, but her heart wasn't in it. She had been running so hard and for so long she wasn't sure what to do with herself. In what seemed like eternity, Gina had focused on Angus, Arbalest, and Sight-Clops to the exclusion of everything else. She had been able to compartmentalize, to put aside matters not relevant to the pressing issues that needed to be addressed.

Now, for the first time in weeks, she had time to think. Gina wasn't sure if that was a good thing.

Ned commented to Bennie, "I just about choked when Gina, cool as a cucumber, told those stiffs in suits, 'Oh, yeah, you're also going to cough up fifty million for a wounded soldiers' fund. And that was after I thought I had already pushed them to their wall by asking for five hundred million. That little bit of extra was not in the script. Where did that come from?"

"I was remembering Cara's affidavit from her meeting with Private Jones," said Gina. "Here's a soldier with a textbook case of

PTSD, and in obvious need of healing, and the only person who's listening to him is a twenty-four-year-old lawyer from Florida. We can do better than that."

"Yeah, agreed," said Ned.

Gina pretended to nod off, and then her pretense became reality. She opened her eyes only when their company plane was on its short final approach for Spanish Trace at just before eleven. Old habits caused her to look at her phone first thing. There was a text from Carol Morris: *You, Deke, Martin, and me to meet in fifth-floor conference room at 8:30 a.m.*

"Home sweet home!" said Ned.

"While you were sawing wood," Bennie told Gina, "I arranged for Steve to have your back tonight. He'll give you a ride to your place."

"You didn't need to do that, Bennie," said Gina. "The case is over."

"As soon as I hear that from Deke and Carol," Bennie said, "you'll no longer have a security detail."

When Ned and Bennie entered the terminal, their families rushed in to give them hugs. After both men finished kissing their wives, Gina thanked Tina Williams and Andrea Stokes for letting her borrow their husbands. The woman seemed to be in remarkably good moods Gina noticed—expensive flower arrangements can sometimes work wonders.

Gina also met Bennie's four children; Dylan was nine, Faith was six, Hope was four, and Charity was three. Two of the girls were in Bennie's arms; the third was holding on to his left leg. Dylan, a spitting image of his father, stood at his side.

"She's Colestah, right Dad?" asked Dylan, pointing to Gina.

Bennie looked embarrassed, but nodded.

"Colestah?" asked Gina. "Who is that?"

"She was a great Yakama warrior," said Dylan. "Colestah carried a stone war club with her. She was always ready for battle. I wrote a report on her and got an *A*. My dad says you're just like her."

"Your dad is the *real* warrior," said Gina. "I probably couldn't even lift a stone war club."

Still, she turned her head and found herself wiping away a few tears. Gina knew she was no Colestah, yet couldn't help but be pleased at the name Bennie had bestowed upon her to his family.

━━◆◆◆━━

Even though it was getting close to midnight, Peter still wasn't home, and neither was Gina's Porsche Cayenne. Even though she'd been out of town, she couldn't help but feel annoyed. Peter seemed to be getting awfully fond of her car.

Her brother's absence, though, allowed her to go to sleep right away. Being in her own bed felt like a luxury. When her alarm went off at six in the morning, she wished she could have slept in.

There were signs that Peter had returned sometime during the night, but when Gina didn't see her car keys, she had Steve drive her to work. When she walked into her office at eight fifteen, she found a handwritten note from Carol: *Please leave your cell phone behind for our meeting. I'll be collecting it afterward.*

For once, Gina wasn't the first to the meeting. She and Martin Bergman arrived at the fifth-floor meeting room at the same time and found Carol and Deke already deep in conversation.

"Good morning," said Carol. "Please come in. I've made sure we can all talk in here without fear of being overheard. We were just discussing these."

She opened up her hand; in her palm were half a dozen wafer-like devices about the size and thinness of a fingernail.

"These are bugs," said Carol. "Two were found in Gina's office, two in her car, and two in her home. There is another even more elaborate bug in her cell phone."

"Son of a bitch," said Gina. "Was I the only one targeted?"

"You seem to have been the focus of interest ever since being given the Arbalest case," said Carol. "Prior to that, I believe Angus was the main target, even though there were others. I feel I am partly to blame for not picking up on the surveillance. In the past we've concentrated on providing security inside the building without considering that we should be doing it beyond these premises as well. The man who I am calling Mr. Wizard—the individual who was hired to do the surveillance—initially bypassed this building. Mr. Wizard performed his black magic in houses and vehicles. It appears he was also able to do his dirty work through home personal computers. And also through property security systems that he turned into his listening and viewing posts.

"The good news is that I am fairly certain no more monitoring is going on now; the bad news is that I had hoped to find a way to use these bugs to find him. Something must have alerted him, though, because no one is on the other end now.

"Mr. Wizard did leave more than a calling card, however. These bugs aren't something you can buy online; they're original and handmade. We have his signature on his bugs and his electronic programming. And because I firmly believe that sometimes it takes a criminal to catch a criminal, I have arranged to go see Foul Henry today."

"Who is Foul Henry?" asked Gina.

"He is someone who most especially wants to meet you," said Carol.

"And why is that?"

"He is a fan of yours, especially since you took on the whistle-blower case against Arbalest. But he's also made it clear that he finds you attractive."

"Carol is the only one in this room who has met Foul Henry," said Deke, "although Martin and I have both helped him on a few occasions to get out from under the thumb of the feds."

"Henry sees himself as a patriot," said Martin, "and believes it is his duty to expose the workings of tyrants everywhere."

"Like Snowden and Assange," said Deke, "Henry can be a bit of a megalomaniac. There's also the problem that what he categorizes as whistle-blowing, the US government might call criminal espionage."

"Foul Henry wants quid pro quo in this," said Carol. "He says in addition to paying him for his work, he also wants a marker for the future. According to Henry, he's working on something that will make WikiLeaks look like 'Mini-leaks.' Because of that, he is certain that in the not too distant future the government will be coming after him. He wants our guarantee to lead his legal defense."

Martin and Deke looked at one another; the firm's founding partner spoke for them: "We'll get you that documentation to give to him."

"So what you're saying, Carol," said Gina, "is that we're seeking out the help of a good wizard to go after a bad wizard?"

"Good wizard might be overstating it," said Carol. "Foul Henry is more like a very independent wizard."

"But why do you call him Foul Henry?" asked Gina.

◆◆◆

During their flight to St. Louis, Carol told Gina and Bennie the story of Foul Henry. "I've been working investigations for a long time," she said, "and have heard a million stories. It was around ten years ago that Henry's name first surfaced. At the time he was known as 'Robin in the Hood.' It's probably the name he's best known as, and I imagine it's the one he prefers. I thought it was all an urban legend, but the stories of this digital Robin Hood going after the Sheriff of Nottingham in his various forms persisted. As the years passed, I began to believe our Robin Hood might actually exist and that we might have a need for his services, so I decided to track him down.

"It wasn't easy. Robin in the Hood sent me down many a wrong path. Maybe he finally took pity on me. Or maybe he's just a pervert. He liked the idea of a woman going to such lengths to meet him, even one he considers of 'advanced years.' So, much to my surprise, Robin decided to invite me to his house. He lives in the slums of East St. Louis. Robin bought up an entire cul-de-sac, and pays a street gang to keep an eye on his digs. Which means invading his turf is like invading gang turf. It is almost like he has his own castle and army. According to him, it's a very sound investment and costs him far less than buying a fortress and staffing it.

"By then I'd found out his real name was Henry, not Robin. Before his twenty-fifth birthday, Henry had been the toast of Silicon Valley. Then he had a breakdown of sorts and fell off the radar. Anyway, Henry recovered from his breakdown, or at least recovered enough to do the kind of work he now does. Over the past five years he's helped Bergman-Deketomis on several occasions."

"Am I ever going to hear why you gave him the name 'Foul Henry'?" asked Gina.

"All too soon," said Carol, "you will smell why he has the name Foul Henry. After Henry bought his street in East St. Louis, every stray cat in town seemed to find its way to his home. He now lives with hundreds of cats and seems to be impervious to their smells."

Gina's face contorted. She wondered if she would be able to stand the acrid smell of all those cats.

"I almost regret having initiated a personal relationship with Henry," Carol said. "As far as I know, I am the only creature with two legs he's allowed in his house. And now he specifically asked for you. If he wasn't the best, there's no way I'd be here. I already sent him pictures of the listening devices and the reverse engineering that was put in place on our computers and security systems, but Foul Henry also wanted us to bring along the electronic surveillance devices that we located."

"Sounds like we should have also brought along some Meow Mix and kitty litter," said Gina.

◆◆◆

With Bennie at the wheel of their rental, they drove through the city and across the Poplar Street Bridge over the Mississippi River. Once across, with the St. Louis Gateway Arch in their rearview mirror, their surrounding circumstances abruptly deteriorated. Luckily Carol knew where they were going. She recognized that you don't want to bet your life on the accuracy of GPS in East St. Louis. They drove through what looked like a war zone and finally arrived at Henry's street. Although they couldn't observe anyone watching them, everyone was sure they were being observed. They pulled up to the end of the cul-de-sac. Behind a wrought iron fence was an old mansion that looked about as welcoming as the one in the movie *House of Usher.*

Carol reached into her purse and brought out a bottle of Vicks VapoRub. She opened the bottle, stuck her finger in, and put a dab under each nostril.

Then she held out the bottle and asked, "Anyone?"

"I'm afraid the cure might be worse than the disease," said Gina.

"Your stomach," said Carol.

Bennie didn't hesitate and dabbed some under his nose. Gina followed suit, although her eyes began to tear up right away.

Carol led the way to the gate and pressed her finger on the bell. From inside the old house they could hear a ring.

"Henry smokes a lot of dope," said Carol. "Sometimes I have to ring the bell for ten minutes until he responds."

She rang the bell a second time. A few more seconds passed before the front door opened. Foul Henry stepped out into the light and tried to fend it off with his right hand. If he'd been wearing black clothes he might have pulled off the vampire look, but he had on cut-offs, a tie-dyed shirt, and Chuck Taylor Converse All Star High Tops.

Gina thought Foul Henry looked a bit like a stoned Johnny Depp, with dark hair and wispy facial hair. The man's slightly uneven eyes took their time running up and down Gina's figure. As Henry made his way to the gate he smiled at Carol and then scowled at Bennie.

"Ladies are welcome," he said. "Chief Broom Bromden stays behind the gate."

"I come in peace," said Bennie, speaking like a John Ford Indian.

"You will welcome Bennie," said Carol, "as you will welcome Gina, as you will welcome me."

"Mom has spoken," said Henry, unlocking the gate.

Even with the Vicks VapoRub running olfactory interference, Gina caught a scent of the "cat house" and almost gagged.

As they were led in, Gina saw the cats weren't the only things contributing to the stench. Henry was a hoarder. There were piles of books, mountains of magazines, and heaps of electronic parts. The living room was a graveyard of old computers and their operator manuals. Amidst the computers were boxes of old and mostly consumed pizzas along with forgotten cans and jars.

And, of course, everywhere there were cats.

"You must really like cats," said Gina.

Henry shrugged. "It's not like I sought them out. With the economic conditions around here, they were looking for a refuge. But then I don't have to talk about economics with you. I have studied some of your cases. It would seem to me you must be political."

"I am," Gina said, "but mostly to the extent of giving to causes I believe in. I understand you're an activist."

"Like Diogenes," Henry said, "I take my lantern and go out on the fruitless search for an honest man. Or woman. And when I find lies, I expose them. Right now the Republicans are blaming the Democrats for leaking material, and the Democrats are accusing the Republicans of the same thing. What they're not saying is that each party is guilty of lying, which they are. The person who believes that either side has the moral high ground is a damn fool."

"And you are Diogenes?" Gina asked.

"More like Guy Fawkes, I think," said Henry, "except instead of setting off actual explosives, I explode secrets."

He motioned to the living room. "Sit down."

His invitation was more easily said than done. Carol, Gina, and Bennie had to shoo away cats so that they could sit down on chairs and a sofa. Henry sat down on an old piano bench. It wouldn't have surprised Gina if she suddenly heard the music to *The Phantom of the Opera* playing.

"All right, Henry," said Carol. "Quit ogling Gina."

"If you insist," he said. "Now, besides her, where are the goodies I asked you to bring?"

# 36
## ROUND AND ROUND
## THE BAGGAGE CAROUSEL

During the flight back to Spanish Trace, the main topic of discussion was Henry. Instead of being repulsed by him as Gina had expected, she both admired him and felt sorry for him. In his moldering house of cats, Henry was fighting what he believed was the good fight.

"If anyone can find who was spying on us," Carol said, "Foul Henry can."

"He said he detected a similar electronic fingerprint in the way Angus's car computer was hacked," said Gina, "and in the bugs planted in my office and home."

"I think Henry already has a good idea of who our guy is," said Bennie.

"It's a small pool of weird wizards," Carol admitted.

Bennie said, "What I wasn't following was Henry's rambling explanation about the Black Knight Richard and Ivanhoe fighting side by side on the deep web."

"The deep web is just the kind of place where I'd expect to find our Mr. Wizard," Carol said. "You want to hire a hit man? Are you a pedophile looking for child porn? That's the place you go. If it had been around during Dante's time, I'm sure the deep web would have been a circle of hell."

"Abandon all hope," said Gina, "ye who enter here."

Carol nodded. "It's a place you don't want to enter unless you have to. When I have to spend time there, I always feel as if I'd had a tar bath."

"Henry said he'd contact us when he had something," Gina added. "I've got my fingers crossed that we hear from him soon."

◆◆◆

During the flight, Gina asked Carol if she could help her to track down a number that no longer seemed to be working. Carol took down all the information, and half an hour later handed her a slip of paper with a number on it.

"I always say there's no such thing as an unlisted number," said Carol.

"Thanks so much," said Gina.

◆◆◆

Gina made the call as soon as she got home. The conversation lasted for fifteen minutes. When it was done, she cried for even longer than she'd talked.

Afterwards, she went to her bookcase and pulled down a book that was near and dear to her heart. Gina found wrapping paper and did her best to wrap the volume. She had never been very good at wrapping, but this time she tried to make her efforts look at least presentable.

Peter was out, as usual, and so was her Porsche Cayenne, so Gina called for a taxi.

—◆◆◆—

Gina tried to remember a time when she'd felt so nervous and decided there had never been such a time. This was it. She felt exposed and vulnerable. She felt like throwing up. Gina hated being so dependent on another human being for her happiness. That wasn't something she did. That was a sucker's game. Flee, Gina thought. Leave a note. Write a card. Recite a cute message. Do anything but avoid this face-to-face.

He had every right to be angry. He had every right to hate her. She was the one who caused their breach, not him. By now, he would likely have gotten over the pain. By now, he might have realized she was toxic and that he was better off without her.

Passengers emerged from the gate. Gina scanned the heads. More and more people walked out, but Bryan wasn't there. He must have taken another flight, Gina thought. Or maybe he fell in love in Australia with a woman who deserved his love. Maybe he had decided there was nothing in Spanish Trace worth coming home to.

A couple came into view. A beautiful woman was walking with Bryan. Gina wanted to run away. She didn't want to see this, even though she deserved it.

And then a voice called out, "Amy!" And the woman went running into the arms of a man waiting for her in the terminal.

That's when Bryan saw her. She smiled for him, but he didn't return her smile. Gina opened her arms for him, but he didn't come for a hug. He just looked at her, his face giving away nothing. Tears started falling from her face. She tried to control herself, but couldn't. She was an absolute mess; there was no masking how she felt. It was all there on display, and Gina felt terrible for that. But that was the very thing Bryan needed to see.

He ran to Gina and lifted her in his arms. "You put me through hell."

"I was . . . was . . . was . . . right there with you," she sobbed.

"I love you," he said.

And right back she said, "I love you."

She handed him a wrapped present. "What is it?" he asked.

"Open it. It's yours"

"And ruin your wonderful wrapping job?" he teased.

"I tried," said Gina, as he ripped away the wrapping. "You said you'd never read *To Kill a Mockingbird*. It's a first edition, one of only a few with a Harper Lee signature. It might seem like an odd gift, but it was one of my few real treasures before you walked into my life. It's the most sincere way I could think of to say how sorry I am and how sorry I am for what Peter did."

"It wasn't your fault. But never mind that now. Let's just go to my house."

"What about your luggage?"

"It can wait. Right now, I need one of those kisses that last all week," he said.

# 37
## TOUGH LOVE

It wasn't an intervention, or at least, not exactly. Gina knocked loudly on her brother's door. She heard some groaning sounds and knocked that much harder.

"Let me sleep," said Peter.

Gina opened the door slightly. "Get your clothes on," she said, unable to hide the fury in her voice, "and get downstairs. Now!"

Two minutes later Peter walked downstairs. Seated in chairs were Gina, Bryan, Bennie, and Carol.

"Sit down," said Gina.

"Don't I get coffee first?" he asked. "Or how about a blindfold?"

"Shut up," said Gina.

Peter suddenly seemed to awaken to the seriousness of his situation. "Look, Gina," he said, "I know there are a few things we need to work out, but can't we do them in private?"

"Sit down and shut up," she said once more.

This time Peter complied.

"I talked to your wife yesterday," Gina said. "She was out of her mind with worry. Apparently, she thought you were in Canada contemplating suicide. According to Sara, she had to talk you out of killing yourself the last time the two of you spoke."

"Sara is—"

Gina interrupted him. "Not another word. I'll tell you when you can speak. Everything you told me about your situation was a lie. Sara is carrying your child. Kumar never had an affair with her. And he wasn't the one who gambled away your business with a derivative scheme. You were.

"Just so you know, as if it might actually matter to you, in your absence Kumar and Sara have being doing their best to try and make things right with your investors. They have promised them that over the next three years, they'll see that they get fifty cents on the dollar. With a miracle, that might save you from being arrested for securities fraud."

Peter nodded to show that he was listening.

"It wasn't enough for you to make a shambles of your own marriage. You did your best to sabotage my relationship and my happiness. When Bryan was in the picture, it was harder for you to play poor little Peter, wasn't it? So you managed to make me think Bryan was hooking up with the bartender at Snooki's, the same bartender that you've been seeing. How am I doing so far? That's how you were able to get that graphic and disgusting footage, substituting Bryan's face for yours.

"Of course, I know you don't have the technical skills of a third-grader. Someone else was in on this—the same someone who happened to send you the footage on a phone you'd just borrowed from Bryan that night at the restaurant.

"I was blind, Peter, because I never expected my own flesh and blood would betray me time and again. I should have been aware of the timing, but you played me like a fool, didn't you? Like when I *lost* my cell phone. You took it, hid it, and then gave it to your psycho partner in crime so that he could put a bug in it. That was the same partner who you allowed to place bugs in my office."

Gina stared her brother down. "Is that about right?"

"You mean I can talk now?" he said. "No, Sis, that's not completely right. You left out the part about me being desperate and broke and needing a few crumbs thrown my way. So, was it wrong earning some cash for a few business transactions? My guy, Larry, was willing to pay me some good coin for getting a little insider information."

"Bryan saw you talking to some character before we met for dinner. Was that your *guy*, "Larry," as you call him?"

Peter nodded.

"We need to hear about your guy," said Gina. "We need to hear every detail."

Carol joined in on the questioning. She learned all she could about "Larry," and how Peter communicated with him. Carol was able to get times and places and specifics. Soon, they would be able to put a face to "Larry," even while Henry was trying to place a name to him.

The physical description provided by Peter and Bryan was good enough for Bennie: "That sounds like the squirrelly guy who was spying at Angus's wake."

"And he sounds just like the bastard who caused the crash," said Gina, "and who almost killed me."

"I didn't know that," said Peter. "I just thought he was hustling for another law firm. He told me all he wanted was the inside scoop to help the other team of legal sharks."

"You betrayed me in the ugliest kind of way," said Gina. "You lied and connived and could have even caused my death."

"I'm sorry. I made some mistakes."

"I don't forgive you," she said. "It's doubtful I ever will. I am sending Sara a check for fifty thousand dollars. That money is to be used for the care of my not-yet-born niece or nephew. I will make provisions so that you will not be able to touch a penny of that money.

With his best abashed little boy manner and voice, Peter said, "Come on, Gina. You don't mean that."

"Have you ever known me not to mean what I say? As of this moment, you are dead to me. The best thing you can do for yourself now is to make things right with the rest of your family. We don't have to be like our father, Peter. You can be better than him." Tears formed in Gina's eyes. She wasn't sure if her words were more for Peter or for her.

"I can understand why you're pissed," he said. "But I'm going to need some money to get back on my feet."

"Then you had better earn that money. It's time to grow up, Peter. It's time to be a man. As you know, Sara had to sell your home. She's now living in a one-bedroom apartment. I have bought you an airline ticket to go home to her. Even after all you have done, Bryan has volunteered to accompany you."

"But we're family," Peter pleaded. "The two of us have always looked out for one another."

"Your flight leaves in two hours," said Gina, turning her back on him and walking out of the room.

# 38
## INTO BONDAGE

"I have a name for your guy," said Henry.

"I'm all ears," said Carol.

"His name is Ivan Verloc. I don't have his address yet, but that might be a good thing."

"Why is that?"

"You ever hear of a troll hole that wasn't defended? I imagine he has all sorts of booby traps. I know I do."

"Remind me not to make unannounced house calls," said Carol.

"He's in the Midwest," said Henry. "In fact, I'm pretty sure he's in Ohio. I can probably have his address in twenty-four hours, but I've got something that might be better than that right now."

He waited for Carol's response. "You need heavy breathing, Henry? You need applause? I am listening closely and then some."

"I'd like to hear Gina's heavy breathing," he said.

"Quit insulting me," said Carol, "and quit being a pervert."

"Bingo," he said.

"Bingo?"

"The old advice about catching crooks is that you follow the money. But it's even easier following the kinks."

"What kinks are those?"

"She calls herself Queen Dominique. On the third Wednesday of every month, she is visited in her Hinckley, Ohio, home by a man her QuickBooks scheduling software identifies as Ivan Cannon. Queen Dominique's accounting software doesn't have a credit card on file for Mr. Cannon; like much of her clientele, Mr. Cannon is a cash customer. He supposedly pays her eight hundred dollars in cash and no doubt a hefty tip as well. But even without a credit card, I am all but certain Ivan Cannon is an alias for Ivan Verloc."

"How do you know this?"

"I did some searching on Queen Dominique and Ivan and found correlating matches."

"And Queen Dominique is a dominatrix?"

"Yes. Or perhaps I should say, 'Please, Mistress, may I have another?'"

"Try not to be naughty, Henry. What can you tell me about Queen Dominique?"

"Her real name is Jessica Hill. She's thirty-one years old and very attractive, both in leather and out—"

"Details!"

"Her business name is Controlling Enterprises. Last year she had gross revenues that exceeded six hundred thousand dollars."

"And she's able to do this in Hinckley, Ohio? Isn't that a Cleveland suburb?"

"It's a very well-off Cleveland suburb."

"What's a dominatrix doing in Hinckley, Ohio?"

"She can hide in plain sight," said Henry. "According to property records, her home is situated on a little more than an acre.

When you take a look at Google Maps, the place is pretty much an upscale, fairly secluded, modern brick home. She doesn't have to worry about nosey neighbors. Maybe I should move to Hinckley."

"Animal control would have you busted inside of a week," said Carol. "I seem to remember Hinckley for something else."

"Would you like a hint from a little *birdie*?"

"Buzzards," said Carol, remembering.

"They're actually turkey vultures," said Henry, "even though Hinckley says that every March fifteenth the buzzards return home. The town even holds a festival welcoming them back."

"And tomorrow our buzzard is supposed to return to Queen Dominique?"

"At eight in the evening."

"We owe you, Henry."

"Will you be wiring the money, or would you prefer I steal it electronically from your company bank account?"

From their vantage point, Carol, Bennie, and Gina monitored the home of Jessica Hill, a.k.a. Queen Dominique. According to her QuickBooks timetable, the Queen scheduled clients at ninety-minute intervals. They had watched a car pull into her driveway at six thirty. That same car was now leaving at seven forty-five.

"It looks like the Queen tries to give herself fifteen minutes between appointments," said Bennie.

"She probably has to tidy up the dungeon," said Carol.

Gina said nothing. They were parked far enough away so as to not spook Ivan, but she was still nervous. Gina wished neither Carol nor Bennie were there. She had passed on Henry's information to Deke; during that initial conversation both of them had wondered if they could handle Ivan without involving Carol or Bennie. Neither of them wanted their friends to be potential accessories to the crime each was contemplating.

That's why Gina had visited Carol's office earlier in the day and had closed the door behind her so that no one could hear what was being said. Without offering specifics, Gina had said, "Carol, you might consider sitting this operation out. I was thinking maybe Bennie could get Louis to go in your place."

That had gotten a smile out of Carol. "Funny," she had said, "Deke called me a little while ago and suggested much the same thing. And I'll tell you what I told him: Angus was my friend too. And it was on my watch that his home was bugged and his car was electronically hijacked. So there's no way I sit this one out. I've been a hands-on, in the trenches investigator for decades. I've put myself in much more dicey situations than what we're looking at here. "

Gina had tried to explain. "I will need to . . . *talk* . . . to Ivan to learn what he knows. That will require breaking some laws."

"You'll get your chance. You, Bennie, and I will be team one. We're the out-of-towners. The second team will primarily be there to transport our boy. They're the locals. I already discussed my plan in detail with Deke and he approved it. Does that work for you?"

"It works for me," Gina had said.

"I hope you brought rainwear," Carol had warned. "We're flying out in two hours and it's supposed to be pouring in Cleveland."

-◆◆◆-

The weather prognosticators had gotten it right. It *was* raining. Gina didn't know if that was good or not.

"Normally, I would prefer to have at least two ground teams working the initial takedown," Carol said to Gina, "but because of the circumstances, we will do our best with just the three of us."

"Four of us," said Bennie. "I'm counting on Queen Dominique to do her part."

"He's hoping she'll tie Ivan up," Carol explained. "I understand that's the usual MO for most dominatrixes. That would make our job considerably easier, especially as we have to assume the worst from Ivan. But Queen Dominique will still be the wild card. While Bennie and I are taking down Ivan, you'll need to be convincing Dominique that we're recovery agents just doing our job."

"Recovery agents?"

"Bail agents," explained Carol, "although more commonly known as bounty hunters. What I'll want you to do is show Queen Dominique our identification which shows we're recovery agents and calmly explain to her that we are apprehending a felon wanted for murder."

"You brought along identification for me?"

"I did," she said, "but just flash it at her. We don't want her reading the fine print. Even though we're representing ourselves as bounty hunters, what we're doing is in no way legal, and if it weren't for Angus I would never be taking chances like this."

Carol passed Bennie and Gina slickers emblazoned with the wording, BAIL ENFORCEMENT AGENT. "Bennie and I also brought a few items to help in the raid. Before we go into the house, Bennie will identify where Ivan and the Queen are with a thermal imaging device. He's also carrying an electronic door pick, and both of us are packing pepper spray, tasers, and batons."

"What about me?" Gina asked.

"We're the brawn," said Bennie. "You're supposed to be the brains."

◄►

"Car coming ," said Bennie.

"The time is seven fifty-seven," said Carol.

"The car is turning," he said. A few seconds later he said, "He's parking in the driveway."

Both Bennie and Carol took out viewing scopes. The seconds passed, and no one said anything. "He's now is in the house," Bennie finally said.

"The time is eight o'clock," said Carol.

"The figure appeared to match everything we know about Ivan Verloc," said Bennie.

"Agreed," said Carol.

Neither Bennie nor Carol made a move to get out of the car. "Shouldn't we get going?" asked Gina.

"In half an hour we'll move the car," said Carol. "That will allow Bennie to take a closer look and give us some confirmation of where our boy is in the house."

◆◆◆

An eerily quiet half an hour passed. Very little traffic passed by. The only break in the silence was when Carol once more went over what everyone would be doing at the start of the operation. Bennie started the car, and when they were within fifty yards of the house, he turned off its lights and let it drift forward in neutral. The vehicle came to a stop just short of the driveway.

"It's eight thirty-three," said Carol.

Bennie opened the door and disappeared into the darkness. Five minutes later he returned. "There are two people down in the basement. I couldn't find any other heat sources in the house. Someone is moving around; the other is stationary."

"You think he's tied up?" asked Carol.

"I do. Grandma always told me timing is the key to any good rain dance. It's time, ladies."

"Then let's go."

All three of them exited the car; Gina followed Bennie and Carol's lead. Staying low to the ground, they crossed the lawn and climbed the porch steps. Bennie had already disabled the porch light. He hunched over the lock; there was a sound like that of a bug zapper, and then he turned the handle and opened the door.

Using hand signals, Bennie pointed the way. All three of them huddled together for a moment at the top of a stairway leading down to a basement, and then Bennie began his descent. A few of the stairsteps didn't cooperate, announcing their passage with loud cracking, but no one slowed. Bennie tested the basement door; it was unlocked. He opened it an inch, and they heard voices from within.

"You are a worm. Do you know what I do with worms? I step on them."

They heard the sound of a heel coming down and a muted scream.

"You have been bad, haven't you?" a female voice said. "I know what bad boys want."

A whip sounded; there was another muted scream and some gurgling. They had heard enough. Bennie threw the door open and began running. Behind him, Carol and Gina both began shouting, "Recovery agents! Do not move!"

As it turned out, Queen Dominique was too frightened to move. And because Ivan Verloc was as trussed as a Thanksgiving turkey, he wasn't going anywhere either.

"Queen Dominique," said Gina flashing her badge, "Ms. Hill, we're recovery agents. This man you know as Ivan Cannon is a felon wanted for two murders."

Dominique looked to be in shock. She was wearing a black leather outfit with crisscrossing lashes that exposed plenty of cleavage. In her hand was a cat-o'-nine-tails. And her stiletto heels hadn't been used only for walking; their indentations could be seen in Ivan's exposed derriere.

He was secured facedown onto a large white-painted cross, where his hands had been bound by leather ties. The leather chaps he was wearing didn't conceal much. Covering his face and head was a mask; it had been tightened from behind causing a red rubber ball to be pushed deep into his mouth. No muzzle could have worked as well. The most Ivan could do was gurgle. He raised his head and looked at Carol and Bennie with panicked eyes.

As Gina continued to talk to Dominique, the dominatrix never saw Carol slip a needle into Ivan's vein.

# 39

## SOMETHING TO CHEW UPON

**"I** think you should consider yourself lucky to be alive, Ms. Hill," said Gina. "The man you were entertaining has been doing bad things to people for years. Now we can call the police in if you would prefer, or we can deal with this matter ourselves."

"No police!" she said. "Please!"

"Whatever you think is best."

Carol had already called team two. She said they were ten minutes out and then announced the time as "Eight fifty-five."

"We'll be out of your hair by nine fifteen at the latest," said Gina. "That will give you a little time to compose yourself before your next client, won't it?"

Queen Dominique was still shaking. "Yes," she said.

"Why don't you sit down right here?" said Gina, leading her to a leather chair that looked like a throne. "I know how upsetting this must be. How about I get you a cup of tea? Does that sound good?"

"Please," she said.

Gina left the room, but she didn't go to the kitchen.

◆◆◆

Bennie had removed Ivan from the dominatrix's punishment cross and carried him upstairs to the study. Instead of putting a gag in his mouth, Bennie had left on the mask and ball and kept his hands and feet bound. He laid him face down on the floor. Gina could see that Carol's sedative was already beginning to work on the prisoner. That would make it easier, thought Gina.

Deke had a family. He and Teri had a storybook marriage, and Deke's two children adored him. She was meant to do this by herself.

"I'm doing this for Angus," Gina whispered into Ivan's ear. "Say goodbye, you dirt bag."

She had convinced herself that a naked man choking on a big red bondage ball in an "S and M" parlor by accident might actually be a plausible story. Plausible or not, she was committed. He must have realized her intent. Ivan began bucking up and down. Gina used her knee against his back to minimize his squirming and pulled hard on the bondage straps entwining him, forcing the red ball deeper and deeper into his throat.

She could hear him gagging and the sounds of throwing up. There was no place for his vomit to go. It was filling his windpipe. He was retching and bucking, even as he was dying of asphyxia. Gina pulled all the harder, trying to wedge the ball deeper into his throat as Ivan's struggles began to diminish.

And then Gina found herself being lifted in the air. Bennie had her in a bear hug and had pulled her off of Ivan.

"No!" she screamed.

"Yes," said Bennie. "Deke talked to me. He warned me you might try something like this. And he said if you did, then I was supposed to tell you that this guy carried out the order, but we need to know who gave the order."

"No, it's here and now," Gina insisted.

"We've got to keep the scumbag alive for now," said Bennie. "We need to do it Deke's way."

Gina finally nodded. She staggered out of the room while Bennie worked to remove the mask and save Ivan's life before he died from the aspiration of his own vomit.

Out in the kitchen, Gina made two cups of tea. And then she rejoined Queen Dominique.

# 40
## THE FISHING EXPEDITION

Although there were very few eyes to bear witness anyway, Ivan was hidden in plain sight as he was transported like any other hospital patient would have been. From the dominatrix's home, he was carted along in a gurney and then lifted into an ambulance. An oxygen mask covered his face, although he was inhaling an oxygen mixture that guaranteed sweet dreams.

Ivan was taken to a small airport outside Cleveland, where the "patient" was put aboard the Bergman-Deketomis private jet. The patient's care team boarded after he did; there were two women and one man.

The next stop was Florida.

At the same time, another private aircraft was flying toward Spanish Trace. Nick Deketomis would also be tending to the same patient.

◆◆◆

The *Jean Louise* had been readied for departure, but Captain Dave had been told his services wouldn't be needed that day. Nick Deketomis had said he would be at the helm.

Captain Dave was surprised. Deke was proficient in handling the yacht, but it was rare for him to take out the *Jean Louise* on his own. Still, bosses did what bosses wanted to do.

Deke arrived at port an hour before dawn. Captain Dave gave him the latest weather reports, including water conditions and tides. "The winds are gonna be gentle. You'll have a one-foot chop, but overall, today should be a good day on the water."

Deke didn't volunteer where he was headed, or who would be on board. He did tell Captain Dave the passengers would be along shortly, which was signal enough for the captain to leave and ask no more questions.

◆◆◆

Bennie wheeled Ivan along the dock. After they'd landed in Spanish Trace, Ivan had been moved out of the gurney into a wheelchair. Their prisoner was wrapped up in clothes to make him look like an infirm elderly man on oxygen. No one even gave him a second look as he was wheeled along the dock and aboard the *Jean Louise*.

The rest of Deke's crew came along five minutes later. Deke stopped Carol before she boarded. "I want you to go home, Carol."

She shook her head. "In for a penny," she said, "in for a pound."

"But not in for ten years," he said.

"Who made you God?" she asked.

"No one," said Deke. "But I am your boss. And I would ask that you respect your boss's wishes and go home."

"Just leaving feels wrong to me."

"It feels right to me," said Deke.

"Bennie has a small bag of his belongings hanging from the wheelchair," she said. "Our friend had a knife and a gun that we dumped in Ohio. In his wallet, we found two thumb drives. I imagine he must have some interesting material on those. We also have his phone, which is password protected, of course."

"Thanks, Carol."

"Are you sure? I want you to know that I'm okay all the way, even if it comes down to drawing straws."

"I know you are," said Deke, "but not this time."

Carol nodded her head and then walked away. From behind her Deke said, "Let's get ready to depart."

Deke set course due south. He was in no hurry. He wanted to get the feel of the *Jean Louise.* At first it seemed that everyone was holding their breath, but as time passed the tension abated. They moved beyond potential prying eyes. There was an ocean for them to get lost in, and that's what Deke planned to do.

They initially traveled in a southwesterly direction and passed a couple of small oil rigs. Drilling in the Gulf of Mexico accounted for a sizable portion of US crude oil and natural gas production.

The morning haze burned away, and gradually the coastline became more illusion than not. By Deke's calculations, they were at least fifteen miles offshore with no obstructions on the radar for twenty more miles. He put the *Jean Louise* on autopilot, pulled back power to barely a snail's pace, and then he joined everyone on the aft deck.

Ivan was no longer in his wheelchair. Bennie had duct-taped his arms to a deck chair and secured his roped feet to the hydraulic pins. Their prisoner still looked groggy, but at the sight of Deke he sat up straighter.

"*O captain! My captain!*" Ivan said.

"Hello, Ivan."

"I'm honored. Nick Deketomis knows my name."

"Don't be honored. You murdered one of the best men I've ever had the pleasure of knowing. That's what I've come to talk to you about."

"Talk? That sounds like a euphemism."

"We need answers."

"And you're supposed to be my confessor?"

"If that's what you'll let me be."

"I have trouble saying much of anything before I've had my morning cup of coffee. That will get my brain working better."

"That can be arranged."

"And I need my sugar fix as well. I usually start the day with a few doughnuts."

"I'll see if there are any in the galley."

Bennie and Gina split their time watching Ivan and the horizon ahead of the boat while Deke made coffee. As much as Ivan tried to ignore Gina, he was unnerved by her cold stare. This was a woman who had already shown her willingness to kill him. Ivan liked strong women. He'd always been attracted to them. But this lady was like a black widow or praying mantis. She'd chew off his head sooner than give him a quickie.

Deke came with coffee for all four of them and some croissants as well.

"*Garçon*," said Ivan, "unless you want to feed me, I'll need a hand freed."

Bennie pulled out a finely honed knife; it cut right through the duct tape. Ivan squeezed his left hand open and closed, getting his circulation back. Then he reached for the coffee cup.

Gina continued to watch his every movement, much to Ivan's displeasure. "Did you know this witch tried to kill me last night?" he said.

"No," said Deke, "nor am I interested. If you want to talk about something that interests me, tell me how you tried to kill her."

"That was a mistake," Ivan said. "I had everything set up. I was in like Flynn. No one would ever have questioned a traffic accident. But what I didn't take into account was your guy having a passenger with him. She should have died in the crash. I wish she had."

"Who hired you, Ivan?"

"Geez, Deke, I thought you were supposed to be a lawyer. I expected you to finesse this better. And I really thought you'd offer up flowers and dinner before screwing me."

"I'm not amused, Ivan. This isn't a joke."

"What is it? Is this your idea of a trial?"

"This is a fact-finding expedition."

"And here I thought it was a fishing expedition." Ivan looked around at the water. "Is there good fishing around here?"

"Not a lot of fish in this particular area," said Deke. "But it's possible to land a big shark. They call this area shark alley. It's where the big boys pass as they travel from one feeding and breeding ground to another."

Ivan looked north. "How far away is shore?"

"It's more than fifteen miles as the crow flies, but then you're not a crow."

"Is this where you're planning on killing me?"

"That's up to you," said Deke.

Ivan started to slowly eat his croissant. His every bite seemed to be a thoughtful chew. "Florida is a death penalty state, isn't it?"

"It is," said Deke.

"So if I wrote out a confession, would you be okay with handing me over to the law?"

"It's a start. But you'd also need to provide me with evidence of who hired you and proof of their guilt in Angus's murder."

"I can do that and more."

"What do you have?" asked Deke.

"Would you like to hear an audiotape of a second murder committed by those who hired me?"

"Why are we even listening to him, Deke?" asked Gina. "He's lying. Everything he's saying is just a way for him to try and buy time."

"Are you willing to take that chance?" Ivan asked. "Who is guiltier? Is it the party that kills or the party that hires the killer? And are you all right with settling for a little fish and letting the big fish go free?"

"I'm okay with that," said Gina. "And your death would spare us from your bullshit."

"The lady lawyer is right. I'm just bullshitting you. So what harm would it do to give me a computer with a Wi-Fi connection and five minutes? That's all I'm asking for."

Deke shrugged. "The boat is equipped with Wi-Fi, Ivan, so I don't see what harm it would do to give you your five minutes. Of course I hope you're okay with a Glock being aimed your way while you work."

◀◆▶

Bennie cut off the second wrapping of duct tape, allowing Ivan two free hands to operate the computer. His fingers moved too quickly to be followed, but it clearly took him several passwords to jump through the hoops of his own creation.

Then, with the volume turned up as far as it would go, Ivan played back the last testament of Kendrick Strahan.

"Thursby," said Gina, recognizing his voice.

"Yes," Ivan agreed. "And he was ordered to kill Strahan by Tom Lutz."

"You have proof of that?" asked Deke.

"I have many tapes proving Lutz's guilt," he said. "I even have him on tape when he hired me to kill your lawyer."

"Knapp and Carter had no part in Angus's death?" Gina asked.

"They're innocent, at least in that one death."

Deke and Gina looked at one another. Neither of them totally trusted what they were hearing. "Hand me over to the state," Ivan promised, "and I'll give you what you need to get Lutz and Thursby. And if you want other white-collar players and politicians, I have plenty of audio of Strahan handing out bribes."

"Write everything down," said Deke. "Leave out nothing about your two murders. We'll also need the details of where you buried your driver and how he died. That will be your first step toward ever making it back to shore. And I want you to list what you have on Lutz and Thursby."

"I am not going to tell you how to access all the tapes and information I've assembled," said Ivan. "That's my ace card for staying alive."

"But you will access it for the Florida authorities?" asked Deke.

"As soon as you hand me over to them," Ivan said.

◆◆◆

Ivan filled half a legal pad with writing before complaining of a cramp in one leg. Deke told Bennie to untie the rope, so that he could move his legs freely. The morning passed into afternoon, and Ivan continued to write. Every so often Deke came and looked over his prisoner's shoulder. From what he could see, Ivan's account was very thorough. The confirmation of Ivan murdering his driver and the location of the corpse would be the first place for Carol to begin before the day was over.

In the midst of writing his confession, Ivan suddenly sat up straight. He could hear the sound of his cell phone ringing.

"That's not right," said Ivan. "I need to see my phone!"

"I'll get it," said Bennie.

"Hurry!" Ivan yelled.

When Bennie reappeared the phone began offering up a different noise. Now it sounded like a cicada; it was whirring, whistling, and clicking.

"There's been a breach of my defenses!" Ivan shouted. "My systems are under attack. I need that laptop! And my phone! This is an emergency!"

Ivan turned to Deke; his desperation was pouring out of him. "I need to protect my recordings. They're proof of what I told you!"

"Give him his phone," Deke said, "and the laptop."

Ivan was all fingers and commands. He typed in passwords and moved through firewalls, managing to get into his own home security system. Deke, Gina, and Bennie came over to see, wondering what had gotten their prisoner so amped. Then images began to appear. With each one Ivan screamed, "No! No! No!" Some with closed-circuit video streams went blank; they had been fried. In others, gray-black smoke made it difficult to see what was going on. But most of the closed-circuit cameras showed a conflagration; hungry fire was consuming Ivan's home, turning his computer screen into a glowing orange.

"Over a million in cash burning up," Ivan said. "Those fuckers."

His hands moved over the keyboard; using CCTV feeds, Ivan stalked his own home. Then one of his cameras caught Lutz and Thursby in an area untouched by flames. The two were remedying that by applying some kind of accelerant.

"Bastards!" screamed Ivan.

From his phone came the sounds of a raging fire. At a typed command, Ivan's computer went split screen. On one side of the display Thursby and Lutz could be seen setting fires; on the other side there was a familiar yellow and black image denoting radiation and the word **CAUTION**. Ivan's fingers moved feverishly. "I'm in," he muttered, and then he tapped in a password. A five-second countdown appeared on the screen.

"Three," whispered Ivan, "two."

Ivan's phone suddenly roared. Then it spat out static and its connection to Ivan's house was lost.

The explosion destroyed almost all of the security cameras, but Ivan found one camera still operating. Through its lens, the wreckage of the house could be seen. And it showed something else; Lutz's head was on the ground. It was mostly intact, although completely separated from his body. Thursby wasn't as identifiable. His large body was scattered in scores of pieces. Like Humpty Dumpty, he wasn't going to be put together again.

"Take that you motherfuckers!" Ivan screamed.

Smoke, flames, and body parts filled the monitor. Into that mix could be seen the reflection of Ivan's gloating face. Everyone stared at the computer screen, transfixed by the horrific images.

Ivan took advantage of that. He leaped from his seat and began running. Bennie went vertical, but was too late. Gina and Deke ran after him, but Ivan wasn't going to be caught. He jumped over the railing and plummeted into the ocean.

# 41
## THE BOUNTY

From the porch, Cary Jones called, "Welcome to the Peach Capital of South Carolina."

"Are you pulling my leg?" asked Cara.

"No," he said. "That's what Gaffney likes to call itself. Of course I've heard some of the residents refer to us as the Peach Pit of South Carolina."

Cary joined Cara on the sidewalk and shook her hand. "I told you I'd come to Gaffney one day," she said.

It had been months since she'd talked to Private Jones at Fort Bragg. His quiet desperation had struck a chord in her. She knew he needed help and feared what he might do without it.

"I thought we'd sit on the porch," he said, "if that's okay with you. At least there's a little breeze out here."

"That sounds fine," said Cara.

After Private Jones' honorable discharge, he had returned to the family home in Gaffney. It was a run-down-looking structure, as were most of the homes on the street.

Cara followed him up the steps and he motioned for her to sit down. "I brewed some sun tea," he said. "Would you like some?"

"I would," she said. "It's crazy hot out here."

"Summer kind of sucks in Gaffney," he said.

He went into the house and returned with two glasses of ice tea. They clinked their glasses together and each said, "Cheers."

At the same time, out of each of their mouths flowed, "So, how are you doing?" Then both of them laughed.

"I would say, 'Jinx, owe a Coke,' but I'm afraid we don't have any," he said.

"The tea is just fine," she said.

Both of them sipped and reflected. Cara spoke first. "That case is over," she said. "We won. That's sort of why I'm here. Our firm was able to get a fifty million dollar settlement that's being called the Angus Moore Wounded Soldiers Fund. It's supposed to provide physical and mental therapy for soldiers who've served in Afghanistan and other combat areas. I thought about you."

"That's a good thing your firm did."

"So is that your way of telling me, 'Thanks, but no thanks?'"

Instead of directly answering, he asked, "Who is Angus Moore?"

"He was my Uncle Angus. That's what I called him when I was a girl. Angus was a partner in Dad's firm. He was murdered because of the work he was doing with Sight-Clops and Arbalest. I know it probably sounds silly to you, but his death made it feel like our law firm went to war."

"Death sometimes just hangs around too long," he said.

"You wouldn't believe all that's happened," she said. "The case exposed this trail of corruption that led to politicians and lobbyists and union leaders—and just about everywhere. It's still being worked out. We know of at least five people who were murdered because of it."

"It does sound like a war," he said.

"We had Angus's killer in our hands," she said. "My father had him on his boat for questioning. He was writing up his confession for all that he'd done, and then he jumped off the ship. No one thought he could have survived. He was a long, long ways from shore. But my dad wanted to be sure. He had his investigators scouring through CCTV footage. And that's where they caught some images of Ivan Verloc in and around Mobile.

"My dad sort of went crazy. He blames himself for Ivan getting away. That's why he's put up wanted posters everywhere. He's offering a quarter-million-dollar reward for the capture of Ivan Verloc."

"That sounds like a bounty."

"It sort of is. Dad and Gina—she's the lawyer who took over for Angus—can't stand it that Ivan got away after killing so many people. People are calling this Ivan guy the 'Generation Y Killer.' If you saw his picture you'd never guess he was capable of murder. He is this small, light guy, who looks like a teenager even though he's twenty-five."

"With your dad offering up a quarter of a million dollars, I can't imagine he'll avoid capture for long."

"That's what everyone thought. But Ivan seems to have disappeared."

They both sipped at their tea, and then Cara said, "That was a good job of misdirection, by the way, of getting off the topic of the wounded warrior fund. Is that what you did with the shrinks?"

"Busted," he said.

"Just so I know I asked the right question, are you telling me you want to pass on getting any help from the fund?"

"It's not for me."

"I'm no mental health professional, Cary, but I'm wondering if anyone gave you a PTSD diagnosis when you were discharged."

"PTSD is just another name for bad shit that happened."

"You said our program isn't the right thing for you. What is the right thing for you?"

He shrugged his shoulders, unwilling to voice his pipe dream.

"No reason to shut me out, Cary. What do you think would help?"

"I'd just like to get away from it all for a while," he said. "I'm happiest when I'm alone in the woods. That's where I feel at peace. I don't like being boxed in by buildings and people. I think it would be a lot easier to heal with open space."

Cara nodded. "Far from the madding crowd."

"That sounds about right."

Cara suddenly smiled. "Are you serious about living in the woods?"

"That's my fantasy," he said.

"Yesterday I heard my father talking with his partner Martin Bergman. He said they'd need a caretaker for the place in Montana owned by Angus—that's the lawyer who was murdered. The firm bought it from Angus's widow supposedly as a company retreat, but in reality it was a way of putting more money in her estate. For now though the place is just sitting empty."

"Your father is really going to hire a caretaker?"

Cara made a gesture of crossing her index finger over her heart: "Cross my heart," she said.

"Hired," he said.

# 42
## A MEAL OF TROUT

For so long, Cary Jones had felt like a bird without wings. Now, with every passing moment, he was feeling more alive and more grateful to Angus Moore. In a way, the man might have actually saved his life.

Angus had purchased the hundred-acre spread as his getaway. It was a shame the lawyer hadn't used the mountain paradise more often while he'd been alive. He had picked a spot in northwestern Montana bordering national forests. On Angus's spread, there were three creeks. In Gaffney, they would have been called rivers. And on the northwest edge of the property, the Clark Fork River meandered by having branched off from the mighty Columbia River.

After only a few days there, the place was feeling like home. He'd already seen elk, white-tailed deer, wild turkeys, and brown bear. He kept a .45 automatic strapped to his side, not for the brown bear but for the two grizzlies who seemed too comfortable within the immediate vicinity of the main residence.

Cara had worried he'd be too cold and too isolated in Montana, but then she'd never visited Angus's paradise. What he had built was really more of a house than a cabin; nevertheless the structure was mostly made up of red cedar and lodgepole pine. There were two river stone fireplaces; each generated lots of heat. It would be up to Cary, though, to cut enough firewood. Five cords were already cut and stacked; Cary would restock as needed. Even though the cabin was off the grid, it was equipped with a solar system and generator.

Cary took a deep breath. Thank you, Angus Moore, he thought. You gave me a gift I could never have imagined. You gave me a chance to recover.

Today, Cary decided, was a fishing day. The biggest creek on the property was only a few hundred yards away from the cabin. Yesterday, he must have seen at least a dozen fat brown trout in the shallows. And for every brownie he saw, Cary knew there were three he wasn't seeing. The place had been well-stocked with fishing equipment. Cary knew very little about fly-fishing, but thought he'd give it a try. He'd also bring along a spinning rod. The bait would be a no-brainer. There were lots of grasshoppers. That was probably why there was a butterfly net in the house. He'd catch a bunch of live hoppers. If they didn't bring the fish, nothing would.

◆◆◆

Ivan Verloc was getting increasingly pissed. He hadn't counted on having to camp out for as many nights as he had. The situation sort of reminded him of a T-shirt he used to own that showed one vulture talking to another and saying, "Patience, Hell. I'm Going to Kill Somebody!"

Ivan was reaching the same conclusion as the vulture. He had hoped the interloper would only stay for a few days and then move on. But now it was clear; instead of moving on he had moved in.

Angus's Montana getaway had seemed like the perfect place for Ivan to hole up. When Angus had first offered it to his whistleblower, Richard Diaz, Ivan was immediately intrigued. And though Diaz had never taken the lawyer up on his offer, Ivan had.

When Ivan was taken out on that little cruise, it was supposed to have been his last outing. Even as he was writing up his confession, he'd been plotting his escape. There was no way that bitch would have let him live. Her green eyes were like neon signs. They flashed "Murderer! Murderer!" And that sanctimonious prick Deketomis wasn't any better. He'd wanted Ivan to confess his crimes as a way to justify what he intended to do to him.

Screw you, Deketomis.

Ivan had waited for just the right time to jump overboard. The sun was getting lower in the sky, and the chop was building. He'd calculated his best chance was to jump overboard and grab hold of the boat's stabilizer that was just below the surface. From above they wouldn't be able to see him. Of course if he'd missed, the next stop would likely have been the prop.

Luckily he hadn't missed, and he held on to the stabilizer while Deketomis slowly maneuvered the yacht around in figure eights. This offered Ivan his chance to make his break from the boat right before he passed out from lack of air. The big Indian and the bitch had done their best to spot him, but Ivan had remained invisible in the chop and the glare from the setting sun. He kept his head from barely breaking the surface. They'd stayed in the area until it was dark. Sometimes their voices carried, and Ivan had heard them talking. They had tried to convince themselves that he was dead.

Finally, they'd headed back to shore. Still, his survival was anything but assured. The direct route to shore was about ten miles away, but Ivan had let the prevailing current take him. He'd been able to rest at a few unmanned oil rigs on the way in. When he'd finally crawled ashore, barely able to move, he wasn't far from Mobile.

He'd broken into a house, taken some money and some clothes, and then he'd done his great disappearing act. Interstate 10 beckoned, and Ivan had gotten rides going west. He'd portrayed himself as a college freshman out to see the country. Along the way he'd picked up some traveling money and left at least one body behind.

Ivan always appreciated irony; he thought it ironic that his destination was the remote Montana getaway of the lawyer he'd murdered. It was there he had planned to regroup. It was there he would plan his new life. The lawyer had told his whistle-blower, Diaz, that it would be an easy place for him to hide and never be seen. That sounded like the perfect hidey-hole to Ivan.

What he hadn't counted on was the visitor. Ivan was barely able to get out of the cabin unseen when the interloper had moved in. Since that time, Ivan had been forced to camp all the while keeping a close watch on the intruder. Now Ivan was convinced the man was some kind of caretaker. The cabin did have some pricy things inside. Ivan was holding one of those items: a Remington .223 bolt-action rifle. Ivan had watched the caretaker spend a day reattaching some fencing and part of another day clearing a trail.

But today, Ivan thought, the caretaker had decided it was a fishing day. The man caught some grasshoppers and put them in a bag, and now he was walking toward one of the creeks with two fishing poles swinging over his shoulder.

The kid sort of looked like an older version of Opie from the TV classic *The Andy Griffith Show*, Ivan decided. Every episode began with Opie and his dad walking toward the water with their fishing poles.

Ivan hoped Opie would be lucky, because if he caught a fish, tonight Ivan would be eating trout.

---◆◆◆---

Afghanistan had taught Cary to trust his instincts. On his way to the creek, he'd heard sounds that were out of place. He was certain the noises weren't coming from animal movements; years of hunting the South Carolina woods had attuned him to those sounds. He played it cool, though, never looking around, pretending like he didn't have a worry in the world.

Once he was at the creek, Cary walked along the bank. Behind him, every so often, he heard noises of someone on his trail. Whoever was stalking him knew very little about stealth or maybe didn't care if he was heard. Cary looked for just the right spot; his concern wasn't so much in locating the best area to angle for brown trout as it was to find a place that might afford him protection from being ambushed.

Finally, Cary came to a stop. He cast his line in the water and waited. Then he retrieved his line and tried again. No one could have been more surprised than Cary when a trout hit his hopper. The struggle was brief, almost anticlimactic. The trout was reeled in and with a rock Cary ended the fish's life.

The rock was still in his hand when a man stepped into the opening and raised his rifle.

Cary hurled the rock at the gunman. The man ducked and almost fell. Then he righted himself and raised his rifle again. But Cary was already in a shooter's stance. He fired four rounds from his .45 and headed for the trees to his right.

Ivan dove for cover behind the remains of a tree trunk that had washed up along the river. His right thigh had been hit with a round and was spewing blood.

He'd need a tourniquet to survive, but first he needed to locate the man who had shot him. The same man he still intended to kill.

Cary scrambled up the bank into the tree line directly behind
Ivan. That's where he would sit silently watching the armed preda-
tor slowly bleed to death.

–◆◆◆–

Where was the son of a bitch? Ivan thought as he looked around.
His vision was getting blurry. His heart raced as a stream of blood
poured out of his body. He felt as if he were looking through a narrow tunnel as he turned his head side to side trying to get a visual
on the man who had shot him. He was losing it. He was dying.

Ivan knew what he needed to do to stop the bleeding. He could
visualize the tourniquet. It was nothing more than a piece of cloth,
a belt, and a strong stick. He knew what was needed, but his body
refused to respond to what his brain was commanding him to do.
He tried to speak, but no words came to his mouth. He had the
sensation of being suspended in the air and looking at his body
lying in a pool of blood.

Ivan had grown up playing hundreds of video games where
computer graphics splattered virtual blood everywhere. But those
were just games. He struggled to suck in two more breaths. Dying
in real life was no fun. Game over.

–◆◆◆–

Cary watched the man die. It wasn't like watching Ahmad's grandfather pass on. This man had stalked him and had raised his rifle to
kill him. He hadn't expected Cary to shoot first.

Cary walked down from his observer's position. He was sure
the man was dead, but he still wasn't taking any chances. Cary
kicked the man's rifle away from his body and reached down to be
certain there was no pulse. For the first time, he could confirm
what had crossed his mind as he watched the man bleed out. He
had killed Ivan Verloc.

Cara's story about her father's campaign to find Verloc had prompted Cary to read everything he could about him on the internet. He had no doubt about the identity of the bloody corpse lying at his feet.

Ivan's eyes were open. Cary reached into his pocket for Ahmad's coins. He took two of them and placed one on each eye.

It felt right. The coins looked like they belonged.

Even the shooting felt right. It had been a situation of kill or be killed, and he had chosen life.

Cary took out his cell phone. The nearest cell reception was in a town more than ten miles away. Cary didn't make calls with his phone; he carried it to take pictures. And now he took a picture of the dead Ivan Verloc. The picture was clear; there was no mistaking his features. Ahmad's special coins seemed to tell a story as well. Cara's father would want to see a picture of Verloc, he knew. Later, he'd go into town and send Cara the picture and ask her what he should do about the body.

First, though, Cary was going to eat some trout.

# 43
## THE NOBLEST VENGEANCE

**D**eke walked into Gina's office and found her staring off into the distant waters of the Gulf of Mexico. "Are you receiving visitors?" he asked.

"Today, all forms of escapism are welcome," she said. "Please join me."

Earlier that morning Deke had called four trusted friends into his office and told them that Ivan was dead. There had been a few amens, a few remembrances of Angus, and a few tears. Deke had asked everyone not to speak of Ivan's death to anyone outside of that room. Cary Jones had endured enough trouble in his life; he didn't need to go through another investigation or trial. In lieu of the cash reward, Cary had asked if he could continue to maintain Angus's Montana home. If he was still of the same mind a few years down the road, Deke said he would transfer the home into Cary's name.

"I am still feeling numb," Gina said.

"That's understandable."

"I would have killed Ivan that day we were out on the ship," said Gina. "I had no intention of letting him escape alive."

"Nor I," Deke said.

"I felt so cheated when we came into port. We were all just guessing—was he dead, or was that sick bastard still walking around?"

"I felt that same disappointment. I thought I had failed Angus. But in the days that followed, I came to realize how lucky both of us were. Had I killed Ivan, I think there would have been this infection inside of me, an infection that ultimately would have impacted me, and my family, and this entire law firm."

Gina nodded. "I'd like to pretend that I would have been tough enough to weather those consequences, that I was up to the task of revenge killing and that it wouldn't have changed me. But the truth is my childhood already left me with more baggage than I can carry on most days. I didn't need any more."

"You and Bryan should get married," said Deke. "The two of you should have kids."

"You sound like Bryan." She smiled and added, "I was sure that ship had sailed. But now maybe I'm reconsidering."

"I hope you do."

"My goal is to never have to plot to kill anyone else, okay Deke?"

"Let me know ahead of time if you do get that urge," said Deke with a laugh, "and I'll send you on a long exotic vacation far away from people."

He surprised Gina by opening his suit jacket and pulling out a rectangular frame he'd been hiding. A surprised Gina accepted his offering.

"I commissioned Rachel Frank to do the calligraphy," Deke said, "and to add her special touches."

In addition to being the firm's best paralegal, Rachel was a talented artist. Gina looked at the elaborate writing she'd penned: *The*

*Noblest Vengeance is to Forgive.* Around her calligraphy, she had added some artwork. Gina studied the intricately drawn images; there was a dove in flight, a fish, a tree, and a mandala.

"I love it," Gina said, "I really do. And I'm going to put it right here on my desk as a daily reminder to try to be that noble."

"We both can try," said Deke.

The two of them shared a smile; each knew that was far better than forever sharing a dark secret. But Gina couldn't let herself appear too warm and fuzzy. "You better not be expecting some miraculous transformation, Nick Deketomis. I'm a girl from Jersey. Deal with it."

"I love you too, Gina," he said.

# ABOUT THE AUTHOR

**MIKE PAPANTONIO** is a senior partner of Levin Papantonio, one of the largest plaintiffs' law firms in America. He has handled thousands of cases throughout the nation involving pharmaceutical drug litigation, tobacco litigation, securities fraud actions, and many of the nation's largest environmental cases.

"Pap" is one of the youngest trial lawyers to have been inducted into the Trial Lawyer Hall of Fame.

In 2012 Mr. Papantonio became President of the National Trial Lawyers Association, which represents forty thousand trial lawyers nationally.

For his trial work on behalf of consumers, he has received some of the most prestigious awards reserved by the Public Justice Foundation,

The American Association for Justice, and the National Trial Lawyers Association.

He is the author of the legal thriller *Law and Disorder* as well as four motivational books for lawyers.

He is also coauthor of *Air America: The Playbook* listed by the *New York Times* as a "political best seller."

Papantonio is the host of the nationally syndicated radio show *Ring of Fire* along with Robert F. Kennedy, Jr., and Sam Seder. In addition to the radio program, Papantonio hosts *America's Lawyer* on the RT America network.

He has also served as a political commentator who has appeared as a regular guest on MSNBC, Free Speech TV, RT America Network, and Fox News.